GHOSTS,
MONSTERS,
AND DEMONS
OF
INDIA

GHOSTS, MONSTERS, AND DEMONS OF

INDIA

RAKESH KHANNA
AND
J. FURCIFER BHAIRAV

WATKINS
1893

Ghosts, Monsters, and Demons of India
Rakesh Khanna
and J. Furcifer Bhairav

This is an updated edition of Ghosts, Monsters, and Demons of India
first published in India in 2020 by Blaft Publications
This edition first published in the UK and USA in 2023 by
Watkins, an imprint of Watkins Media Limited
Unit 11, Shepperton House
89–93 Shepperton Road
London N1 3DF

enquiries@watkinspublishing.com

A CIP record for this book is available from the British Library.

ISBN: 978-1-78678-807-8 (Hardback)
ISBN: 978-1-78678-830-6 (eBook)

10 9 8 7 6 5 4 3 2 1

Printed in the United Kingdom

❦ CONTENTS ❦

Author's Note ix

Aavi 1
Ahmaw 3
Airi 5
Ajaju 7
Alakhani 8
Alchi 8
Aleya 10
Alha and Udal 12
Alvantin 13
Ambi Jakbyryt 14
Anangu 14
Anchheri 15
Angra Mainyu 17
Aonglamla 18
Apasmara 19
Apsara 20
Arakkan 20
Ashwatthama 22
Asura 23
Avittam 26
Baak 26
Baalu 28
Bai Thappikne Seithaan 29
Bakasura 30
Balishtamaru 31
Balvala 35
Ban Jhakri and Ban Jhakrini 35
Banji-Banmang 38
Banshira 39
Barambha 40
Barola 40
Bayangi 41
Bembong 43
Beri 43
Bhoot 45
Bhoota (Tulu Nadu) 50

Bhoota Vahana Yanta 54
Bhurey 56
Bido Tech Lau 56
Bira 58
Blemmyae 59
Boba 59
Bonga 60
Bootham 64
Brahmadaitya 66
Bram Bram Chok 67
Btsan 69
Budangma 69
Buga 70
Bugarik 72
Bullet Baba 73
Burha Dangoriya 74
Buru 75
Cetea 76
Chawmnu 77
Cheda 78
Chedipe 78
Chekama 80
Chetkin 81
Chhongchhongpipa 82
Chol 82
Chon 84
Chordeva 84
Christalina 86
Chual Chhongal 88
Chudail 89
Churgin 91
Chuti 93
Crocotta 93
Daayan 95
Dakini 98
Dakkhin Rai 99

Daula 100
Dev 101
Devchar 104
Deyyam 105
Doht 106
Dragon 107
Duma 108
Eaka 110
Eenampechi 113
Elmakaltai 113
Farasi Bahari 113
Faru Fureta 114
Firangi Bhoot 115
Flying Horses 120
Fravashi 121
Gaali 122
Gaantiyal Dangoriya 123
Gandharva 123
Garuda 124
Gata Loops Ghost 124
Ghar Jeuti 125
Ghorapaak 125
Ginggrek Mikdalong
    Gingthongreng 126
Gobhoot 127
Gog and Magog 127
Goggayya 128
Hadal 129
Hamzad 130
Hanal 131
Hedali 131
Helloi 132
Hidimba 133
Hi-i 133
Hingchabi 134
Hinn 135
Hmuichukchuriduninu 136
Hmuithla 138
Huai 138
Ichchhadhari Nag 143
Ifrit 143
Iliphru 144
Ilvala and Vatapi 145
Indus Worm 147
Inene 147

Ingennangkwe 148
Iwi-Pot 148
Jadaamuni 151
Jaukaar Paal 151
Jhunjharji 152
Jimu-Tayang 153
Jinn 154
Jokhini 156
Jol Kuwori 157
Jurua 158
Kaathu Karuppu 159
Kabandha 159
Kali 161
Kalystrioi 161
Kaniam Pey 163
Kanni Pey 164
Kanva 165
Kaoshe 165
Kappiri Muthappan 166
Karinthandan 167
Karna-Pisachini 168
Keertimukha 169
Keimi 170
Kenglong-po 171
Ketu 172
Khabish 172
Khais 173
Khavees 173
Khawhring 174
Khetor 174
Khond 175
Khuavang 177
Khuba and Khubi 178
Kimidin 178
Kinnara 180
Kokaachi 180
Kolavo 182
Kollivay Pey 182
Kondhokata 184
Kroni 184
Ksuid 186
Kuli 192
Kundra 192
Kungumi 194
Kurali Pey 196

CONTENTS

Kuttichathan 197
Lai-Khutsangbi 199
Laqa 202
Lasi 202
Lavsat 204
Lha 205
Lhadam 205
Lhangnel 206
Maadan 208
Mahoraga 208
Makara 209
Maltong 209
Mamadev 210
Man-Eating Boulder 210
Mande Burung 212
Mangermachh 212
Manticore 213
Maru 214
Marudyl 214
Masaan 215
Matiya 217
Mayel 217
Memang 219
Merching 220
Mirchuk 220
Mishing 221
Mohini Pey 222
Moila Deo 222
Momiyaiwala Sahib 223
Monkey Man 224
Monocoli 225
Morakon 225
Morua 226
Mudmudiya-Gudgudiya
    Bhoot 226
Mughal Ghosts 226
Muhnochwa 228
Mung 230
Muni 244
Munjya 246
Mura 247
Naale Ba Bhoota 247
Naar Mokal 248
Naga 249
Nakshatra Meenu 252

Nasu 252
Nawang 253
Nazar 254
Neeli 255
Nelhao 256
Newand Dokka 256
Nila 257
Nim-Tan 258
Nipong 258
Nirrti 260
Nishi 261
Noeri Simeri Jahpramma 261
Nongshohnoh 262
Nyalmo 263
Odiyan 265
Odontotyrannos 266
Onida Devil 267
Onkoboykwe 268
Otte Molechi 270
Padosomaru 271
Pandubba 272
Paubi Lai 272
Pavagada Wolves 273
Penchapechi 273
Penu 274
People with No Anuses 278
Peri 279
Peshwa Narayan Rao 280
Pey 281
Phi 282
Pheichham 284
Phung 284
Pisacha 285
Pitr 288
Pogeyan 289
Polydactyl Warriors of the
    Himalayas......................... 289
Pramatha 290
Preta 290
Printer's Devil 293
Pu Pâwla 293
Pugri Naad 294
Rahu 295
Rakhondar 296
Rakshasa 296

Railway Ghosts 297
Rantas 299
Ratha Kaateri 300
Rau 302
Ret ka Pret 303
Ro Langs 304
Rose 305
Rukh Balu 306
Ruleipa 306
Rulpui 307
Runiya 311
Ruru 311
Saamri 312
Sakainjeek 313
Salyasura 314
Sambandh 314
Samon 315
Sanamahi Apoiba 315
Sanu 316
Sanvari 317
Saroi 317
Seven Sister Spirits 319
Shaitan 321
Shakini 322
Shankhchunni 323
Sheep-Killer of Niali 323
Silesaloma 324
Simekar 327
Sivatherium 328
Skondhokata 329
Songduni Angkorong Sagalni
    Damohong 329
Sonum 331
Srin Mo 333
Sungur Bhoot 334
Svarbhanu 334
Swkal 335
Takte Ragre 337
Tandei 338
Tasma-pa 338
Tasrufdar 339
Teghami 339
Tengte 341

Terhoma 341
Than-Thin Daini 343
Thendan 343
Thilha 344
Thla Ai 347
Thlarau 347
Timitimingala 349
Tisso Jonding 350
Tsine Nat 351
Tsungrem 352
Tualsumsu 353
U Diengiei 353
U Ksuid Tynjang 354
U Thlen 355
Uchu 358
Uka 359
Unicorn 360
Vanchungnula 362
Vantri 363
Vetal 363
Vir 369
Virika 369
Vritra 369
Vriyabhoot 370
Wakmangganchi Aragondi....... 371
Wai Whop 373
Wan Mohniyu 373
Werehyena 374
Wereleopard 375
Weretigerman 375
Wiyu 377
Yach 378
Yakshi 379
Yali 385
Yam Bhaya Akhoot 386
Yamaduta 388
Yantra-Purusha 389
Yatudhana 390
Yeti 391
Zasam 392
Zoting 392
Zoumi 393
Zunhindawt 394

Bibliography............................ 395

⤙⟶ AUTHOR'S NOTE ⟵⤚

I have been a fan of spooky stories, pulp horror novels, and monster movies since childhood. I also love reading Indian folklore, especially tales about supernatural creatures. Blaft, the publishing company I co-founded twelve years ago, has had some success with horror fiction and books about monsters; our readers seem to enjoy such stories as much as I do.

Bhairav and I began compiling this book because, though India has an astounding diversity of mythological fiends, the vast majority of them are unknown outside a particular region or language group. This situation is a little surprising, since horror stories usually travel well across cultures.

There's something comfortable about sharing monster legends. It's a great way to make friends. When people of different faiths start debating the relative merits of their gods, there's always a danger that they'll end the conversation by drawing weapons; but if the same group sits down to compare their demons and devils, they're more likely to break out the popcorn.

India is an intensely spiritual place. It's also a very superstitious one—a country where politicians see no shame in consulting astrologers, and where almost every house has some talisman for warding off the evil eye. Some of these practices are harmless, approached primarily out of a reverence for cultural tradition and the aesthetics of ritual. On the other hand, witch hunts still result in lynchings with appalling frequency, and there are very real evildoers who believe that conducting a human sacrifice will help them attain magical power.

Unfortunately the situation seems to be getting worse. Dangerous superstitions are flourishing—encouraged by religious and political leaders, nurtured by a post-truth media environment, and unopposed by a struggling education system. Outspoken sceptics have, in several high-profile cases, been murdered. One victim was Narendra Dabholkar, a doctor-turned-activist from Maharashtra who spent decades campaigning against phony miracle cures and belief in black magic. He was gunned down in August 2013 by two masked assailants who escaped on a motorcycle. Investigations into the assassination unveiled a large conspiracy against Indian advocates for rationalism. The case against five accused by the Central Board of Investigation is still working through the courts; meanwhile, there may be other culprits still at large.

With all of this going on, we must beg the reader to take our book in the right spirit (so to speak). Some of the tales in these pages come from ancient folklore, and can be appreciated as cultural heritage; others are just gory spook stories meant for cheap thrills. A few entries describe rituals for summoning demons or warding them away, but we suggest you don't take these instructions too seriously. In case you start feeling haunted, I recommend switching over to a good science book—ideally, one on palæontology or astronomy. The slice of spacetime we live in is really very tiny, and I find that keeping this fact in mind makes ghosts less scary.

Or, in case you find cosmic insignificance just as terrifying as the malevolent undead, then perhaps try a nice book about flowers.

Linguistic regions don't always align perfectly with national boundaries, and the same is true for endemic ranges of ghosts. We have used the word "India" in the title, but some entries describe spirits that haunt parts of Pakistan, Afghanistan, Iran, Bangladesh, Nepal, Tibet, Myanmar, and the Maldives as well. We trust this won't be misunderstood as an attempt to claim territory for a chthonic Akhand Bharat. It's just that lakhs of Indians speak Tibetic languages like Bhutia and Ladakhi, and so share folkloric traditions with Tibet—not to mention India's sizeable community of refugees from Tibet proper, and their descendents. Millions more Indians speak Sindhi or Nepali. The country is home to more Zoroastrians than any other in the world, despite the faith having originated far to the west. In the east, the line between India and Myanmar goes right through the homelands of the Kuki, Chin, and Mizo people, in fact cutting across the legendary path taken by souls on their final journey to the afterlife. Like most of India's international borders, this line has been drawn within living memory—hardly long enough to make an impression on the world map of the eternal dead.

Not all regions of the country are equally represented in these pages. There are clear necrodiversity hotspots—the Konkan coast, Kumaon, Chhotanagpur, Sikkim, and the seven sister states of the Northeast—where a startling variety of supernatural beings are concentrated in a small area. Even within each of these regions, some traditions are better attested than others. Folklorists from Mizoram, for example, have published and translated a wealth of their stories into English, with multiple versions widely available in bookstores and on the internet. The Bathouist mythology of the Boros of Assam, on the other hand, is much harder to come by.

Any attempt to collect mythology from a variety of languages and cultures opens itself to allegations of appropriation. We have done our best to take this issue seriously, seeking out input on the book from people all over the country. It was impossible, though, for us to get feedback from every state and every tribe. Dear Reader, if you come across anything we have misrepresented or goofed up in any way, we would greatly appreciate it if you would contact us, so we can correct it in a future printing.

The human brain seems to have a natural predilection for describing and classifying demons. Every culture on earth has invented a complex pantheon of bad guys. Whether they are called devils, rakshasas, lords of Xibalba, daikaiju, or Batman supervillains, each character comes complete with an origin story and a distinctive set of powers and weaknesses.

I have wondered, while compiling this book, whether we *evolved* this tendency. Did it confer some selective advantage on our ancestors? Consider that 100,000 years ago, there was a much richer megafauna. Early hominids who had memorized the hunting schedule of a sabre-tooth tiger, who could recognize the pugmarks of a cave lion, or who knew the best way of dodging an angry woolly rhino might have been more likely to survive. Perhaps our brains are *designed* to store knowledge about a large number of different dangerous monsters; and now that the deadly beasts are mostly extinct or confined to cages, we make up stories to fill the empty space.

Or, perhaps, we tell ghost stories to protect our own sanity. Many people find that a belief in some kind of afterlife—even one filled with everlasting torment—is less psychologically disturbing than the idea of perpetual void.

But "believe" is a fuzzy word. There are things we believe in as children that we reject as adults; and then sometimes in old age we go back to believing them again, in a wiser, less literal way. Hardcore sceptics can be great storytellers, and they can do as much to popularize myths and legends as their more credulous friends. This range of "belief" is worth keeping in mind when reading folklore, especially when reading about tribal superstitions that strike us as bizarre or backward or primitive.

This book should not be considered a work of anthropology. It has not gone through an academic peer review, and we confess to being less than perfectly up to date on contemporary theory. While the relativist nature of the philology of the vernacular as it pertains to demonopathy is certainly worthy of study, our focus here is on fangs and blood and severed heads. Of course, we are heavily indebted to the legion of anthropologists and folklorists whose research we have mined (and who we hope will not be too horrified by our approach)—as well as all the amateur enthusiasts who have shared the stories their grandparents told them, in print, online, and in person.

We have taken some pains not to distort things, and to draw on multiple accounts that can be traced back to different primary sources whenever possible.

But in retelling the tales, we've removed a lot of information about where and when and how the originals were collected. For anyone who wants to delve deeper into the particulars, our main sources are listed in the bibliography.

We've also taken a few liberties. For one thing, we have tried to omit mention of caste. Many works of Indian demonology extend the caste system into the afterlife: Spirit A is the ghost of a Caste X person, Spirit B is the ghost of a Caste Y. We find this distasteful, and not just because of the affront to social equity. It seems to us that in a good spook story, the nature of a person's spirit should depend on their actions in life and the circumstances of their death, rather than on the circumstances of their birth.

Some may object that this approach is naïve, for belief in supernatural entities intersects with caste in all sorts of complex and interesting ways. In the Theyyam and Bhoota Kola traditions of Northern Kerala and Tulunadu, for example, spirit-channelling mythologies can be seen as an assertion of lower-caste cultural heritage against the dominance of Brahmanical religion. Countless pages have been written on the politics of the wars between the godly Devas and demonic Asuras of Hindu mythology, debating whether or not those conflicts should be read as metaphors for the subjugation of indigenous peoples by Aryan invaders. There are also prickly questions about where "tribe" ends and "caste" begins, and how tribal deities change when they are subsumed within Hinduism. But these issues are better dealt with in a more academic book. We have tried to sidestep them, hopefully not too clumsily.*

Yet another problem is how to decide what counts as a demon and what doesn't. Indian religions don't emphasize good-versus-evil binary dualism the way Western Christianity does. Some of India's most fearsome undead fiends are worshipped and prayed to on a regular basis; and conversely there are deities—such as the goddess Kali—who go about wearing necklaces of skulls and skirts of severed legs, but whose devotees would be offended if you called them demons.

The line we have drawn is somewhat arbitrary. We have attempted to include the union of the following sets: 1) all those supernatural or mythical entities who are primarily malevolent towards humankind, 2) all those who are the ghosts of dead people, and 3) all those who are clearly not objects of worship.†

One final technical note on a thorny issue: spelling.

....

* There are a few cases where mentioning caste is unavoidable—for example, a ghost like the Brahmadaitya has its certificate baked right into its name.
† It was of course impossible to cover them "all". But we tried anyway.

India's languages all have competing schemes for writing words in the English alphabet. One way to standardize everything would have been to use the International Alphabet of Sanskrit Transliteration, the way academic Indologists do; but we decided against this. For Indians who read English, *cuṛail* is much harder to recognize than *chudail*—and that diacritical mark makes the word look strangely clinical. Also, many Northeastern languages use the Roman script with their own established systems of orthography, and it didn't seem right to alter the standard spellings of Khasi or Karbi words to match a system devised for a totally unrelated ancient language.

Instead, we have gone with the transliterations that most bilingual speakers of each source language would use, or else the spelling most commonly found in our references—without regard for consistency across languages.

The result, though, is that the spellings in this book are a bit of a mess. For example, for the /ɑ:/ sound, we've used "a" sometimes and "aa" other times; in a few cases, there's inconsistency within the same word. We considered putting together a pronunciation guide—but given that many of the words are used across several languages and dialects with a range of local pronunciations, the project was simply too daunting. If you want to be sure how to pronounce something correctly, you'll just have to look that up that yourself.

Many, many people contributed to this book: of course all the artists, poets, and translators whose work is featured within; all the writers and researchers in the bibliography; and over a hundred other informants—friends, acquaintances, people we chatted with at comic cons and book events, and people who answered questions online. We would like to give special thanks to the following people who made especially important contributions: Misha Michael, for editing and suggestions; Anannya Baruah, credited elsewhere for her featured translation, for her research assistance and translations of Assamese source material; P.S. Nissim, for general suggestions and corrections; S. Divyapriya, Adarsh Yadav, and Sowmya Vaidyanathan, for their help in research assistance and compiling the bibliography; Nahim Abdullah, who provided sources of Kaasrote Baase folklore and more; Jaywant Michael, for his notes on the ghosts of Uttarakhand; Dr. M. Thanuja and Dr. S. Ponnarasu, for providing sources and answering questions on various Dravidian ghosts; Kuzhali Manickavel, for her input on Yakshis; Monidipa Mondal, for tips and leads on Bengali spirits; and Musharraf Ali Farooqi, for providing sources on the Jinn.

Rakesh Khanna
Chennai, October 2020

*Reference numbers *Ref* at the end of each entry relate to
the bibliography which begins on page 395.

AAVI

Aavi means "vapour" in Tamil. It is the word used for the steam from an idli cooker, the morning haze above a village lake, or the misty cloud of a person's breath on a chilly night in the Nilgiris.

The word also signifies the vital spirit of a living thing: the sigh that leaves the body at the moment of death, to linger on as a ghost.

Most ghosts in Indian stories can take on a physical form. They disguise themselves as real, solid people that can be touched and felt. They can pick things up, wield weapons, do chores, eat food. They are often colourful: in cartoons and picture books, they're drawn with bright blue or green or orange skin. They usually have fangs. When they *aren't* in corporeal form, they either become invisible or transform into thick purple smog. They tend to be raucous and loud and vicious and bloodthirsty, whether or not they had that sort of a personality when they were alive.

The Aavi is an anomaly. In many ways it resembles the ghosts of Western stories more closely than Indian ones. It is wispy, white, forlorn, and brooding. It retains a lot of its personality from life, recalling its friends and loved ones as well as its enemies and its unfulfilled desires. Aavis can have only limited interaction with objects in the material plane, and they have a tendency to disappear into thin air when threatened.

Not to say that they can't be scary. An Aavi might stretch its spectral arm through a wall, slowly moving its fingers as though grasping for something, sending any witnesses screaming away in terror. Or on a still and moonless night, its transparent head might roll out from underneath a cot, give a few anguished sobs, and then vanish.

But they almost never *eat* anyone.

An Aavi that retains ties to the world of the living is typically a murder victim, or perhaps a lover driven to suicide. It can possess people, but it rarely causes illness or madness. Instead, the Aavi provides information to help others avenge its death. When it enters a living person, it causes them to start speaking in an unnatural voice; or else it makes the spirit-medium fall into a trance and set its secrets to paper in strange and unfamiliar handwriting.

Some of the similarity between the Aavi and the ghosts of Europe may be traced to the Tamil country's ancient Christian community, or to the long centuries under colonial rule. But much of the influence is probably due to a more specific band of travellers: the Theosophists.

In the late 19th century, a religious movement known as Spiritualism was
ascendant in the Western world. Its adherents believed that the human soul
was distinct from matter and that it remained active after death. Many of them
rejected mainstream Christianity and set out eastwards in search of ancient
secrets and esoteric knowledge.

Several prominent Spiritualists—including Annie Besant, Henry Steel
Olcott, Charles Leadbeater, and Helena Blavatsky—made their way to Madras.
In the 1880s, on a 260-acre campus on the south bank of the Adyar River,
they established the International Headquarters of the Theosophical Society, an
organization devoted to "investigating the unexplained laws of Nature".

Their major preoccupation was making contact with ghosts. The members
of the society, and Madame Blavatsky in particular, were famous for holding
séances, during which spirit-mediums would channel energies from "the other
side". Some of the mediums would ooze ectoplasm, a viscous supernatural goo
that supposedly flowed from the orifices during a visitation. Others would
engage in a practice called automatic writing, letting paranormal forces move
their pens across the page without their conscious effort.

Not all of the early Theosophists were pure in their motives. Blavatsky was
accused of being a fraudster who used cheap magic tricks to fool people. Others
confessed to darker crimes. Nevertheless, their "occult investigations" had an
outsized impact on the South Indian imagination.

For example, Blavatsky had a theory, expounded in her 1888 book *The Secret
Doctrine*, regarding an ancient sunken continent called Lemuria. In the ancient
past, this continent was supposed to have occupied most of what is now the
Indian Ocean, connecting Sri Lanka to Madagascar and Australia. Blavatsky
proposed Lemuria as the land of what she called the "Third Root Race"—
ancestral humans who had lived alongside the dinosaurs. Her idea was taken
up by native writers of the Tamil renaissance, who gave the ancient landmass
the name Kumarikandam (or Tamilagam). A popular pseudohistory emerged in
which Kumarikandam was the birthplace of Tamil civilization. Some said it had
been a land ruled by a succession of powerful women; others asserted that it had
been the seat of the Pandian Dynasty for 10,000 years, before sea levels rose and
the ocean claimed it.

By the 1950s, the scientific community had turned to embrace the theory
of plate tectonics, which showed that Lemuria could never have existed. The
southern landmasses of the world were indeed once connected—but that was
some 150 million years ago, long before the evolution of humans. They have
been drifting apart ever since.

Despite these revelations, the legend of the lost continent endures. Tamil politicians and orators still draw allusions to a mythical homeland sunk beneath the waves, and Kumarikandam remains a popular subject in Tamil poetry and speculative fiction.

Though Blavatsky died in 1891, the Theosophists' efforts to contact the spirit world continued into the 20th century. Indeed, the Society remains active today, though it is less focused on generating ectoplasm than it once was.

In the meantime, the city of Madras, now Chennai, expanded and grew around it, developing into a major centre for publishing and filmmaking. Generations of writers grew up hearing stories about spirit-mediums and astral bodies. It would seem that the Aavi of Tamil popular culture, of countless television serials and pulp horror novels, is modelled at least in part after the spirits that were channeled at the séances in Adyar.

Akin to the Aavi, but more powerful and malevolent, is the **Pey**, sometimes called Pey Aavi. These more volatile South Indian spirits probably represent an older stratum of belief. The word Achuthaavi or "unclean spirit" is also used, especially in Christian contexts, for a possessing demon which must be exorcized.

Ref: 1, 15, 174, 291, 577

AHMAW

Ahmaw is a sort of vampire soul or jealousy demon found in the traditional belief of the Mara people, whose homeland is an autonomous district in the southeast corner of the state of Mizoram, on the border with Myanmar. This spirit can project itself from one body into another.

If a person is Ahmaw, he is perpetually envious. When he covets something that belongs to another—it might be fancy clothes, jewellery, or real estate—he sends part of his spirit inside the owner. This causes an excruciating stomach ache, so severe that it can be fatal if untreated. The affected person dreams of being chased by a horse or a dog, or of a leech crawling over his body.

When a person falls sick and the cause of the sickness is believed to be someone else's Ahmaw, the victim's relatives make offerings in order to satiate the spirit and drive it out of the afflicted person. If the sickness does not subside, the gifts become progressively more generous. First, a large gourd-spoon full of food is offered; then a slaughtered chicken; then a slaughtered pig; then expensive jewellery; and finally a lick of human blood, drawn from the big toe of a loved one.

The head of someone who is Ahmaw can detach from the body at night.* The head goes rolling around into kitchens in search of meat to gobble up, or outside in search of livestock to kill. Some say the head can fly through the air in the form of a flickering flame. The head can also reduplicate itself; an Ahmaw may have as many as ten ghost-heads prowling for food. If *all* of these heads are captured and confined before they can roll back to rejoin the body at dawn, then the host body as well as the heads will die.

In days past, people suspected of being Ahmaw—that is, those who were thought to be the cause of the sickness—were shunned and ostracized by society. If a woman was believed to be Ahmaw, she might find it impossible to get married. A shopkeeper might be unable to attract customers. Accusing someone of being Ahmaw, therefore, was a very serious matter, and anyone who made an allegation later judged to be false could be forced to pay fines of restitution.

The Mara believe that Ahmaw is not native to Maraland. It is thought to have been introduced by a visitor from the east, a man who befriended a Mara family and sometimes came to stay with them. Whenever this man visited, there would be sudden and mysterious deaths of handsome men and beautiful women. Pigs and cows would die as well. Eventually becoming suspicious, the villagers burst into the man's room one night to find his headless body lying there. They prevented the wandering head from reattaching itself, thus killing him. Then they threw the Ahmaw's corpse into the river.

A little while later, a pheasant bird called *fachari* came to feed on the worms that were eating the corpse, and in this way the Ahmaw possessed the body of the pheasant. Later on, the catfish called *ngalei* also nibbled the decaying flesh, and so the Ahmaw entered the fish's body as well. Later on, both the pheasant and the catfish were caught and eaten by some Mara people, and this is how Ahmaw came to infect people in Maraland.

Some say that there are two distinct types of Ahmaw: the Ngalei Ahmaw, descended from the catfish, is more dangerous than the Fachari Ahmaw, descended from the pheasant. The condition is believed to run in families, and to be transmittable through sexual intercourse.

---

* Thus the Ahmaw bears some resemblance to the **Than-Thin Daini** of Garo lore and the Krasue of Thailand. However, unlike these demons, the Ahmaw host is often male.

Today, though nearly all Mara people have converted to Christianity, belief in Ahmaw persists. It is sometimes discussed in the context of Christian theology as one of the works of the Devil.

Ref: 33, 216, 259

AIRI

Airi haunts the dense and hilly jungles of Kumaon in Uttarakhand. He has a hideous face with eyes on top of his head. Some say he has four arms which carry different weapons; others say his arms themselves are bows and arrows.

Airi is said to be the ghost of a wealthy man and avid hunter who died while on shikar. He can be heard in the middle of the night crashing through the trees with his hunting party. Airi is carried aloft by his two ghostly litter-bearers, Sau and Bhau, who call out "Sau, sau" as they walk. He is also accompanied by his loyal ghost-hounds and a pair of **Anchheri** bodyguards with backwards-turned feet. Other attendant ghosts beat the bushes ahead of the palanquin to drive out the animals.

Airi is in the habit of spitting a lot. His saliva is extremely poisonous. If a glob of it lands on someone, that person is doomed to die within a few days unless healing rituals are performed.

Getting spat on is bad enough; but coming face to face with Airi is *instantly* fatal. The unlucky person who looks him in the eye will either be burnt to a pile of ashes or ripped into shreds by his ferocious dogs.

Though human blood is not his main source of nourishment, Airi enjoys a taste of it from time to time. To get it, he uses his supernatural powers to inflict wounds on people. One way in which he does this is to cause small accidents, making people trip and scrape themselves as they walk through the forest or as they work in the fields. Another method is to stir up arguments between friends and relatives, pit them against each other in fistfights, and wait for someone's nose to get busted.

Airi is also blamed when people wake up to find themselves partially paralysed or extremely weak. It is thought that this happens because one of his invisible arrows has flown through a smokehole in the wall and struck the victim. Thus the Kumaoni proverb *Dalamuni se jano, jalamuni ni seno*: "Stoop under a branch, but never sleep under a niche."

Despite all this, many Kumaonis consider Airi Devata to be a benevolent deity and protector of livestock. There are temples devoted to him throughout

the region. Airi's shrines are roofless; the deity within is represented by a trident, around which stones are placed to represent his dogs and attendants. Devotees give offerings of bows and arrows. Goat kids are also sometimes sacrificed to Airi, and pieces of cotton cloth stained red with their blood are flown as flags above the temple. The tail is cut off and kept beside the trident.

It is believed that if he is properly worshipped at the time of conception of a child, Airi protects the young life in the womb, in infancy, and all the way up through adolescence. However, if the child grows up and waits too long to get married, Airi will turn against him or her.

Some devotees associate Airi with Arjuna, the archer hero of the Mahabharata epic. Connections can also be drawn to the "Wild Hunt" of European folklore—a roving nocturnal band of supernatural game-hunters, usually led by the god Woden.

An even closer relative is Hantu Pemburu, the spectre huntsman of Malay legend. This spirit, too, travels with demon-hounds, spits venom, carries different weapons in his four arms, and has eyes on the top of his head. Hantu Pemburu is said to be on an eternal search for a buck mouse-deer that is pregnant with male offspring; and since he has failed to find one on Earth, his eyes have turned upwards to scour the heavens.*

Ref: 4, 163, 165, 323, 337, 511

ᐛ AJAJU ᐛ

The Ajaju is a species of man-eating monster from the Garo Hills of Meghalaya. These bizarrely constructed creatures have the heads of giant chameleons and the arms and bodies of monkeys, but their legs are like bamboo stalks—long, straight, stiff, and skinny. These legs cannot bend, for they have no knees.†

This makes it very difficult for Ajajus to walk on open ground. In forested areas, though, they can move quite rapidly by swinging from tree branch to tree branch.

The Ajaju makes a shrill call as it swings through the forest: "Wa-oh, wa-oh." If any person mistakes this sound for a human voice, and calls back in answer, the Ajaju will come closer and closer until the person is near enough to attack.

An Ajaju has twelve long forked tongues which lash out from its mouth like ropes. As soon as these tongues make contact with the victim's skin, the flesh starts to liquefy. The tongues constrict around the person's half-melted body and reel it into the Ajaju's mouth. Afterwards, the monster spits out the bones.

If you happen to encounter an Ajaju in a hilly forest, you should always run downhill, as the monster finds it quite difficult to follow on its kneeless legs.

* Hantu Pemburu is in turn related to the character Hantu Seburu, a folkloric spirit hunter of the Temuan people, a tribe of Orang Asli (the aboriginal people of Malaysia.) Lists of Indian ghosts compiled by foreigners sometimes include the "Hanh Saburo" or "Bantu Saburo", described as an "Indian forest vampire" or "black hunter ghost". The name is apparently a misspelling of the Orang Asli spirit. It is an intriguing mystery how the Airi/Hantu Pemburu legend apparently travelled from Kumaon to Malaysia, or perhaps in the other direction, without leaving similar folk stories anywhere in between.
† Compare with the Karbi monster **Kenglong-po**.

If you try to run uphill, the Ajaju is certain to catch you with its long, lashing tongues.

The bones of an Ajaju are thought to have magical properties. They are an ingredient in spells to reincarnate the dead. When fashioned into amulets, they offer protection against disease and evil spirits.

Ref: 51, 126, 306

ALAKHANI

The Alakhani is a tiny pixie-like spirit that lives under the sheltering leaf of a plant called the *alakhani-bah*, which grows in thickets of bamboo. It is found in the northeastern state of Assam.

A female Alakhani is energetic and mischievous. She roams the jungle in search of fun. If she finds a man out walking by himself she will possess him for a lark, causing him to act bizarrely, wander off, and get lost. When the man comes to his senses (usually in some strange and embarrassing position, such as lying naked in a mud puddle, or strapped upside-down to the trunk of a tree), he might hear a tiny giggle as the quick-footed spirit dances off into the undergrowth.

Male Alakhanis are more rarely encountered, and this is lucky, for they are far less friendly. An attack by a male Alakhani can cause heartburn painful enough to knock a man unconscious, triggering lasting health problems.

Ref: 159, 294

ALCHI

In the traditional religion of the Malto people of Jharkhand and Bihar, who are also known as the Maler or Paharia, an Alchi is a fearsome evil spirit. There are various types. All Alchi are usually invisible, showing themselves only very rarely.

Masani Alchi lives near the village graveyard and attacks people who pass by there at night. Women who come to the graveyard in the middle of the night and dance naked for this spirit's pleasure are rewarded with supernatural power (see **Churgin**).

8

A **Pori** is the ghost of a human man, woman, or child. It too lives in the graveyard, but sometimes wanders outside its boundaries wearing a dirty cloth. It appears black with wide white eyes. When a Pori attacks someone it causes gastric distress.

A **Jampori** is the ghost of a *demno* or Malto shaman. After death, he goes to live at the base of a tree—usually a banyan—where he is sometimes seen around noon or midnight. He has long hair and gaint, round, fearsome eyes. He is especially dangerous to pregnant women. He carries a staff to beat his victims with.

Dinde is a black ghost with yellow eyes who lives in mango trees. One account says it is the ghost of an unmarried woman who troubles men and women indiscriminately, while another says it is a male spirit who only molests women.

Mara Kambe is another tree-dweller with long matted black hair, white eyes, and backwards-turned feet and hands. He is sometimes seen swinging on vines through the forest. Mara Kambe is very dangerous to pregnant women, whom he always attacks.

Jame is another male spirit who lives on a black stone. He attacks both men and women, and also murders infants. He is propitiated with black chickens or black pigeons.

The **Narrah** is a shapeshifting spirit who haunts stagnant pools of water. At night it takes the form of an animal (a boar, muskrat, or tiger), sneaks into people's houses, and licks them as they sleep, causing agonizing diseases such as œdema.

Am Narrah is a smaller version of the Narrah that lives in clean springs. Offerings of puffed corn and bread are thrown into the river for Am Narrah; in case of more severe illness, a black chicken is sacrificed as well.

Umat Narrah lives under rocks and causes epilepsy.

Other Alchi whose names are mentioned in studies of Malto religion are **Ampacha**, **Simadandi**, **Umble Cheno**, **Erbekker**, and **Mari**. A large bamboo pole is placed in front of Malto homes to ward these spirits away.

Ref: 17, 48, 392

~~ ALEYA ~~
(AND OTHER GHOSTLY LIGHTS)

Reports of unexplained ghostly lights that flicker and move about in the dark are common the world over. The Latin name for these radiances is *ignis fatuus*, meaning "fool's fire". Scientists say they are photon emissions caused by the oxidation of methane and other gases released into the air by rotting organic matter.

But many witnesses refuse to accept this explanation, insisting instead that the lights are supernatural in origin.

In Bengali, they are known as Atoshi Bhoot or Aleya. They are most often seen over marshy areas and water bodies. Some say they are the ghosts of women who were burnt to death; others say they are the spectres of those who passed away with unfulfilled desires. Fishermen out late at night can get transfixed by the Aleya and follow them into muddy overgrown bogs, where their boats get stuck. The lucky ones manage to wade their way out onto solid earth. The unlucky ones are drawn further into the swamp to drown.

A brave person who keeps his wits about him can sometimes manage to catch an Aleya and chop it up into pieces. This is thought to be a merciful act, since it releases the spirit from torment.

In Kumaon, the phantom light is called Tola, and he is said to be the ghost of a bachelor. He is seen only on lonely hills, for the other ghosts refuse to associate with him.

In Kashmir, mysterious lights in the hills are thought to be the flaming eyes of the **Bram Bram Chok**.

In other parts of North India, ghost lights over water are attributed to the snake-like **Nagas**. This belief stretches eastwards into Thailand, where giant Nagas that live in the Mekong River are said to produce the annual phenomenon known as the Phaya Nak Lights, or Naga fireballs.

Dumas Beach, a black-sand beach dotted with ancient graveyards near Surat, Gujarat, is supposed to be haunted at night by glowing orbs and unexplained whispering voices. These are said to be manifestations of the restless spirits of the dead.

Ghost lights have also been reported from above the salt flats in the Rann of Kutchh, where they are called Chir Batti. These spirits are playful, engaging onlookers in games of hide and seek.

In Karnataka and Tamil Nadu, the ghost lights are attributed to a malevolent spirit who lives in the hills—the **Kollivay Pey**, also known as Kolli Deva, Kolli Pisaasu or Thikolli Pisaasu.

Up until a few decades ago, a different sort of ghost-light, called Kuliyande Choote, was reported from Kasaragod in Kerala. These lights came from the sea. Observers claimed that on moonless nights they would appear at first in ones and twos, and then quickly multiply into hundreds and thousands and even millions of small torch-blazes, streaming along the beach in pulsating waves. Some of them came in far enough inland to climb up trees and jump back down, forming orderly queues of moving serial lights as they did so. The Kuliyande Choote ran from anyone who had a fishing net, and they would disperse quickly at the sound of the *azaan* from the local mosque. Like many other supernatural phenomena, the Kuliyande Choote are said to have disappeared after electric lights became prevalent.

The Chote Naga tribe of Northeast India call the fireball spirits Lammeithanpi. Though not often seen anymore, they are said to have once been common, inhabiting rocky crevices and inaccessible places along mountain streams. In Kalimpong, such spirits are called Rakhae Bhoot.

The Garos of Meghalaya believe that the witches called Skal (see **Swkal**) can take the form of fireflies. In some stories, they can detach their heads, which fly around at night like glowing balls.

The Kuki tribes call the faint and flickering ghost lights of the hills Kaomei. It is thought that the vampire spirits **Kaoshe** take this form when they wander abroad at night.

The Kukis also tell of another ghost-light, called the Gamkau, with a different sort of behaviour. This spirit moves at great speed when it moves; when it stops, it does so suddenly and stays fixed in one place, its light intensely bright and pulsating. Gamkaus are usually noticed by people who go fishing in the nighttime. It is considered very unlucky to point at them or look at them too closely, and actual contact with a Gamkau is supposed to be immediately fatal.

Ref: 39, 59, 74, 123, 219, 412, 418

ALHA AND UDAL

Alha and Udal were two legendary generals in the army of Raja Parimardi of Chandela who warred against the king Prithviraj Chauhan in the year 1182. Ballads about the exploits of these two heroes have been sung for centuries in different Central Indian dialects, especially Bundeli. The epic poem *Alha-Khand* gives descriptions of fifty-two different wars in which the two brothers fought side by side.

Not only are Alha and Udal said to have been the best swordsmen of their time, they were also skilled in the art of *kushti* (traditional mud wrestling). They lived in Maihar, now in Madhya Pradesh. They were great devotees of Sharda Mata, the deity whose temple sits at the top of a hill outside town.

Today, the ghosts of these warriors are said to visit the temple every day in the wee hours of the morning to worship the goddess. Entry to the temple building is strictly prohibited between the hours of 2 and 5 a.m. to ensure the spirits are undisturbed. Alha arrives riding on the ghost of his elephant, whose name is Pachsawad, while Udal rides on a ghostly pegasus named Bendil.

It is believed that the goddess will not accept worship from others before the two ghosts arrive, and that anyone foolish enough to defy the rule will die.

Ref: 131, 398, 400

⊱⊰ ALVANTIN ⊱⊰

This name is used in Goa and other parts of Western India for the ghost of a woman who died in childbirth, but whose child survived. In some communities, it can also be used for a woman who died just before she was about to be married.

These spirits are incorporeal and invisible, and usually don't bother the living. They never haunt strangers. Alvantins only cause trouble to members of their own family, and even then only if someone is about to experience the major life event which fate denied to the deceased.

Suppose a woman dies in childbirth. When her widower remarries, the ghost of the dead woman might become envious at the idea of a different woman mothering her child. The Alvantin may then possess the new wife and harass and torment her.

Or suppose a woman dies the night before her wedding. Then, when a younger sister or a niece gets married, the Alvantin may return to haunt the bride.

An Alvantin may haunt a family for centuries, over many generations, even after the name of the deceased is long forgotten and the house she lived in has crumbled to dust. But the ghost only troubles women—that too, only those women fathered by, or married to, members of the male line of descent from her father or her husband. For example, the dead woman's brother's daughters, or her brother's sons' wives, are at risk; but her sister's descendants are immune.

A woman exorcist is required to drive an Alvantin out of a possessed person. Male exorcists are ineffectual against this spirit.

Ref: 29, 575

~— AMBI JAKBYRYT —~

In the folklore of the Atong people of Meghalaya—a subgroup of the Garo tribe—Ambi Jakbyryt is a ghostly hand, with no body attached.

When people walk on jungle paths on dark and moonless nights, the Ambi Jakbyryt will begin to follow them, floating silently behind in mid-air. When they least expect it, it reaches forward and claws their back.

When the person turns around, yelping in pain and alarm, they see the disembodied hand flying into the shadows.

Ref: 51

~— ANANGU —~

Ancient Tamil literature has a wide variety of terms for ghosts and demons: Oozhi, Paasam, Yaadam, Savam, and Veri being a few of them. But there is not much to say about these beings by way of description. If the words ever referred to *specific* types of spirits, those shades of meaning are now mostly lost to the mists of time.

Another ancient term is Anangu. This word occurs in the *Tholkappiyam*, the oldest surviving work of Tamil literature, and is still used today. Its meaning has varied widely over the centuries, making the Anangu a rather difficult spirit to characterize.

But we shall hazard a try.

The most common understanding seems to be that an Anangu is a demoness of hysterical grief—an embodiment of the rage stemming from women's oppression.

The Anangu has been described as a preternaturally beautiful celestial damsel, an attacking deity from the mountains who wears bright flowers in her long flowing hair; but also as a shapeshifter, or as a formless entity. Some poems paint her as a succubus or **Mohini**—a temptress who feeds on the souls of weak men drawn to her by lust. Others say that she is the demon unleashed by a woman with disruptive sexuality: a married slut, an unchaste widow. But the Anangu's activities are driven by a thirst for vengeance rather than by physical desire.

In the ancient Tamil epic *Silappathikaram*, or "The Anklet Story", when Kannagi learns that her husband has been wrongly executed, she is described as an Anangu. The term has also been connected to Suparnakha—the **Rakshasi** of the *Ramayana* who was humiliated and disfigured for the crime of desiring the wrong man—and to the folkloric character **Neeli**.

Anangu is also the name of a modern Tamil feminist literary movement and magazine, founded by the Puducherry-born poet Malathi Maithri and associated with other writers like Salma, Kutti Revathi, and Sukirtharani. Their work has been translated into English in a collection called *Wild Girls, Wicked Words*, and perhaps this title encapsulates the sense of the word Anangu as succinctly as can be hoped.

Ref: 441, 442

⊱⊰ ANCHHERI ⊱⊰

The Anchheri live high in the hills of Kumaon and Garhwal in Uttarakhand. Sometimes, at night, they descend to lower altitudes to play near the shores of lakes and in flowering meadows. They appear in groups, cavorting and chasing each other in what appears to be a frolicsome mood. But if you look closely you will see that their eyes are hollow and sunken, for these are the ghosts of girls who died unnatural deaths—either from murder, disease, or neglect.

Despite their playfulness, they are very dangerous. If a living girl sees them and tries to join their games, she will die. It is unsafe to visit the favoured playgrounds of Anchheri even during the daytime after they have left. When little girls or elderly people fall sick, it is thought to be because the shadow of an Anchheri has fallen on them.

Anchheri hate the colour red. Some say that the best defence against them is to tie a red ribbon around one's neck. But according to other stories, the colour makes the Anchheri fly into a rage, so red clothing may invite an attack rather than repel it.

These ghosts appreciate gifts—especially jewellery, kajal for the eyes, and colourful saris or shawls. If they are regularly propitiated with such things, they cause less trouble for the living.

Anchheri play a role in a famous Garhwali folk ballad known as *Jeetu Bagdwal*. This is the tragic tale of a young man named Jeetu, said to have lived around 500 years ago during the reign of Raja Man Singh.

According to this story, Jeetu had to make a journey to his sister's village to invite her for a pooja. It was a long journey, and after travelling some distance, Jeetu stopped to rest and play his flute.

The Anchheris who lived on the nearby mountain of Khait Parvat heard his music. They floated down through the trees and started to dance around him in a circle. The sound of the bells on their anklets hypnotized Jeetu, and he slowly fell asleep. Then the ghosts entered his body through his eyes, his ears, and his hands, and began to drink his blood.

Shaking himself awake, he insisted that the spirits let him go so that he could meet his sister. He promised that once he had returned and the pooja was done, they could take him.

The Anchheri agreed.

Jeetu finished the journey to his sister's village, brought her back home, and conducted the rest of the pooja successfully. But as soon as the rituals were over, the Anchheri swept down from the hills and stole him away; and as they left, they caused a calamitous landslide which killed his sister and every other member of his family.

"Native American" Anchheri

Many Western websites on supernatural phenomena describe a spirit called the "Acheri" from the folklore of the Chippewa, a Native American tribe also known as the Ojibwe. This appears to be an error caused by misunderstanding of the term "Indian" in lists of spirits from around the world. The most likely explanation is that at some point in the last decade or two, a non-indigenous American author spuriously assigned the legend to the Chippewa to make it sound more authentic. "Acheri" was the spelling used in British accounts of Kumaoni folklore from as long ago as 1859, and the *Jeetu Bagdwal* story suggests a much older pedigree than that; on the other hand we have found no approximation of either the word or the myth in any book of genuine Ojibwe or Anishinaabe stories.

Nevertheless, in a case of cultural-appropriation-gone-haywire, the supposedly Chippewa "Acheri" has successfully propagated around the internet, inspiring spooky artworks, stories, and even whole novels set in the North American Midwest, featuring Native American spirits with all the characteristics of a Himalayan ghost.

Ref: 74, 165, 185, 511

ANGRA MAINYU

In Zoroastrianism, Angra Mainyu—also called Ahriman—is the adversary of God in the great cosmic battle between good and evil. He is the king of all the Daevas (see **Dev**), the grand demon of deceit, chaos, and destruction.

Zoroaster taught that in the beginning Ahura Mazda, the creator, made twenty-four great Yazatas. He placed these angels inside a celestial egg. But Angra Mainyu created twenty-four evil Daevas to oppose them, and they bored holes through the egg to attack. This war between the Yazatas and the Daevas has raged ever since.

In Persian tradition, Angra Mainyu was a primordial entity. He came into being at the same time as the Ahura Mazda, and was considered nearly his equal in power.

However, among the Parsis of India, he has been pulled down a notch in the hierarchy: he is merely the destructive emanation of Ahura Mazda, rather than his rival.

This demon is associated with foul smells. He can take on the shape of a worm, snake, fly, or lizard.

In the Pahlavi language, the word Ahriman was always written upside-down, as a sign of contempt.

Ref. 443

AONGLAMLA

Aonglamla, also called Alonglemla or Aonglemlatsü, is a diminutive jungle spirit known from the folklore of the Ao Naga people of Nagaland. According to most accounts—but not quite all—she is female. She stands just about two feet tall, with wild hair that falls all the way from her head to the ground. Her feet are turned to point backwards, and there is hair that grows on her legs and feet as well. She is sometimes encountered bathing in lonely jungle streams or cave pools, talking or laughing to herself, or singing songs in an alien language.

This spirit—it has been argued that "entity" is a better word—has a tendency to *flicker*. One moment she's there, the next she's gone. The reason for the flickering, some say, is that she becomes invisible whenever she makes direct contact with the ground. You can only see her when she is floating in a pool of water; or if she hops; or if she steps on her hair while she's walking. Others say that she moves backwards and forwards in time. She appears young and healthy one second, then suddenly old and wizened—and then she blinks out of existence entirely for a while.

The sighting of Aonglamla is very unlucky. Those who catch a glimpse of her can expect to fall very ill soon afterwards, perhaps even die; or they might see a close friend perish in an gruesome accident. However, Aonglamla is not malevolent by nature. Instead, she has a sort of melancholy detachment from the human realm.

After a woman dies, her ghost meets Aonglamla on the way to the village of the dead. Aonglamla accosts her, demanding a gift. It is for this reason that a round pink swordbean seed is placed beside a woman's corpse on her corpse-platform. When the dead woman rolls the seed along the ground, Aonglamla excitedly runs after it, thinking it's a toy—thus allowing the ghost to continue on her way.*

It was claimed in recent years that Aonglamla was captured and killed by hunters. The perpetrators met their own ends in a grisly accident not long afterwards. The people who came to be in possession of Aonglamla's remains were trying to sell them, distributing images on Whatsapp that showed a bizarre blackened skeleton with elongated legs and gigantic eye sockets.

There have, however, been multiple sightings of Aonglamla alive since then, and it seems likely that the strange skeleton probably belonged to a Hoolock gibbon, a small ape native to the region.

Or perhaps, due to her ability to skip through time, Aonglamla is simultaneously alive and dead.

Ref: 30, 201, 265, 332

APASMARA

Apasmara, also called Muyalaka, is a Hindu demon of ignorance and ego. He appears as a dwarf, and is usually depicted with his hands in the *anjali mudra*, or "namaste pose".

One story goes that Apasmara was brought to life by a sect of powerful rogue sadhus. These ascetics, who lived in a mangrove swamp, created him in an attempt to kill Lord Shiva. But Shiva, in his avatar as Nataraja, began his cosmic dance—the *tandava*—and stamped Apasmara underfoot.

The demon can be seen in most images of the dancing Nataraja.

It is said that Apasmara can never be killed, so Shiva must stand on him for all eternity.

Ref: 444

....

* Similar underworld guardian figures, encountered by a person's ghost on its way to the village of the dead, are found in many other mythologies from Northeast India. For example, compare with the Garo ogre **Nawang**.

APSARA

In mainstream Hindu and Buddhist mythology, Apsaras are beautiful celestial angels or nymphs—dancers, singers, and seductresses in the service of the gods. Their Sanskrit name, *a-psaras*, means "shameless"—a reference to their promiscuity.

The best-known of them are Urvashi, Tilottama, Menaka, Rambha, and Ghritachi, all of whom are important figures in mythology. Dozens more Apsaras are named in the *Mahabharata* and *Ramayana* epics. For the most part, they are benevolent, though they sometimes throw curses when they are very annoyed.

In some local traditions, the Apsaras can be more sinister. They may simply be amoral creatures, who think nothing of murdering humans on a whim. In the ancient *Atharva Veda*, too, Apsaras take the role of malevolent possessing demons; but they are also revered as deities of gambling.

The word is sometimes used as a synonym of **Peri**, or of the Kumaoni ghosts called **Anchheri**.

In Assam it is said that a person who steps on an Apsara's shadow, or who angers the Apsara in some other way, will be put under a magic spell that will cause him to wither away and die.

Apsaras are always women. Their male consorts are the **Gandharvas**.

Ref: 119, 391

ARAKKAN

In Tamil folklore, Arakkans are gigantic humanoid monsters, usually depicted as muscular male creatures with red skin. They live in solitude at the tops of forested hills.

An Arakkan will rarely bother humans unless they trespass in his lair or offend him in some way. In this case the angry Arakkan might hurl a giant boulder at the intruders, instantly crushing them to death.

Alternatively, the Arakkan might decide to take the humans captive. Such captives usually end up wishing they *had* been smashed by a boulder, for Arakkans are sadistic taskmasters who force their prisoners to do backbreaking, repetitive work.

One folktale tells of a Paataal Arakkan from the jewel-studded netherworld of Paataal Lok, who became enamoured with a human woman and abducted her. This Arakkan had the power of turning his enemies to stone. He also had the power of hiding his soul outside his body, so that he would be impossible to defeat in battle.

The imprisoned woman kept refusing to marry him. Finally, she agreed, but on a condition: he should tell her where he kept his soul, so that as his dutiful wife she might be its caretaker. The Arakkan told her that he kept it in the form of a snake.

Luckily for her, the woman was able to pass this information on to a man who found the snake and killed it, thus destroying the Arakkan and setting her free.

There are different theories about the etymology of the word "Arakkan". Many believe it came from the Sanskrit **Rakshasa** through Maharashtri Prakrit, while others claim it is a native Dravidian word. Whatever the truth, "Arakkan" has been used in ancient Tamil texts to refer to the character Ravana from the *Ramayana*; in Tamil translations of European fairy tales, such as *Jack and the Beanstalk*, to mean "giant"; in environmental writing to refer to the spectre of nuclear disaster; and in astronomy to mean the supermassive black hole at the centre of the Milky Way.

Ref: 107, 220, 247, 356, 434, 438, 439

ASHWATTHAMA

Ashwatthama is not exactly a ghost, for he never died; but he still manages to haunt the present, thousands of years after his birth.

The *Mahabharata* tells us that Ashwatthama's father was the sage Dronacharya. For many long years before his son was born, Dronacharya had practised intense asceticism, praying to Lord Shiva for a boon.

As a result of his father's devotions, Ashwatthama was born with a magic jewel in the middle of his forehead. This gem gave him special powers. No illness could affect him; he could feel neither hunger, nor thirst, nor tiredness. He could stay alive even without needing to breathe. He was a *chiranjeevi*—one of the very few "immortals" who will survive until the end of Kali Yuga, the current æon, more than 400,000 years in the future.

In the Kurukshetra War, Ashwatthama fought on the side of the Kauravas against the Pandavas, led by Arjuna. He was a ferocious warrior with deadly skill on the battlefield, and he dispatched many opponents.

Then the Pandavas killed Drona, his father, and Ashwatthama became even more dangerous. Consumed by murderous rage, he aimed a powerful supernatural weapon called the *brahmashirastra* at the womb of Uttara, Arjuna's daughter-in-law, in an attempt to put an end to the Pandava lineage.

In this he was thwarted by Lord Krishna, who restored Uttara's child to life. Krishna then removed the gem from Ashwatthama's forehead, and as punishment for having targeted an innocent unborn child, he cursed him to suffer for the whole of Kali Yuga. He left Ashwatthama roaming the forests, howling in pain and wishing for death, with his skin slowly melting away.

Some say that Ashwatthama is still living out this curse, and that he haunts the Asirgarh Fort in Madhya Pradesh and neighbouring areas along the Narmada

River. Several people claim to have encountered a freakishly tall man—it is believed that human beings were much taller in the days of the *Mahabharata*, averaging eight or nine feet—with a weird dent in his forehead, oozing blood and pus from sores all over his body.

In other versions, the period of Krishna's curse was 3,000 years, rather than the full length of the Yuga. Since the historical Kurukshetra War is thought to have occurred around 3000 BCE, Ashwatthama should have been released from the curse by now. This may account for other sightings of a friendlier, less hideous giant—with the strangely misshapen forehead, but without the nasty dermatological disorder.

Ref: 445, 446

ASURA

Commonly translated into English as "demon", the word Asura is very ancient, and its meaning has shifted over time. It is related to the Persian word *Ahura*, which signifies a kind of angel in the Zoroastrian faith. Many linguists believe it comes from the same Proto-Indo-European root as the word *Æsir*—the clan of deities in Norse Paganism that includes Frigg, Odin, and Thor.

In the oldest Hindu texts, the word Asura is used for any and all supernatural beings. The *Rig Veda* refers to gods such as Indra, Rudra, and Agni as Asuras.

In later texts, the pantheon of deities is divided into two main camps: the mostly benevolent Devas and mostly malevolent Asuras.

The Asuras are further subdivided into many clans. A few of the major ones are:

- The ***Adityas***, led by the god Varuna. In most stories, these deities are pious and good.

- The ***Daityas***, descended from the earth goddess Diti and the sage Kashyap. These beings have a mixed reputation. Some are worshipped as deities, but many other legendary Daitya kings became power-mad and warred with the Devas. In several Indian languages, *Daitya* is used to mean "giant", or any enormous monster.

- The ***Danavas***, sons of Danu. These are usually evil, or at least up to no good. The monstrous drought-demon **Vritra** is the eldest of the Danavas.

- The ***Nivatakavachas***, beings who wear impenetrable armour and reside at the bottom of the ocean. In the *Ramayana*, they are allied with Ravana, the Asura king of Lanka. In the *Mahabharata*, they are finally destroyed by Arjuna.

Over time, the word *Asura* began to be associated primarily with evil demons. A few characters from mythology have *-asura* appended to their name if they acted in evil ways, even if they were technically Devas by ancestry. The term **Rakshasa** is used for particularly fearsome Asuras.*

Many well-known Hindu myths tell of Asuras who subjected themselves to gruelling rituals of asceticism and purification. They did this in order to gain supernatural powers, which were granted to them as boons by the god Brahma as reward for their devotions. Thus strengthened, the Asuras proceeded to try to conquer the universe, until they were thwarted by the Devas.

The Asura brothers Sumbha and Nisumbha, for example, were granted a boon that ensured neither humans nor demons could kill them. They were eventually defeated by the goddess Kali, to whom the boon did not apply, since she was neither human nor demon.

Another Asura, Raktabeeja, had the power that whenever a drop of his blood dripped onto the ground, a new Raktabeeja would spring up from it.† He, too, was dispatched by Kali, in her avatar Kaatyayani (see **Ratha Kaateri**). After killing thousands of Raktabeeja clones, Kaatyayani managed to drink the blood from his wounds before it could spill.

The Asura king Hiranyakshipu was granted a boon that he could be killed neither inside a building nor outside of one, neither during the day nor at night, neither on the ground nor in the sky, neither by a human being nor by an animal, nor by any weapon. Though he firmly believed he was invincible, he was finally killed by Narasimha, the lion-headed avatar of Lord Vishnu. As a half-human and half-animal being, Narasimha laid Hiranyakshipu across his thighs in a doorway at twilight and ripped open his belly with his claws.

Jvalasura, the fever-demon, born from the sweat on Shiva's brow as he sat before a sacrificial fire, tried to strike the gods down with epidemic disease—but was tamed by the goddess Shitala.

Trishiras, also known as Vishwarupa, was an Asura with three heads. One drank alcohol, one drank *soma*, and one ate food. He was killed by Indra, who

---

* Some scholars believe that the term Asura (or Rakshasa, or both) was used by Indo-European-speaking Aryans to describe the Dravidian or Adivasi peoples they encountered in Central and South India. This is a matter of ongoing debate, much of it rancorous.

† Compare with **Kuttichattan**.

sent a carpenter to cut off his heads and make sure he didn't come back to life. The heads then turned into birds.

There are many other Asuras in Hindu mythology who challenged the Devas for power and were ultimately defeated by them. Andhaka, Hiranyaksha, Mayasura, Narakasura, and Darika are a few of the better-known ones. Special mention must be given to ten-faced Ravana, Lord of Lanka, antagonist of the *Ramayana*, abductor of Sita; his giant-sized brother Kumbhakarna, who sleeps for six months at a time, wakes up for one day to go on a rampage and gorge on food, and then falls back asleep; and Mahishasura, the shapeshifting buffalo-demon who fought and defeated the Devas in æons long past—only to be vanquished in turn by three-eyed Durga, in a battle commemorated in sculpture on thousands of pandals every year during the festival of Navaratri. Yet another famous Asura king is Mahabali, worshipped throughout the state of Kerala during the festival of Onam.

Though these characters are often called "demons" in English, many of them are known for positive qualities such as loyalty, wisdom, and piety. Their stories— and the stories of the gods who fought them—belong to Hindu mythology, and are not covered in detail in this book.* We have chosen to showcase only a few Asuras who are especially monstrous in their appearance, bloodthirsty in their behaviour, and/or cannibalistic in their eating habits.

Asur is also the name of a small tribe of real people from Jharkhand, variously reported as numbering between 7,000 and 30,000 individuals, who speak a language related to Santali. According to their own legend, they are descendants of Mahishasura, the buffalo-demon, whom they continue to venerate. Their traditional occupation is iron-smelting, and many continue to be employed in the region's mines.

This iron-smelting Asur tribe appears in a myth common to many tribes of Central India, including the Oraon and the Munda. In this story, the Asur's smelting industry is causing devastating pollution and heat. The trees are drying up and all the animals are in distress. The creator god sends a young boy to trick the Asur men into their furnace, where they are all burnt to death. The Asur women then turn into the spirits of the mountains and streams.

Ref: 411, 438, 447

---

* Nandita Krishnan's *The Book of Demons*[447] is an excellent reference for these stories.

✦ AVITTAM ✦

Avittam is the Tamil name for the star Dhanishta, or δ-Delphini as it is known by Western astronomers. This star gives its name to the twenty-third of the twenty-seven lunar mansions in the Hindu astrological calendar. One night every month, the moon is in Avittam.

This star manifests as a grotesque demon that lives in the cremation ground. If someone dies on the night of Avittam, then the demon visits the house of the deceased every month on the same night for the next few years. The relatives of the deceased are supposed to leave offerings for it on the *thinnai*, a raised platform outside the house: a little water in a snail shell, a handful of rice. They are also supposed to spread some sand on the thinnai so that Avittam can lie down for a while after it eats.

Failure to propitiate the demon in this manner can have dire consequences. When Avittam is angry, it grows in stature until its head touches the sky. Then, at midnight, the humongous monster stomps out of the cremation ground. In this form, it has huge bells hanging from it that clang when it walks, and smaller **Rakshasas** that ride along on its shoulders and limbs.

In its rage, Avittam is capable of destroying the house of the family that neglected to feed it, or even levelling the whole village with fire.

Ref: 291, 292

✦ BAAK ✦

The Baak is perhaps the best-known monster of Assamese folklore. It inhabits swamps, lonely ponds, and abandoned temple tanks. It is constantly in search of fish.

In its natural form, a Baak appears as a very tall, lean, gangly, shadowy humanoid. It has long fingers and toes and messy hair, and it stinks like rotten seafood.

However, a Baak can change its shape. It can become a mist floating through swamp grass, with tendrils that reach out to snatch the catch from a fisherman's boat. It can also take the shape of a human.

It is thought that in order to survive, a Baak needs to occupy a human corpse once in a while, drawing its energy from the dead. The more peaceable among the Baaks satisfy this need by inhabiting the bodies of the drowned, or

of people who have been murdered and thrown in the water. Other Baaks have no compunctions about killing in order to obtain a fresh corpse.

A Baak always carries a small pouch or bag. This bag appears to be made of black fishnet, but it is really of some otherworldly material. If a person is able to steal a Baak's bag, he will gain complete control of the monster. He can even make the Baak assume human form and work for him like a servant. However, the Baak will always be on the lookout for a chance to reclaim its bag, and if it does, then woe betide the thief!

There is substantial overlap between legends of the **Doht**, the **Ghorapaak**, and the Baak. These may all be different names for the same creature, or they may be related varieties.

Ref: 448

⤐— BAALU —⤓

Baalu is a dwarf-spirit that lives high in the mountains of Ladakh.

It is said that if you stand at a crossroads and wait for a Baalu to walk by, you can catch him. Keeping a captive Baalu brings tremendous luck and riches to one's household.

However, the Baalu will continually throw tantrums and demand to be let out. It is vitally important to ignore it. As soon as you let yourself get drawn into a discussion with a Baalu, it will hypnotize you and persuade you to let it out of its cage.

The people of the remote Himalayan settlement called Sumda Chen claim that they are descended from Baalus. There is also a ruined fortress in the area called Baalu Mkhar, or Dwarf's Castle, which is so inaccessible that not many people even from the closest village have ever set foot there. The fort is said to have been built a thousand years ago by Baalus. To support this claim, people point to the tiny doorways, and the fact that the architecture is very different from other ancient structures in the surrounding area.

Tibetans claim that Baalus derive their power from the Yül **Lha,** the ancient gods of the soil.

Ref: 397

BAI THAPPIKNE SEITHAAN
(AND OTHER SPIRITS OF MISDIRECTION)

Many parts of the country have a folkloric spirit that causes people to lose their way at night. Afflicted travellers start wandering around in loops and circles, unable to find their bearings, even when they are very close to their destination.

Bai Thappikne Seithaan, a spirit from Kasaragod, Kerala, belongs to this category. The word *Seithaan* is the local Kasrod-Malayalam dialect version of **Shaitan**, so the demon is presumably some sort of evil **Jinn**; but in most tales, he is actually fairly harmless.

After he selects a person or party to confuse, he simply follows some distance behind them in the shadows. He chuckles silently at all the anxiety he's causing as they get more and more lost and distressed.

Luckily, there is a method by which the spirit's enchantment can be defeated. The lost person should pick up seven stones and proceed to drop them one by one as he walks, letting go of each stone a few paces apart, as if leaving a trail. As he drops the stones, he should count them out loud. Finally, as he drops the seventh stone, he should confidently say, "EIGHT."

The demon gets terribly confused at this, and rushes back to see where he lost count. In the meantime, the spell is broken, and the person can find their way again.

People who claim to have successfully used this trick report that they have heard Bai Thappikne Seithaan's deep bass voice behind them, counting and recounting the stones, sounding very perplexed.

*

In Assam, the spirit responsible for getting travellers hopelessly lost is the *Poruwa*, a sort of a mischievous fairy. She stands unseen at a crossroads in thick jungles, especially at a point where three paths meet. She plays an instrument called the *toka*, a sort of bamboo clapper.

If a lonely traveller approaches her—especially if it's a young man—the Poruwa surrounds him with a thick magical fog, so he cannot see where he is going. Once he has left the path, she goes off in a different direction and starts talking in what sounds like a human voice. The traveller will follow the voice, hoping to get back on the path. Then the mist will clear, and he will find himself hopelessly lost, surrounded by thick vegetation.

A person who is *Poruwa powa*—possessed by a Poruwa—ends up wandering lost in the jungle until someone finds him.

The Poruwa can sometimes be glimpsed through the mist in the form of a beautiful woman dancing. However, if the apparition is chased, it will vanish.

In the folklore of Maharashtra and the Konkan coast, the ghost of misdirection is called the Chakwa (not to be confused with the bird of the same name). It makes people go in circles, always returning to the same place even if they were sure they were walking in a straight line. It is said that if the Chakwa is only heard and not seen, then the spell will be broken by morning; but if he appears as a beckoning traveller, the person may wander so far into the jungle that they never return.

People of the Baiga tribe call this sort of spirit a Kari Bhulin. There is a folktale about how god turned one of these ghosts into a bear and got her married to the Earth; this is why bears play with termite mounds, which are the Earth's breasts.

In Nagaland, the spirit Muzamuza plays a similar role. He is one of the **Teghami**.

The Bhoolandara of Madhya Pradesh is a mysterious plant that grows low to the ground. It has the strange power that if you step on it, you will become completely confused, unable to tell which direction you came from, which direction you were going, or how to get back to any landmark. You will end up walking in aimless loops.

Because of the disorienting effect, no one is sure what the Bhoolandara looks like.

Ref: 115, 268

BAKASURA

Bakasura is a **Rakshasa** who appears as a character in the *Mahabharata*.

A gluttonous demon who lived in a cave in the forest, Bakasura had made an arrangement with the raja of the nearby city of Ekachakra, whereby the raja would send him a bullock cart loaded with food once a week. Bakasura would devour not only the food, but also the bullocks and the man who drove the cart.

The citizens of Ekachakra held a weekly lottery. The chosen household had to volunteer one of its members for the grim duty of driving the cart to Bakasura's cave. In return, the city was spared from the ogre's wrath.

It was around this time that Kunti and her sons the Pandavas (the five brothers who are the heroes of the epic) were wandering through the forest. They had been exiled from their homeland and were trying to keep a low profile. Near Ekachakra, they met a villager who lived with his wife and two children. He kindly welcomed the travellers into his house and let them stay on as guests.

Shortly after they arrived, it happened that their host's household was selected by lottery to provide the weekly sacrifice to the Rakshasa. Every member of the family was willing to sacrifice themselves to spare the others; but Kunti insisted on sending one of her own sons. As guests, she said, they should be the ones responsible.

Kunti chose to send her second son, Bhim, who was the strongest of the Pandava brothers. He was also the hungriest, renowned for his gigantic appetite.

Bhim traveled to the city, loaded the cart high with provisions, and drove it towards Bakasura's cave. But on the way, he started feeling peckish, so he decided to have a snack.

By the time he reached his destination, Bhim was polishing off the last of the week's worth of food. Bakasura emerged from his cave and saw an empty cart, with Bhim sitting at the reins, licking his lips. A murderous rage came over the Rakshasa, and he attacked.

Bhim and Bakasura wrestled furiously, but neither could gain an advantage. Soon they began uprooting trees to throw at each other. It was such a fierce fight that they cleared half the forest.

Eventually, though, Bhim prevailed. In the end, he threw the Rakshasa so high into the air that when he crashed to earth, every bone in his body was shattered.

The whole town rejoiced that Bakasura was dead. But Kunti and her sons had to slip away quietly, so their identities wouldn't be discovered.

Today, Bakasura's legendary appetite has inspired the name of a Bangalore-based chain of all-you-can-eat buffet restaurants.

Ref: 447

BALISHTAMARU

The Kumbri Marathi community of the Karnataka coast speak a dialect that combines Marathi and Kannada. They are thought to be the descendants of troops in the service of the Maratha warrior king Sivaji during his invasion of Karnataka in the 1670s, who then left the army and settled in the hills.

In the Kumbri Marathis' complex taxonomy of ghosts and spirits, a Balishtamaru (plural: Balishtamarava) is an extremely malignant spirit, even more evil than a **Padosomaru**. Possession by this type of demon causes serious illness. It sometimes happens that a person is afflicted by a Balishtamaru and a Padosomaru at the same time, and these cases are the most deadly of all.

Interestingly, a Balishtamaru is not the ghost of a single dead creature. Instead, the spirit is formed as a result of a rare and unlucky event when the deaths of several people or animals occur simultaneously.

There are different types of Balishtamaru listed below. Each one arises from a different set of circumstances.

A *Devati* comes into being when three cats die at exactly the same moment. This spirit causes fever, weakness, cough, cold, and vomiting in humans.

A *Rav* is created when seven tigers die all at the same moment.

This cruel demon causes its victims to vomit blood. A person afflicted by a Rav will die within three to twelve days unless a ritual is performed for them by a *gadiga* (diviner) assisted by a **Yakshi** spirit.

An *Akashmurchi* is created when seven buffaloes die all at the same moment. This demon, like the Rav, causes a person to vomit blood, which may result in death.

When seven pregnant she-buffaloes die at the same moment, the spirit created is called a *Murchi*. A Murchi causes a raging fever, and is more difficult to ward off than an Akashmurchi. Even if cured, a person who has been afflicted by a Murchi is doomed to die within twelve years of the initial attack.

When seven pregnant she-buffaloes AND seven pregnant human women all die at exactly the same moment, a Balishtamaru called *Hemmalati* comes into existence.* This spirit takes the shape of a human woman with a single breast. She lives in dense jungles.

If a man should happen to encounter a Hemmalati in the forest, the Hemmalati will ask him for some betel-leaf and betel-nuts to chew. When the man hands it to her, she pretends to accidentally drop it to the forest floor. As the man bends to retrieve it for her, she removes her huge breast from her

---

* This is the Kumbri Marathi version of the **Otte Malechi** of Kasaragod.

blouse and flops it onto his head. At this moment the traveller gets struck with a frightful panic. He runs back home as fast as he can, but once he gets there, he is stricken with fever. At night he dreams horrifying nightmares, and soon he begins vomiting blood.

The intervention of a spiritual healer may save the afflicted person from a quick death. But it is said that no one who meets the Hemmalati will survive longer than three years, even with the best efforts of the most skilled doctors.

Nagadevati: when a mongoose kills a cobra, it cuts the snake into seven pieces. The head of the cobra then spreads out its hood, flaps it like a pair of wings, and flies away.

If the shadow cast by this serpent-head as it flies through the sky should fall upon a person, that person will be afflicted with the Nagadevati spirit. This causes instant paralysis. The person must seek out a skilled spiritual healer immediately, or else forfeit his life.

Holtandmarava are classed as a type of Balishtamaru, but unlike the other types, they are not brought into existence by simultaneous deaths. Instead, they are thought to be born to Holtandmarava parents, and to live in family structures much as humans do. They are meat-craving hunter-spirits who roam the forest in groups, casting magical nets to snare their prey. They prefer to hunt wild animals, but if there is not enough game to sustain them, they turn their attention towards domestic cattle, or even towards humans.

If a human gets trapped in one of the Holtandmarava's magical nets, he will usually be devoured alive. Even if he manages a lucky escape, he will be stricken with fever and a sort of insanity.

A person afflicted by a Holtandmaru is especially susceptible to possession by other spirits as well, either Balishtamarava or Padosomarava. He is also likely to become violent in his mad ravings. The best way to restrain a person thus afflicted is to bind his limbs in shackles made from the wood of *Nux vomica*, the strychnine tree. (All types of **Maru** are said to avoid this wood.)

Certain areas of the forest along the Konkan coast were once thought to be home to Holtandmarava, and people had to be very careful going to these places. The Kumbri Marathi practise a ritual hunt called a *baundi* to prevent the Holtandmarava from infesting a region of forest; this involves letting a little blood from the kill soak into the ground. These practices are said to have been successful, and today Holtandmarava have been driven out from most areas.

Ref: 32, 161

⤙⤳ BALVALA ⤝⤲

Balvala is an **Asura** who appears as a character in the *Mahabharata*. He was the son of **Ilvala**, and shared his father's hatred of sages and rishis. Like many other Asuras, he had the power to conjure storms of filth.

The story goes that Balvala was tormenting the rishis of Naimisharanya, a forest near the Gomti River in what is now Uttar Pradesh. Whenever the rishis who lived in this forest lit a sacred fire to perform a *yajna* ritual, Balvala would summon downpours of disgusting, putrid rain to extinguish the flames.

Frustrated, the rishis pleaded to Lord Balarama, elder brother of Lord Krishna, for assistance. And soon, he came to their aid.

But just as Balarama arrived in Naimisharanya, Balvala sent a dust storm which filled the sky. Hailstones started to fall. A noxious stench filled the air. Then angry torrents of pus, hair, blood, liquor, piss, shit, raw meat, and bone began raining down from above.

Finally the demon appeared. He flew through the sky towards Balarama brandishing his trident. He was gigantic, with shining coal-black skin; his hair, beard and moustache were the colour of blazing copper. He had a terrible scowl on his face, and long yellow fangs protruded from his mouth like blades.

But Lord Balarama easily dragged Balvala to earth and smashed him in the centre of the forehead with his club, cleaving his head in two.

From then on the rishis of the forest could perform their rituals in peace.

Ref: 449

⤙⤳ BAN JHAKRI ⤝⤲
AND BAN JHAKRINI

This being occurs in the mythology of the Tamang people, many of whom reside in the Darjeeling district of West Bengal and the state of Sikkim, as well as in Nepal.

Ban Jhakri means "shaman of the forest" in Nepali. He is a Himalayan teacher-spirit who appears as a short (three to five foot tall) dark-skinned ape-like man with large ears and matted golden dreadlocks. He usually goes about entirely naked, though he sometimes wears a skirt made of feathers. According

to some, he is a small type of **Yeti**. There is disagreement as to whether there are many Ban Jhakris or only one.

Ban Jhakri is a nocturnal shapeshifter with the power to turn himself invisible. He can see well in the dark. Like other types of Yeti, he eats from the backs of his hands; but unlike them, Ban Jhakri is a vegetarian. He plays a golden frame drum, called a *dhyangro*.

Ban Jhakri searches for human children who are pure of heart and body and who show promising spiritual talents. Once he identifies such a child, he abducts him. He usually selects boys between the ages of six and ten, but there are a few stories of Ban Jhakri abducting girls as well.

Once the child has been captured, Ban Jhakri brings him to his lair to train him to become a shaman. This lair is a beautiful golden cave in the mountains. It is said to be a blissful place, where one has a view of the whole world.

But there is a complication. As long as the child stays in the cave, he is in danger of being eaten by Ban Jhakri's wife, Ban Jhakrini.

The she-yeti is taller, fatter, more vicious, and more bloodthirsty than her husband. Whereas Ban Jhakri appears to be half man and half ape, Ban Jhakrini appears to be half woman and half bear. She has thick dark fur, large sagging breasts, and backwards-turned feet. She carries a golden kukri, or curved dagger. While her husband refuses to eat meat, Ban Jhakrini constantly craves it.

If Ban Jhakrini is feeling hungry and happens to come around while her husband is teaching, Ban Jhakri has to quickly hide his pupil from her sight. He does so by flinging him up into one of the large cobwebs that hang in the corners of his ceiling, leaving him stuck there until the ferocious she-yeti leaves.

Ban Jhakri communicates with his students telepathically. He insists that they go naked, as he does, and that they eat their food off the backs of their hands, as he does. (Some of the food on offer is rather squirmy; Ban Jhakri likes to feed his students pink earthworms.) If a student should break any of these rules or refuse to do as asked, Ban Jhakri will call his wife to administer punishment. Ban Jhakrini then takes the badly behaved students and gives them a sound beating, and perhaps a few little warning jabs with her kukri.

Students typically stay in Ban Jhakri's cave for thirty days of training before they are returned to their homes. This is long enough to learn the fundamentals of shamanism; besides, Ban Jhakrini's appetite for human flesh makes it dangerous to stay any longer.

But Ban Jhakri is strict and easily angered. He may choose to discontinue the training for even the slightest of infractions. If the student finds it difficult to focus and memorize the mantras, Ban Jhakri will throw him from the cave. If the student is found to have any blemish on his skin, Ban Jhakri will throw him from the cave. If the student farts in the middle of a lesson, Ban Jhakri will throw him from the cave.

Ban Jhakri is tremendously strong. When he throws a student out of his lair, he tosses him so far that he can get seriously injured. Those who claim to have been abducted by Ban Jhakri as children and then thrown out before their training was complete can usually point to a scar they carry as a memento.

Ban Jhakri keeps a pet porcupine that can shoot quills out from its body at high velocity. This animal plays a role in the training sessions. By practicing blocking and dodging the porcupine quills, the student learns to block magical arrows fired by evil spirits and tantric sorcerers.

Ban Jhakri also teaches his students how to fly, how to shapeshift, how to shoot thunderbolts from a slingshot, how to destroy an enemy's brain with a fire arrow shot from a magical bow, and how to turn invisible.

Once the thirty days are over and the student is returned to his home, Ban Jhakri may continue to teach him for years afterward by appearing in his dreams.

Ref: 269

BANJI-BANMANG

In the mythology of the Donyi-Polo faith, as practised by the Adi people of Arunachal Pradesh, Banji-Banmang is the first-born son of the primordial couple Pedong Nane and Yidum Bote, who are also the ancestors of humans. He is an evil and bloodthirsty spirit.

The term Banji-Banmang is also used to describe this first-born son's progeny—a whole clan of destructive, malevolent supernatural beings. The Banji-Banmang reside in their own land or plane of existence, separate from our own.

Occasionally they visit us. A Banji-Banmang comes in the shape of an eagle, flying high over the land in search of smaller birds and mammals to prey upon. Sometimes they take human babies.

They can also assume a humanoid shape when they need to walk on the ground. In this form, they are always seen to be carrying a gourd full of human blood.

It is believed that the spirits of soldiers who have died in wars travel to the plane of the Banji-Banmang to spend the afterlife.

The Banji-Banmang once tried to take control of our world as well. They were thwarted by a goddess named Misum-Miyang, who cut off her own fingers one by one and planted them in the earth. Her severed fingers then grew into the sacred ginger roots that bind the worlds together. This legend is recounted during the Adi marriage ceremony, in which several varieties of ginger (galangal, cassumunar ginger, etc.) have ritual significance.

When a woman cannot conceive, the Banji-Banmang are thought to be responsible.

One of Banji-Banmang's daughters is Banji Medeng Sene, the spirit of lies, treachery, and vanity. She remains active in the human realm today as the force that inspires con-men and scam artists.

In the Adi Christian bible, in Daniel 7:4–8, the term Banji-Banmang is used to describe the beasts that rise out of the sea in Daniel's dream. There are four of them: a beast like a lion with eagle's wings; a beast like a bear, raised up on one side, with three ribs between its teeth; a beast like a leopard with four bird-wings and four heads; and a beast with large iron teeth and ten horns.

Ref: 70, 166, 364

BANSHIRA

This powerful spirit from the forests of Himachal Pradesh has a taste for old, rusty metal. It makes its home in a deodar tree—the Himalayan cedar. In old British accounts of folk beliefs in the region, Banshira is described as a **Bhoot** or hobgoblin; today he is also worshipped as a Hindu deity, a lord of the forest.

The Banshira has some limited shapeshifting ability. It can appear like a giant ape, a monkey, a jackal, or a goat, but it seems to always be covered with short fur.

If any branches are taken from its tree for firewood, the Banshira becomes furious and attacks the perpetrator.

On the other hand, if the spirit is treated with respect, he can protect a village against malevolent spirits. Whenever someone from his village has to go on a nighttime errand, the Banshira will walk nearby unseen; and since all other ghosts tremble in fear of him, the person will reach their destination safely.

In olden days, iron sickles and other implements used to be left on the branches of the Banshira's tree. Today, Banshira shrines contain piles of rusty machine parts and old automobile number plates.

Whenever a new village is to be founded in a fresh area, a few pieces of metal from an old Banshira's tree are brought to a new deodar tree, and thus a new guardian spirit is created. It is said that the guardian spirits of all the villages in Kullu Valley are descended from eight original parent Banshiras in this way.

Ref: 67, 98, 187, 234

⤖ BARAMBHA ⤎

A Barambha is a male spirit in the mythology of the Warli tribe of Maharashtra. The Thakurs* call the same spirit Munja.

A Barambha is usually invisible to human eyes, though when he does choose to show himself, he appears as a tall and handsome albino. His skin and hair are pure white. So are his shirt, his loincloth, and the towel which he always keeps draped over his shoulder.

Most of the time, though, he keeps himself invisible.

Some say that he carries a long staff with a bell fixed to the top, and that even when he is invisible, the faint, rhythmic tinkling of his bell can be heard.

Barambhas live in peepal trees.†

This ghost often becomes enamoured with young human women. During the day, he follows the object of his affection through the forest as she goes about her work. Then, at night, he sneaks into her room and tries to lie with her.

If the woman isn't happy about this, she can tie a piece of leather cord around her neck, and sprinkle a few drops of water from a cobbler's pot on her skin. A Barambha abhors the smell of leather, and as long as a woman wears this protection he cannot touch her.

On the other hand, if the woman is willing, she may let the Barambha visit her every night. She may even make love to the invisible Barambha secretly, while lying next to her sleeping husband.

The Warli once believed that albino children were fathered by a Barambha.

Ref: 450

⤖ BAROLA ⤎

The Barola is a whirlwind or dust devil. There is a folk belief in some Punjabi villages that these whirlwinds have evil spirits in their centres, and that people

---

* An Adivasi tribe, not to be confused with the feudal title *Thakur*.
† The peepal tree or Indian sacred fig, *Ficus religiosa*, is commonly associated with ghosts. It has a long lifespan, ranging from 1,000 to more than 2,000 years. It is an abode of Yama, the Hindu god of death, and is often planted near crematoriums.

who get caught up in them will be afflicted with mental problems. Some even say the Barola can be fatal to young children.

The spirit of the Barola is thought to be wealthy. There is a superstition that if you urinate into an old shoe and throw it into the whirlwind, the shoe will be full of coins after the wind passes.

Ref: 50

⊱ BAYANGI ⊰

In the folklore of Maharashtra and the Konkan coast, a Bayangi (or Bayangi Bhoot) is a spirit that can make a person fabulously rich and successful. But the wealth often comes at the ultimate cost of their life, or the life of a loved one.

Occult practitioners who know how to summon a Bayangi are, oddly, almost always very simple people themselves. They typically live in small huts and avoid fancy clothes or vehicles. They charge a fee—as of this writing, 10,000 rupees is the going rate—to capture the spirit in a coconut, or in a small white cloth doll. The ritual for binding the spirit involves lemon, supari, and black pepper. It must be conducted on the night of a new moon.

A sort of contract is made at this point. The owner agrees to make regular offerings to the spirit in return for its service. Sometimes these offerings are to be made whenever the moon is new or full; sometimes it is only at the new moon, or just once a year.

At any one of these intervals, the buyer may decide to release the Bayangi and exit the contract. Alternatively, a fixed time period of service may be specified—typically seven years.

The exact nature of the offerings is left unspecified. The buyer must agree to give the spirit whatever it asks for.

The owner of the spirit must then take the coconut or doll containing the Bayangi and hide it somewhere in their home where no one will find it. It is crucially important that no one but the owner should get a glimpse of the thing.

The owner must keep the Bayangi's hiding place clean and tidy. If there is a *devhara* (pooja cabinet) in the house, it must be covered with a sheet. Likewise any other images of gods must be covered or removed from the walls.

The spirit itself remains invisible, but the owner—and the owner alone—can hear it speak. If the spirit is housed in a doll, the figure may be able to gesture with its arms or change its facial expression, but it will not move from its hideaway.

The Bayangi starts out with simple demands, asking only for coconut sweets or plantain bajjis.

The owner of a Bayangi Bhoot can go from rags to riches in very little time. The spirit has a knack for removing obstacles to money, and it acts as a magnet for windfalls. A long-drawn-out legal case might suddenly be settled in the owner's favour, with unexpected compensatory damages paid. An acquaintance from the past could suddenly reappear, flush with business success, and offer a lucrative franchise. A forgotten antique inherited from a distant relative could turn out to be worth crores.

A Bayangi can bring fame, too, if fame is desired.

The luck the Bayangi brings to its owner is said to be siphoned off from the owner's neighbours. Nobody else's business ventures seem to take off; the surrounding houses fall into disrepair. On the same day the Bayangi's owner buys a new car, the neighbour's scooter starts giving engine trouble.

All this breeds envy and suspicion, of course.

As the owner's wealth increases, the Bayangi begins to demand bigger and bloodier sacrifices. First it asks for roosters, then goats, then buffaloes.

But if the owner has any misgivings, they are offset by the designer clothing, the vacation homes, and the gold.

The usual outcome is that the run of good fortune becomes addictive. The owner refuses to release the Bayangi, heading towards a gambler's ruin, keeping it longer than the agreed-upon time period.

Then the Bayangi demands human sacrifice. The first time, it is content with the life of a stranger. But soon afterwards, it demands the life of a family member.

Should the owner refuse these demands, he forfeits his own sanity, and the story ends in suicide.

The other possibility is that a suspicious friend or neighbour may hit upon the truth before the sacrifice has been carried out. For instance, if they decide to snoop for clues in the house when the owner is not at home, and they happen to remove the sheet from the devhara, they will see the wooden cabinet and all the idols within it instantly crumble to a strange grey ash.

If they ransack the house and discover the Bayangi's hiding place, the Bayangi will vacate the premises. It will throw a furious tantrum as it does so—usually burning and bruising a few people in the process, punching holes in the walls and destroying a few large appliances—but without having satisfied its thirst for human blood.

Ref: 115, 451

⤳ BEMBONG ⤝

In the folklore of the Kuki tribes of Northeast India, a Bembong is a tiny dancing female fairy-spirit.

To summon a Bembong, one must hold a small bamboo basket in one's palm, and then place a particular sort of bead inside the basket. Then a friend should play a tune on the gourd-flute known as a *goshem*, while the person holding the basket sings a short song:

We ask God above
to let Bembong dance below.

At this, a Bembong will fly in and begin to dance in the basket. When it is time to send the Bembong away, the singer must sing:

Rush back home, shameless Bembong,
Enemies are attacking your village.

Ref: 123

⤳ BERI ⤝

The Beri is a very ancient thing that lives in the Lakshadweep Sea.

Most of the time it looks like a large log of driftwood. It can spend years, decades, even centuries at a time in this shape, dormant, floating in the open ocean.

Barnacles, mussels, and other marine animals make their homes on it. They live out their lives bobbing in and out of the waves and the scorching sun, until one day they die. Their empty shells fall away, and the space where they grew is occupied in turn by the creatures' descendants.

Generations live and die.

The Beri sleeps.

Eventually, the log is washed onto the shore of one of the atolls of Lakshadweep or the Maldives. There it lies on the beach, unmoving.

If the island is an uninhabited one, the Beri will be swept back out to sea at the next high tide. However, if the island has a village, and if a young woman from that village goes out walking on the beach and should happen to sit on the log or stand astride it, the Beri will slowly begin to wake up.

A few days pass before it shakes off its long slumber. Then, late at night, the Beri begins to transform itself. Slowly it takes the shape of a handsome, slumbering young man, stretched out on the sand.

An hour or so before dawn, the man gets up, stretches, and brushes himself off. Then he walks towards the island's village, where he introduces himself as a visitor from a different island, claiming that he was dropped off by a passing boat.

The disguised Beri proceeds to seek out the same young woman who woke him up on the beach. Since he can make himself appear irresistibly attractive, he usually succeeds in marrying her. Then he settles down on the island and pretends to live a normal life.

Secretly, though, in the dead of night, the Beri keeps sneaking off to the island's cemetery to dig up corpses, bring them home, and eat them.

Once it has eaten all the bodies in the graveyard, the demon starts causing other people in the village to sicken and die, so that it can eat their corpses as well.

It might happen that the Beri's nocturnal activity is discovered. (Sometimes, it is given away by the funeral shrouds that begin to accumulate at home.) When the islanders get wise and band together to attack it, the Beri will change its shape once more. This time it turns into a tall, slimy, hideous monster with gigantic teeth. In this form it can gobble up living people, too.

But if the monster finds itself badly outnumbered by angry villagers, it will run back into the sea and swim away. Once safely out of range of any pursuing boats, it slowly changes back into a sleeping log, and goes to sleep for another age.

On the other hand, it might happen that the Beri's true nature is not guessed until there are too few people left alive to fight it. In this case, the last few survivors will flee the cursed island to escape the monster.

There are several islands of the atolls that used to have settlements but are now uninhabited, and these are said to have been abandoned on account of the Beri.

Long ago, there lived a powerful *fandita* man* by the name of Vaadhoo Dhanna Kaleyfanuu, who lived on Kinolhas Island in the Maldives. He was said to have captured the Beri. He used his powers to shrink the monster down to a very small size and confined him in a bottle. Then he threw the bottle out onto a reef. Even today, this place is still called *Beriyanfanu*, the Reef of Beri; but it is not known whether the demon is imprisoned there still.

Ref: 3, 209, 303

....

* The word *fandita* means "shaman" in Dhivehi; it is derived from the Sanskrit *pandit*.

꯶ BHOOT ꯶

In most Indian languages derived from Sanskrit, Bhoot or Bhoota means "ghost". The word usually refers to the spirit of a person who died in an accident, committed suicide, or was murdered. A person may also become a Bhoot if they died suddenly of some acute illness, or because they passed away with some unrequited desire, or because their funeral rites were not performed correctly. The word can also be used as a catch-all term for any sort of ghost or evil spirit, especially in combination with **Pret** (*Bhoot-Pret*).

Bhoots abound in mythology, folklore, and popular culture. Though their description depends on community and geography, there are several elements that are common to most stories.

Bhoots are shapeshifters; but most of the time they appear in human form. In many tales, they try to fool people into thinking they're not ghosts at all. One way to discover their true nature is to check their feet. Bhoots don't like to make contact with the earth, so they float just a tiny bit above the ground. Also, some of them have their feet reversed—their toes point behind them, rather than in front. Their ears are often pointy and bat-like.

Bhoots don't cast shadows. They speak through their noses with a nasal twang. They are most active on warm nights and on hot, dry days when the sun is directly overhead.

Bhoots are usually confined to the house they died in. If the house is abandoned and dilapidated-looking, it's called a *Bhoot bangla*. Or they may be confined to a village, the boundary of which they may not cross; or to a flat complex, or an office building. Old stone ruins are often said to be full of Bhoots: Bhangarh, a 17th-century fort in Rajasthan, is one of the best-known such haunted locations. Some stories tell of large households of Bhoots, including several generations of family members and domestic workers, all of whom died in the same building and go on cohabiting in the afterlife much as they did when they were alive.

A Bhoot who died outside often makes its home in a peepal tree, and may attack unwary travellers who sleep beneath its branches. It is considered bad luck to take shelter under a peepal tree for this reason. A Bhoot can never enter the house of another person without being invited.

Young Bhoots are mischievous but fairly harmless figures—as shown, for example, in this famous Assamese children's poem.

Kumpu's Dream

by Jyoti Prasad Agarwala (1903–1951)
translated by Anannya Baruah

Ma, in my dream, I saw two baby ghosts,
And with them were two little **jokhini** girls,
So teeny, so tiny, big eyes and bright noses!

One black and one white bhoot, both nakedly nude.
When they spoke they made noises like *Takut takut kut*.
Poot poot poot, said one bhoot.
Dhoot dhoot, said the other one, scrunching his nose.

Ma, how they played! And what fun to watch!
They were singing a song that went *Foos foos faas*,
bustling quietly, *khoos khas khas*,

Twisting and turning and dancing along,
And if ever the jokhinis fell out of step,
They'd pull on their hair to give them a scare.

Slapped in the face, the jokhinis
Swayed at the waist
Kutuk kutuk ghutuk ghutuk
They danced around the place,
The little ghosts leaping and
whirling and lunging.

Ma, but you told me
Ghosts gobble up children, or turn them upside down
And push-push-push them headfirst
neck deep into pond mud.
Why, ma, but these ghosts would do nothing to harm me.
They didn't even dare to come too close to me.
I think ghosts only bother the scaredy-cat boys.

No, Ma, I'm not afraid of ghosts.
How they were whirling in the jokhinis' arms
When I caught hold of both of them tight by the ears.

What long, long ears, and what fun to twist them!
How loud they shouted! They brought the whole house down!

Those two little ghosts, ma, I finally got them.
I grabbed them—I'd just put them into my toy drawer
When you called and woke me.

No, Ma, I'm not in the least bit afraid of ghosts.
Do you know, they didn't even dare to come close to me?
I think ghosts only bother the scaredy-cat boys.
No, Ma, I'm not afraid of ghosts.

*

So much for the cute baby dream-Bhoots. The older ones are generally more dangerous, and some are purely malevolent and murderous towards the living.

An evil Bhoot's favourite way to kill someone is by twisting their necks around, leaving their corpses sitting upright in bed with their heads facing backwards. They can also attack by choking, or by magically removing a person's liver or kidneys. This is done without leaving any mark on the skin (which tends to be perplexing for the doctor performing the autopsy).

Bhoots have fantastically flexible limbs.* While a Bhoot is standing in one room of a house, it can stretch its arm all the way into another room to grab something off a shelf or to shut a window.† In many tales, the Bhoot who is pretending to be human does this absentmindedly, thus betraying its true nature.

Aside from their prodigious reach, Bhoots are strong, with tremendous endurance. This makes them efficient workers, both around the house and in the field; so if a Bhoot can be tamed, or if it lives with a human family undetected for some time, it can prove to be quite useful.

When Bhoots take non-human shapes, they can appear as ferocious animals or as hairy, grim-faced giants. Another common form is that of a greyish-purple

---

* Limb-stretching is one of the most common and iconic features of Indian ghosts. It is a standard trope in modern Indian horror movies, and in the 1980s even made its way into the *Street Fighter* video game franchise as the special attack of the Indian character Dhalsim. The same characteristic is found in a few Southeast Asian spirits as well, for example in the Thai ghost Mae Nak.

† One source puts the upper distance limit—the farthest a Bhoot can stretch one of its limbs—at ten *yojanas* (about 120 kilometres.)

smoggy cloud. In this gaseous state they are able to zoom about and squeeze through tiny cracks and keyholes. Bhoots can also become completely incorporeal, manifesting as nothing but an eerie sound or chill feeling. They do *not*, however, commonly appear as transparent, white, floating, anthropomorphic vapours, the way Western ghosts do. And while they can turn themselves invisible, they don't have the same tendency to "ghost"—that is, to disappear suddenly without warning in the middle of an encounter.

Bhoots have an affinity for milk. If a glass of milk is left out, a Bhoot in smog-cloud or incorporeal form may inhabit the liquid. If a person then proceeds to drink the milk, the Bhoot gets inside them. (A Bhoot imparts its strength, endurance, and flexibility of limbs to anyone it possesses.)

Bhoots are immortal souls. They cannot be killed. Yet certain materials can offer protection against them. They flee from burning turmeric, water, and salt. They also hate anything made of brass or iron; the steel *kara* bracelet worn by many Punjabis, for example, is supposed to ward them off.

The fact that Bhoots cannot touch iron means that it is difficult for them to cook for themselves. This explains why there are so many stories about Bhoots stealing food.

Mechho Bhoot

A Mechho Bhoot is the ghost of a Bengali person whose love for the taste of fish has persisted into the afterlife. These ghosts are ready to do absolutely anything for a bite of fish: they will steal, they will cheat, they will threaten, and they will kill.

Mechho Bhoots reside in trees near fish ponds, lakes, and marshes. They are usually pictured as skinny humanoid creatures with two downwards-pointing fangs. They also have some fish-like physical characteristics, such as scaly skin, fin-like protrusions at the side of the head, puckered mouths, or webbed feet.

Gecho Bhoot

This ghost, known from the folklore of Bengal, is a bloodthirsty tree-dwelling Bhoot that ambushes passers-by. She lies in wait on a branch just above a path, swinging her dangling legs. Then she jumps down onto her victim's shoulders, places one hand on either side of his head, and snaps his neck.

In most depictions, Gecho Bhoots are lean and lanky, with cone-shaped heads, large protruding ears, and glowing eyes. They prefer to live in *shaora* trees (*Streblus asper*).

Pencho Bhoot

The Pencho Bhoot is known from the folklore of the Bauri people of West Bengal. This ghost takes up residence in abandoned houses, neglected storerooms, and dirty corners where junk is piled. It preys upon newborn babies, especially those who aren't watched carefully enough by their parents. The Pencho Bhoot can cause discolouration, bloodshot eyes, fits, and other problems for infants.

Pencho Bhoots are afraid of brooms.

Puwali Bhoot

In the folklore of Assam, a Puwali Bhoot or **Jokhini** Puwali is a small ghost that steals sweets and snacks. They can be annoying, but are fairly harmless. Puwali Bhoots are able to cast sleep spells, ensuring that the residents of a house won't disturb them while they clatter about raiding the kitchen.

Begho Bhoot

Begho Bhoots are the ghosts of victims of tiger attacks.

Possession and Exorcism

Possession by Bhoots is considered by many Indians as the primary cause of mental illness. Afflicted people travel many kilometres to sites famous for exorcism to banish these ghosts from their bodies.

One such place is the Mehendipur Balaji Temple in Rajasthan, where devotees worship Shri Pretraj Sarkar, the Ghost King. This deified former ruler was said to have subdued thousands of Bhoots and **Jinns** and made them his slaves.

Another site is the Malajpur Temple in Madhya Pradesh, where devotees visit the samadhi of Gurusahib Baba, a 17th-century saint. After a possessed person makes a few rounds of the tomb, the Bhoot is supposed to leave the body to take residence in a nearby banyan tree. People who have been cured are asked to offer their weight in jaggery, so the temple always has massive quantities of sweet jaggery on hand. It is considered a miracle that, despite this fact, it is *not* swarmed with flies. The temple holds an annual *Bhoot mela*, or ghost festival, where mass exorcisms take place.

Other famous Bhoot melas are held at Haidarnagar in Jharkhand every Navaratri (late September or October), and in Hajipur, Bihar, on Karthik Purnima (late November or early December). *Ojhas*—witch doctors, or black magicians—travel from surrounding areas to congregate at these melas and flog their services. For a small monetary fee and a gift of liquor and ganja, an ojha will drag a possessed woman around by the hair and beat her with a birch stick until the Bhoot leaves her body.

Belief in Bhoot possession is not limited to the rural poor. Some educated people view mental illness through this lens as well. The Benaras Hindu University, and some other prestigious institutions where Ayurvedic healing is taught, have recently included *bhoot vidya* (ghost science) certifications among their course offerings. Bhoot vidya is claimed to be a scientific approach to treating psychosomatic disorders, but the courses include traditional methods of ghost-warding, exorcism, and apotropaic magic as well.

Ref: 317, 322, 418, 456

BHOOTA (TULU NADU)

In Tulu-speaking communities around Mangalore, the word Bhoota is used for a rather different sort of spirit than the **Bhoot** of North Indian stories.

While outsider accounts often refer to the Tulu Nadu Bhootas as devils or demons, many are worshipped as benevolent deities—or at least, deities that *can* be benevolent if correctly propitiated. Some of them are nature or animal spirits, while others are the ghosts of legendary human heroes.

Many of these Bhootas are represented by intricately detailed brass masks. In a ritual folk performance known as Bhoota Kola, dancers in elaborate costumes go into trances, and are possessed by these spirits.

A few of the well-known Bhootas are listed below.

Bobbariya Bhoota is the ghost of a legendary fisherman and sea merchant who was prominent in the trade between North Africa, the Persian Gulf, and the Malabar coast. He is supposed to have lived at least 500 years ago.

According to one account of his origins, Bobbariya was born near Goa. His mother was a Tulu-speaking Jain woman named Durgu Shetty. She had been married forty times, but every one of her husbands had died in their sleep on the first night after marriage.

Her brothers finally arranged for a forty-first wedding. The groom was a man named Madhava Bayri, who may have been of black North African Muslim ancestry.

After the marriage, Madhava Bayri took Durgu Shetty home. That night, while she slept, he got up and arranged some cloth in a bundle so it looked like he was still sleeping next to her under a sheet. Then he stood by a banana tree a short distance away and waited and watched.

In the middle of the night, Madhava Bayri saw a white snake slither out of his wife's right nostril. It stretched itself towards the bundled-up sheet and bared its fangs, preparing to bite.

As soon as it clamped its mouth down on the fabric, Bayri leapt forward, caught the snake, and killed it.

A few moments later, another snake came out of Durgu Shetty's left nostril—a black one this time. Bayri caught and killed that one too.

When his wife woke up, he told her what had happened. Durgu Shetty was overjoyed. At last she was free from the curse of the snakes that had been killing all her husbands! She and Madhava Bayri went straight to the mosque, where she converted to Islam and changed her name to Bibi Fatima.

Soon afterwards, she gave birth to a son, Bobbariya.

Bobbariya was immensely tall and strong, even at a young age. When he was only six years old, he dug out a boat for himself from the trunk of a large tree, and took it out to sea to fish.

Before long he had grown into a huge man with an imposing moustache who was one of the most successful fishermen up and down the coast. He began commissioning more boats from the carpenters who lived in the uplands, and soon built up a thriving maritime trade business which helped his whole community flourish.

After a few years, though, Bobbariya was caught in a storm at sea. His ship was wrecked, and he and all his sailors drowned.

Bobbariya's ghost is said to be very restless, partly because he travelled so much during life, and partly because he feels guilt about the sailors who died along with him. His spirit is venerated today, especially by Tulu-speaking fishermen of the Karnataka coast, who believe he protects them in rough seas and brings them a bountiful catch. He is often pictured holding a giant mace in one hand and a bell in the other.

There is an alternate account of his death, sometimes enacted in the Bhoota Kola performance, according to which Bobbariya was killed in a fight with a rival; his leg was chopped off, and he bled to death.

Chinikara Bhootas: from the 13th to 15th centuries, Indian ports along the Karnataka coast played host to a huge number of Chinese ships. These merchants were involved in a vast Indian Ocean trade network that stretched from Zanzibar to Singapore.

Shipping was a dangerous business in those days, and several Chinese ships were caught in cyclones and sunk off India's west coast. The ghosts of the hapless sailors lost in such accidents are known as Chinikara Bhootas.

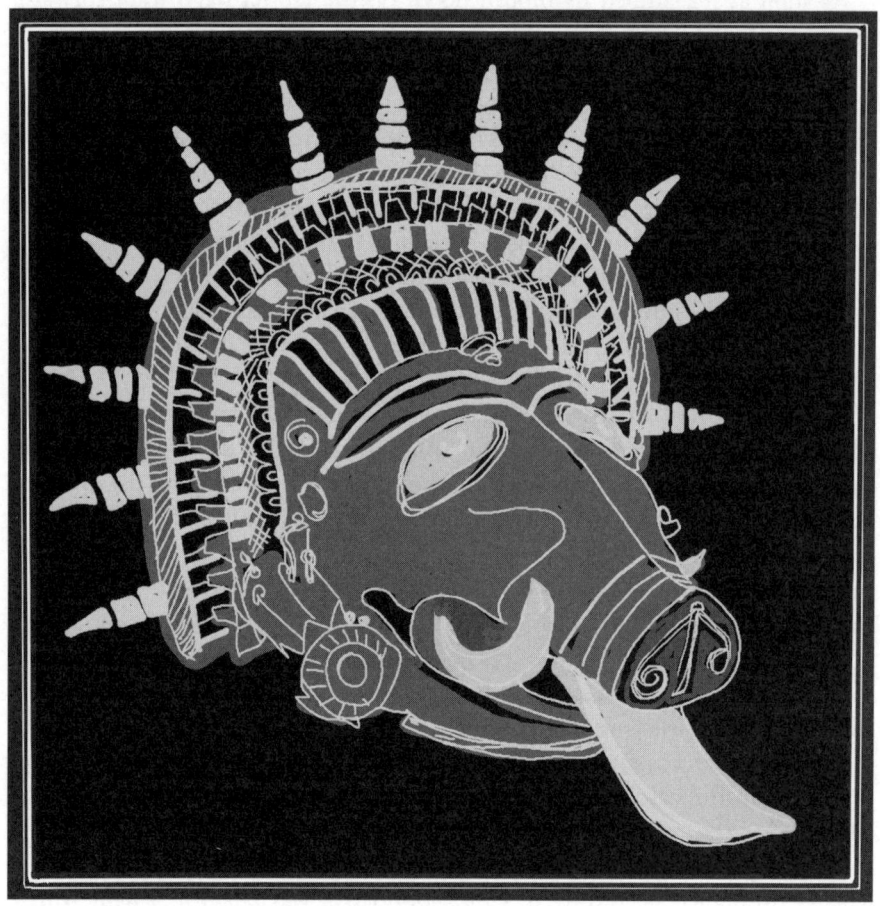

Panjurli is a wild boar ghost, said to be the result of an incestuous relationship between a brother and sister spirit. According to one legend, Panjurli once trampled a banana grove belonging to the goddess Parvati, and so was cursed to be reborn on Earth. He causes illness and various other calamities, and must be propitiated by the building of shrines.

It is said that Panjurli once encountered a group of Chinikara Bhootas who began making fun of him. He got angry and captured five of them, and their idols now stand alongside him in some of his shrines.

Pilichamunda is a tiger-spirit. It is said that Lord Shiva once saved the life of a bird. In gratitude for saving her husband, the bird's wife gifted him a magical egg. From this egg hatched a tiger, and Lord Shiva gave it the job of watching over his cattle. One day, however, the tiger gave in to temptation and killed and ate one of the cows, and so Shiva banished it to Earth.

Koti and *Chennaya* are the ghosts of two heroes from the Billava caste of toddy-tappers and soldiers, who lived perhaps in the 17th century.

Their story begins with a feudal chieftain, the Ballala of Padumale, who was out on a boar hunt when he impaled his foot on a giant thorn. The wound became septic and he seemed close to death. Luckily for him, a pregnant, widowed herbalist named Deyi Baidethi was able to cure him.

Not long afterwards, the healer woman died, and the Ballala decided to repay his debt to her by raising Koti and Chennaya, her orphaned twin sons, in his estate. This didn't go down well with the Ballala's ministers or other high-caste residents, however. The twins were bullied relentlessly and finally driven out.

After that Koti and Chennaya became warriors for social equity, and fought many battles. They were eventually martyred in Yenmooru village, now in Karnataka, where their tomb still stands.

Jumadi is an androgynous spirit with insatiable thirst, associated with the Hindu mother goddess Dhumavati and with **Naga** worship. One origin myth of Jumadi goes as follows. Shiva and Parvati were about to do battle with Dhumasura, a mighty Asura demon who had a boon that he could be killed neither by man nor by woman. Parvati felt hungry, and thought she should eat before the fight. She ate and ate and ate but for some reason was never satisfied. Finally, Lord Shiva told her to eat him. She did so, and swallowed him up to his neck, but his head wouldn't go down her throat—it remained sticking out of her mouth. At this point, the two bodies merged to form Jumadi, a being having the body of a woman but the head of a man. Since they were neither, Jumadi was able to defeat Dhumasura in battle.

Nandigona is a bull-spirit. Nandigona never speaks, but the touch of its tail is purifying.

Kalkuda is the spirit of a sculptor of great artistic genius who had one arm and one leg hacked off by an evil rajah. **Kalluruti** is his twin sister who committed suicide along with him after his mutilation.

Kanodevera is a spirit that used to angrily wreck ships at sea, but has since been tamed.

Guliga is the astrological shadow of the planet Saturn; a wild spirit that dances in a frenzy around the fire.

Ref: 13, 25, 164, 263, 359, 440, 452

⤐ BHOOTA VAHANA YANTA ⤇

Bhoota Vahana Yanta means "spirit movement machine". The term is used for several varieties of robot drone assassins and sword-wielding machine-men mentioned in the *Lokapannati*, a Pali-language text written between 1000 and 1200 CE by Saddhammaghosa of Thaton, but concerning events that took place much earlier, around 500 to 200 BCE.

According to the story, robots were first invented by engineers of the early Roman Republic. These robots were used for commerce, in agriculture, as a police force, and as executioners. The secret of how to build these spirit-engines was fiercely protected. If any engineer dared to take the designs out of the city, one of his own executioner robots would come after him and kill him.

At that time, in Pataliputra (then in the kingdom of Magadha, now Patna in the state of Bihar), there lived a young man who had heard of the Romans' magical androids. He became so determined to learn the secrets of their manufacture and share them with the people of Magadha that he arranged his own death. Then, on his deathbed, he vowed to be reincarnated as a Roman.

This indeed took place. In his new life, the man grew up to join the Roman guild of engineers. He even married the daughter of the Master Robot-Maker, and had a son by her.

Once he learned the secrets of the Bhoota Vahana Yanta, the man resolved to transfer the information back to Pataliputra. But he was well aware that now, since he was a member of the guild, he would be killed as soon as he left. So he cut a gash in his thigh, inserted the plans in his flesh, and sewed the wound back up.

Then he told his son: "I am going to Pataliputra. As soon as I leave, they will send one of their flying executioner robots after me to kill me. Once I am dead, you must arrange to take my body to Pataliputra for the funeral. Once you get there, cut open my thigh and remove the secret plans I have kept inside. Inform my family from my past life, who live there still. Then you may earn your livelihood by means of these spirit-engines."

Soon afterwards, the man left the city. He had not made it far from Rome when, as expected, one of the drone assassins descended from the sky and cut off his head.

The bereaved son followed the instructions he had been given and accompanied the body to Pataliputra. There he cut open his dead father's leg and removed the secret technical diagrams. Before long, he had made a career as a renowned engineer.

Later on, the son received an interesting commission from Raja Ajatashatru, the King of Magadha. The raja wanted him to build an army of robot warriors to guard the relics of the Buddha—one of eight sets of pieces of the Awakened One's body—which were to be entombed beneath a stupa. It was thought that android guards would be best for the job since they themselves would not become attached to the relics, and so would not try to steal them.

The engineer acquitted himself admirably, and the relics and their deadly robot guardians were buried underground.

Much later, the Mauryan Emperor Ashoka the Great, who was Ajatashatru's descendant, went in search of the Buddha's relics. He was guided by prophecy and assisted in his search by a wise elephant and a 120-year-old nun. Eventually he found the stupa, but could not find a way to get past the robot swordsmen.

Ashoka then sent his elephant out to roam around the country, offering a reward of one thousand gold pieces for whoever could deactivate the machine-men. Soon the call was answered by the same engineer who had built them, who was somehow still alive.

Once the engineer had successfully disarmed the Bhoota Vahana Yantas and claimed his reward, Ashoka took the relics and redistributed them to 84,000 different stupas around his empire, with an army of **Yakshas** aiding him in construction.

However, because of all the publicity that Ashoka put into finding the engineer, the Romans finally got wind of the fact that their secrets had been stolen.

One day an elaborately carved wooden box arrived for the engineer. It was supposed to be full of gifts. But when he opened it, one of the mechanical assassins emerged from within, and cruelly decapitated him.

Then the robot lifted off into the air and flew back to Rome.

Ref: 130, 200, 300, 352

⟞⟝ BHUREY ⟞⟝

The Bhurey legend comes from the hilly jungles of Darjeeling and Sikkim. This spirit appears as a boy in his early teens with chicken-like wings and claw-like hands. He is an adept tree-climber and can fly for short distances.

The Bhurey lives in thick jungles, but visits human habitations to abduct young children, especially those who are neglected or ill-treated by their parents. The abducted children are thought to also become Bhureys.

Bhurey means "brown" in Hindi, and in English he is sometimes called "Brown Boy" or "Chicken Boy".

Ref: 142, 253

⟞⟝ BIDO TECH LAU ⟞⟝

In the folklore of the tribes of the Andaman Islands, Lau are ghosts of the dead. (They were called *Chauga* in the language of South Andaman.) The Bido Tech Lau or Ti-Miku Lau are jungle spirits, one of the two main varieties of Lau. The other type is the **Jurua**, or sea-spirits.

Bido Tech Lau are usually invisible, but they can show themselves to the living whenever they wish to do so. Humans who have seen them describe them as fearsome and ugly. They have light skin and long, flowing hair and beards (in stark contrast to the dark skin and afro-textured hair of living Andamanese). The spirits are also said to have small, dwarf-like bodies with elongated limbs.

They live in villages deep in the jungle. These villages are protected from the outside world by impenetrable thickets of *Calamus tigrinus* ("*bido*"), a thick cane covered with sharp thorns. Bido Tech Lau translates as "Spirits of the Calamus Leaf".

The Bido Tech Lau sometimes catch mortals who venture too close to their encampments. If the captured mortal shows any fear, they kill him, and his spirit

becomes one of them; but if he is brave, they may allow him to visit their village, keeping him there for some time before releasing him back to human habitation.

A person who has undergone this experience becomes endowed with magical powers. He may disappear again from time to time to visit his spirit-friends for a few days at a stretch.

Bido Tech Lau rarely visit human settlements, but they will attack any person who wanders alone late at night in the forest, making him fall suddenly and violently ill. Therefore, it is always safer to travel in a group. Lau are scared of fire, arrows, human bones, beeswax, and red paint, so these can be used to ward them away if one is compelled to make a solo nighttime journey.

It is believed that the Bido Tech Lau eat the corpses of people who are buried on land.

The words Lau and Chauga were also used by the Andamanese to describe mainland Indians, Europeans, and most other outsiders (with the exception of black Africans, who were considered fully human in appearance).

Ref: 54, 182, 467, 475

BIRA

The Bira or Bira Mwdai is a troublesome poltergeist-like female spirit from Assam. In the wild they rarely bother humans, but they can be caught and domesticated by black magicians, who then set them against their enemies. In the house of their owners, they live in the guise of rats; the owner feeds them and offers them an occasional animal sacrifice. When they attack, they turn invisible.

Bira hauntings result in rocks raining down through the roofs of houses, clothing getting mysteriously ripped to shreds in the almirah, dirty slippers appearing in pots of cooked food. Biras harass babies and leave bite marks on their legs. They can also possess people and make them forget things, or cause hysterical fits.

A Churuni Bira is a type of Bira that specializes in stealing food from kitchens.

Some believe that Biras are the ghosts of women who died by suicide. Others class them as a variety of **Khetor**.

Ref: 170, 285

BLEMMYAE

The Blemmyae or Akephaloi are a race of people without heads. Their eyes and mouths grow on their chests (though in some depictions, females of the race have their eyes on their shoulders).

The first known mentions of Blemmyae are found in European descriptions of the Nile Valley in Africa. Many later texts say that they lived in India as well. *The Wonders of the East*, a thousand-year-old manuscript written in Old English, describes the Indian Blemmyae as giants, eight feet tall and eight feet wide.

Ref: 251, 454

BOBA

The word Boba means "mute" in Bengali. It is also the name of the evil spirit who is the personification of sleep paralysis.

While scientists would refute the existence of most of the entities in this book, sleep paralysis is a real and well-documented phenomenon. Medical doctors explain it as certain aspects of REM sleep intruding upon consciousness. It typically occurs in patients who are sleep-deprived, or who suffer disturbed sleep.

Sleep paralysis is experienced either just before falling asleep or just after waking. One finds oneself lying supine in bed, conscious but completely unable to move or speak, with an intense and painful pressure on the chest. Some people claim to see a witch or ghost sitting on top of them, staring into their faces.

This ghost has many different names in different world languages. In Tamil, for example, it is called Amuku **Pey**; in the Shona language of Zimbabwe, it is called Madzikirira; in old English folklore, it is called the Night Hag.

Bengali accounts differ as to what Boba looks like (if indeed it is visible at all). Some stories say that if Boba returns too often—that is, if the person keeps experiencing the paralysis night after night—then Boba will eventually strangle them to death.

Ref: 34, 418

⤙ BONGA ⤚

The Munda languages are a group of twenty-two tribal languages spoken in East and Central India. The best known of these is Santali, with about eight million speakers. It is also the only one with official status at the national level. Mundari—spoken by the Munda tribe, which has given its name to the whole group—has just over one million speakers. The Ho language has about the same. A few of the others, such as Gutob and Turi, have so few speakers that they are seriously endangered.

These languages are not Indo-Aryan languages, like Hindi or Bengali. Neither are they Dravidian languages, like Tamil or Telugu. Nor yet are they Sino-Tibetan languages like Ladakhi, Mizo, or Bodo. They belong to a fourth family: the Austroasiatic languages, which includes faraway relatives like Vietnamese.

Most people who speak Munda languages have a traditional faith that bears little resemblance to Hinduism. Many instead call it Sarnaism or *Sarna Dharam*, a term which unifies the faith of the different tribes.

Bonga, in Sarnaism and related belief systems, is a general term for a supernatural entity. This includes deities, such as the creator god Sing Bonga (also known as Thakur Jiu), as well as ambivalent spirits, malevolent entities, and ghosts.

Anthropologists who have studied the Santals and other tribes have remarked on how believers do not talk much about the Bongako (the plural form)—partly out of fear of divine power, and partly because of the spirits' unknowability. Furthermore, the deities of Sarnaism are not worshipped as idols, but in a sacred grove of sal trees, called the *sarna sthal*. As a result, there is little in the way of physical descriptions of these entities.

One class of spirits, conceived in a similar way by many of the Austroasiatic-language-speaking tribes, are the ghosts of the ancestors. These are called Hapramkoren Bonga by the Santals, Haram-Horoko by the Munda, Haram Hapram by the Kora, and Hapram by the Birhor. They are the shades of forefathers who lived full and admirable lives: those who got married, looked after their children, and were generous with their meat whenever they returned from a successful hunt. They are benevolent spirits who look after the well-being of their living descendants. On festival days, they are venerated in a shrine kept in the northeastern corner of the main room of the house.

Some of the tribes do not actually consider these ancestor spirits as Bongas, but rather as mediators between the Bongas and the human realm. Among the Birhor people, there are two classes of Hapram: Burha Burhi and Chaurasi. The Burha

Burhi (literally "old man old woman") are the spirits of recently dead ancestors, whose names are still remembered by the living. The Chaurasi are the older and more numerous spirits of those whose names have been forgotten. The word is borrowed from Hindi, meaning eighty-four: a reference to the 84 million earthly lifetimes which constitute a complete cycle of transmigrations of the soul.

When animal sacrifices are made to the Hapram, the animals are clubbed over the head to kill them. This method is different from the one used to propitiate the Bonga deities: in a sacrifice to the Bongas, the animal is beheaded.

The list below gives some of the more demon- and ghost-like Bongas from the folklore of the different tribes. Many Bongas are common to the religious tradition of several tribes, while others are specific to one.

Marang-Buru Bonga, also known as "Lita", is a powerful Bonga worshipped by the Santals and the Hos. Marang-Buru means "Big Mountain". The homeland of this spirit is thought to be far to the north, on a mountain perpetually covered with snow. Sometimes he is said to be the king of all evil Bongas; he is equated with Satan by some Christian converts. But he is more often described as a jocular grandfather spirit, and may even be considered as the head of the pantheon.

The identification with the biblical Satan is due to a mythological tale about Marang-Buru Bonga being sent by Thakur Jiu to meet the first human couple on Earth. He taught them carpentry and farming, as well as the art of making alcohol to overcome their sexual inhibitions. When Santals drink rice beer, they sprinkle a few drops to the ground for Marang-Buru Bonga first.

Pargana Bonga is the Santal spirit who teaches witchcraft. He is represented by one of the sal trees in the sacred grove. When witches hold their meetings in the funeral ground at night, Pargana Bonga is supposed to appear with them, dressed in royal garb. He has command over the minor wandering Bahre Bongas, and at the request of a witch, he can direct these Bongas to do harm to others. But Pargana Bonga is the spirit who teaches the art of catching and defeating witches as well, so some worship him as a benevolent deity.

Sima Bonga (or *Simi Bonga*) is the guardian of the boundary of a Santal village. He is a ferocious being who attacks farmers in the fields in the form of a venomous snake or other dangerous animal. He is propitiated with offerings of human blood, usually drawn from the thigh of the *kudum naike*, the priest's assistant.

Bahre Bongas are a class of minor demons that live on the outskirts of a Santal village, taking up residence in abandoned structures, tree stumps, or holes in the ground. They are known for fooling thirsty travellers with mirages. They are propitiated by sacrificing roosters. A ritual is performed before beginning any new construction to ward the Bahre Bongako away from the site, and to discover any cursed objects they may have left buried in the ground.

Bagut Bongas are water-spirits who become enamoured with young men.

One story tells of a schoolboy who put his books by the side of a tank to bathe. The Bagut Bonga who lived there watched him bathe and become infatuated with him. Quietly she stole his books and hid them. When the boy went to try to retrieve the books, the Bagut Bonga trapped him and made him her husband. The boy kept complaining of missing his parents, and eventually—after extracting a promise that he would only stay a few days—the Bagut Bonga let him visit home. But he did not come back, so the Bagut Bonga went to his house in the shape of a venomous snake, fatally bit him, and then abducted his ghost.

Gudro Bongas or **Kudra Bongas** are small dwarf-like spirits that can be used as thieves. See also **Kundra** and **Chordeva**.

The **Kisar Bonga** is another spirit who can make a person rich. One folktale tells of a poor farmer who found a brass pot full of money while ploughing his field. Ecstatic, he took the money and buried the pot under the floor of his house, and began to live extravagantly. As the years drew on, though, bad luck seemed to follow his family; they were always in ill health, and his grandchildren kept dying. Only after digging up the pot and doing a ritual to banish the Kisar Bonga did he regain any peace.

Rog Bonga is the Munda demon of cholera and dysentery. She is also known as Baran Bonga, Ote-Baran, or Deb Mai. This Bonga is of no fixed address. She is found wandering sometimes in the jungle, sometimes in the streams, sometimes in the village itself, always hungry. She is propitiated with sacrifices of several different-coloured roosters, which should be left outside the village for her.

A **Banita Bonga** is a lesser evil spirit, generally the ghost of a Munda ancestor who died a violent or unnatural death. While they are inclined to be troublemakers, these spirits are not usually dangerous unless they are brought under the control of a sorcerer and weaponized against his enemies. Curiously, though Banita

Bongako are the ghosts of Mundas, the sorcerers who control them are often not Mundas themselves.

Ikir Bonga is the Munda demon of very deep lakes and wells. It is told that he was originally a protector demon, but fell under the influence of witchcraft, and has now become malevolent. By some accounts, other spirits such as Karam Bonga, Hankar Bonga, and Nasar Bonga are manifestations of Ikir Bonga.

A *Mua* is the ghost of a person who has been beheaded, especially a victim of human sacrifice. They come to haunt the home of their killer, driving the children in his family insane. A Mua is usually invisible, but sometimes appears as a walking headless corpse. This ghost is common to the folklore of the Kurukh tribe, as well.

Hankar Bonga is another Munda demon of disease and death. The term actually encompasses four different spirits with varying levels of malevolence. Regular Hankar Bongas cause cattle to sicken, but they usually don't take life immediately. Vehankar Bonga demands a sacrifice at once, or else he will kill. Hisingahankar Bonga is still more demanding, and mounts repeated attacks, coveting the wealth of a family. Tunduhankar Bonga, the most dangerous sort, threatens to wipe out entire families and all of their cattle.

Nage Bonga or Nage-Era is the Munda version of the **Naga**, a demon that causes leprosy, as well as all sorts of rashes and skin diseases. He is said to haunt certain ponds and springs, and will infect anyone who bathes there. Among the Ho, Nage Bonga is a more benevolent river-spirit, said to be the wife of the creator god Sing Bonga. She is very fond of pigs.

Nasam Bonga is an evil spirit who causes mental illness and gastrointestinal problems.

Churdu Bonga is a lecherous spirit that possesses women and makes them infertile.

Jugini Bonga is related to the Yogini of Hindu mythology, the companion of the goddess Kali.

Bagia Bonga is the tiger-spirit, who must be propitiated if anyone dreams of a tiger, to prevent him from killing. But this spirit is also considered a protector of cattle.

*

There is a Munda myth which says that the Buru Bonga, Ikir Bonga, Nage Bonga and other troublesome Bongas are the descendants of the wives of the **Asuras**.

In this legend, the Asuras were smelting iron day and night, causing noxious pollution and disturbance. Sing bonga played a trick on them; he trapped them all in their own furnace and burnt them to death. Once this was done, he began ascending back into the sky. But the wives of the dead Asuras held onto his loincloth, and were carried up into the air along with him. So Sing bonga grabbed them by the hair and flung them to the ground. The ones that fell on the mountains became the Buru Bongako, the ones that fell into ponds became Nage Bongako, and so on.

Ref: 128, 348, 393, 455

BOOTHAM

Although the Tamil word Bootham is etymologically related to the Hindi Bhoot, the two terms describe very different spirits.* The Bootham is the more powerful of the two. While Bhoots tend to be restricted to the house or the village they died in, Boothams are free to roam the Earth. They can assume practically any form at all.

In older Tamil texts a Bootham was a ferocious guardian spirit. The epic tale *Silappathikaram* ("The Anklet Story"), set in the time of the early Chola Kingdom, tells of a huge statue that stood at the intersection of four roads at the entrance to the port city of Poompuhar. This stone monster was called the Sathukka Bootham. It was supposed to protect the city from liars, hypocrites, and thieves. If anyone spoke slander about a woman of Poompuhar, the

---

* In Malayalam, *Bhootham* can be used in either sense. Bhoothams in stories from Kerala are often employed by black magicians; they also feature in the ritual dance performaces called Theyyam.

Bootham would come to life in the nighttime, drag them out of their houses, and wring their necks.

In later stories, Boothams have come to bear a strong resemblance to the **Jinn** of Muslim lore. Like the Jinn-in-the-lamp from the tale of Aladdin, a Bootham is capable of supernatural speed, approximating instantaneous movement. It is also immensely strong. If a Bootham is given the task of building a thousand palaces, he can finish the job before you snap your fingers. Boothams can cause things to move without touching them. They can also conjure objects from thin air.

In its natural form, a Bootham is usually obese. It may appear as a dwarf, as a giant, or of an average human height. Male Boothams typically have long, styled facial hair, and female ones have elaborate braids. They are partial to colourful turbans and fancy caps.

Boothams live alone or in small groups in secluded caves on remote hills. They can be good-humoured, and may treat certain favoured humans—especially children—with affection and indulgence.* They even grant wishes. However, they are also prone to boredom and quick to annoyance. Caution must be exercised when making a request of a Bootham, lest it decide to devour the beneficiary upon fulfillment of the wish.

Though they appear all-powerful, Boothams can be stumped by certain challenges. One Tamil folktale tells of a Bootham that threatened to destroy a kingdom unless he was given some interesting jobs to do. The raja set it to work deepening reservoirs, widening roads, and renovating temples; but the Bootham completed all these tasks in no time, and the raja soon began to despair. Finally the rani pulled a long hair from her head and asked the Bootham to cut it into 108 pieces of exactly equal length. The Bootham retired to his cave to puzzle over this problem, and never came out again.

Ref: 291, 292

* The hit Tamil television serial *My Dear Bootham*, which ran from 2004 to 2007, featured a young boy who collaborated with a troupe of friendly Boothams to thwart the designs of an evil black magician.

BRAHMADAITYA

A Brahmadaitya is the ghost of a dead brahmin man. He usually appears wearing wooden shoes and a white dhoti, with a sacred thread across his chest.

Apart from this physical description, not many generalizations can be made. Some Brahmadaityas are kindly spirits, while others are vindictive and murderous. Some are known for obnoxiously showing off their knowledge of Sanskrit. Others are content to let the living alone unless their tree of residence is disturbed.

Some say Brahmadaityas are the ghosts of brahmins who died without ever marrying. Others say they are the ghosts of brahmins who were murdered or died unnatural deaths. Still others use the word as a synonym of **Munjya**, meaning the ghost of a brahmin who died shortly after the ceremonial tying of his sacred thread.

*

One well-known tale tells of a poor brahmin (one that is still alive) who is on the verge of starvation when he hears about a haunted *vakula* tree (*Mimusops elengi*). The tree is known to be home to a legion of evil ghosts who attack anyone who approaches. The zamindar of the area has offered a huge plot of land to anyone brave enough to cut a branch from the tree.

The brahmin, who figures he has nothing to lose, decides to take up the challenge, and walks bravely towards the tree. One hundred evil ghosts advance towards him menacingly; but among them is a Brahmadaitya, who speaks kindly to the poor brahmin. They become friends. The other ghosts, following the Brahmadaitya's instructions, cut a branch from the tree and give it to the poor brahmin.

The brahmin presents the branch to the zamindar, who recognizes that it really has come from the haunted tree. So the brahmin claims the land as his reward, and proceeds to plough and plant it.

When harvest season comes around, the brahmin requests the Brahmadaitya's help a second time. This time, the Brahmadaitya gets the one hundred other ghosts to help reap the crops.

Finally, the now-staggeringly-rich brahmin desires to provide a feast for one thousand other brahmins. Again the Brahmadaitya and the legion of ghosts who do his bidding come to his aid, obtaining the food for the feast, and cooking it, and serving it. After it is all over, the Brahmadaitya has earned so much merit that he is released from his earthly bonds and carried into heaven.

In folktales like this one, the Brahmadaitya appears benevolent (to the living brahmin, at least—to the other ghosts who work for him, not so much!) But these spirits can also be deadly. They are fiercely protective of their trees, and have been known to snap the necks of people who try to climb them. Other stories tell of Brahmadaityas who develop a taste for meat in the afterlife. Regretting having wasted their living years as vegetarians, these ghosts have intense cravings to eat as much non-veg food as possible. Some Brahmadaityas consider rotten fish a delicacy. Others dine on human flesh.

Such cannibalistic ghosts are often called *Brahmarakshas*. However, this term is usually reserved for the ghost of a brahmin man who committed unpardonable sins while he was still alive, or who died consumed by hatred. These spirits are most active around noontime and on warm evenings. Malevolent Brahmadaityas and Brahmarakshas must be propitiated on full moon nights to prevent them from tormenting people.

Ref: 326, 418, 456

⊱ BRAM BRAM CHOK ⊰

The Bram Bram Chok, also called the Ram Ram Chok, is a monster from Kashmiri folklore. Its distinguising characteristic is the light that shines from its torchlike eyes, which are placed on the very top of its head. The rest of its body is more rarely glimpsed, but it is said to be covered with long dark hair.

There is some dispute as to the creature's size. Some say it is just two or three feet tall, and lopes like a wolf; others describe it as a hulking giant. It may be able to shrink and expand at will.

Bram Bram Choks normally inhabit marshes and caves, but on winter nights they can wander far from home, especially during heavy snowfall. Most often they are seen as mysterious lights racing along lonely mountainsides; but there are also stories of Bram Bram Choks making noctural forays into towns, even into densely populated neighbourhoods of Srinagar. They are thought to be very ancient creatures, but despite this they can move very quickly—much too quickly to be caught.

People who cross the path of the Bram Bram Chok tend to get lost. In the city, this can be inconvenient and frustrating; in the snowy wilderness, it can be deadly. It is also said that anyone who looks upon the monster's hideous face will fall unconscious. Then the creature drags them to its lair. It is unknown what fate awaits them there.

Ref: 94, 457

ᐳᐊ BTSAN ᐊᐸ

Btsan are warrior demons who live in the mountains of Ladakh and Tibet. They wear red silk with leather helmets, carry red lances with blood-soaked pendants, and ride red horses.

From the front, they look like human beings, but from behind, their backs appear to have been ripped away, exposing all their bloody internal organs. The unlucky sight of this horror can cause illness and death. Most Btsan are very malefic, and only very great sages can hope to pacify them or calm them. However, they can sometimes be held captive in cages made of iron.

Legends tell of vast armies of Btsan warriors who ride invisibly across the land. If a house obstructs the path of one of these campaigns, it can bring disastrous luck, as the occupants will be struck by the Btsans' poisoned arrows.

Probably India's best-known Btsan are the Seven Rong-Btsan Brothers, who are guardian spirits of Ladakh. These demons were originally from Bodh Gaya in what is now Bihar. They were once wild and ferocious. They caused so much trouble that eventually they were caught and imprisoned in an iron cage. Later on they managed to escape and travel to Tibet, where they caused much havoc. But after a while they got homesick and decided to make their way back towards Bodh Gaya.

On the way they passed through Ladakh, and they found it very beautiful. Two of the brothers stopped at the Ladakhi town of Gya and decided to remain there. Another two stayed at Matho; another two at Stok; and the last one at Skyurbuchan.

In each of these places there is now a famous monastery over which the Btsan preside.

Ref: 458

ᐳᐊ BUDANGMA ᐊᐸ

Today, the Garo people of Northeast India, who also call themselves A·chik Mande, are mostly Christian. Before their conversion, they practised a religion known as Songsarek, which still survives in some villages.

In the mythology of this religion, Budangma was an ogress—an extremely ugly and deformed cyclops-woman who liked to carry children away in the middle of the night to eat them alive. She was as tall as the tallest tree on Earth, with a huge protruding nose, thick pouting lips, and earlobes that reached down to her ankles. Her earlobes were stretched so long that when she slept, she would pull them over herself like a bedsheet.

Budangma was eventually killed by Goera, the hero-god of strength, who knocked her down with one blow from his club and hacked her body to pieces.

Ref: 306

BUGA

In Garo mythology, the Buga are a race of shapeshifting mermen that live in streams and rivers, especially in the Brahmaputra. They bear many similarities to the **Nagas** of Hindu and Buddhist mythology.

There are many well-known tales in which a Buga falls in love with a human. In some of these legends, the human is abducted, while in others the couple may try to live consensually either above ground or in the aquatic realm. However, the stories usually end tragically.

Bugas have the power to keep humans alive underwater, though some say it is only the spirit of the human that the Buga takes, discarding the body as food for the crocodiles.

Buga Raja and Dombe

One famous story tells of a couple named Dombe and Joreng, two newlyweds who were head over heels in love with each other. Joreng could never stop talking about how lucky he was to be married to such a beautiful woman.

One day, he made the mistake of talking about her to a friend while they were walking over a bridge on the way to Dareng market. It so happened that the Buga Raja, king of the mermen, was at that very moment swimming in the stream beneath the bridge. He overheard what Joreng said.

The Buga Raja was very curious about Dombe. He sent his spies to verify that she really existed, and that she was as beautiful as Joreng claimed. The spies went out and came back and told him that it was true.

Now the Buga Raja came to visit Dombe's house himself in the guise of a bangle-seller. He arrived when Joreng was away. He gave Dombe a pair of bangles to try on, and after she put them on her wrists, she found that they were stuck; she couldn't get them off, no matter how hard she tried. The Buga Raja gave her a smile, and told her that she could keep them without paying.

Perhaps it was because he was suspicious about the bangles, or perhaps he had some other clues. In any case, Joreng began to suspect that a supernatural creature had designs on his wife. Determined to keep her safe, he moved her far away from the river and built a house for her in a giant peepal tree.

But the Buga Raja commanded his giant army of electric eels and crocodiles and sharks to excavate a tunnel through the earth towards her house, forming an underground river. One day the river opened into a huge pool right under Joreng's peepal tree, and swallowed the tree with Joreng's house and Dombe in it.

The lake is still there. It is called Dombe Wari, a tourist attraction in the South Garo Hills.

Buga Rani and Saora Spora

Another story tells of a human man named Saora Spora who fell in love with the Buga Rani, the beautiful queen of the mermaids. This couple actually got married and had a lavish underwater wedding, complete with a jewelled chariot pulled by a team of **Bugarik.**

However, the relationship went sour when they went to visit Saora Spora's maternal relatives above ground. Saora Spora spent days on end getting sloppy drunk with his friends and cousins and ignoring his wife. Meanwhile, the Buga Rani found she could not eat the surface-people's food. She quickly became bored and hungry. But Saora Spora was too busy partying to pay her any attention.

Eventually the Buga Rani's rumbling stomach got the better of her. Giving up on her drunken husband, she went back underwater.

When Saora Spora finally sobered up, he searched everywhere for his wife. But he was unable to find her. He went back to the river and tried to swim down to her, only to discover that he had lost the power of being able to breathe underwater.

As he sat disconsolate at the edge of a rock near the river, the Buga Rani, looking up at him from below, decided that she was done with him. She called two of her servants, the longest of all electric eels and the most gigantic of all crocodiles, and sent them to Saora Spora.

The eel shocked him to death and the crocodile ripped his corpse apart.

Ref: 306, 459

☙ BUGARIK ☙

The Bugarik are a race of water-wights, subordinate to the **Buga**. They are also called Sangkinnies.

The Bugarik appear as giant serpents, occasionally with beautiful human heads. They are thought to inhabit deep pools and rivers, such as Tasek Lake in Meghalaya. They have supernatural powers, and occasionally they pull hapless humans to their deaths. But for the most part, they stay hidden.

The progenitor of the Bugarik is Bugarik Bugasil, who is a servant of the Buga Raja. Another Bugarik, by the name of Sarenchi, is credited with naming the days of the week of the Garo calendar.

Ref: 306

⌐ BULLET BABA ⌐

On December 2, 1991, a twenty-one-year-old man named Om Singh Rathore was riding his Enfield Bullet motorcycle down National Highway 65 in Rajasthan when he lost control, struck a tree, and was instantly killed.

In the morning, the motorcycle was taken to the local police station and parked in the evidence room.

But the next day, it was missing.

The bike was soon noticed back at the site of the accident, in the same ditch it had been taken from.

The police took the bike back to the station. This time they locked it up with a heavy chain. But in the morning the evidence room was again found empty,

and the bike was discovered back in the ditch once more, near the tree it had crashed into.

As legend has it, this kept on happening; no matter how securely the motorcycle was stored, it mysteriously returned to the site of the accident in the middle of the night. People soon came to believe the bike was being ridden there in the night by the ghost of Om Singh Rathore, now known as Om Banna, or Bullet Baba.

Today the motorcycle stands in a temple at the site, where it is venerated as an idol. Devotees do aarthi for it every morning, tie red threads on the front tyre, give offerings of whiskey to Bullet Baba's ghost, and pray for safe travels. It is thought to be unlucky to pass the shrine on a two-wheeler without giving, at the bare minimum, a slight bow of the head.

Sometimes, in the middle of the night, the bike is said to mysteriously turn on by itself.

Ref: 460, 461

⤛ BURHA DANGORIYA ⤜

This is a well-known, well-respected, and benevolent spirit from Assam. Burha Dangoriyas are ghosts of pious and dignified elderly gentlemen. They are tall; they dress in spotlessly white dhotis and kurtas with perfectly tied turbans; they live in trees.

Burha Dangoriyas don't usually meddle in human affairs, except to attend an important pooja or some other ceremony. On rare occasions they may possess a person, but only in order to speak some sage advice to the person's friends and family.

The only time one of these ghosts will ever cause harm is if someone tries to cut down its tree. In this case the offender may be struck ill or suddenly weakened before they can finish. If other people gather to try to complete the job, they may find that the tree becomes as hard as steel and impossible to cut. Or they may find that, even when the trunk is chopped all the way through, the tree refuses to fall over—no matter how hard it is pushed or pulled—and regenerates its trunk overnight.

In case it is really essential to chop down a Burha Dangoriya's tree, the spirit should be approached respectfully, and a logical case laid out. If a convincing argument is put forward with impeccable manners, the ghost can sometimes be persuaded to move to a new home.

The Burha Dangoriya also has a seat in a special enlarged pillar in the Namghar—the community prayer hall of the Ekasarana sect. No one is allowed to sit next to this pillar, and the ghost gets offered the first prasad after a service.

A similar protector spirit from Assamese villages is the Gaon Roja. This ghost, too, is tall, dignified, good looking, and dressed all in white, though he is not as old. During the day, the Gaon Roja is invisible; during the night, he makes his rounds of the village on a ghostly white horse. He is often seen in the wee hours of the morning, just before dawn, standing guard over the Namghar.

The Gaon Roja will never harm anyone—except an outsider who comes into the village with criminal intent.

Ref: 294, 448

BURU

The Apatani people of Arunachal Pradesh have a legend explaining how they migrated to the Ziro Valley, where they are now settled. When they first arrived, they say, the valley was a vast swamp; and in the swamp there lived dangerous giant reptiles called Burus.

Descriptions of the Buru vary. One report says an adult was around four metres long, bluish-white, with four stumpy legs and a powerful tail. Its triangular head ended in a snout, and its mouth was full of sharp teeth. There was a row of spines along its back. In the winters, they were said to hibernate in mountain caves.

Buru mothers were fiercely protective of their young. Once, an Apatani hunter killed a baby Buru. Not long afterwards, he was hunted down in turn by the mother, who crushed him to death with one blow of her mighty tail.

Eventually the Apatani drained the swamp, and most of the Burus died. But the last one dug a deep hole in the centre of the swamp so that it could hide in the water. The people were afraid that it might attack.

To the people's rescue came two large brass plates, called Mwamwa, that were being kept in a nearby house. These were sacred plates, sometimes used as shields, and they were sentient. One was male and one was female. They ventured out together to the swamp to challenge the last Buru.

The female Mwamwa died fighting the monster, but the male Mwamwa managed to chop off the Buru's head, killing it.

The male Mwamwa came back to the house to find that the son of the man who owned it was home. The Mwamwa was still full of battle-lust and so furious at the death of its companion that it chopped off the boy's head as well. When the boy's father came back and discovered that his son was dead, he howled with despair and angrily chased the Mwamwa away. It flew off into a bamboo grove, where it poked out its eye on a bamboo stump.

These two brass plates are still kept by the Apatani. The hole in one of them, where it lost its eye, can still be seen.

Some say this was the end of the Burus. But according to another story, many years later, a young woman saw one while getting water at a spring at night. She ran back to tell the other villagers, and the next day they filled up the spring with stones and clay.

In the 1940s, the legend of the Buru came to the attention of an Englishman named Ralph Izzard, a reporter for the *Daily Mail*. He travelled to the Ziro Valley in 1948 and later wrote a book called *The Hunt for the Buru*, in which he speculated that the Buru might be a sauropod dinosaur that had somehow survived the end-Cretaceous mass extinction. Ever since, the Buru has found a place on lists of cryptid creatures from around the world, along with the Loch Ness Monster and Bigfoot.

Ref: 41, 122, 145, 186

CETEA

The ancient Greek writer Ælian, writing around 200 CE, described a species of sea monster inhabiting the waters around South India and Ceylon. He called them the Ketea Indikoi, or Indian Cetea. (*Cetos* was the Greek term for any giant sea creature, including those slain by the mythical heroes Heracles and Perseus; *Ceto* was a sea-goddess and the mother of several monsters, including the gorgon Medusa. The name is the root of "cetacean", the modern scientific term for whales, dolphins, and porpoises.)

The Indian variety of cetea were amphibious beasts. They had the bodies of fish or dolphins but the heads of other animals—lions, leopards, wolves, rams, or even women (but with spines instead of hair). Some of the beasts had huge coiling tails.

During the day, the Cetea would swim in the ocean. At night they would climb up onto the land and graze as though they were cattle. They liked to eat dates, which they obtained by wrapping their coiled tails around date-palm trees and shaking them. As dawn began to break, they would head back into the water.

Some fishermen were said to hunt these creatures for their meat.

Ref: 462

 CHAWMNU

In the folklore of Mizoram, especially among the Hmar clan, a Chawmnu is a giant female demon with enormous breasts. She lives in the deep ravines formed by mountain streams.

Chawmnus are hungry always, but they are most active at dusk. They are known for stealing domestic livestock, and they sometimes eat humans as well. In many stories, they approach people who are cooking food outdoors and threaten them: "Would you like to give me what you're cooking, or should I eat *you* up instead?"

People generally choose the first option.

Chawmnus are especially fond of drinking the blood of children.

If one is able to kill a Chawmnu, one should extract the brain, for it is said to have magical properties. For example, a bit of Chawmnu brain rubbed across the eyes can restore sight to a blind person.

Ref: 229

CHEDA

There are a few conflicting descriptions of this ghost, which hails from the west coast of India. Some say a Cheda is the ghost of a young shepherd who died unmarried. Others say it is the ghost of a greedy, miserly man who hoarded wealth but never got any enjoyment from it. He takes the form of a salamander, a frog, or a snake, and lives around the spot where his treasure is buried. He can cause serious illness to anyone who tries to dig up his treasure.

Many villages on the Konkan coast have a Cheda stone, where this spirit lives. After milking the cows in the morning, the first taste of milk should be offered at the Cheda stone. If this is done consistently, the Cheda can be a steadfast guardian and protector to the village. But if the offering is missed, the Cheda can become furious. An angry Cheda can cause cows to stop giving milk, or turn into a tiger at night and kill the livestock.

Chedas can be tamed, and sometimes even sold for use as personal bodyguards, bulwarks against black magic, or guardians to watch over a piece of property.

A Cheda can never cross a body of water. If the image or stone of a Cheda is dropped into a river, it will become harmless and quiet—until the river should happen to dry up.

Ref: 463, 464

CHEDIPE

A Chedipe is an evil sorceress known from stories of the Koya people, most of whom live near the Godavari River in Andhra Pradesh.

The Chedipe looks and acts like a normal woman during the day. At night, though, she removes all her clothes and rides a tiger silently through the streets of seven villages in search of victims, returning home in the early morning.

The Chedipe usually preys on men. However, in a few tales her victims are women, or even whole families.

When a Chedipe attacks, she walks naked to the door of her victim's house. The door swings open silently, by magic. As the Chedipe enters the house, she casts a spell on the occupants, causing them to fall into an impenetrable slumber. She makes her way to the place where her victim is sleeping and kneels by his feet. Then she begins sucking his blood out through his toe.

The next morning, the man may feel uneasy and light-headed, as if he were a little stoned. If he is smart, he will consult a *wadde* (a Koya shaman or healer). If the wadde correctly diagnoses the problem, he will give the man medicine to

ward off the Chedipe, and his condition will improve in a few days. But if the man does not get proper treatment, the Chedipe will return the next night, and the next, until he slowly withers away and dies.

Sometimes, if a man has insulted a Chedipe or wronged her in some way, she may kill him more quickly, by ripping out his tongue.

Most tales have the Chedipe riding a tiger; but by some accounts, she can change into a tiger herself. Not completely, though—one foot will always remain human-looking. A Chedipe in tiger form is called a *Marulupuli*.

A common trick of the Chedipe is to go into the forest saying she's planning to gather roots. Once there, she undresses, transforms into a tiger, and hides in the undergrowth near a path. When someone passes by, she jumps out and devours him. Later, she re-assumes her human form, gets dressed, and walks back to the village as though nothing happened.

Older British accounts of the Chedipe legend associate her with courtesans or sex workers, and one text translates *chedipe* as "prostitute". However, the word means "spoil" or "ruin" in Telugu, so "The Ruiner" may be a better rendering of the name of this spirit.

Ref: 379

⊱━⊱ CHEKAMA ⊰━⊰

A Chekama is a type of a maleficent being or **Hi-i** from the folklore of the Karbi people, most of whom live in the Karbi Anglong district of Assam.

This spirit has the strange property that if you look it in the eyes, it grows in height, stretching to enormous size; but if you look at its feet, it diminishes until it becomes a harmless dwarf. It shares this trait with another Karbi spirit, the **Tisso Jonding**.

The Chekama is a fish-loving demon, and is known for stealing fish from fish-traps. It carries a staff, called a *chin*, that it uses to smack people around. Those unfortunates who have encountered a Chekama bear bruises and scars where they have been whacked. A Chekama can hypnotize people and cause them to do dangerous or harmful things, such as walk for kilometres through thorny bushes, or to hurt themselves with blades. The Chekama always carries a *bor*, a sort of amulet, in its armpit; if a person manages to steal this from the Chekama, the Chekama will pay any ransom to regain it.

A beehive hung at the entrance to the house will ward off a Chekama.

Ref: 93, 276

CHETKIN

Chetkin is a Marathi word, usually translated as "witch" or "sorceress".

Chetkins are mortal women who have become skilled in black magical arts. They have the ability to change shape—for example into a cat or a smoky vapour. However, unlike **Daayans**, they rarely bother to disguise themselves as young and beautiful women. Instead they are content to appear old, haggard, and ugly when they are in human form. And whatever shape they may take, they emit a nauseating stench.

The Chetkin walks with aid of a cane, which she can magically turn into a black krait if she chooses.

A Chetkin may take possession of people, especially young girls, causing them to cackle madly. By possessing their bodies, she can make those she dislikes suffer accidents. Others she presses into service, forcing them to perform black rites or gather materials for her spells. Once she is done with a victim, she eats part of him.

Chetkins are fond of taking human trophies. They often have taxidermied heads, hands, or legs of their victims decorating the inside walls of their huts.

Ref: 465, 466

CHHONGCHHONGPIPA

In the folklore of the Mara tribe of Mizoram, a Chhongchhongpipa is the ghost of a man who died a virgin. Such ghosts are condemned to wander forever in the limbo between the earthly realm and the afterlife.

Chhongchhongpipa have another role, and that is to meet other dead souls, or Thlapha, and direct them onwards to their final destination. The souls of people who have died natural deaths (i.e. from old age) take the right-hand road to Athikhi, the village of the dead. The souls of those that have died unnatural deaths (accidents, murder, killed by tigers, virulent disease, etc.) must take the left-hand road to another realm, called Sawvawkhi.

Before the Chhongchhongpipa send these souls on their way, they like to steal their clothing. This is why dead bodies were buried with a spare set of clothes. The Chhongchhongpipa also make the dead souls pick a few lice or ticks from their bodies, and then force them to eat them. For this reason, dead bodies are buried with a handful of sesame seeds, so that the soul can bite them and pretend to have done the job.

Ref: 259

CHOL

The Chol are a race of supernatural beings mentioned in anthropological accounts of the folklore of the Great Andaman archipelago in the Bay of Bengal. They are spear-wielding spirits of the air, associated with the racket-tailed drongo. "Chol" is the sound of this bird's call: *chol, chol, chol.*

It is said that in the distant past, Maia Chol, the ancestor of these beings, stole a pig from another mythological figure named Maia Kolwot.

Maia Chol took his prize and climbed up into a tall gurjon tree to eat it.

Maia Kolwot, who was incredibly strong, was not ready to let this deed go unpunished. He set up sharp spikes in a circle all around the tree. Then he grabbed hold of the trunk and with mighty heaves started pulling the tree straight down into the ground.

Maia Chol felt his perch getting lower and lower. He realized that if he didn't get off the tree soon, he too would be stuffed into the earth. So he jumped—only to be impaled on the spikes Maia Kolwot had set up around the tree.

Usually, when people die, their soul travels over an invisible cane bridge in the sky that connects our world with the world of the dead. But when Maia Chol died, his soul did not cross all the way over the bridge. Instead, it took up residence on the bridge itself, where it was joined by all his progeny, the racket-tailed drongos.

Sitting in the sky and looking down on us, the Chol sometimes take offence at certain human actions—for example, if someone does a shoddy job of butchering a pig. When this happens, they punish the person by hurling invisible spears at them. The Chol live so high above the Earth, though, that they can't hope to hit a moving target, nor can they see well enough to aim at night. They can only get a clear shot when someone is standing absolutely still in the daytime. Thus the spears of the Chol are blamed when people suffer from sunstroke.

The Great Andamanese tribes are thought to be descended from ancient seafarers who settled the islands around 26,000 years ago. Isolated on their remote island chain for millennia, they were decimated by the disease and violence that followed British colonization in 1789. Today they number only a few dozen individuals, and their languages have mostly died out.

The description given above is based on records of Andamanese folklore from the 1870s. Scholars of the culture have noted that tribal mythology tended to be dynamic, changing drastically with each new teller, with listeners placing a higher value on style and delivery than on consistency. Indeed, a record of Great Andamanese folklore from a few decades later gave a quite different account of the Chol, in which they are simply birds with some limited supernatural powers.

Ref: 467

CHON

This weird nocturnal creature lives in the Kinnaur region of Himachal Pradesh. It has the body of a horse and a human-like head that has a single luminous, glaring eye in the centre of its forehead.

Chons are the riding-horses of the ferocious Kaalis—black-clad, ageless fairies with waist-length golden hair who are said to live on the mountain peaks. The Kaalis let the Chons out at night so they can wander down into the valleys and lick up the ashes from the cremation ground. (This is the Chons' favourite snack.)

If a Chon fixes you with its stare, you are certain to fall severely ill—perhaps even perish. Luckily its gaze is easily avoided, for the Chon can only ever look straight ahead. It is unable to turn its neck from side to side or up or down. Furthermore, it wears a strap of jingle-bells around its neck, and this sound announces its presence. If you hear a Chon coming, the smart course of action is just to sit down off to the side of the road, and wait for it to pass.

At the boundaries of villages, piles of Mani stones, inscribed with the Tibetan mantra *Om mani padme hum*, serve to keep the Chon away.

Ref: 82, 249

CHORDEVA

A Chordeva is a thief-spirit, common to folklore in many parts of India, especially among the Kurukh and other tribes of Jharkhand, Chhattisgarh, Odisha, Bengal, and Assam.

In the form of a short little man, about one-and-a-half feet tall, it wanders from house to house late at night holding a bag. When it finds a small entrance, it changes into a cat and sneaks inside to steal things. Chordevas are usually searching for materials needed for black magic: a lock of hair cut from a person's head, nail clippings, articles of clothing. They also hunt for bones, so they are sometimes encountered in graveyards.

It is believed that if you offer rice crackers and milk at your doorstep after everyone else has gone to sleep, a Chordeva may come to eat them. If this is repeated for a few nights, the Chordeva may come and live in your house. Then you can send it on errands to steal from your neighbours. You can become very wealthy this way.

However, there are dangers associated with fraternizing too closely with one of these spirits. It is said that if a Chordeva leans over while you're sleeping and licks you on the lips, you'll never wake up.

In some traditions, the male Chordeva is accompanied by a female spirit, the Chordevi. The male spirit can possess female humans, and the female spirit can possess males. These are agricultural godlings propitiated by farmers; according to some, they are a pair of **Yakshas**. In seasons when the harvest is poor, the spirit couple is said to go out in search of more fertile fields in neighbouring villages, steal the crops, and bring them back for their worshippers.

Ref: 281, 339, 379

⊱⊶ CHRISTALINA ⊷⊰

Christalina was a young and very beautiful woman who lived in the village of Saligão, Goa in the Estado Português da Índia during the 19ᵗʰ century. She married a wealthy man who worked for a trading company. Shortly after marriage, her husband left for Mumbai on what was supposed to be a temporary assignment. But he got delayed there for weeks, and then months, and then years, leaving his wife alone in a large bungalow.

Christalina was a fun-loving type who made friends easily, and she refused to just sit around feeling bored and abandoned. She began hosting parties. Her house soon acquired a reputation for drunken revelry. She took lovers, and not just a few of them.

Then, one day, Christalina's husband sent a letter saying he was coming back. The wording indicated that he had heard something about her behaviour in his absence.

Christalina began to despair. She had become notorious all over town for her dalliances, and she knew that as soon as her husband returned he would learn everything. Fearing that he would kill her, she tried to convince some of her lovers to run away with her, but no one was willing.

Finally, feeling that she had no other recourse, she drowned herself in a well. Ever since, her spirit has haunted the banyan tree at the top of Saligão hill.

The Goan poet Joseph Furtado wrote the following poem about Christalina's ghost and its shapeshifting abilities.

The Ghost of Saligáo Hill
by Joseph Furtado (1872–1947)

Dong! Dong! Dong! Clear the Angelus
Is ringing down below.
"Ave Maria!" he exclaims,
"How slow the horses go!"

It is a cleric, young and hale,
So late returning home.
The cabman cracks his whip and makes
The horses fret and foam.

But fast the beasts they dare not go
So narrow and so steep
The road is, while the dell anear
Is dark and dangerous deep.

"What dismal howls are these that rise,
Good driver, in our rear?"
"'Tis but a hungry dog that howls;
Your Reverence need not fear."

"But, there, good driver, tell me, pray,
What figure may that be,
That still white figure standing alone
Beneath the banian tree?"

"A still white figure – ah, 'tis but
A woman I see there,
A woman waiting for someone
Or saying her vesper prayer."

A woman, yea, it was, both young
And lovely to behold;
Dressed in an *ôll* of stainless white
And decked with gems and gold.

Upon this hill no man may drive
But he must needs allow
The panting beasts a breathing space:
So did the cabman now.

She came and sat beside the priest
Without the least ado;
Crack went the whip! And down the hill
Away the horses flew.

So fair and young was she, the priest
Felt tempted – who would not?
But, in his sin, the wretched man
To cross himself forgot.

And woe to such! – what makes him now
Paler and paler grow?
Protect him, Heaven! – he knows not why
The woman's staring so.

The while each moment she appears
Less lovely and less young;
Oh! – can he trust his eyes? – he thinks
He sees a forky tongue ......

A hideous speckled coil—O Christ!
He staggers in his seat:
With hood erect there glares defiant
A cobra at his feet.

And whoso sees this cobra fiend
Not long alive may be;
His Reverence thus, his journey done,
A corpse all cold was he!

Furtado's poem is said to be based on a real incident which occurred in the 1880s, in which a young clergyman died.

Another locally famous incident took place in 1952 when a Portuguese padre, who had travelled from Lisbon to oversee work on the Saligão seminary, was attacked by Christalina's ghost while out on a walk. He was found lying senseless, face-down in the mud, on the verge of suffocation. Once he was removed to the hospital and revived, he began speaking fluent Konkani... in a female voice.

Some Hindu residents of the area identify Christalina's ghost with **Devchar**.

Ref: 108, 151

CHUAL CHHONGAL

In Garo mythology, Chual Chhongal is a long-tongued monster dressed in light. He is associated with bright streaks in the night sky—large meteors, rather than everyday shooting stars—which are believed to cause blight to crops.

Chual Chhongal is a thief of souls, not just of people but of things. During the harvest, he tries to steal the spirit or essence of paddy. Farmers tie knots in the stalks to prevent this.

He is propitiated once a year at harvest time.

Ref: 306

CHUDAIL

The Chudail is one of the most feared of all ghosts. It is prevalent in legends, folklore, and horror movies across the length and breadth of South Asia, from Iran to Indonesia, though it goes by different names in different regions. Pakistanis and Indian Muslims often call it the Pichal Peri—the backwards-footed.

It is the ghost of a woman who died while pregnant, or in childbirth.

All Chudails are extremely powerful and deadly. A young wife who was abused by her husband and in-laws, or an unmarried woman who was murdered by the father of her unborn child, become particularly bloodthirsty in the afterlife. The first aim of these vengeful ghosts is to seek and destroy the father or family members who ill-treated them. Once they have killed these offenders, they continue to attack others, especially unmarried young men or new mothers.

In her natural shape, a Chudail appears as a hideous hag with wild hair, a bulging belly, long claw-like fingers, a thick black tongue, and feet that are turned backwards, with the heels in front and the toes pointing behind.

But the Chudail can also make herself appear as a beautiful young woman. In this guise she usually wears a white sari or a dress smeared with blood. There are many stories of Chudails appearing on lonely highways late at night. When a male traveller stops to offer her a ride, the Chudail accepts… and then seduces him, draining him of his life fluids and vitality. The man is found dead the next morning.

When they are not haunting lonely highways, Chudails hang around cemeteries, old battlefields, swamps, dirty toilets, and cremation grounds.

In Kumaon, it is thought that Chudails haunt the crematorium invisibly, waiting for dead bodies to turn up. As soon as a corpse does arrive, the Chudail gobbles up its brain before it can be burnt. Mourners sometimes tap the skulls of the deceased prior to immolation; if the head sounds hollow, this means the Chudail has had her meal.

Traditionally, women who died while pregnant were buried rather than cremated. This practice is still current in many parts of the country. Various macabre rituals were followed to prevent a Chudail from coming back to torment her family. The corpse would be removed from a side door rather than the front—the logic being that this would make it harder for the ghost to find its way back to the house. As soon as the funeral bier was carried outside the village boundary, an iron nail would be driven into the path to prevent the ghost's return. The corpse would be buried face downwards. Heavy stones would be placed on the grave so that the spirit would find it difficult to rise, and mustard seeds sprinkled along the path leading out of the graveyard.

These mustard seeds had a dual function. Firstly, some of the tiny seeds were believed to sprout and bloom in the world of the dead; their fragrance was supposed to distract the Chudail. Secondly, it was thought that the ghost would try to gather all the seeds that didn't sprout. This difficult task would take her so long that she would not finish before morning. Then, when the sun rose, she would rush back into the grave without having troubled anyone, throwing the mustard seeds she'd collected back to the ground as she fled the breaking dawn.*

In some parts of the country, the corpses of women who died while pregnant used to be mutilated. The eyes would be sewn shut and rubbed with chilli powder, or else gouged out of their sockets; the ankles would be broken and thorns pushed into the feet—so that when they became Chudails, they could neither see nor walk.

Such customs tended to shock foreign observers, who were astounded that a woman accused of no wrongdoing in life should be treated with such fear and loathing after death. Those who took part in the rituals were often traumatized themselves; there are several reports from Christian missionaries and Muslim da'is indicating that those who witnessed or participated in such mutilations were among those most likely to seek out a new faith.

Kunwari Chudail

While the term Chudail is usually reserved for the ghosts of women who died while pregnant, in modern usage it is applied more broadly. For instance, in the folklore of Rajasthan and other states of the Hindi heartland, a Kunwari Chudail is the spirit of a young woman who died a virgin. These ghosts typically wear red saris and live in thickets of bamboo. They look for men who wander

---

* Sometimes cotton is used instead of or in addition to mustard.

alone outside late at night or during the hottest part of the day. They attack them, use them sexually, and then murder them.

In many stories, Kunwari Chudails pretend to be human, and their true nature goes undetected for a long period of time. An alluring young Kunwari Chudail might seduce a much older man—a bachelor or widower—and convince him to marry her over the protests of his friends and relations. Under the cover afforded by her position in the family, the Chudail begins attacking all his extended relatives and heirs, and finally her husband himself, eventually laying waste to his entire clan.

The Kunwari Chudail is a material being—an animated corpse, rather than merely an ethereal spirit. If she is killed (again), she crumbles to bits.

The bone of a Kunwari Chudail is thought to be an immensely powerful talisman, much prized by black magicians.

Chudails of Kuldhara

The Rajasthani village of Kuldhara, in the Thar Desert, is home to some of India's most famous Chudails. It is said that back in the early 19th century, when the area was under the rule of Maharawal Mulraj of Jaisalmer, there was a wicked and lecherous minister named Salim Singh who preyed upon the local women. The village has since been abandoned, and the angry spirits of his victims now roam the streets at midnight.

A local hotel has turned this opportunity into a tourist attraction with a late-night excursion known as "The Chudail Trail".

Ref: 2, 121, 312, 318

CHURGIN

A Churgin is a malevolent entity known from the folklore of Central and Eastern India, especially in tribal communities. The stories told about it vary a good deal from tribe to tribe. Some say a Churgin is the shade of a person who died an accidental or unnatural death, cursed to float about in the sky forever. Others say it is the ghost of a woman who died in childbirth; for these, the Churgin is almost the same as a **Chudail**. Among most tribes, it is considered very fearsome and dangerous.

One legend is that the Churgin hates all those people whom it loved during its life, and loves all those whom it hated. Therefore it will haunt and harass its former friends, and give supernatural aid to its enemies.

The Malto tribe of Bihar and Jharkhand believe that Churgins are witches who have the power to launch attacks in the form of supernatural locusts against their opponents.

Among the Birhor tribe of Jharkhand, the word Churgin is an umbrella term for evil spirits in general. The Birhor recognize eight different types of Churgin:

- **Dainee**, or witches. In Birhor folklore, they live in tangles of vines and creepers in the forest.

- **Pangri**: evil spirits that live on the banks of forest streams. They are small and blind.

- **Churni**: evil spirits that live in trash or junk heaps. They especially like piles of broken bits of clay pots.

- **Draha**: evil spirits that live in the ground beneath large trees.

- **Khut**: evil spirits that live in the ground beneath giant boulders.

- **Bhulah** and **Bhulah Chandi**: evil spirits cursed to wander for eternity. They can often be found living under small bushes. Bhulah and Bhulah Chandi are thought to be the spirits of ancestors for whom funerary rituals were not performed correctly. They can cause serious illness.

- **Bhagat**: evil spirits that live in dense jungles.

The word Churgin may be related to the Marathi witch **Chetkin**, as well as to the Chirkun or Chirkuni, a diminutive blood-sucking witch from the tribal folklore of Odisha who hides in the undergrowth and casts spells on the cows as they come home in the evening to sicken them.

In one folktale from the Tea Tribes of Assam, a Chirkun has two heads growing from a forked neck. In this story the ghost can breathe fire, and it likes to eat corpses. Its method is to roast a human limb with the flame from one mouth and then munch on it with the other.

Also possibly related is the Sorgoni **Dumma**, a whirlwind ghost from the Parengi Porja tribe of Andhra Pradesh. These spirits torment people by calling to them with strange voices.

Ref: 30, 258, 272, 345, 362

CHUTI

A Chuti is a variety of **Yeti** that lives in the Himalayas. They walk sometimes on four legs, sometimes on two; when they stand erect they are about seven to eight feet tall. This makes them taller than some Yetis, but not as tall as the biggest (see **Nyalmo**). They have long arms, huge hands, and feet that are human-like except for long claws. Their bodies are covered with grey or reddish fur.

These Yetis are omnivorous. They are known for stealing goats and other livestock, but when food is scarce they may also raid human habitations for vegetables. They are found at altitudes between 8,000 and 10,000 feet. Chutis may attack humans if disturbed, but they are not typically man-eaters.

Some people believe that sightings of this Yeti are in fact sightings of the Himalayan red bear. Others insist the Chuti are supernatural creatures with the power to shapeshift and turn invisible. They are also said to have excellent senses of sight and hearing, and to be able to communicate telepathically.

According to one myth, Chutis grow in size over the course of the day as the sun rises, reaching their largest at night; then they shrink back again.

Ref: 269

CROCOTTA

The Crocotta is a man-eating, hyena-like monster fabled to live in Northwest and Central India. It was mentioned in ancient works on the natural history of the subcontinent by the Greek authors Ctesias and Strabo, the Roman author Pliny the Elder, and the Byzantine author Photius, among others. One account claims that Septimus Severus, Emperor of Rome from 193 to 211 CE, brought a Crocotta from India to keep in his personal menagerie.

A Crocotta can imitate the voices of other animals—anything from birdsong to mooing cattle to human speech. It uses a human voice to call shepherds out from their homes at night so it can attack them and prey on them.

If the shadow of a Crocotta should fall across any animal, such as a dog, that animal will be rendered mute. The beast also has a petrifying gaze; anyone it fixes with its stare becomes paralyzed, completely unable to move or speak. The effect takes hours to wear off. Together, these two attributes allow a Crocotta to enter a human settlement in silence and go about its hunting without raising an alarm.

Some authors believe the Crocotta is a cross between a dog and a wolf, or perhaps between a hyena and a lion. Its teeth are tremendously strong—capable of piercing thick metal—and it can digest nearly any substance. It is fond of carrion, and is known to dig human corpses out of graves to feed upon them.

The Crocotta is said to be a sequential hermaphrodite, meaning that it alternates its sex from male to female, spending a year in each state. It is parthenogenic; that is, the females are able to conceive and bear young on their own, without a male (which raises the question of why the male phase is necessary at all.) The female Crocotta is supposed to be especially hard to catch; and since Crocottas held in captivity do not change sex as they would in the wild, the female phase is almost never observed.

The eyes of the Crocotta are brilliantly coloured, and of a different hue in each individual. According to some writers, these eyes are gems with magic powers. It is rumoured that if you place a Crocotta's eyeball under your tongue, you will gain the ability to predict the future.

In his *Natural History*, Pliny the Elder mentioned a similar animal called the Leucrocotta that lived in Ethiopia. Its range is sometimes said to have included India as well.

This animal is reportedly about the size and shape of a donkey or hyena, but it has a lion's tail, a badger's head, cloven hooves, and a ridge of bone in place of teeth. The corners of its mouth open all the way back to its ears. The Leucrocotta is an extremely fast runner.

Like the Crocotta, the Leucrocotta is a man-eater, capable of imitating the human voice to lure its prey within attack range. One theory held that it was the hybrid offspring of a Crocotta and a lioness.

Ref: 251, 468

⊱— DAAYAN —⊰

In most North Indian languages, the word for witch—Daayan, Dain, Dainee, Daken, etc.—is derived from the Sanskrit term **Dakini**. Since the original Sanskrit meaning of Dakini in Hindu and Buddhist texts is rather different, we deal with it in a separate entry; but Dakini, like Daayan, is sometimes also used in modern Hindi to mean an evil witch.

The Daayan is a fixture of Indian superstition and popular culture, from Hindi television serials to Malayalam comic strips. In many of these narratives, the power of the Daayan is contained in her hair braid, and the secret to defeating her is to chop off her plait.

Belief in witches and their magical powers varies from region to region. In some stories, they are undead women who have sacrificed children to obtain immortality. On new moon nights, their illusions lose their power and they show their true age, appearing as ancient hags with decaying flesh. They have the power to turn invisible; only by tucking the flower of a betel-leaf plant behind one's ear may one see them. In yet other stories, they are jungle-dwelling spirits who waylay and abduct young men. They can keep these hapless youths imprisoned for years or even decades, using them as sex slaves and draining them of their life force. Only when a man is too old and weak to be of service any longer does the Daayan return him to his village and whatever surviving family members may remain.

But none of the nefarious deeds described in these fictional tales are anywhere near so monstrous as *daayan pratha*, the very real practice of witch hunting.

Witch Hunts

Records of witch hunts in India date back at least to the time of the Moroccan traveller Ibn Battuta, who lived in Delhi from 1334 to 1341, during the reign of Sultan Muhammed bin Tughlaq. He wrote that the witches of Delhi were called Kaftar, perhaps from the Urdu word for hyena. Kaftars were said to be able to eat the heart of a person without touching them.

Ibn Battuta witnessed the trial of a woman who was accused of cannibalizing a young boy in this manner. At the order of a lieutenant of the sultan, four jars of water were tied to the woman's arms and legs, after which she was pushed into the Yamuna River. She floated, which meant she was a witch; and therefore she was burnt to death.

Abul Fazl, the court historian of Emperor Akbar in the late 1590s, wrote of a similar type of witch and the tortures to which they were subjected.

> But the greatest of all wonders is the *Jigar Khwar* or "Liver Eater", an individual who by glances and incantations can extract a man's liver.* Some aver that under certain conditions and at certain times, he renders the person senseless upon whom he looks, and then takes from him what resembles the seed of a pomegranate, which he conceals for a time in the calf of his leg. During this interval the person whose liver is stolen remains unconscious, and when thus helpless, the other throws the seed on the fire which spreads out like a plate. Of this he partakes with his fellows and the unconscious victim dies. He can convey a knowledge of his art to whomsoever he wills, by giving him a portion of this food to eat and teaching him the incantation. If he is caught in the act and his calf is cut open and the seed extracted and given to his victim, the latter will recover. The followers of this art are mostly women.
>
> They can convey intelligence from long distances in a brief space of time, and if they are thrown into the river with a stone tied to them, they will not sink. When it is desired to deprive one of these of this power, they brand

----

* This type of witch is still well known today in Punjabi witchlore, where she is called Kaleji Khane. In other regions, such as Kashmir, the Daayan is thought to consume a person's kidneys.—J.F.B.

both sides of his head and his joints, fill his eyes with salt, suspend him for forty days in a subterranean chamber, and give him food without salt, and some of them recite incantations over him. During this period he is called Dhachrah. Although his power then no longer exists, he is still able to recognize other Liver-Eaters, and these pests are captured through his detection.*

Centuries later, there was a rash of witch-killings coincident with the 1855–56 Santal Rebellion and the 1857 Indian Mutiny. For patriotic Indians used to thinking of the rebels in these conflicts as the good guys, the details of these murders make decidedly uncomfortable reading. The killings were concentrated in Chhota Nagpur (now Jharkhand and Chhattisgarh), but occurred in Rajasthan and elsewhere as well. A belief had taken root among many communities that Daayans were thriving in their midst under the protection of British law; and when the grip of that law was loosened, there was a massive and murderous purge of women suspected of witchcraft.

The problem persists to the present day. According to India's National Crime Records Bureau, more than 2,500 people were murdered on suspicion of witchcraft between 2000 and 2016—substantially higher than the death toll due to terrorism over the same period. Most of those killed were women. Some of the accused witches were burnt alive. Others were suffocated, beheaded, electrocuted, or hacked to death. Thousands more—perhaps millions—have suffered torture, rape, public humiliation, or confinement. The widespread belief in witchcraft can be weaponized: accusing a woman of being a witch is a tried and tested method of stealing her property.

The majority of reported cases are from disadvantaged tribal communities, concentrated in the states of Odisha, Jharkhand, Madhya Pradesh, Andhra Pradesh, and Assam. But these statistics are probably biased. The scourge of witch murder affects wealthier, more literate sections of society as well; killings of accused witches occur even in the swankiest neighbourhoods of India's global cities. While such incidents do sometimes make the news, the role of superstition is more likely to go unreported.

Most distressing of all, *daayan pratha* murders don't seem to be declining much. They peaked in 2011, a year in which 240 accused witches were killed

* Translation by Colonel H.S. Jarrett,[149] with minor edits.

across the country, but the numbers are still higher today than they were in the 1990s.*

Over the past few decades, several states have enacted new legislation against witch-hunting. Among various programmes to change the public mindset, a memorial statue to the victims of witch hunts was unveiled in Kheonjar, Odisha; it portrays a woman standing with arms raised in protest, her hair falling over half her face. On the pedestal, it says, "IN MEMORY OF ALL INNOCENTS WHO WERE KILLED BEING BRANDED AS WITCH".

Choti-Katne-Wali Daayan

In 2017, a series of reports erupted from Rajasthan, Delhi, and Uttar Pradesh about a black-clad figure, the Choti-Katne-Wali Daayan or "hair-cutting witch", who would sneak into houses and chop off the braids of women and girls in their sleep in order to use them for black magic. Witnesses claimed that the figure could change its shape and take the form of a cat. Police investigators later determined that most of the women had actually cut their hair themselves; they had wanted to try out short hairstyles, but were so afraid of condemnation from their families that they invented a witch story as cover. Unfortunately these revelations didn't stop a woman who was accused of being the Daayan from being lynched in Agra. Many others, too, were harassed and beaten.

Ref: 24, 137, 144, 149, 242, 246, 329, 377, 437

DAKINI

Dakinis are flesh-eating female demons who accompany the goddess Kali. They appear in ancient Hindu texts such as the *Bhagavata Purana*. The male version is Daka.

---

* Of course, this form of violence against women is hardly unique to India. Witch purges have occurred intermittently throughout history and in many parts of the world. The European witch trials of the late 16th and early 17th centuries resulted in some 50,000 people being burnt at the stake. In Saudi Arabia, as recently as 2011, a woman was convicted by a court of law of practicing witchcraft and sorcery and publicly beheaded. The practice is thought to persist into modern times in rural China, too, though it is difficult to find reliable data.

The word evolved and came into North Indian languages as Dakan, Daayan, Dain, or Dainee. These terms indicate a folkloric witch or ghost who is almost always diabolically evil.

In Buddhism, though—as well as in the Bön religion of Tibet—Dakinis have a much more wholesome character. They are manifestations of energy in female form, used as a focus for spiritual meditation.

There are many different Dakinis, including:

- *Jnana Dakinis*, Dakinis of wisdom.

- *Karma Dakinis*, Dakinis of action.

- *Simhamukha*, the lion-headed Dakini, who can overcome and subdue negative energy.

- *Kurukulla*, the lotus-blossom Dakini. She is a goddess of sex magic. She is associated with the colour red, the heat of the sun, and the goddess Tara.

- *Ulukhamukha*, the owl-headed Dakini.

- *Makaramukha*, the **Makara**-headed dakini, who can bestow supernatural powers on believers.

Another meaning of the term Dakini is any highly realized human female tantric or Yogini, especially a practitioner of *kamamudra* (sexual yoga). The word is also used to refer to the power of the lowest chakra, at the base of the spine.

Ref: 469, 470

 DAKKHIN RAI

Dakkhin Rai or Dakshin Rai, literally "King of the South", is a fearsome and bloodthirsty deity worshipped in the Sunderbans mangrove forest of Bengal—where his realm is called *athero bhatir desh*, the "Land of the Eighteen Tides". He commands an army of swamp tigers and crocodiles and is said to be hungry for human sacrifice. He himself is said to be half-human and half-tiger, and he can assume the form of a tiger at will.

Some believe that the character is a deified historical figure. In his temple in Dhapdhapi, his idol appears wearing a jacket and boots, and holding a rifle.

Honey-gatherers who work in the Sundarbans often wear a mask on the backs of their heads bearing Dakkhin Rai's face, so as to ward off any man-eating tigers that may be stalking them.

Dakkhin Rai appears as the antagonist in the legend of the forest goddess Bonbibi, a tale retold in folk performances throughout the region. Bonbibi and Dakkhin Rai have both Muslim and Hindu devotees, and their worship is highly syncretic. A pooja is held for Dakkhin Rai on the first day of the month of Maagh (January–February).

Ref: 578

DAULA

Daulas are small, mischievous spirits from Assam that look a bit like monkeys. They live in thickets of bamboo.

Daulas harass people who walk too close to their homes by pelting them with clods of earth. Another of their favourite tricks is to hide at the side of a path just ahead of a traveller, and bend a bamboo stem down to the ground. Just as the traveller approaches, the Daula releases the bamboo, which snaps up and gives them a hard and painful *whack!*

Daulas will not stand their ground in a fight. As soon as you start throwing dirt clods back at them, they will scurry away quickly, cackling.

Most encounters with wild Daulas occur in Assam's Nameri Forest Reserve. Some ojhas are said to keep Daulas as pets, even breeding them in captivity.

There are similar spirits in other folkloric traditions, such as the Cheijunpa of the Chothe Nagas. This spirit is also known for its bamboo attack, but unlike the Daula, it can never be seen by human eyes. Cheijunpas are active at any time of day or night. In Bodo folklore, the bamboo ghost Fagon is said to fear human urine.

Another example is the Besho Bhoot of rural Bengal, who is larger, stronger, and more deadly than the other sorts. When it strikes with its bamboo rod, the blow can be hard enough to snap a spine.

In bamboo groves that are haunted by one of these spirits, the bamboo stalks sway and rub against each other, making eerie creaking noises… even when the air is perfectly still.

Ref: 34, 418, 448

DEV

Six thousand years ago, in Eastern Europe and Western Asia, there lived a people known to linguists and archaeologists as the Proto-Indo-Europeans. They were sheep and cattle herders, probably nomadic, which is why they left few archaeological sites. They had no written script, so we cannot directly read their stories. But the language they spoke is the progenitor from which over four hundred modern languages evolved—everything from Assamese to Sinhala to Gujarati to Greek to Gaelic.

By fitting together clues from these latter-day descendants, some bits of the ancient language and culture can be reconstructed. Among the Proto-Indo-European words the linguists are surest of is the name of a god, *Dyeus*, the Sky-Father. The name of this powerful deity became *Zeus* in Greek, *Deus* in Latin, *deva* and *devata* in Sanskrit; it is the root of the English word "deity" itself, as well as "devil". It has been borrowed into Dravidian languages too, becoming *theyyam* ("spirit") in Malayalam and **Deyyam** ("ghost") in Telugu.

In Avestan, the ancient Iranian language of Zoroastrian scripture, the word became Daeva; and in later Persian, this evolved to Dev.

In Zoroastrianism, the Devs are a class of demonic giants or "rejected gods". They were created by **Angra Mainyu**, the destructive spirit and principle of evil, from the demonic essence, to battle the Yazatas or angels of Ahura Mazda.

There are six arch-Devs:

- *Akoman*, the Dev of evil intent.

- *Indar*, the Dev who constrains virtuous thought.

- *Savar*, the Dev of corruption, lawlessness, and drunkenness.

- *Naikiyas*, the Dev of discontent.

- *Taprev*, the Dev of thirst, fever, and destruction.

- *Zairich*, the Dev of poison.

Ahriman also created countless other Devs who fly out from hell every night to cause torment. The names of some of these lesser Devs are:

- *Jeh*, the Dev of lasciviousness, Ahriman's wife and queen of hell.

- *Eshm*, the Dev of wrath, who carries a bloody mace.

- *Bushasp*, the long-armed Dev of sloth and procrastination.

- *Taromat*, the Dev of disobedience and scorn.

- *Mitrokht*, the Dev of lies.

- *Arashk*, the Dev of the evil eye.

- *Vizaresh*, the Dev who torments the recently dead.

- *Uda*, the Dev who attacks people who talk with their mouths full, contaminates their food and water, and makes them incontinent.

- *Akatash*, the Dev of perversion.

- *Zarman*, the Dev of old age and decrepitude.

- *Chishmak*, the Dev of whirlwinds and other disasters.

- *Vareno*, the Dev of illicit sex.

- *Sej*, the Dev of annihilation.

- *Niyaz*, the Dev of poverty and distress.

- *Az**, the Dev of greed and gluttony.

- **Nasu**, the Dev of contamination.

- *Friftar*, the Dev of deception.

- *Spazg*, the Dev of slander.

- *Arast*, the Dev of falsehood.

- *Aighash*, the Dev who smites mankind with his eye.

- *But*, the Dev worshipped by Hindus (see **Bhoot**).

From Zoroastrian roots, Devs became monstrous ogres in Persian folklore, and eventually found their way into Urdu fantasy literature.

....

* Az later became a major demoness in Manichæism, the religion founded by the 3rd-century Persian prophet Mani, which flourished for some time in Northern India. This demon is also connected to the Persian dragons called Azi or Azhadar, and to the Vedic drought-demon **Vritra**.

In Urdu stories, they are usually evil. There are a few good ones—in particular, those that have been converted to Islam—but they are less likely to be benevolent than **Jinns**. Devs are often said to be enemies of the **Peris**. In some folktales, a Dev will keep a beautiful Peri imprisoned in a box, and take it out once in a while to watch it dance.

The average Dev is a bit larger than a human. Powerful ones can be *much* larger. The strongest Devs are capable of throwing giant boulders weighing up to 100 tonnes. They fight using tree trunks as weapons, and occasionally bludgeon their enemies with giant serpents.

Devs appear frequently in the *Hamzanama*, the Persian/Urdu epic tale that relates the exploits of the swashbuckling Amir Hamza, an uncle of the Prophet Muhammed ﷺ. The most famous version of this story was produced in India between 1562 and 1577, during the reign of Emperor Akbar, as a 48,000-page illustrated manuscript. In these illustrations, the Devs look similar to the **Rakshasas** of Hindu mythology. They are humanoid, but with animal features, such as orange skin with leopard spots, shaggy white fur, or bird-like talons on their feet. Sometimes they have protruding fangs or spiralling goat horns.

In a later 1855 version of the *Hamzanama* by Ghalib Lakhnavi, one Dev is described as being as tall as a tower and having the head of a peacock. Kharchal and Kharpal, two Dev generals who lead an army of ten thousand other Devs, are described as having the features of a donkey: one has donkey ears and the other has a donkey's nose and face.

The homeland of the Devs is the city of Ahrimanabad, named after the Zoroastrian god of primordial evil. This metropolis is located on Mount Qaf, a mythical mountain on the far side of the world ocean.

In Kashmiri folktales, Devs live underground, and emerge once in a while through caves or springs or fissures to cause trouble amongst the humans.

They are pretty easy to fool, though. One way to trick this sort of Dev is to show it a box with a small mirror in it. Seeing the reflection and not recognizing it as their own, they will believe that you have defeated another Dev and trapped him in the box. Thus convinced that you are dangerous and powerful, the Dev will run away quickly.

Another usage of the word Dev is common among the tantric magicians of Gujarat and Maharashtra. Here Devs are captive or co-operative spirits who give the tantrics information. So, for example, if you ask, "When will I get married?", the tantric will make a show of listening to someone invisible, and then answer, "Dev says you'll be married within a year."

Ref: 94, 191, 471, 472

❯❯❯ DEVCHAR ❮❮❮

Devchar, also called Zagevoilo or Bandevoilo, is a spirit of the Konkan coast. He is variously described as a guardian deity, a devil, a mischievous spirit, the ghost of a man who died soon after marriage, or as a forest-dweller who lures people to follow him.

Those who do follow Devchar into the woods are sometimes found dead, other times alive; if they survive, they are likely to be discovered far from home, unable to explain how they got there.

The Catholic Church of Goa translated the Portuguese *Diablo* ("Devil") into Konkani as *Devchar*, so the spirit has often been equated with Christian devils, or with Satan himself. However, many Hindus, and those with syncretic beliefs, reject this. Instead, they revere Devchar as a protector who resides at the four corners of a village boundary. This Devchar is propitiated with offerings of feni (the local Goan liquor, made from coconut or cashew). He also likes toddy, leavened bread, and country cigarettes. These offerings are sometimes left quietly behind Christian crosses, such as those placed at the sites of road accidents.

Devchar is also associated with **Rakhondar**, another guardian deity of Konkan villages; with Betal, the King of Ghosts (see under **Vetal**); and with the demon-god **Maru**.

In the spring, during Shigmo (a Goan holiday coinciding with Holi), Betal temples hold a festival called Gadyachi Zatra. During this festival, in the middle of the night, Devchar is said to appear as a faceless, shadowy form. He delights the crowds by holding flames in his palms and walking in the air. Cameras are strictly forbidden at the festival, and there are several modern legends about would-be photographers falling unconscious or deathly ill.

Male devotees, called *gade*, play hide-and-seek with Devchar on the nights of Shigmo. They roam through the forest following his torch, or else go searching for other gade whom the spirit has captured and hidden. On the last night of the festival, the gade visit cremation grounds and cemeteries, gather up bits of corpses, bring them back and dance with them for some time, before finally returning them to the graveyard.

There are stories of gade disappearing during this festival, or being so well hidden by the Devchar that they are only found the following year.

*

According to a belief current among the Kumbri Marathi tribe of Karnataka, the Devchar are usually kindly spirits. However, if taboos pertaining to purity and cleanliness are not followed, they can cause great affliction. In the Kumbri Marathi pantheon of demons, the term Devchar is also applied to certain types of **Balishtamaru**, in particular the Rav, Devati, and Akashmurchi.

Ref: 32, 86, 161, 575

DEYYAM

Deyyam is a Telugu word derived from the Indic word **Dev**. It is usually translated as "ghost", though not all Deyyams are spirits of the dead.

In folk stories of Andhra Pradesh and Telangana, Deyyams have many attributes in common with the Hindi **Bhoot**. But there are some differences. While Bhoots can stretch their arms and legs to reach a great distance, the Deyyam prefers to do this trick with its *tongue*—extending its glistening, prehensile pink muscle into another room to adjust the volume on a radio, or to turn off the gas burner of a stove. Deyyams also have the ability to transfer their spirit to any other living thing through a bite or a scratch. Sometimes these scratches seem to come from invisible entities hovering in cool air, in which case they are called *deyyam barukulu*, or ghost scratches. Deyyams are susceptible to fire, and appear to die a second death if they are burnt.

Thus, in one folktale, a marauding Deyyam who had been feeding on the livestock of a certain village was caught, and the villagers burnt it to death. Just before the ghost died, it managed to grab hold of a chicken and claw a gash in its side. The chicken then became a demon-chicken that laid cursed eggs, out of which hatched bizarre feathered Deyyams with human heads. The demon chicken was later caught and killed and cooked, and all those who ingested its flesh turned into Deyyams as well.

Some Deyyams are bound to certain objects. A famous story from the Guntur district tells of a farmer who found a beautiful glass bead in his field. He took it home and hid it in the pooja cabinet. Soon afterwards, an old woman showed up at the house. She introduced herself as Peki, and asked if there was any work for her to do around the farm.

Almost immediately, doubts arose about Peki's true nature. For one thing, she was freakishly strong, working better and faster than any of the men in the fields, despite her wrinkled face and stooped back. And late one night, the farmer's mother, who was half-asleep, observed her stretching her tongue far across the room to adjust the wick of an oil lamp.

Distraught, the family tried to move to a new house to get away from Peki. As was the custom, they left behind their stone mortar and pestle, to ensure that any evil spirits residing in the old house did not follow them. But Peki simply lifted up the mortar and pestle and carried them to the new house.

Finally, the family brought magicians to chant mantras of protection to banish the spirit. Peki, from outside the gate, shouted at them, "Just give me my glass bead and I'll leave you alone!" For though she had searched everywhere else in the house, the pooja cabinet, with all its images of the gods, had remained off limits for her.

The farmer threw the bead out to Peki. She caught it and left, and after that the haunting stopped.

Ref: 473, 474

DOHT

Dohts are spirits known from the folklore of Assam. They are pitch-black, gaunt, and enormously tall—about 5 or 6 metres (16–20 feet). Their fingers and toes are unnaturally long, as are the claw-like nails that grow from them. They have oily, slippery bodies: it is nearly impossible to grab hold of one of these beings, or to wrestle it down. They have dishevelled mops of hair on their heads. Male Dohts always go naked, whereas female Dohts sometimes wear tattered rags.

Like the **Baak**, a Doht always carries a little round black pouch under its armpit, similar to the kind used to carry betel-leaves. This bag is made of a supernatural net-like cloth.

Dohts live in family groups near mosquito-ridden swamps, ponds, or slow-moving rivers. They love to eat fish, and sometimes steal them out of fishermen's traps, or even creep along behind a person to silently snatch fish out of his bag. They also eat shellfish and the cocoons of Assam silkworms, which they consider a delicacy.

All Dohts are spiteful towards humans, but to varying degrees. If they encounter someone by chance, they might beat them black and blue, or they might stick them upside down in the mud with their heads buried until they nearly suffocate. Some Dohts refrain from attacking if they see a way to steal some fish. Others are merciless killers, ready to take a human life at the slightest provocation.

Male Dohts are most ruthless and dangerous when they are on their own, away from their families. They are less prone to violence while their wives are watching them.

A thicket of tall bamboo at the water's edge is often a home to a Doht. If you notice one of these thickets suddenly starting to shake, it is because the Doht that lives inside is trying to scare you away.

Like many other ghosts, Dohts fear fire, iron, and mustard seeds. Anyone who carries any of these things is protected from an attack. Fisher-people sometimes wear steel fish-hooks on threads around their necks to ward off Dohts.

If a person manages to steal a Doht's magical pouch, he should bury it in a pile of mustard seeds to ensure that the Doht cannot retrieve it. By doing so he can make the Doht his slave. As soon as a Doht loses its pouch it also loses its supernatural powers, and takes the shape of a mortal human who will obey his master's every command.

Dohts can change their shape and take human form, sometimes even coming to human markets to shop. On these visits male Dohts sometimes abduct human women and mate with them. The half-human children of a Doht have curiously lanky, weak limbs, streaks or marks on their arms, and may have reddish, curly hair.

Ref: 294, 448

⤟⟿ DRAGON ⟾⤞

In much of the world, Dragons are the most familiar of all mythological beasts; but they are rarely associated with India today. However, long ago, things were different. The area around the Jhelum and Chenab rivers, in what is now Punjab and Kashmir, was once thought to have been a home to Dragons. They are mentioned in the works of several ancient Greek and Roman writers, whose descriptions of India were based in turn on the accounts of European or Persian travellers.

These dragons did not have wings, nor did they breathe fire. Instead they resembled oversized snakes. It is possible that Western legends of the *drakon indikos*—the Indian dragon—are based on the **Nagas** of Hindu mythology.

The Greek author Ælian, writing in the 3rd century CE, described a species of Indian dragon that preyed upon elephants. These dragons would climb up into large trees and hide there. When an elephant came to the tree to feed on its leaves and branches, the dragon would spring at it and bite out its eyes. Then, keeping its tail anchored to the tree, it would wind itself around the pachyderm's neck and constrict it to death. Finally, it would swallow the animal whole.

According to Philostratus, a Greek author who wrote around the same time as Ælian, India was chock-full of dragons. He described three sorts.

Marsh Dragons were the smallest, around 30 cubits (14 metres) in length. They were also the most sluggish. They had large, black scales on their backs and smooth heads without crests.

The Plains Dragons were larger and very fast-moving. These were silver in colour. Young plains dragons started out with small crests on their heads which grew taller as they aged; a serrated dorsal fin developed as well. The plains dragons were said to have magical stones in their eyes and huge indestructible teeth.

Finally there were the Mountain Dragons, the largest of all. These had golden scales, bushy golden beards, and crests which flashed with a fiery light. Mountain dragons could burrow into the earth, making an incredible racket while doing so. In addition to their valuable eyes and teeth, the skulls of mountain dragons contained multicoloured gems which had tremendous magical powers (see **Ichchhadhari Nag**).

Abisares, a king who ruled part of the Punjab during the time of Alexander the Great, was said to have kept two captive dragons, one 140 cubits (64 metres) long, and the other 80 cubits (37 metres).

Philostratus wrote that some Indians knew the secret of charming mountain dragons. This was done by means of occult symbols woven in gold thread into scarlet fabric. When these cloths were waved at the entrance of a dragon's burrow, the monster would come out to gaze on them and fall asleep, at which point the people would hack off their heads with axes in order to obtain the gems inside. Dragon hearts and livers were also harvested; eating these organs was supposed to give a person the power to speak to animals and to read their thoughts.

Perhaps it was these methods that eventually drove the Indian Dragon extinct.

Ref: 14, 270

 DUMA

The word Duma (or sometimes Dumma) means "ghost" or "ancestor spirit" in several tribal languages of Andhra Pradesh and Odisha.

In the Gadaba tribe, for example, there is a process of transformation from life to death to benevolent ancestor spirit. For some time after a person dies, their Duma roams the village, visiting the houses of family members. People who died of natural causes don't cause much trouble; their relations leave them offerings of rice and beer, and gradually they withdraw. After a few weeks, their individual life-force becomes reincarnated in the womb of a mother.

But those who die bad deaths stay volatile, their spirits wandering in the forest with malicious intent. Women who die in childbirth become Sunguni Duma; those who fall from trees, Mursu Duma; those killed by tigers, Bag Duma; those who hang themselves, Utshki Duma; and those who are struck by lightning, Betani Duma. Pacifying these spirits requires a special sacrifice of twelve animals. If the ritual is not done correctly, the Duma transforms into a horrifying demon called a Sagbo Duma, who causes people's necks to swell up and makes them vomit blood.

It is said that some magicians can capture a peaceful Duma and turn it into a Betani Duma, using it as a weapon against their enemies.

Every three or four years, when there is a good harvest, a *Gotar* or Duma Puja is performed. This is an elaborate month-long ceremony in which the spirits of the deceased are pushed into a buffalo. The ceremony culminates in the sacrifice of many buffaloes, by slicing open their bellies and tearing out their intestines while they are still alive.

It is thought that the Gotar ceremony brings the Dumas peace, allowing them to join the benevolent ancestor spirits. Without it, the Dumas would go on wandering restlessly, attacking people and causing crops to fail.

The Ganda of Odisha are another community who believe in a complex process by which the *jeo* or soul is absorbed into a larger ancestral Duma. After a Ganda person dies, a feast is held on the tenth day. The deceased is eulogized in song to the accompaniment of drums, and a goat is sacrificed and offered to the jeo. Then, that night, in a more private ceremony, close friends and family head home, carrying a brass plate with a wet ball of wheat flour on it. Whatever insect or other creature falls into the flour and is trapped there becomes the symbolic jeo; it must be guarded, lest it be attacked by other roaming evil spirits. The jeo is brought home to the *pidar*, the household shrine of the ancestral Duma, and a covered plate of flour is left next to the shrine.

The next morning, the plate of flour is inspected by the elders to know what sort of Duma the jeo has become. If they see the shape of a bunch of paddy, then the Duma will bring peace and prosperity. If they see the shape of an elephant's paw, the Duma is less auspicious, but still peaceful. If they see the shape of a cat's paw, then the Duma is a troubled spirit, who died unfulfilled.

Ganda people believe that every Duma has a different favourite *paar* or rhythm, which is used by a ritual drummer to invoke them in ceremonies.

The Parangi Porja tribe recognizes several varieties of Dumma, including:

- **Bagh Dumma**, the ghost of a person who was killed by a tiger in the forest and whose body was never recovered. It is said that the half-eaten corpse regrows so that it is half-human and half-tiger.

- **Dongria Dumma**, a mischievous spirit who wanders on hilltops on new moon and full moon nights. This ghost likes to pull hair, rip clothes, and pull other such pranks.

- **Nor Dumma**, the ghost of a person who died with unfulfilled wishes. These ghosts appear human. They wander around at night making a low hum or moaning noise, and if anyone ventures outside to investigate, the Nor Dumma will possess them.

- **Kamini Dumma** or **Pathala Kamini Dumma**, a female demon who lives in streams and springs. She afflicts new mothers and their babies with fever and diarrhoea unless she is propitiated on the fifth day after birth with a ritual involving cow dung, charcoal, eggs, soil of different colours, and bangles. Kamini Dumma can also act as a seductress, preying upon lonely men or boys.

- **Sorgoni Dumma**, a whirlwind spirit.

- **Merching Dumma**, an infant ghost and ruler of the cemetery.

Ref: 111, 345, 542

EAKA
(AND OTHER BEINGS FROM THE LOWER PLANES)

The Eaka are a class of ghostly beings in the folklore of the Onge tribe of Little Andaman Island.

The Onge are a highly endangered tribe. In the 2011 census, their population numbered just 101 individuals. Their society, culture, and language have been devastated by colonization and settlement of the islands. As a result, anthropological understanding of their traditional mythology and folklore is limited. What follows is based primarily on interviews conducted by the anthropologist Pranab Kumar Ganguly between 1953 and 1957.

In Onge mythology, there are thirteen planes of existence, six that lie above our world and six that lie below. The six higher planes have no ocean, only endless land. Each of the six lower planes consists of an island about the same size as Little Andaman, surrounded by an ocean. Even lower, beneath them all, is Kwatannange, the primordial ocean, which is full of turtles.

This entry covers the beings who live in the six planes of existence that lie below Little Andaman Island. The residents of the higher planes are discussed in the separate entry on the **Onkoboykwe**.

The plane directly beneath Little Andaman is inhabited by the Eaka. Like the Onge, they are black-skinned, but have large distended bellies and bald heads. Food is plentiful in their world. They eat fruits, tubers, edible roots, and pork, in addition to meat caught from the sea that surrounds their island: fish, turtles, and dugongs.

The Eaka sometimes come to the human plane and kidnap Onge under cover of darkness. When they catch a person, they bring him down below and turn him into another Eaka.

The Eaka themselves are the ghosts of humans—at least, some of them are.

The Onge believe that if a person dies a "normal" death (of illness or old age), then a few days after his body is buried, a tiny humanoid form called an Embekete emerges from his corpse. The Embekete digs itself down through the earth and dives into the sea below it. Then it swims across the ocean until it reaches the faraway land of the **Inene**, another class of spirits. At that point the Embekete transforms into one of the Inene, and proceeds to live a life in that form.

The day after the Embekete departs, a second spirit, this one an Eaka, emerges from the corpse. The Eaka digs himself slowly into the ground by wiggling back and forth until it drops through the bottom of the Earth and into the lower plane. There, other Eakas come to greet it, and they offer it food and shelter.

Onge who die unnatural deaths have a different fate (see **Onkoboykwe** and **Ingennangkwe**).

Despite being ghosts, the Eaka are considered still to be mortal; the afterlife comes to an end eventually. In fact, this is true of the inhabitants of all the planes, both the higher and the lower.

The Taoere

Below the plane of the Eaka is the plane of the Taoere. The beings who dwell in this plane appear mostly human, but with reddish-brown skin. They subsist on seafood caught in the ocean surrounding their island. Their world has no jungle, and therefore no pigs; but they still have a taste for pork, so they sometimes travel two planes up to visit Little Andaman and hunt for pigs.

The Tege-ele

Below the plane of the Taoere is the plane of the Tege-ele. This world has both a sea surrounding it and a forest with wild pigs. Nevertheless, the Tege-ele sometimes come up to hunt for pigs in the human plane. The Tege-ele resemble the Onge, but they are uglier; they fear humans, and are considered harmless.

The Toranchu

Below the plane of the Tege-ele is the plane of the Toranchu, who are described as being in all respects similar to the Tege-ele.

The Burage

Below the plane of the Toranchu is the plane of the Burage. This world too has both a jungle and a surrounding sea. The Burage are light-skinned with extremely long noses. They live in huts and hunt pigs. They do not visit the human plane.

The Kochay

Below the plane of the Burage is the plane of the Kochay. The beings who dwell in this plane are black-skinned like the Onge, but with protruding jaws. In their land there are no pigs, so they subsist on fish, turtle, and dugong. They, too, appear uninterested in visiting the human plane of existence.

Ref: 475

⥱— EENAMPECHI —⥆

In the folklore of Kerala, pangolins—called *eenampechi* in Malayalam—were thought by some to be the spirits of aborted human fœtuses, most likely because of the way they curl up when threatened.

These scaly nocturnal mammals rest in burrows during daylight, but emerge at night to feed on ants and termites. They are sometimes encountered in paddy fields. They are now an endangered species—threatened by habitat loss, hunted for use in Chinese medicine, and killed by superstitious people who think they are evil spirits.

In folk stories, the Eenampechi is a sort of bogeyman who carries off children in the night.

Ref: 181

⥱— ELMAKALTAI —⥆

According to a legend about the town of Kolhapur, in Maharashtra, the area was formerly inhabited by a fierce **Rakshasa** who refused to let anyone build there. The pandits conferred about what to do. They finally decided that to appease the demon, a human sacrifice would have to be made, and the person to be killed would have to be a mother with seven sons.

Elmakaltai is the ghost of this mother, who was killed to placate the Rakshasa and buried beneath the city walls. It is said that she still haunts the city. She appears as a ghostly form wearing a black sari, with seven small child-ghosts playing around her.

When Elmakaltai visits a house, food stores mysteriously start to vanish, cattle begin to sicken, and milk will fail to turn to butter no matter how hard it is churned.

Ref: 92

⥱— FARASI BAHARI —⥆

The Farasi Bahari is often found on lists of mythical Indian beasts compiled by foreigners. Sometimes, they even appear in lists of creatures from Hindu mythology. They are supposedly a species of long-maned, emerald green horses that live at the bottom of the Indian Ocean, where they graze on seaweed. They do not need to breathe air, and normally never surface.

In descriptions of this creature, it is claimed that ancient coastal people who owned regular land-dwelling horses would graze their animals close to the shore, in hopes that the Farasi Bahari would emerge from the ocean at night to mate with their mares. Horses with Farasi Bahari ancestry were believed to have extraordinary speed and endurance, and to be very long-lived.

The origin of this myth is murky. It is almost certainly not Indian. Farasi Bahari means "sea horse" in Swahili, which is spoken along the east coast of Africa; but the term is used in that language to mean the real animal—the fish with the prehensile tail—rather than any supernatural creature. It's possible that the legend is of recent vintage, perhaps invented by someone foreign to both Indian and Swahili culture.

On the other hand, the description of the Farasi Bahari is similar in many respects to the mythological Hippocampus of ancient Greek and Phoenician mythology, which was half-horse and half-fish. Some dictionaries of mythology mention an Egyptian counterpart to this creature called *Sabgarifiya*. There are also parallels with the legend of the **Cetea**. It's possible that during the Middle Ages, African merchants and sailors from the Swahili coast brought tales of such beasts to India.

Ref: 476, 477

❧⟞ FARU FURETA ⟝❧

Faru Fureta means "reef monster" in Dhivehi, a language spoken in the Maldives and on remote Minicoy Island, the southernmost point of the Lakshadweep Archipelago.

The Faru Fureta is a large, slimy, toad-like creature that can stand as tall as a tree. While on land, though, it usually prefers to crawl about on all fours. It has a huge, wide mouth full of teeth like crystal daggers, each one larger than a man's hand. This monster has a nasty smell, like sea sponges and corals that have been sitting in the sun for a while.

The Faru Fureta sometimes comes ashore in the dead of night, calling out a person's name in a human voice. In the darkness, the monster makes itself look like a shadowy human form. It beckons the person to follow as it walks to the beach. It leads them to the edge of the water. Then it drags them into the surf and eats them.

Despite being fearsome and bloodthirsty, Faru Furetas are quite cowardly and easy to fool. One way to scare a Faru Fureta away is to noisily crunch breadfruit chips. It will think you are crunching bones. This will convince the monster that *you* are much more dangerous than *it*, so it will hightail it back into the water.

Ref: 3, 209, 303

❧ FIRANGI BHOOT ❧

There are plenty of ghosts of foreign origin in India, ranging from the Chinese or "Chinikara" **Bhootas** of Mangalore to the African-origin **Kappiri Muthappan** of Kerala. The term Firangi Bhoot, though, is usually reserved for the spectres of dead Britishers.

Some of these Europeans died in military forts at the hands of rebellious colonial subjects. Others can be found haunting the old summer mansions of the hill stations. A few well-known examples are detailed below; but as there are probably thousands of ghost legends dating from the two centuries of colonial rule, we can only hope to skim the surface. Besides, this class of spirits already has an illustrious and prolific annalist in the person of British-Indian writer Ruskin Bond.

*

One of the most famous cases—on which Bond has written extensively—was that of Frances Garnett-Orme. Garnett-Orme was a wealthy unmarried Englishwoman who travelled to India in 1894 after the death of her fiancée. She soon found her way into the strange subculture of European spiritualists and occultists who were wandering the subcontinent at the time.

By 1909, Garnett-Orme was living in Lucknow with a younger companion named Eva Mountstephen, whom she had met in Nainital a few years earlier. The two women had studied the art of scrying from a Lucknow-based clairvoyant named Mrs. Cardeux; they purchased a crystal ball from her, which they carried wherever they went. According to later testimony, Orme frequently used the ball to make contact with a ghost called Mrs. Winter, whom she referred to as her guardian angel. During their seances, Mrs. Winter would inform the two women about events that would happen in the future.

At some point, Garnett-Orme made Mountstephen the sole beneficiary of her will.

In September 1911, the two Englishwomen travelled to the hill station of Mussoorie, then known as "the pleasure capital of the Raj". They stayed at the Savoy Hotel, one of the fanciest properties in India at the time—it had hosted the Princess of Wales just a few years before.

After they had been there a week, Mountstephen returned to Lucknow, ostensibly to pack up their things from their house and prepare for a move to Jhansi.

Two days later, Garnett-Orme was found dead in her room. She was laid out on the bed as if posed by a mortician, with the door locked from the inside. The postmortem showed that she had died from ingesting prussic acid, also known as hydrogen cyanide.

Mountstephen was arrested in Jhansi that December and charged with murder. Garnett-Orme's relatives alleged that Mountstephen had somehow killed her by suggestion. They claimed she had convinced the gullible older woman that her death had been foretold by the ghost of Mrs. Winter.

Eva Mountstephen's version of the story, on the other hand, was that Orme had been predicting her own death.

Mountstephen was eventually cleared of the murder charge, but she didn't get the money. The Allahabad courts turned down her application on the grounds of "fraud and undue influence in connection with spiritualism and crystal-gazing".

The case made international news. "Weird Occult Practices Revealed in a Murder Trial in India", read the headline in the *Kansas City Star*. "She Looked at Friend's Death in a Crystal", said the *Vancouver World*. The story was passed by the India-born writer Rudyard Kipling to Arthur Conan Doyle, who considered basing a Sherlock Holmes episode on it. But even more significantly, it may have drawn the attention of a young Agatha Christie—her first novel features a poisoning which is similar in some details to the Garnett-Orme case. Thus a murder in a Mussoorie hotel helped launch the career of the world's all-time bestselling fiction writer.

It is said that the Savoy, bought and refurbished by the ITC Hotel group in 2009, is still haunted by Garnett-Orme's ghost today. A variety of paranormal phenomena has been reported, including pianos that play with no one at the keyboard; billiard balls that roll across the table with no one striking them; toilets that flush spontaneously in empty rooms; locked doors that mysteriously swing open; and a misty apparition that floats down the hallways at night, grasping a crystal ball in its hands.

*

Captain Pole—or perhaps Captain Powell, or Poole, or Pooley—is the legendary ghost of a British man who was mortally wounded during the Travancore Rebellion against the East India Company in 1809. He was shot by a musket ball in a battle which took place in a pass through the Western Ghats. The story goes that he tried to make it back to get medical care in Madurai or Thirunelveli, but died on the way, in a tiny village called Ittamozhi near Suviseshpuram.

The local people buried him there beneath a banyan tree, and soon they came to worship him as a ferocious demon. His violent death transformed him into an agent of madness and violence. When he was angry, he could sicken a whole herd of cattle with fatal disease. The ghost of Pooley Sahib had to be propitiated with cigars, meat, brandy and soda water on a daily basis.

According to some, the town of Polepettai in Thoothukudi district is named after Captain Pole.

*

The ghost of Mary Warwick is thought to haunt the village of Jeolikot, near Nainital in Uttarakhand.

The story goes that Mary, having divorced her husband, travelled alone to India in 1913 at the age of 45. A few years later, her youngest brother, her son, and her son-in-law were all killed in World War I.

The next anyone heard of Warwick, she was living in a mansion on a hilltop in Jeolikot and going by the name of Michael. Everyone thought she was a man. Some people remembered her as being "the quintessential Sahib; he enjoyed drinks with his kind at the bar, and was very much part of the social scene and ran charitable organisations". Her house was palatial; it was said to have taken nine years to build, and had a huge library boasting thousands of volumes. Many of those books were signed "Major M. Warwick". Whenever Warwick rode into Nainital on horseback, she dressed as an army major and sported a thin moustache; in this guise she attended many official functions.

In later years, the socializing stopped, and "Brother Michael" became a solitary monk. He had a chapel and a dispensary built outside his house, and hired a pharmacist to work at the dispensary, distributing medicine to the poor. Michael also did much to support St. Anthony's Mission at the bottom of the hill.

It was only after his death from heart failure in 1944 that the doctor who wrote the death certificate confirmed that "M. Warwick" was biologically female.

It is unclear to this day why Warwick chose to live this way. One version has it that when she first moved to Nainital, a British officer warned her that it would be dangerous to live alone as a woman, and that she took this advice very seriously.

The house was kept just as Warwick kept it for years after her death. Visitors say they can feel a strange presence there. They have also remarked upon the unusual placement of two human skulls next to the statues of the Virgin and Baby Jesus in the small Catholic shrine where Warwick worshipped. Many people believe that her prayers were focused on keeping something out of the house.

There is a legend that Warwick's ghost still rides around the village at midnight. Residents claim to have heard the sound of pounding hooves, or caught a glimpse of the major in uniform, trotting through the dark.

*

Warren Hastings was born in Oxfordshire in 1732 and travelled to Kolkata at the age of seventeen with the East India Company. He was destined to become one of the most important and powerful administrators of the British Empire in South Asia.

But throughout his life, he had problems with money. He nearly bankrupted himself on his visits to London through extravagant spending. He fought against corruption amongst the traders of Bengal, but was often accused of embezzlement himself. When a tax collector alleged that he was accepting bribes, Hastings retaliated by accusing that collector of forgery and having him executed. He financed military raids against French outposts by raiding the treasury, angering his political rivals. Then, shortly after he resigned the post of Governer-General of Bengal in 1785, he was dragged into the London courts to face accusations of corruption. It took the prosecution two whole days to read the charges, and Hastings had to fight the case for seven years before he was finally acquitted. He lived out his old age in elegant English stately homes, but at the end, he was broke.

Though Hastings died in England, it is said that his ghost still haunts Kolkata. Every New Year's Morning, his spirit visits Hastings House, now home to the Institute of Education for Women. A carriage pulled by four spectral horses stops outside the entrance and the ghostly form of Hastings jumps out, running up the steps in a great hurry. Some say he's looking for a black bureau; it contains important papers that could be used as evidence against him in the corruption trial, and he wants to destroy them. Others say the bureau contains evidence exonerating him. Still others say he is looking for a stash of precious stones he left behind when he quit Kolkata for Britain—a treasure that could have solved his financial problems forever, a treasure that may still be hidden somewhere in the grounds of Hastings House.

*

In 1857, Brij Raj Bhawan Palace in Kota, Rajasthan was being occupied by a British officer named Major Charles Burton and his family. When the mutiny broke out, a group of Indian soldiers broke into the building and murdered the major along with his children. The Raja of Kota had the bodies buried in the central courtyard.

But Major Burton's ghost is said to still haunt the place. He appears as a very old man, with long white hair and a walking stick, doing the rounds of the building at night. If he catches any security personnel sleeping on duty, he gives them a tight slap and a scolding.

*

Brigadier General John Nicholson hailed from Ireland. He began his career as a soldier in 1839, fighting on the losing side in the First Anglo-Afghan War, where he spent six months as a prisoner. Later, in India, he became renowned by some for his sadism and cruelty to the native population. He was hated and feared by many, but others were so impressed with his bravery and command that they worshipped him as a living saint, "Nikal Sen".

He is most famous for his brutal suppression of the Mutiny of 1857. He killed hundreds of rebel soldiers, and famously executed a kitchen full of cooks for trying to poison a soup about to be served to a table of British officers. He advocated flaying all the mutineers alive, saying, "I would inflict the most excruciating tortures I could think of on them with a perfectly easy conscience."

He was finally killed by a sepoy sniper in September 1857.

On new moon nights, his headless, horse-riding ghost is said to ride through the Nicholson Cemetery, outside the Kashmiri Gate in Delhi where he was killed.

*

Perhaps the most stereotypically British of all British ghosts is Owen Tomkinson, who haunts the town of Gaya in Bihar. A solider who died of cholera in 1906, he was buried in the Durbar Cemetery at Iqbal Nagar. His ghost is said to rise up out of his grave at night, approach passers-by, and demand tea and biscuits.

Ref: 43, 44, 63, 64, 194, 211, 239, 248, 321, 327, 357, 373, 374, 386, 389, 491

⮜⟶ FLYING HORSES ⟵⮞

The best-known Flying Horse in Hindu mythology is Uchchaihshravas, the divine seven-headed snow-white steed who serves as the *vahana* of Surya the Sun God. He was born from the churning of the Ocean of Milk, along with the nectar of immortality and many other wondrous things.

There is a folktale about a mechanical flying horse told among the Baiga people of Madhya Pradesh. In one version of this story, there is a smith who is doing a roaring business in metalwork, and a carpenter who is struggling to make ends meet. The carpenter is frustrated, for he feels he is more talented than the smith. So he calls for a competition, and asks the raja of the kingdom to judge who is the better craftsman.

The carpenter proceeds to build a beautiful winged horse out of wood, complete with a working wooden engine inside. The smith only makes a simple flat iron pan.

When the two craftsmen bring their creations to the raja, the rani says, "We have plenty of horses in the stables already. I don't need anymore. But I do like that iron pan." The carpenter starts to tear his hair out in exasperation when the raja's son comes into the room, lays his eyes on the horse, and decides that it looks like a fun toy. He jumps astride it and accidentally turns on the engine. The horse flies off into the air with the prince on its back, and travels over many countries before the boy finally chances on the button that will make it land.

The prince goes on to have many adventures on the flying horse. He uses it to sneak into the bedroom of the princess of another kingdom, and eventually to steal her away from the palace.

But the poor carpenter who built the horse is jailed by the raja for many years.

*

Several other flying horses are mentioned in the Bundeli-language epic of **Alha and Udal**, set in the late 12th century CE in Bundelkhand. Papiha is the name of the first of these horses, and the only one who possesses the power of speech. Lord Surya gave Papiha to Parmal, the Chandela king, as a reward for his devotion. Papiha then fathered several more flying horses by his mate Harini. Their offspring were:

- *Karilya*, also known as Hansaamani, a terrifying black stallion ridden by Alha.

- *Manoratha*, a pale horse who shared Harini's womb with Karilya, ridden by Prince Deva.

- *Rasbendul*, also known as Bendula or Bendil, a golden stallion ridden mostly by Udal.

- *Harnaagar*, also known as Balahaak, a snow-white stallion ridden by Parmal's son Brahma, who was born at the same time as Rasbendul.

- *Kabutri*, a mare, ridden by Alha and Udal's cousin Malkhaan (though some versions say Malkhaan rode Harini, the mother of the others).

In Manipuri mythology, the deity Ibudhou Marjing, God of the Northeast Direction and inventor of the game of polo, rides a flying horse named Samadon Ayangba.

Ref: 36, 400

FRAVASHI

In the Zoroastrian faith, a Fravashi (also called a Fravad or Faravahar) is a personal spirit. The ghost of a dead person is a Fravashi, as is the guardian angel of someone living—and the spirit of a person yet to be born. There are Fravashis of animals too, and plants, and even rocks. But nothing man-made or manufactured has a Fravashi.

The Fravashi is different from the *Urvan*, or soul. After a person's death, both the Fravashi and Urvan separate from the body. The material corpse is occupied by **Nasu**, the corpse-demon, while the Urvan travels to the Chinwad Bridge to be judged by the angel Mihir. If the good deeds the person performed in life outweigh the bad, then the Urvan passes onwards to heaven; if the bad deeds outweigh the good, then the Urvan is damned to hell.

The Fravashi, on the other hand, is an incorruptible and pure life essence. After death it always goes to join the other Fravashis high in the air. The Fravashis have existed from the beginning of time; indeed they helped the god Ahura Mazda to create the universe, and even now they help to hold up the Earth and the sky.

There is a period at the end of the Zoroastrian calendar called Frawardagan, during which the Fravashis of the ancestors are invited into the home. Zoroastrians clean their houses and light lamps to welcome the spirits, and carry sandalwood to the Towers of Silence to burn.

The concept of the Fravashis and their annual worship bears some similarity to the Vedic Hindu worship of the **Pitrs**, as well as to the ancient Greek concept of the Daimon.

Ref: 49, 231

GAALI

Gaali is the Kannada word for "air" or "wind". It is also used for a type of invisible evil spirit which wanders through the atmosphere.

It is thought that Gaalis travel on their own paths and thoroughfares, laid out on a plan which is completely independent of the human geography of a place. If a person should unwittingly cross one of these paths, or linger in the middle of one, there's a good chance that a passing Gaali will enter them.

Once a Gaali is inside a person, and no longer wandering through the air, it is referred to as a Duratma, or "bad soul". Possession by this type of spirit can cause physical pain, mental anguish, bizarre behaviour, and madness. Typical symptoms include frequent blinking, grinding of teeth, and speaking in languages one has never learned.

A Duratma can also take up residence in a house. There it will possess the different members of a family in turn, stoking disagreements and fights and even causing material damage.

Certain human beings possess a mysterious quality called *suli*—the word also means "vortex" or "swirl"—which makes them especially attractive to these spirits. Such unfortunate people may play host to multiple Duratmas at the same time.

Duratmas find it tortuous to be inside churches, temples, or dargahs. If a possessed person goes into such a place of worship, they will be overwhelmed with crushing despair and begin sobbing uncontrollably. In this manner, possession by a Duratma can be recognized—but not cured, since the Duratma cannot exit the body into the air of a sacred place.

Instead, to remove the Duratma, one must bring the sufferer home, and take advantage of the spirit's attraction to certain objects. These include lemons, locks, and needles. A spiritual healer will attempt to cure the possessed person by teasing the Gaali out of them and into one of these objects, and then setting the spirit loose into a neem tree.

At certain ancient sites in Karnataka, there are to be found stones known as *Gaali kallu*, or "devil's stones". These are monoliths in which a gap has been carved, just barely large enough for a person to squeeze through by doing some complex contortions of the shoulders. It is believed that if a person gets stuck while crawling through the gap, then they are possessed by a Gaali. No one should offer a helping hand, or else the spirit will be transferred to them.

Ref: 261

⤙⤙ GAANTIYAL DANGORIYA ⤚⤚

The Gaantiyal Dangoria is a ghost from the folklore of Assam. Like the **Burha Dangoriya**, these spirits are wise and benevolent.

A Gaantiyal Dangoria is typically the custodian of a horde of treasure buried at the base of a tree. If the ghost witnesses someone performing a selfless and charitable deed in the vicinity of his tree, he will appear and reward the person with gold and jewels.

Ref: 294, 448

⤙⤙ GANDHARVA ⤚⤚

Gandharvas are a race of supernatural beings in Hindu and Buddhist mythology. They are the husbands of the **Apsaras**, the heavenly nymphs. Gandharvas are nearly always male.

Gandharvas are sky-dwelling musicians with singing voices of superlunary beauty. Many have virtuosic control over stringed instruments or flutes as well. They act as guardians over the ritual mind-altering drink of the Vedic prayers called *soma*, and they are in charge of producing it for the gods. But they do not partake of it themselves. They derive their own nourishment from fragrance, and are attracted to sweet smells.

Most Gandharvas are handsome, with an atmospheric or extra-dimensional quality; ancient texts often describe them as "wind-haired". But some ancient texts feature more monstrous individuals. For example, one Gandharva character in the *Sama Veda* is a huge ogre with three heads who dwells underwater.

In Hinduism, the chieftain of the Gandharvas is the horse-headed Tumburu, who plays the veena. He is a close associate of Kubera, the king of the **Yakshas**. In Buddhism, their leader is Dhritarashtra, Guardian of the East Direction.

Gandharvas are often lustful and possessive, with a special attraction to married and/or pregnant human women, over whom they have a hypnotic power. Thus possession by a Gandharva, or interference by a jealous Gandharva lover, was once held to be a cause of infertility or miscarriage.

In wars between the Devas and **Asuras**, Gandharvas typically take a neutral role.

Ref: 136

GARUDA

The name Garuda is most commonly used for one particular mythological figure, the bird-like deity who is the *vahana* or mount of Lord Vishnu. This character is the king of a whole race of bird-creatures, also called Garudas, which are common to Hindu, Buddhist, and Jain mythology. In Tibetic languages, they are called *Khyung*.

The Garudas live in Himavanta, a jungle around the base of Mount Meru, the five-peaked mountain at the centre of the multiverse.

According to Pali-language scripture, Garudas in their natural form are impossibly huge birds, with a wingspan of 330 yojanas (roughly the distance from Delhi to Singapore). When dealing with humans, they can reduce their size and appear as humanoids with wings and bird-like faces. At least some of them can change their appearance so much as to be indistinguishable from a human.

Garudas are almost always portrayed as benevolent creatures, but there are exceptions. At Singye Dzong, a fortress-monastery in Bhutan, there is a rock which serves as a prison for 108 evil Garudas who once tried to poison the Earth.

The Garudas are also one of the *astagatyah*, the eight classes of supernatural beings in Buddhist mythology, along with the **Gandharvas**, Devas, **Asuras**, **Yakshas**, **Kinnaras**, **Mahoragas**, and the Garudas' sworn enemies, the **Nagas**.

Ref: 478

GATA LOOPS GHOST

Gata Loops is a high-altitude stretch of the Manali–Leh highway: a series of twenty-one switchbacks on a mountainside in the high, cold desert of Ladakh, a desolate place of great scenic beauty.

It is said to be haunted by the ghost of a trucker's assistant who died there one winter. When the truck broke down on the nineteenth loop, the driver decided to make the trek on foot to the nearest village to get help, leaving his assistant with the vehicle to guard the goods. But just as the driver arrived at the village, a snowstorm started, and the roads became impassable.

The assistant was stranded in the cold for eight days. By the time help could reach him, he was dead.

Since that day, there have been sightings of a lonely man on the highway, flagging down travellers and begging for water and food. But whatever is placed in his hands falls right through them.

A shrine has come up at the spot, where people place offerings of bottled water, cigarettes, and packets of biscuits.

Ref: 479

~→— GHAR JEUTI —←~

Ghar Jeuti means "light of the house" in Assamese. It is also the name given to a small and very rare female spirit that sometimes takes up residence in the home of a single man. She is invisible except as a small light, barely glimpsed out of the corner of an eye. On quiet evenings, she can be heard making soft ticking sounds.

If the man sleeps with his body across his doorway, he may feel the Ghar Jeuti lightly tiptoeing over him on her way in and out of the house.

Ref: 294, 448

~→— GHORAPAAK —←~

The Ghorapaak is an Assamese evil spirit, similar in many respects to the **Baak**. It too is a marsh-dwelling fish-eater that can change its shape. When it comes onto land, it appears in the form of a horse with a human head.

Ghorapaaks can cause fever and delirium through possession. They are also known for luring fishermen to their deaths.

It is said that these spirits somehow know the name of every human they meet without being told.

Ref: 170, 383

GINGGREK MIKDALONG GINGTHONGRENG

In Garo folktales, Ginggrek Mikdalong Gingthongreng is an ogre with a huge long and pointy nose. This nose is as hard as an elephant tusk, and it is very sharp.

Ginggrek lives in a comfortable house hidden in the forest, where he often welcomes lost travellers. He cooks elaborate meals for them, serves them good wine, engages them in pleasant conversation, and gives them comfortable beds to sleep in.

Then, in the night, he sneaks into the guest room and spears his guests to death with his nose.

It is likely that this monster is related to the witch of Mizo legend named **Hmuichukchuriduninu**.

Ref: 306

GOBHOOT

A Gobhoot is the ghost of a cow who died before its time, usually in a traffic accident. They appear at night to haunt the roads where they died. A Gobhoot is sometimes encountered limping slowly along, dripping phantom blood from its wounds, fixing passers-by with a ghostly stare from its empty eye sockets.

In tribal communities of West Bengal, a Gomua Bhoot is the ghost of a cow who died while delivering a calf. This ghost has the ability to shape-change into a goat, a cat, or even a pumpkin; it can climb trees and hover near the top. They follow people who are carrying mutton or fish. They are mostly harmless, though they can sometimes frighten a person badly enough to cause a fever.

There is also a tale from Tamil Nadu about a giant demonic cow called Pasuvarakkan. She was summoned by a group of Jain black magicians who wanted to show their dominance over the city of Madurai. They knew that because of the holiness of this animal, Lord Shiva would refuse to kill it.

The demon was instead defeated by Shiva's bull Nandi, who had no such compunctions.

Its body became the hill Pasumalai ("Cow Hill").

Ref: 84, 208

GOG AND MAGOG

Gog and Magog are legendary figures who first appeared in the Hebrew bible. Their roles in Jewish, Christian, and Islamic mythology are different, but they are generally thought to be evil allies of Satan, associated with the End of Days—i.e. the apocalypse.

Some versions of the *Romance of Alexander*, a medieval legend about the exploits of Alexander III of Macedon, place Gog and Magog in India.

In these stories, they were vassals of Porus, a king who ruled Punjab around 326 BCE. Gog and Magog presided over a degenerate society of Punjabi cave-dwellers with singularly repulsive culinary habits: they ate worms, human fœtuses, and dead bodies.

Gog and Magog are described as very short—only half the height of normal men—with long claws, hooked noses, and hairy tails.

Gog and Magog and their armies were defeated by Alexander (or, in Islamic tradition, by a two-horned hero named Dhul-Qarnayn), who sealed them behind a giant wall. Ever since, they have been scratching at the wall trying to break through. During the day, they make some progress, but every night, while they sleep, the wall is magically repaired.

There is a prophecy that in the time of Armageddon, Gog and Magog will finally succeed in digging through the wall. Then they will escape from their prison to join the Antichrist.

Ref: 480

⟩⟩⟨⟨ GOGGAYYA ⟩⟩⟨⟨

Goggayya is a bogeyman character in Karnataka, often used by parents to threaten their children. "If you don't finish your food, Goggayya will come and take you away!"

The physical description of Goggayya is usually left up to the child's imagination, but he has been pictured as a hunched-over man with a long beard, a shawl over his head, and a sack slung over his shoulder in which he stashes captured kids.

There are close equivalents for this character in many other languages. In Tamil, he is called *Boochandi*; in Telugu, *Boochodu*. In Rajasthan, *Buddha Baba* is used in approximately the same way, and the Karbi people of Assam call the child-snatcher *Kong Kong Do*. Outside India, especially in Spain, Portugal, and Latin America, he is simply known as the Sack Man.

Ref: 481

 HADAL

Hadals are female ghosts in the folklore of Maharashtra and the Konkan coast, the shades of women who died childless. They are wanton, lusty spirits who wear dishevelled green saris and keep their hair loose. They have more than the usual amount of body hair, and they stink; a strong odour hangs about them, described as a combination of rotting eggs and burnt hair.

Hadals live in trees, most commonly tamarind or babul. They sometimes haunt old wells or crossroads where three roads meet. They are especially active on nights when the moon is either full or new. Though they don't always show themselves, their presence is announced by the tinkling of their glass bangles— and by their awful smell.

Hadals can cause trouble for young mothers and their children, whom they attack out of jealousy, and handsome young men, whom they try to molest.

Luckily, it is fairly easy to escape from a Hadal, or to chase one away. They can't walk very quickly, and since their hair often hangs in their face, they don't see too well. They are afraid of sticks and canes, and if beaten with one will hobble away as fast as they can. They also abhor cleanliness, and will never enter a house or any other place that is kept neat and tidy. A Hadal will never possess a living person.

The presence of a Hadal is said to cause malfunctions in nearby electrical equipment. In areas frequented by these ghosts, unexplained nighttime power cuts or surges are common. Transformers blow out when they pass. Car and motorcycle batteries die without warning. Lights dance and flicker in strange patterns. If you stand at a road junction haunted by a Hadal and look up, you're likely to see the charred corpse of a large fruit bat, still entangled in the power line that electrocuted it during the ghost's last high-voltage tantrum.

Hadals are sometimes pushed into the service of powerful **Yakshis** or evil tantric magicians. They are made to do dirty work such as digging up corpses and body parts or gathering other materials for black magic.

Ref: 482, 483, 484

⟩⟩━ HAMZAD ━⟨⟨

In Islamic belief, every time a child is born, a supernatural double of the child is born, too. This spirit, which follows the person throughout his or her life, is called a Qareen in Arabic and a Hamzad in Persian and Urdu. Some religious scholars classify it as a **Jinn**, while others say it is a distinct type of spiritual entity.

An evil Hamzad perches like an invisible devil on a man's shoulder, encouraging his worst instincts. It urges him to indolence and crime and sometimes helps foster a morbid fascination with the occult. A better-tempered Hamzad can inspire its human to create great art or to become a renowned poet. The choices a person makes in life affect the disposition of his Hamzad, in turn—though it is said that a Hamzad is always basically malignant at its core. (The only exceptions are the Hamzads of the prophets. The Prophet Muhammed ﷺ was said to have converted his Hamzad to Islam, while the Hamzad of Jesus Christ is better known as the Holy Spirit.)

Some Islamic scholars claim that spiritually advanced people can master their own Hamzad, and that this brings them incredible power. But it takes years and years of work and prayer and reciting verses from the Holy Quran to achieve such a result. Greedy people who try to take a shortcut and capture their Hamzad by means of dark magic risk having the process backfire on them. An angry Hamzad fighting for its freedom can tear apart a house, smashing glass, throwing furniture, lighting fires, and opening up a deep, gaping hole in the earth.

The idea of the Qareen has found its way into folklore outside the Muslim community, too. Manohar Shyam Joshi—the Hindi writer best known for the smash hit 1980s TV soap opera *Hum Log*—later wrote a novel called *Hamzad* in which the idea of the evil spirit-double is used to explore a man's progressive moral dissolution.

The Jism-e-Latif in Sufism and the Sukshma Sharir or Chaya Purush in Hindu Transcendental Meditation are sometimes associated with the Hamzad. Each of these terms can be translated as the Subtle Body, the Astral Body, or the Shadow Soul. These traditions are more optimistic about one's chances for mastering the spirit, and generally ascribe it a less malign character.

Ref: 106, 277

⤙⤙ HANAL ⤚⤚

Among the various Gond tribes of Central India, a Hanal is the ghost-spirit of a human being.

During life, the Hanal is sometimes able to leave the body and travel abroad— in vivid dreams, for instance. When a person yawns, it is said that the person's Hanal is "dancing in the mouth".

After death, the Hanal remains in the corpse for a few days before travelling to a carved pillar or megalith in the village burial ground. Eventually, it may experience rebirth in a new body.

There are differences in belief between the Gond tribes. The Muria believe that a person has two or three souls. The Hanal is usually the quietest one; after death it sits in a tree and watches the body being buried or cremated. Then it goes to live in a nearby stream or forest for some time, before finally coming back to stay in a large earthen pot called the *hanal kunda*, the Pot of the Departed. This vessel is kept either in a dark corner of the inner room of the family house or in the store room.

Exceptions are made for those who die from wild animal attacks, smallpox, or cholera, and for women who die in pregnancy or childbirth. These ghosts are far too dangerous to allow inside the house, and no funeral stone is erected for them.

Ref: 99

⤙⤙ HEDALI ⤚⤚

In the folklore of the Thakur and Warli tribes of Maharashtra and Gujarat, a Hedali is a mother-ghost. (The word is related to **Hadal**, but the ghost is quite different in character.)

According to the Thakurs, the Hedali is a dark-skinned goblin-woman who has her head wrapped in a blanket. She has a habit of suddenly erupting into flames. The sight of her can cause fever and delirium; but anyone who carries a bit of leather is protected.

The Warlis say that the Hedali appears under a tree, holding her infant in a cradle and singing to it softly. This ghost can be seen even during the daytime. From the front, she looks as beautiful as she did in life; but if one should walk around and see her from behind, it is another story. The flesh of her back is missing, and all her organs and entrails are visible.* Anyone unlucky enough to see the ghost from this angle will be stricken ill.

This type of Hedali doesn't cause any trouble if left alone, as long as no one looks at her from behind. But a ritual can be performed to free the dead woman and child from their pitiable state. In this ceremony, a human figure made of flour, a cradle made of cloth, a comb made of wood, and a cord made of leather are set ablaze and burnt in a cremation ground.

After this, it is said, the ghost will no longer appear.

Ref: 450, 485

⊱⊸ HELLOI ⊷⊰

In the folklore of Manipur, the Helloi are a group of seven beautiful and mischievous fairy spirit sisters. The seventh and youngest Helloi is the most beautiful of all, and it is impossible for any human who sees her not to fall instantly in love with her.

Helloi spend their time in dense forests, especially along the banks of streams or in marshes. If they find a man wandering alone near their abode, they weave a magical illusion to trap him for a while and play with him. Such a man might believe he is sitting in a golden palace being attended by naked beauties feeding him grapes, while in truth he is lashed to a tree and covered with mud, and the Helloi are feeding him worms and insect grubs.

The Helloi usually let their victim go after a while, but the man's hallucinations may linger on, recurring for years afterwards.

It is said that in the olden days, it was difficult for Manipuri girls who came from a family of seven sisters to get married. Potential grooms worried that they were actually Helloi, and that they would never be able to trust their senses around them.

Ref: 62

---

* The mother-ghost with the hollowed-out back is a common motif across India and beyond. **Chudails** are sometimes described this way. Among the Atong of Meghalaya, there is a particular woman-ghost called Kynkongbang whose name means Hollow-Back. The myth is probably related to the Sundel Bolong of Indonesian lore—the ghost of an unmarried woman who died while pregnant, so that the ghost of her unborn child had to burrow its way out of her body through her back, and then up out of the grave. On the other hand, in Ladakh, there is a male spirit with this attribute: the **Btsan**.

⤙⤙ HIDIMBA ⤙⤙

Hidimba is a Rakshasa character in the *Mahabharata*. He and his sister, Hidimbi (or Hidimba Devi) ruled over the demons of Kamyaka Forest.

Hidimba is described as a fearsome man-eating giant, twelve feet tall and fantastically strong. He had skin the colour of storm clouds, wild red dreadlocks, a red beard, and ears that stuck out like arrowheads. He had just eight teeth, but these were long and extremely sharp. They could pierce through any earthly substance, even the hardest metal.

Hidimba was very fond of eating human flesh. When the Pandava brothers (the heroes of the epic) were camped in Kamyaka Forest, Hidimba smelled them, and felt hungry. He asked his sister to go and kill the men and bring him their bodies so they could feast.

That was the plan; but as soon as Hidimbi laid eyes on Bhim—the strongest of the brothers—she fell in love. She changed herself into the form of a beautiful human woman and went to flirt with him.

After they had been talking for a long while, Hidimbi's brother Hidimba became impatient. He came and found them. As soon as he realized what was happening, he flew into a rage and attacked Bhim.

They had a tremendous battle, which ended with Bhim breaking Hidimba's body and killing him.

Afterwards, Hidimbi and Bhim were married, and Hidimbi bore his son, the half-Rakshasa named Ghatotkach. Today there is a temple to Hidimba Devi in Manali in Himachal Pradesh, and a Veer Ghatotkach temple nearby.

Ref: 486

⤙⤙ HI-I ⤙⤙

The traditional religion of the Karbi people of Assam teaches that there is a duality between two spirits or deities, Hi-i and Arnam. They are always mentioned in that order, *Hi-i Arnam*.

In the ancient past, the god Hemphu created the first Karbi people from the mud of a termite mound. But Hi-i was present at the creation, and immediately devoured the humans. Hemphu tried again, but Hi-i ate the second batch too. A council of the *Arnam Pharo* (One Hundred Gods) was called, and they decided to place two pairs of dogs outside the village, one at the eastern end and one at the western end. When Hemphu created the third group of Karbis, Hi-i came once more to attack them, but was scared away by the dogs. To this day, Karbi people avoid eating the meat of the dog, out of gratitude for saving them from Hi-i.

Hi-i is sometimes considered as a single entity, sometimes as multitudinous. A simplistic picture holds Hi-i as "evil" and the Arnam as "good"; but Hi-i can also be thought of as a caretaker of evil, the force that keeps ill-intentioned spirits in check. Thus the household protector god Peng is considered to be one of the Hi-i.

The word is also used for dangerous demons. Hi-ipi, as female Hi-i are called, like to sneak up on children while they are eating mulberries and gobble them up. **Khetor** is considered by the Karbis to be one of the Hi-i, as is the jungle-dwelling **Tisso Jonding**. A Hi-i called Theng-thon, also called Ok-langno, causes recurring disease; Chomang-ase, also called Keche-ase, causes rheumatism; Ajo-ase causes cholera. These last few spirits demand the sacrifices of various animals.

People with unusually bright, intense eyes are sometimes thought to be Hi-i, or possessed by them. Certain species of animals and plants are also associated with Hi-i, including vultures, crows, banyan trees, and the devil's tree (*Alstonia scholaris*).

Ref: 39, 328, 367

HINGCHABI

A Hingchabi is a child-eating witch known from the folklore of Manipur. The word Hingchabi indicates a female; the male form, Hingchaba, is less commonly heard of.

A Hingchabi typically resides alone in a remote hut in the jungle. She often has children who mingle in society and act like normal people, but who secretly abduct boys and girls and supply them to their mother to eat.

Most Hingchabis have the power to fly. They can rise up high over the trees to get an early warning of approaching enemies, or to scout for unaccompanied children to prey upon.

Hingchabis also cultivate certain magical plants for use as defensive weapons to keep enemies away. The magic is unleashed by plucking a single leaf from the plant and dropping it to the ground. A leaf from the plant *isingchaopbi manaa* will transform into raging floodwaters; a leaf from the plant *kaakpheichaobi manaa* will summon a plague of leeches; and a leaf from the plant *meichaobi* will start a blazing forest fire. By use of these powers, a Hingchabi will almost always remain safe even if her hideout is discovered.

A Hingchabi can change her appearance to impersonate others. If she spies a mother leaving her child unattended, she will impersonate the mother in order to steal the child. Hingchabis are also capable of transforming into incorporeal spirits that possess people—usually adult women, but sometimes young children. A person possessed by a Hingchabi tends to hide in dark corners or under the furniture, muttering to themselves in an unknown language. Various forms of exorcism are practised; these usually involve coaxing the Hingchabi's spirit out of the body by offering her a beedi to smoke, or some chicken to eat, or some pieces of betel-nut to chew.

The wall of a Hingchabi's hut will always have a bamboo bow and a large hollow gourd mounted on it. These talismans are magically connected to the Hingchabi's body: the bow is her back and the gourd is her head. If the bow is snapped, her spine will be shattered, and if the gourd is broken, her skull will be smashed in.

Ref: 132, 250, 256, 333

HINN

In Islamic mythology, Hinn are a race of supernatural creatures which have existed long before the first man. They are similar to the **Jinn**, but predate them. According to the Quran, these two kinds of spirits are made out of two different types of fire.

The 13th-century Arab-Persian writer Zakariya ibn Muhammad al-Qazwini, in his book *Marvels of Things Created and Miraculous Aspects of Things Existing*, claimed that there were Hinn living in India, and that they looked somewhat like dogs.

Illustrated manuscripts of this book depicted the Indian Hinn as a small canine with a single twisted horn extending vertically upward from the top of its head.

Ref: 571

HMUICHUKCHURIDUNINU

In Mizo folklore, Hmuichukchuriduninu is an evil witch who lives in the woods. She looks like a normal old woman except that, instead of a nose and mouth, she has a long hard beak, like a bird.

The famous story of Nuchhimi and Hmuichukchuriduninu bears some similarities to "Little Red Riding Hood" and "Hansel and Gretel".

Nuchhimi was a young girl who was travelling to her aunt's house along with her younger sister. As her parents sent her off with a packet of pork, they warned her that when she came to a fork in the road, she should take the neat and clean path which led to her aunt's house, not the dirty and messy one which led to Hmuichukchuriduninu's house.

Unbeknownst to them, Hmuichukchuriduninu was hiding behind a nearby tree, and overheard this whole conversation. She quickly ran back and cleaned the path to her house, transferring all the dirt and rubbish to the other road.

So it was that when Nuchhimi and her sister came to the fork, they turned down the wrong path.

Hmuichukchuriduninu stood outside her house—a traditional bamboo structure on a raised platform—and welcomed the two girls, pretending to be their aunt. Nuchhimi was surprised by the woman's strange beak, but Hmuichukchuriduninu spoke kindly to them and served them a tasty dinner. Soon Nuchhimi cast her suspicions aside. As the sun set, Hmuichukchuriduninu told Nuchhimi to sleep in the corner, while she cradled the younger sister in her arms.

Late in the night, Hmuichukchuriduninu started pecking the girl's head with her beak, trying to crack her skull. Nuchhimi was awakened by her sister's cries; but Hmuichukchuriduninu reassured her, saying that the girl was only crying because of insect bites. So Nuchhimi went back to sleep.

Meanwhile, the witch proceeded to kill the sister, eat her brain, drink her blood, devour her flesh, and throw her bones into the fireplace.

The next morning, Nuchhimi went to make a fire to cook breakfast, and there she discovered her sister's bones. She realized what had happened and began weeping.

Hmuichukchuriduninu asked her why she was crying. Nuchhimi, thinking it was best not to anger her, pretended that it was just the smoke from the fire making her eyes water.

After breakfast, Hmuichukchuriduninu caught Nuchhimi, bound her hands and feet, put in her a basket, and tied the basket to the roof beams. Then she went out to work in her jhum field, planning to eat the girl for supper that evening.

After she had gone, Nuchhimi heard a rat scuttling about in the house. She whispered to the rat, pleading desperately for it to bite through the ropes and set her free. The rat did so. As soon as she was released, Nuchhimi thanked the rat profusely and ran home.

Her parents, horrified at her ordeal and enraged at the loss of their younger daughter, devised an extraordinary method of trapping Hmuichukchuriduninu.

While the old witch was out, they went to her house and prepared a complicated trap for her. First, they hid an egg inside the hearth. Then they put a snake in her water gourd. Next they placed a nest of termites in her blanket. Next they hid sharp-pointed water caltrops in the bamboo walls of the house. Next they smeared night soil all over her bedpost. Next they placed a large number of tiny biting red ants in her oil can. Next they left a huge wooden pestle at the other door of the hut. Finally they left a ferocious dog, an angry goat, a wild boar, and a bull gayal in the space under the hut.

They spoke to the rat, who was still there, and told it to answer in case Hmuichukchuriduninu called for Nuchhimi. Then they left.

While Hmuichukchuriduninu was out in the field, she had caught a pregnant barking deer which she planned to slaughter. As she was carrying this animal home, she was caught in a torrential downpour, which left her sopping wet. As she got home, flustered and with her arms full, she shouted, "Nuchhimi, open the door."

"I can't," answered the rat. "You tied me up and hung me from the crossbeams, remember?"

Cursing, Hmuichukchuriduninu broke down the door in a rage. The rat quickly hid inside a hollow bamboo.

The old witch realized that Nuchhimi was gone, and this made her even angrier. Still dripping wet and grumbling, she sat down by the hearth and lit a fire. Almost as soon as the fire was going, the hot egg burst and splattered in her eye.

She rushed to her water jug, but the snake leapt out of it and bit her on the face.

"Awi, awi, awi!" she screamed. "I'm in such pain! I'm going to crawl under my blanket and rest."

But as soon as she drew the blanket over herself, the termites started biting her. She grabbed hold of the bedpost to try and pull herself out of bed, only to discover that it was covered with excrement. She tried to clean her hands by wiping them on the wall, but ended up shredding her flesh on the sharp points of the caltrops. Then she tried to pour oil on her wounds, but along with the oil came hundreds of red ants which bit her all over.

"This house is full of pests!" she shouted. "I have to get out!" She tried to run out the other door, but did a faceplant into the wooden pestle.

She stood on the platform at the front of her house, despondent. She realized that she had not only lost Nuchhimi; the barking deer had run away as well.

In a tantrum of agony and frustration, she began stomping up and down. Soon she broke through the platform and fell into the space underneath, where the ferocious dog, angry goat, wild boar, and enraged bull gayal set upon her and quickly tore her to pieces.

Nuchhimi and her parents went home and lived happily ever after.

Ref: 192, 487, 488

HMUITHLA

In Mizo folklore, a Hmuithla is a ghostly white apparition that foretells death. It appears at sundown, hanging around a house where someone is soon to die, making spooky noises. In some tales, these noises are only audible to the victim's family; in others, it is only the victim that can hear them.

Ref: 489

HUAI

A Huai is a non-human spirit or demon from the folklore of the Lushai of Mizoram. Similar beings exist in the mythology of many other Zo and Kuki tribes.

Huai is a broad category of spirits. There are many types of Huai, each with different characteristics and temperament depending on their habitat. Here we give an introduction to the four best-known varieties: Ram Huai (forest-demons), Sih Huai (spring-demons), Tlang Huai (mountain-demons), and Tui Huai (water-demons). Other, less-storied types include Puk Huai (cave-demons), Bung Huai (banyan-tree-demons), and Lungpui Huai (rock-demons).

Ram Huai

Ram Huai are perhaps the most malevolent type of Huai. They live in trees in the jungle, especially strange or remarkable trees, such as trees that have roots on both sides of a stream, and tree trunks that are alive but have no leaves. They may also take up residence in the skulls of dead baby monkeys.

Ram Huai can take a humanoid shape. When they do so, they appear to be of great stature, with giant heads. They wear headdresses and garlands of baby skulls. Some say they have their two eyes set one above the other in the middle of the forehead. The female ones have gigantic, pendulous breasts. But they are shapeshifters, so they can appear in many different guises. They are associated with epilepsy, insanity, and miscarriage.

There is a Mizo superstition that calling a person by their real name invites the Ram Huai to capture their soul (**Thlarau**), making them gravely ill. For this reason many Mizo people use a combination of titles and nicknames; in particular, young children are often given intentionally ugly pet names.

If the Thlarau of a child is stolen by a Ram Huai, it is the responsibility of the child's grandfather to go to the Huai's abode and call it back with the words "Thla ko!" This can be extremely dangerous; the grandfather is at great risk of being killed himself.

One account tells of a young girl who was frequently ill, and used to get possessed by a Ram Huai named Chongpuithanga, who spoke through her on several occasions. This evil spirit boasted of having caused the deaths of ten people in the village. He demanded a pig in sacrifice whenever he spoke.

Another named member of the Ram Huai is called Maimi. He hypnotizes people in their sleep, and is associated with sleep paralysis and sleepwalking.

In the Mizo Tawng language, *Ram Huai* is the common translation of the English "demon" or "devil", so in modern times the term has merged with the Christian concept of Satan.

Ferocious spirits that appear nearly identical to the Ram Huai appear in the folklore of other tribes of the region, such as the Chiru, the Kom Rem, and the Maring Naga. In these languages they are called Rampu, Rampu Pathen, Rampi-Rampu, or Ram Thrai. ("Ram" means forest, "Pu" is a masculine particle, and "Pi" is feminine.)

For the Chiru, there are four chief Rampu. One lives on Kobru, a hill overlooking the Manipur valley, and this is called the Guardian of the North. He is honoured with a sacrifice twice a year.

The other three Rampu live in Kangjupkhul, Makong Hill, and in Imphal Valley itself. These Rampu are only propitiated in case of a serious calamity or illness.

Sih Huai

A *sih* is a type of muddy brackish perennial spring found commonly in Mizoram. Sih Huai are the spirits who live in them.

Most Sih Huai dislike humans, and try to keep them away from their springs. People who disturb the spirits tend to fall ill or have bad luck.

On the other hand, one story tells of a Sih Huai who invited a farmer to visit its home for a beer. The farmer didn't realize it was a Sih Huai at first; it appeared to be a normal human. The farmer accepted the invitation, and walked along with it to its home. He spent a pleasant evening drinking with a small group of friends in what seemed to be a good thatch house before returning to his hut late at night.

The next day he realized that he had left his pipe behind, and decided to go back to the house to retrieve it. Strangely, the path seemed much rougher than it had the previous night—rockier, more overgrown. When the farmer finally arrived at the place where the thatch house had been, he found that it had disappeared; there was only a muddy spring in its stead. And there, laying at the edge of the spring water, was his pipe.

Every sih is home to at least one family of Sih Huai. Sih Huai children are loud and playful, and it is said that their laughter can sometimes be heard coming from the sih.

Sometimes it couldn't be avoided that a jhum plot (used in slash-and-burn cultivation) would be close to a sih. In this case, the farmer used to call a priest to perform a ritual to appease the Sih Huai that lived there. This ritual involved the gift of a set of gongs, a set of clay figurines—a mithun, a fish, and a banyan tree—and the sacrifice of one rooster and one hen.

Chham, King of the Sih Huai

In the bigger springs, many families of Sih Huai live together. A large sih may even be home to the king of the Sih Huai, whose name is Chham.

There is a story about a farmer named Manmasia and his wife, who planted an indigo crop near the sih in which Chham lived. The roots of the indigo plant grew deep into the spring, criss-crossing this way and that, and eventually wound their way into Chham's nostrils. This made him sick, and he tried to leave the sih; but the entrance and exit were blocked by the roots. Immobilized, Chham could hardly do anything but sleep all day. His food had to be brought to him in bed by his subjects, and he couldn't even leave his bed to poop. (Chham's poop is red in colour, and it can sometimes be seen bubbling to the surface of a large sih.)

Chham was greatly annoyed by this, and eventually had Manmasia's wife killed for her transgression.

Even today, when someone is being extremely lazy and not doing anything for themselves, Mizos say they are "laying around like Chham."

Wild animals are attracted to sihs for the water and the salt. There are different varieties of Sih Huai, named according to which type of animal likes to frequent the spring. *Sazuk* Sih Huai live in springs were sambar deer come to drink; they are the gentlest sort. *Sakhi* Sih Huai, from springs where barking deer congregate, are slightly more dangerous. *Zawng* Sih Huai, from springs preferred by monkeys, are the most vicious and deadly variety.

Tlang Huai

Tlang Huai live in the hills and mountains. They make their homes on cliffs, ledges and sheer rock faces.

There are different clans of Tlang Huai, one for each large hill, each with its own chieftain. These spirits are warlike and often battle each other for supremacy.

Tales of warfare between Tlang Huai clans involve complicated military tactics, including feints, ambushes, and espionage. Some of the Tlang Huai can take the shape of *sialsir*, a type of hawk, and attack by air. The Tui Huai of the rivers would sometimes get drawn into the conflict, cutting down mountains by the force of their waters. Many landforms and river courses in Mizoram are explained as resulting from famous battles of the Tlang Huai.

Some clans also form alliances, and these are strengthened through intermarriage. Tlang Huai marriages have customs similar to those of human Mizo marriages; in particular, the groom's family is expected to pay a bride price. In one case the bride price might be the morning mist. Or it might be a grove of pine trees, or a pair of gibbons. Such stories are invoked to explain isolated populations of trees or animals on lonely hills.

Tui Huai

Tui Huai, also called Dil Huai or Tuikuachoi, are demons that live in streams and lakes. They are not so evil as the Ram Huai, and usually don't disturb humans unless humans disturb them first.

Tui Huai generally appear humanoid, but they can take the shape of insects, snakes, or other animals as well.

One story tells of an excellent swimmer named Vanzema, who went fishing in a lake with his friends. When Vanzema dived to the bottom of a lake, he saw a Tui Huai in the form of an old man who was cutting bamboo strips to weave. The old man looked at him and gave a stern warning: "If you value your life, go away from here, and don't come back."

Vanzema returned to the surface empty-handed and told the story to his friends. They scoffed at him, saying he was a poor swimmer and a coward, and that he was fibbing. They refused to believe him unless he could provide some proof.

Vanzema agreed to dive down again, but he asked his friends to tie a rope around his waist, and to pull it up quickly if he tugged at it. They did so, and Vanzema dived in. As soon as he reached the bottom of the lake, his friends felt a tug; but when they pulled him up, his head was missing.

Another story tells of a boastful man named Darkawlchhuna. He claimed he could swim all the way across Rih Dil (a lake across the border with Myanmar which is sacred to the Mizos). When he reached the middle, he stopped and shouted "Here I am swimming across Rih Dil, and I will never drown!" A Tui Huai promptly appeared in the form of a giant water-dragon and dragged him under to his death.

It is said that the king of the Tui Huai once fell in love with a human girl named Ngai-ti. She rejected him, but he would not take no for an answer. He became so angry that he flooded the whole land, trapping the entire human race on the peak of a mountain called Phunlubuk. The flood level kept on rising, and finally, to save themselves, the people had to throw Ngai-ti into the water.

Once this was done, the waters receded, and as they did so, they cut away the hills and valleys of Mizoram, which had formerly been flat.

Ref: 6, 192

 ICHCHHADHARI NAG

An Ichchhadhari Nag (or Nagin, for the female) is a cobra that has lived for one hundred years without ever once using its venom. It is believed that the venom of such a snake hardens inside the gland in its head and becomes a gem, called a *nag mani* or *naga ratnam*, which gives the cobra fantastic powers. These snakes can shapeshift into any living creature and perform many other feats of powerful magic.

The gems retain their powers after the snake's death. They are said to cure sickness, even cancer and terminal illness. In some stories, the gems can grant wishes, or attract great wealth to their owners.

All this makes the naga ratnam a supremely valuable object. It is highly coveted by tantric magicians, and frequently used as a MacGuffin by authors of Indian-language pulp fiction and screenplays—for example, in the cult classic 2010 Tamil film *Pournami Naagam*.

Ichchhadhari Nags are extremely intelligent. They keep to themselves, though, and rarely interact with humans. If one snake of a couple is killed, its surviving mate will stop at nothing to avenge the death.

Ichchhadhari Nags can be controlled to some extent by playing the snake-charming instrument called the *pungi*.

Some stories draw no distinction between Ichchhadhari Nags and the mythological beings called **Nagas**. But while Nagas are usually thought of as being born with the ability to shapeshift, Ichchhadhari Nags are born as normal cobras, and must acquire it.

Ref: 427

IFRIT

In Islamic legends, an Ifrit is a type of evil **Jinn** or **Dev**. Ifritah is the female form. They appear as some of the main villains in the Indo-Persian epic *Dastan-e-Amir Hamza*.

Ifrits are large, fiery, winged beings who breathe gusts of flame. They typically live alone in deep caves underground; but in epic stories, great armies of Ifrit can band together to attack a human city.

It is extremely difficult to capture an Ifrit, but powerful magicians can strike bargains with them in order to make use of their powers. It is believed that governments or terrorist groups sometimes employ them as saboteurs.

The Ifrit are thought to be the wiliest, most cunning, and most technologically savvy of the Jinn. Modern urban legends associate them with security system hacks and malfunctioning office identity card readers, internet phishing campaigns, sextortion rackets, and other types of cybercrime. In particular, Ifrit have been accused of involvement in the creation of the Conficker worm, a malware program targeting Microsoft Windows that caused major economic damage in 2009, and in the 2018 Marriott data breach, which exposed the personal information of over half a billion people. They are also rumoured to have a "supernatural back door" which allows access to sensitive biometric data both at the Unique Identification Authority of India and the National Database and Registration Authority of Pakistan.

There are several tales of Ifrit interbreeding with humans. Some stories portray them as passionate, possessive lovers, while in others, they are heartless and rapacious fiends. The 2018 Hindi film *Pari*, for example, centres around the story of a half-Ifrit, half-human woman whose conception was arranged by a group of occultists. In the film universe, the offspring of an Ifrit in a human woman's womb lacks an umbilical cord, and the pregnancy only lasts one month.

In recent decades, Ifrit characters have been popularized in the West through role-playing games, video games, and comic books. They are now common fixtures in international fantasy literature and anime.

Ref: 428

ILIPHRU

In the ancient Brog-pa religion of the nomadic Dard tribes of Ladakh, Iliphru is a dwarf-spirit with a long white beard and large, sharp canine teeth. Iliphru has three arms, the third one extending from the centre of the chest.

There are other, similar characters called Phatgon and Balutche.

Iliphru rides on the wind after dark. Strange inscriptions that appear carved into rocks in the mountains are said to be written by Iliphru during the night. He is usually only encountered at midnight.

If one should find a shoe or a hat belonging to Iliphru, it can bring good luck. Iliphru will keep returning to visit the possessor of this article of clothing, and may shower them with wealth in an attempt to get it back.

Ref: 492

ILVALA AND VATAPI

In Hindu mythology, Ilvala and Vatapi were two cannibalistic **Rakshasa** brothers who ruled an area in what is now Karnataka. There were many sages and rishis who used to meditate in the forests near the brothers' lands, and Ilvala and Vatapi secretly despised them for their piety.

The two brothers were black magic practitioners. Through long study of the dark arts, Vatapi had gained the power to shapeshift into any other living thing he chose, and Ilvala had gained the power of resurrecting the dead. Together they devised a plan to use these powers to murder the rishis of the forest.

Their method was this: Vatapi would transform himself into a goat, and then Ilvala would invite one of the rishis to come for a meal. Ilvala would slaughter the goat, cook it, and serve it to the holy man. Once the rishi had eaten his fill,

Ilvala would say "*Vatapi atragacha*" ("Come out, Vatapi"), instantly bringing his brother back to life. Vatapi would then spring forth in his natural shape, ripping open the belly of the rishi, who had just a few seconds to be very surprised before dying in a pool of his own blood and guts.

Afterwards, the two brothers would make a feast of the rishi's flesh.

It is said that Ilvala and Vatapi killed and ate around 9,000 holy men this way.

Finally, the great rishi Agastya was invited to eat with Ilvala and Vatapi. Luckily Agastya knew of the brothers' plan in advance; what's more, he had a few magic powers of his own. Once Vatapi had been turned into a goat and Ilvala had killed and cooked him, Agastya sat down and ate heartily, savoring the taste of the meat. As soon as he was done, Agastya licked his lips, rubbed his belly and said "*Vatapi jeernobhava.*" ("Get digested, Vatapi.")

Ilvala then tried to bring his brother back to life, but it didn't work. This time, Vatapi was dead for good.

Realizing what had happened, Ilvala flew at Agastya in a murderous rage, but Agastya used his powers to reduce Ilvala to a pile of ashes.

Ref: 493

INDUS WORM

The Indus Worm, also known as *Skolex*, is a gigantic white carnivorous worm that is said to have lived in the Indus River. This monster was described in the book *Indica* by the Greek writer Ctesias in the 5th century BCE, based on accounts he heard related by travellers from India who visited Persepolis, where he worked.

The worm was said to dwell in the muddy bottom of the river during the day. At night, it would emerge to devour horses, cattle, donkeys, goats, and camels. It had just two huge square teeth, each 40 cm long, one at the top of its mouth and one at the bottom.

According to Ctesias, the body of the Indus Worm contained a volatile chemical called "skolex oil". Indian kings were said to have hunted the worm, using livestock as bait, in order to harvest this substance for use in warfare. When laying siege to a city, ancient armies would set pots of worm oil on fire and launch the flaming missles from slings, thus setting whole forts and armies ablaze.

Ref: 251

INENE

The Inene are ghost-beings in the folklore of the Onge people of the Andaman Islands. If an Onge dies of natural causes and the body is buried, a tiny humanoid form called an Embekete crawls out of the corpse. The Embekete digs itself deep into the earth until it emerges into the ocean below. Then it swims far across the sea to a distant land where it transforms into an Inene.

The word Inene is used to describe all people lighter-skinned than the Onge, including mainland Indians, Burmese, and Europeans. Unless you, Dear Reader, are of Negrito or Melanesian or Black African descent, then you may be an Inene ghost yourself.

Ref: 475

INGENNANGKWE

Another Onge spirit from Little Andaman Island, an Ingennangkwe is the ghost of a person who is either killed by a shark or dies by drowning. These ghosts appear similar to living Onge, but are very short—only about three feet tall—and have huge bellies, bloated by all the sea water they have swallowed.

The Ingennangkwe are thought to reside deep in the ocean near the tiny Sister and Brother Islands in the strait between Little Andaman and Rutland Island. Unlike other types of Onge ghosts, such as the **Eaka** and **Onkoboykwe**, which travel to different planes of existence after death, the Ingennangkwe share the same plane as humans. They hunt dugongs for their food.

Ref: 475

IWI-POT

In the folklore of the Nicobarese people, the Iwi are invisible spirits, some of whom are the ghosts of dead humans. The word *Iwi* means "becoming". The homeland of the Iwi is a place called Henekla, an invisible island which lies to the east of the Nicobar Islands; but the spirits sometimes roam human-inhabited islands as well.

There are two classes of Iwi: the Iwi-Ka, which are benevolent, and the Iwi-Pot, which are evil and malicious. The Iwi-Pot cause sickness—especially elephantiasis—and accidental death. They are also blamed when there is bad weather, a lack of fish, or any other sort of ill luck. There are a few different varieties of Iwi-Pot: they are named Iwi-Kincheha, Iwi-Muka, Iwi-Mahasul, Iwi-Payuh, and Iwi-Rohcan. Some live in the jungle, others in the sea, and others in the sand.

Traditionally, the Nicobarese people built "scare-devils", called *hanta*, and intricately carved wooden boards, called *hanta-koi*, to keep the Iwi-Pot away. They also wore banana-leaf garlands or amulets of silver, and hung coconuts sprinkled with a few drops of rooster blood from the ceilings of their huts. After a ritual feast, they would hang the spinal columns of slaughtered pigs outside for the Iwi to eat. Nicobarese parents are careful to call their children by a name other than their true given name, in the belief that this will confuse any Iwi-Pot who are out to get them.

Another method to get rid of malignant Iwi is to set them adrift in the sea. In this ritual, shamans, called *mineluans*, and their apprentices, called *mafai*, chase

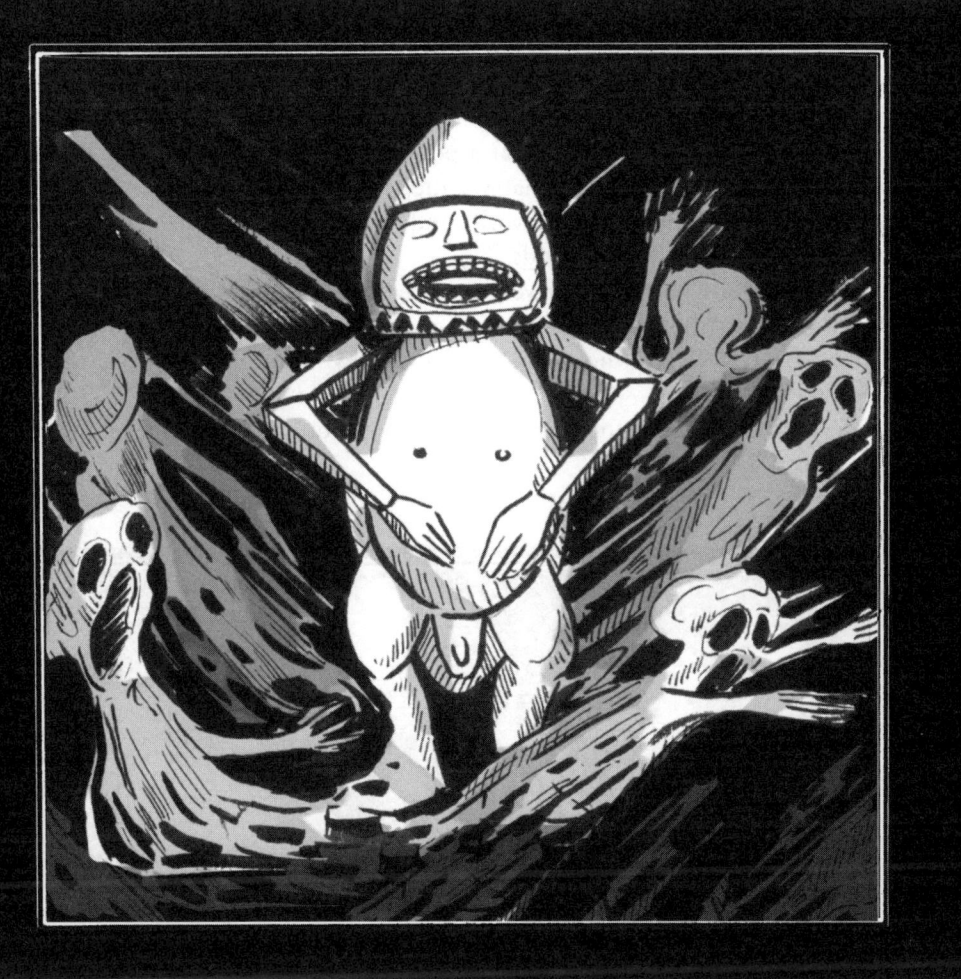

after an invisible Iwi and wrestle it into a catamaran before an audience. Then the boat is towed far out to sea and left to float away.

When a mineluan is called upon to heal a sick person, he extracts the Iwi-Pot who was causing the illness by dramatically capturing it in a boar tusk or in a piece of metal. These talismans are then supposed to be discarded into the sea or the forest. But a few unscrupulous mineluans secretly keep them, and use the spirits contained within for evil purposes.

Sometimes an Iwi-Pot would prove to be very stubborn, and refuse to come out of a person, driving them to do crazy and despicable things. In olden days, it used to happen that a person who was believed to be incurably possessed by an Iwi-Pot would be brutally and publicly killed by the community. This practice was termed "Devil Murder" by the British colonial administrators, who banned and suppressed it. Some have argued that the practice was in fact a sort of indigenous death penalty for a person who had committed numerous crimes and was unrepentant. Whatever the truth, sensationalized news of the practice was reported around the world, and it prompted an influx of Christian missionaries to the Nicobar Islands.

The island of Chowra is believed to be the place where human connection with the Iwi is strongest. Many famous mineluans were said to hail from this island—great sorcerers who could control the Iwi and make them do their bidding.

The old faith is fading on many of the islands, but on Chowra, belief in the Iwi persists.

Ref: 217, 182, 403

⟶ JADAAMUNI ⟵

A Jadaamuni is a supernatural being with a monstrous face whose entire body is covered with long dreadlocks. It appears in very old folktales of Tamil Nadu.

Like **Peys**, Jadaamunis are able to fly, turn into clouds of smoke, and shapeshift, taking the form of normal-looking humans. They are fond of scaring people just for the fun of it. A Jadaamuni may disguise itself as an old beggar and approach a person to ask for a bit of food; then, when the request is granted, it suddenly shows its true abominable form, causing the person to run away screaming in terror.

At least some of a Jadaamuni's power resides in its hair. If you cut its dreadlocks or rip them out of its head, it will become weaker.

Jadaamunis are known to collect magical artifacts. Someone who is able to catch a Jadaamuni—by ripping out some of its hair, nailing it to a tree, and threatening it with fire—may find it willing to barter these prizes for its freedom.

Ref: 107, 291, 292

⟶ JAUKAAR PAAL ⟵

These noisy ghosts are always seen in a group; *paal* means "team" in Assamese. They live near lakes and streams. In their natural form, they look like young, naked children. However, if disturbed by humans, they will suddenly turn into very normal-looking dogs, goats, or even silent fisherwomen. Nothing to see here!

The Jaukaar Paal are said to be completely harmless as long as one doesn't encounter them alone. They quickly shapeshift or escape when a number of people walk into their area, but if a single traveller enters their territory, they may stalk him and prey upon him.

Jaukaar Paal are most active early in the morning and around noontime.

Ref: 294, 383, 448

JHUNJHARJI

This legend comes from Rajasthan, especially from the Mewar region. A Jhunjharji is a warrior who has been decapitated in battle, but who is so brave and fiercely committed to his struggle that he manages to transcend death for a while and keeps fighting without a head.

In some tales, a lotus blossom sprouts from his neck.

A headless Jhunjharji may kill many enemies. He may even emerge victorious and start walking home triumphantly from the battlefield. It's not until a woman sees him, and remarks to her friend "Look! He's got no head!", that the Jhunjharji realizes what has happened; then he falls lifeless to the ground.

The motif of a warrior so virile that he can fight battles in spite of a mortal wound occurs in other Rajasthani stories, such as the epic of the folk-deity Pabuji.

In this tale, Pabuji has a companion named Dhebo—an immense, towering man who loves to eat, drink, and smoke opium. At one point, Dhebo's innards are eaten by a colony of hungry vultures. Once the birds are finished, Dhebo simply pulls his belt tighter and gets back on his horse. Then he rides off to rout an army. It's only on the return journey, when Pabuji offers Dhebo a smoke, that he reveals to his friend he's been disemboweled, and promptly expires.

Ref: 125, 494

JIMU-TAYANG

The myth of Jimu-Tayang comes from the highlands of Arunachal Pradesh in the far eastern Himalayas.

Tani, the first man, had several children. But one day his two eldest sons went missing. He searched for them everywhere, without success.

Finally, following the advice of a bird, he climbed up to the top of a mountain. There he found a dark cave—the lair of Jimu-Tayang, the fierce **Wiyu** of the snowy peaks. Inside the cave, Tani discovered the bones of his children. Jimu-Tayang had abducted and eaten them.

As Tani stood there grieving, Jimu-Tayang himself appeared.

The demon was of enormous size. He was white like the snow, with huge round eyes, a gigantic mouth full of teeth as sharp as spear-tips, and long hair that fell to the ground. He had no feet. The bottoms of his legs simply faded into mist, and he moved by gliding over the icy rocks.

But Tani was not scared when he saw him. Instead, he flew into a rage, demanding that Jimu-Tayang pay restitution for the murder of his sons.

The Wiyu was quiet at first. At some length he agreed that he would pay a blood price. He offered Tani some rare animals and plants—species that had never been seen before at lower elevations. These were the ibex, the takin, the Himalayan musk deer, wild garlic, the mountain reed, and wolf's bane. Jimu-Tayang showed Tani how to use the wolf's bane to prepare a deadly poison, and explained to him that if he rubbed this poison onto his arrowheads, he could bring down an elephant with a single shot.

Tani was amazed by these marvels. He agreed to accept them and to forgive his sons' murders. To seal the deal, he and Jimu-Tayang drank rice beer together.

Tani brought the animals and plants down the mountain to his village. But in the warm and wet jungle, they failed to thrive. None of them were adapted to life at lower altitudes. Soon all the plants were attacked by fungus and insects, and all the animals fell ill and died.

Ever since, in order to hunt and harvest the things that Jimu-Tayang promised, Tani's descendants have had to climb the mountains.

Jimu-Tayang believes that this is a violation of the terms of the original agreement. He has a watchman by the name of Poli-Adi who guards his territory. If men venture too high, or if they greedily help themselves to too many kills, Poli-Adi catches them, tears out their eyes, rips off their testicles, and throws them off the mountain to their deaths.

Ref: 188, 318, 384

JINN

The Jinn are supernatural creatures in Islamic folklore. However, the word *Jinn* predates the Muslim religion. While most agree that the myth is native to Arabia, linguists have argued variously that the word originally comes from Aramaic, Persian, or even Latin.

Every country with a sizable Muslim population has local stories about Jinn. There is also a wealth of written literature about these beings—in many languages, and stretching back several centuries. Jinn lore is vast and varied, and cannot be restricted to India; a short article such as this one can hardly hope to do justice to the subject. Here we limit ourselves to discussion of a few common characteristics of the Jinns of the subcontinent. Readers interested in more in-depth coverage can study the references listed in the back.

According to sources such as the Indo-Persian epic *Dastan-e-Amir Hamza*, the homeland of the Jinn is on Mount Qaf, the farthest point of the Earth. There they are ruled by an emperor, Shahpal bin Shahrukh.*

But many Jinn have travelled far from their ancestral lands, and some have made their homes among humans. They can reside anywhere—in the sky, in the jungle, even in crowded cities. They are generally invisible and undetectable, unless they choose to be otherwise. Only certain spiritually advanced people can see them. There have been recent claims that they are visible under the influence of ayahuasca.

....

* Other sources give the name of the king of all Jinn as Malik Gatshan.

Many Jinn can shapeshift. They can appear as humans, cats, dogs, donkeys, goats, reptiles, or scorpions. They travel across deserts and plains by turning into whirling columns of dust. When they are not travelling—and not trying to appear as something else—they are humanoid in shape, but tall: eight or nine feet at a minimum. They are said to be made out of smokeless flame. They glow, sometimes with an aura so bright that humans cannot bear to look at them for long. Even when Jinn disguise themselves as regular humans, a telltale shining light can be seen in their eyes. They are unable to wink.

Jinn can be good or bad, male or female, cis or trans or non-binary. Some Jinn are Muslims; others are Hindus or Christians or Zoroastrians; still others are faithless. Then there are the **Shaitans**, a class of evil Jinn who live in hell along with Iblis, their father and leader.

The king of the Jinn of India is named Naqtas.* He was said to have been a Hindu who was converted to Islam by Seth, the third son of Adam and Eve.

Muslim Jinn like to take up residence in masjids. They prefer older styles of architecture, especially buildings that feature the small arch-shaped depressions in the walls called *taakh*. Some buildings are famous for housing Jinn who grant wishes—such as the Jinnaaton Wali Masjid in Lucknow, or Feroz Shah Kotla, a 14th-century citadel in Delhi.

Occasionally, a Jinn will possess a person. There might be a malicious motive; the Jinn could simply want to harass the person, or to make them harm one of their friends. A benevolent Jinn, on the other hand, might possess someone in order to convey helpful information.

It is also possible for the reverse to happen—that is, for a human to capture a Jinn. Those who know the right magic spells can bind them to stones, especially carnelian or turquoise. But a person who has a Jinn under his control should be very careful to keep it busy, for Jinns hate to be bored, and a resentful Jinn can easily kill its master if it manages to escape from its bondage.

Jinn fear iron, so much so that the mere mention of the word terrifies them. Some say this is because fire runs in their veins instead of blood, so when they suffer a cut, the flames burst out and consume them. But a different legend contradicts this, saying that for every drop of blood that spills from a live Jinn onto the ground, another Jinn will pop up where it has fallen.

Jinn can be extremely long-lived, surviving for several centuries or even millennia. But most are thought to be mortal. Shaitans are an exception: they are unkillable—that is, until their leader, Iblis himself, is destroyed.

....

* The names of Indian Jinn who were born Hindu typically end in -*tas*; those of Muslim Jinn end in -*nus*; and those of Zoroastrian Jinn end in -*nas*.

The ranks of Jinn are numerous. According to *The Thousand and One Nights*, there are forty troops of them, each consisting of six hundred thousand individuals. Another legend says that for each birth of a human child, a thousand Jinn are born. There are many different subtypes, including the **Ifrit** and the **Hamzad**. Other types of Jinn known from Arabic sources, but less commonly spoken of in Indian tales, include the *Marid* (according to some, a synonym of Ifrit), the Ghouls (corpse-eaters, similar to the **Pisachas** of Hindu mythology), the Shiqq (half-formed beings, possibly synonymous with the **Nim-Tans**), and the Si'lat (female Jinn who are expert shapeshifters).

Ref: 76, 490, 495, 496, 497, 498, 499, 500, 572

❧ JOKHINI ❧

Jokhs and Jokhinis are Assamese versions of the **Yakshas** and **Yakshis**—spirits found in various guises throughout the country.

Jokhinis are diminutive female spirits. They live under rhododendron bushes or near small bodies of stagnant water. They have wild and dishevelled hair. They have cute faces, but are often dirty and lice-ridden. In some stories they have a coat of fur all over their bodies.

As they wander around the jungle, Jokhinis frequently spit. This is supposed to be the origin of the spittle-like secretions of froghopper nymphs found on the stems of plants, which cause a painful rash if touched.

Jokhinis are said to be terrified of the larger, fish-eating Assamese monster called the **Baak**, which preys upon them. They are usually scared of humans, too, running away and hiding whenever someone comes too close. However, they are mad for *pithas*. If they smell someone frying pithas, they cannot control themselves; they will walk up to the person's kitchen and beg, or try to stick a hand in through a window or gap in the wall to grab one.

Many stories describe Jokhinis as mute, able to communicate only by hand gestures. They definitely cannot sing, though they are fond of dancing.

There are tales of Jokhinis falling madly in love with human men. Humans tend to find them repulsive, so these feelings are rarely reciprocated. This drives the Jokhini into a frustrated rage. Usually quite docile, she becomes very dangerous when spurned, and may decide to put the man in a trance and lure him to her lair in the bushes. Then she will have her way with him and/ or kill him.

Jokhinis are also held responsible for incessant crying in young children.

People skilled in the arts of black magic, called *Bhoot Damor*, are said to be able to summon Jokhinis and keep them as spirit-familiars.

As for the male spirits, the Jokhs are fierce warriors. Usually invisible, they can take the form of bull buffaloes, and are sometimes encountered grazing in herds along with normal animals. If the spirit of a Jokh possesses a man, the man will start roaring like a buffalo.

Jokhs are said to be extremely violent, attempting to kill any man that crosses their path—either by invisibly devouring his internal organs, or by transforming into a buffalo and goring him to death.

Some communities in Assam worship the Jokh in the form of an idol wearing a garland of snails, with two javelins stuck into the ground on either side.

Ref: 30, 114, 448

✦ JOL KUWORI ✦

Jol Kuwori means "water maiden", but these spirits should not be confused with mermaids. They inhabit fresh water, not the sea, and they don't have the characteristic mermaid fishtail. They're found in many parts of India, but are most common in the folklore of Assam and Bengal.

In most stories, they appear as beautiful women who abduct attractive-looking young men. But there are also stories about Jol Kuwors, the male versions, abducting women. Then again there are gender-bending stories in which male Jol Kuwor spirits appear as women to lure young boys, and still others about female Jol Kuworis who prey upon women. Jol Kuworis are not the ghosts of humans, but a separate category of supernatural being, so it may be that they have no sex or gender at all unless they choose to wear one as an illusion.

Jol Kuworis live in ponds, lakes, and large wells. They can only harm a person if he gets into the haunted water body to bathe, or if he drinks from it. In the latter case, the Jol Kuwori's spirit may possess the person, causing the victim to jump in and drown.

Sometimes, the bodies of the Jol Kuworis' victims are found dead and floating in the water. Other times, they go missing entirely; this means they have been taken down to the spirit's murky underwater lair. In such cases the victim's friends or family members can plead with the Jol Kuwori to restore the abducted person. It sometimes happens that the Jol Kuwori relents, and returns her captive to the surface.

Ref: 226

JURUA

In the folklore of the Andaman Islands, the Jurua are sea-spirits. They are described either as the ghosts of people who drowned at sea or as the ghosts of coast-dwellers. They resemble the **Bido Tech Lau** or forest-dwelling spirits in that they are usually invisible, but if they do show themselves, they are long-limbed, white-skinned, and have long hair and beards.

The Jurua have the power to call storms. Burning certain varieties of creepers, or burning turtle fat, may offend the Jurua, and result in a terrible cyclone. Damaging a *Ficus altissima* strangler fig tree may anger them as well, and cause a torrential downpour of rain.

Ref: 54

⤳ KAATHU KARUPPU ⤵

Kaathu Karuppu means "black wind" in Tamil. It appears as a small dark cloud, moving quickly, against the flow of any breeze or air current.

A person who is attacked by a Kaathu Karuppu gets knocked senseless, sometimes falling into a coma that can be fatal. Blue-black bruises appear all over the skin.

This poorly understood evil spirit lives in untamed and undisturbed places, rarely venturing very close to human habitation. Its victims, then, are people who wander alone into the wilderness, or those who build their dwellings at its edge.

In such a house at the edge of the forest, a man might be sitting alone, shortly after completing construction. A knock comes at the door. The man opens it, and is surprised to find one of his friends standing there—a friend who lives far away, a person he hasn't seen in years. The friend smiles silently, beckoning him to come outside.

Surprised and confused, the man steps out across the threshold. No sooner is he outside than the shape of the friend dissolves into a Kaathu Karuppu. The spirit sweeps the man high up into the air and spins him around in a dark tempest. Then it smashes him violently back to the ground, shattering both his body and mind.

Kaathu Karuppus can also cause problems for farmers whose fields are at the edge of a forest. They are blamed for drought, blight, or insect swarms.

Ref: 501, 577

⤳ KABANDHA ⤵

Kabandha is a **Rakshasa** from Hindu mythology. Persian writers such as Zakariya al-Qazwini, the author of the 13th-century book *Marvels of Things Created and Miraculous Aspects of Things Existing*, considered him a Shiqq **Jinn**.

He was originally a **Gandharva** with a humanoid body, but he was arrogant and cruel. In punishment for his behaviour the god Indra struck him with the *vajra*, his divine thunderbolt, driving Kabandha's head down into his torso, and pushing his legs into his body up to the knee. Brahma pleaded with Indra to have mercy, and to give him at least one eye to see and a mouth to eat. Indra agreed to do so—but he placed the eye and mouth on Kabandha's chest.

Kabandha now looked grotesque and hideous. His eye was large and round and yellow; he was covered with spiky hairs; and he had a long tongue with which he kept licking his chops.

After his transformation Kabandha went to live in the forest, camouflaging himself among the trees and then popping out to grab wandering holy men with his long arms and eat them.

He was eventually defeated when he tried to catch Ram and Lakshman in this manner. The two brothers cut off his arms. With that the curse was lifted, and the demon died.

Ref: 17, 502, 503

⊱⊱ KALI ⊰⊰

In Hindu mythology, the demon Kali* is the source of all evil in modern times.

Kali loves all vices. His favourite is gambling, but he also enjoys liquor, tobacco, psychoactive drugs, depraved sex, exploitative pornography, rash driving, hyperviolent video games, unbridled consumerism, the hoarding of ill-gotten wealth, toxic chemicals, quack medicines, reckless use of firearms and explosives, deepfake blackmail, irresponsible experiments with nanotechnology, AI-assisted disinformation campaigns, fracking, saturation advertising, random acts of cruelty, cheating, lying, littering, and internet trolling. Kali evangelizes moral turpitude and works to spread corruption and debauchery among all the peoples of Earth.

He presides over the current age of mankind, which bears his name: *Kali Yuga*, the age of strife. Calculations for the beginning and ending dates of Kali Yuga vary, but some say it started in the year 3102 BCE and will end in 428898 CE.

Kali is born from the incestuous union of Himsa (Violence) and her brother Krodha (Anger). According to the *Mahabharata*, he was a **Gandharva** whose machinations started the Pandavas and Kauravas on the road to war. Duryodhana, the eldest Kaurava prince, is said to have been an incarnation of Kali.

Kali has been depicted in different ways by different artists, but he is always very tall, with a long tongue and fangs. The emblem on his war-flag is an owl.

In the Ayyavazhi faith, Kali is the sixth fragment of **Kroni**, whose other avatars include the **Asura** king Ravana and the giant leech demon Kuntomasali.

Ref: 516, 517

⊱⊱ KALYSTRIOI ⊰⊰

Ancient Greek accounts of India from over 2,000 years ago contain several mentions of a Himalayan tribe called the Kalystrioi, which was translated into Greek as *Cynocephaloi*, or "Dog-Heads". These people had human bodies but

---

* The first syllable of the name is short, and not to be confused with the mother goddess Kāli—who, despite her fearsome aspect, is a destroyer of evil.

heads and tails like dogs. While they could understand human language, they could not talk themselves—only bark and howl. They used sign language to communicate with people outside their tribe.

The Dog-Heads hunted wild game for their food. They may have also herded sheep. They lived in caves and slept on grass mats. They traded with the kingdoms of the plains below, exporting fruits, amber, and a kind of red dye made from crushed insects in exchange for swords, spears, and bows. The weapons they imported were only used for hunting, never for war; according to the historian Ctesias, the Kalystrioi were noble, just, and peaceful.

The Dog-Heads were also blessed with long lives. Ctesias reports that the average lifespan was 170 years, and some individuals lived past the age of 200.

A later European book, *The Wonders of the East*, reports that only the men of this race were dog-headed, while the women were fully human and very beautiful.

Ref: 251, 286

⟿ KANIAM PEY ⟿

The Kaniam Pey is a lecherous male evil spirit known from the folklore of Tamil Nadu. It lives in tamarind trees and does its rounds on village streets from midnight until about two in the morning, searching for beautiful women. These ghosts have a keen sense of smell, and are attracted to the scents of sandalwood and jasmine flowers.

When a Kaniam Pey happens upon a woman it fancies, it will abduct her, possess her body, and molest her. After she is completely used up and her beauty has been drained away, the spirit discards her, and she stumbles home. Afterwards, the woman suffers from severe body aches, numbness, and weakness, which last until she receives some sort of spiritual healing.

A Kaniam Pey can be equally cruel to a woman it finds ugly. In this case, though, instead of possessing her, it may just kick her around, insult her, and make her very ill.

If the Kaniam Pey fails to find a woman during its nightly rounds, it will find a stone mortar and pestle, sit down, and grind away at nothing, making an eerie *ghadaghadaghada* noise.

Like other **Peys**, the Kaniam Pey is extremely strong. In areas infested by Kaniam Peys, married couples are afraid to sleep outside at night; for if the spirit wanders by, he may lift up the husband, rip his body into two pieces, and carry off the wife.

Kaniam Peys are invisible while they are alive. However, it is said that when one is killed (for example, by forcefully swinging a red-hot iron rod in the air around its tree at midnight), its corpse appears like that of a charred animal, about the size and shape of a monkey.

Ref: 291, 292

⤙ KANNI PEY ⤚

In the folklore of Tamil Nadu, a Kanni Pey is the ghost of a girl who died a virgin. This description applies to the **Mohini Pey** as well, but the Mohini Pey is usually older and more sexually aggressive. Kanni Peys are generally sweet-natured and innocent; but they are also capable of dangerous tantrums, and they can turn deadly if they don't get what they want.

Like other varieties of **Pey**, Kanni Peys are shapeshifters who can take the form of any other human being. There is usually some tell-tale feature, though: their feet may float slightly above the ground, or else they may be turned backwards.

Kanni Peys typically play in groups. When they are not pretending to look like something or someone else, they appear wild-haired and naked. They are very fond of jewellery, and will use all sorts of tricks to steal diamonds or other valuable pieces. They are terribly afraid of fire.

Some Kanni Peys take up residence in places of worship, where the officiating pujaris treat them with tender care. In one temple, on the slope of the forbidding Rangaswami Peak in the Nilgiris, a priest from the Irula tribal community invites a Kanni Pey to stay for a month every year. He welcomes her with a song

on the first day; a vegetarian feast on the second; and on the third day, a meal cooked with venison from a sambar deer, which must be hunted down for her.

Ref: 291, 292

ᐳ᠆ **KANVA** ᠆ᐸ

Kanvas are a class of evil spirits mentioned in the *Atharva Veda*, Hymn 2:25. There is a Kanva that drinks blood, another that stunts growth, and yet another that causes miscarriage.

The goddess Prisniparni is invoked to ward these spirits away. Prisniparni is incarnate as an herb, *Uraria picta*, which is important in Ayurvedic medicine.

Ref: 119

ᐳ᠆ **KAOSHE** ᠆ᐸ

Among the Kuki and Chin tribes of Northeast India, Kaoshe is an envious vampire spirit that can occupy a person and devour him from the inside, eating his heart and liver.

This legend is related to the evil eye and to the Mizo myth of **Khawhring**, but it differs in some respects. For example, while Khawhring are usually women, Kaoshe can be of any gender.

One story about the origin of Kaoshe goes as follows.

Chongthu, the legendary progenitor of the Thado Kuki tribe, had a son named Sattong. Sattong had recently been married to a woman named Sheichin, who came from Vanlal, the celestial village of sky-spirits (see **Vanchungnula**). Sheichin had come to live with Sattong in Chongthu's house.

In this house there also lived an enslaved man* by the name of Santhuh Kaoshe. Once in a while, Sheichin, the new bride, would make a visit to her father's house. When she returned, she would bring back some choice cuts

---

* Chattel slavery was practised among the Kuki, Lushai, and Mara until the early 20th century. Some slaves were orphans raised from childhood. Others were captives taken in raids of other clans. A third type were debtors or murderers, on the run from those they had wronged, who offered up their freedom to a chief in exchange for protection and a payment of debts or blood-price.

of pork for her husband. But before she could offer any to Sattong, his slave Santhuh would snatch it and eat it all up.

Eventually, Sattong's wife told her husband about Santhuh's behaviour, and Sattong was so enraged that he sliced off the enslaved man's head.

Two blind worm snakes reattached Sattong's head to his neck, but in the process he was transformed into a Hoolock gibbon, a species of noisy ape that lives in the forests of the Northeast. Since then it has been forbidden for anyone to eat gibbon meat; those who break this taboo become hosts to Kaoshe's spirit.

In olden days, people accused of being Kaoshe were treated like evil witches or warlocks—shunned, ill-treated, even lynched. It sometimes happened that one tribe or community would accuse an entire neighbouring tribe of being Kaoshe, and refuse to interact with them.

Ref: 504

KAPPIRI MUTHAPPAN

Fort Kochi in Kerala, originally called Fort Emmanuel, was the first Portuguese fort in Asia. It was granted by the Raja of Kochi to the naval commander Afonso de Alberqueque for his assistance in defeating his enemy, the Saamoothri of Kozhikode. This was in 1503, seven years before Afonso's conquest of Goa. The area remained under Portuguese control until 1663.

During this time Kochi was a major port for the Indian Ocean slave trade. Captive Africans—called *kaafirs* in Arabic—were brought in from Mozambique and Mombasa, often to be sold onwards to become labourers and soldiers in Sri Lanka.*

Legend has it that just before the Dutch took Kochi in 1663, many enslaved *kaafirs*—or *kappiri*, as they were called locally—were bound with chains and mortared up alive within the walls of the Portuguese houses, along with hordes

---

* The Portuguese and the royal families of Kerala also bought and sold enslaved Indians—Dalits and tribal people from the Western Ghats. This despicable trade in human bodies persisted long after Kochi was conquered by the Dutch. During the 17th and 18th centuries, thousands of enslaved Indians were transported to Batavia (present-day Jakarta, Indonesia) and to Cape Town in South Africa. Only in 1855, forty years after Kochi had passed into the hands of the British, was slavery finally outlawed in Kerala.

of gold and treasure at their feet. Their wicked, greedy, superstitious masters are said to have entombed them there to stand guard over their wealth and protect it for their descendants. Centuries later, when the old ruined houses were torn down, the skeletons of these men were found; but the treasures had disappeared.

Some say that there are still ancient walls around Fort Kochi, called *kappiri mathil*, which have the bones of Africans embedded within.

The spirits of these men are now believed to live within the banyan trees and mango trees of Fort Kochi. Kappiri Muthappan is a name applied to one such ghost. He is usually seen on full moon nights, sitting on top of an old wall, drinking toddy and smoking a cigar, humming a tune and softly clinking the heavy chains that dangle from his arms.

Kappiri Muthappan is considered a benevolent spirit who can cure illness and bring good luck. At his shrine in Mattancherry, he is offered flowers and tender coconuts.

Some members of Kochi's Anglo-Indian community have the superstition that when *puttu* is being steamed, the first piece should be promised to Kappiri Muthappan, or else the dish won't come out right.

Ref: 79, 96, 152, 355

KARINTHANDAN

Legend has it that in colonial times, the route through the Western Ghats of Kerala from Thamarassery to Wayanad was known only to the local tribal people, the Paniyas. A British engineer, looking for a way to build a road, enlisted the help of a man named Karinthandan, who was a Paniya chief. Karinthandan showed him the pass that is now the Lakkidi Ghat Road.

On their way back, the engineer said he wanted to climb higher to have a look around, and called Karinthandan to follow him. At the top of a lonely hill, the engineer shot him dead. Then he went back and tried to take all the credit for the discovery himself.

The highway through the hills was built, but Karinthandan's restless, angry spirit remained, haunting the road and the jungles around it. For decades, there were gruesome accidents and unexplained disappearances.

Finally, a priest managed to capture Karinthandan's ghost and chain it to a banyan tree.

This "Chain Tree" is still there in Lakkidi, and draws many tourists. It is said that Karinthandan's ghost remains there too, and that as the banyan tree has grown, the chain has magically grown along with it. The Paniya chief is revered as a martyr, and an annual procession is held in his honour.

Ref: 344

⊷ KARNA-PISACHINI ⊶

In Tantric lore, a Karna-Pisachini is a female demon that has the power to look forward and backward in time.

Though the name would seem to imply that she is a female **Pisacha** or goblin, she is usually described instead as a dazzlingly beautiful but terrifying **Yakshi**.

Karna-Pisachinis are thought to be fairly common entities, roaming invisibly through the atmosphere all around us. But they do not interact with the material plane unless summoned by means of certain mantras and rituals.

The Karna-Pisachini appears before the summoner in the form of a voluptuous naked woman. Her eyes are blank, with no pupils or irises; her legs terminate not in feet but in billows of smoke. The summoner may ask the demon questions, either about events that will take place in the future, or about secrets from another person's past, and then the Karna-Pisachani whispers the answers in the summoner's ears.

But obtaining such forbidden knowledge comes with terrible long-term consequences. Karna-Pisachinis are evil spirits with voracious sexual appetites, and a person who summons one is duty-bound to gratify her, night after night after night. Refusal to do so can result in death. What's more, the spirits are terribly jealous; if they learn that their summoner has other lovers, they will hunt them down and brutally kill them. A Karna-Pisachini may go on to target her summoner's parents, siblings, and children, and anyone else she sees as competing for the person's attention.

Therefore, although it is true that a Karna-Pisachini can help a person achieve great fame and fabulous riches, the material gain will be offset by a life full of tragic personal losses and emotional hardships. Many of those who bargain with Karna-Pisachinis go insane. They develop a propensity to strip naked in public places and shout trivial prophecies at passers-by, or at insects, at plants, at shadows. Even worse, the demon takes possession of the person's soul after death, and subjects it to a thousand years of torture and torment.

Ref: 506

 KEERTIMUKHA

Keertimukha is Sanskrit for "The Face of Glory".

According to the ancient Hindu scripture called the *Skanda Purana*, Lord Shiva was doing battle with **Rahu** when Rahu spoke a vile insult about his wife Parvati. Shiva's rage was so great that a monster was born from the third eye in the middle of his forehead. This monster took the form of a huge, emaciated, voracious, demonic lion. It leapt towards Rahu with its jaws open wide.

Rahu was terrified of the beast, and pleaded with Shiva for his life.

Shiva granted him mercy, and held the demon-lion back. But the creature was still ravenous, and now that it couldn't have Rahu, it demanded something else to eat instead.

Shiva suggested that the demon-lion eat his own paws, which it promptly did. But it was so hungry that it did not stop there—it went on devouring itself until only its face was left.

At this point, Shiva told it to stop. He named the lion-face Keertimukha, and proclaimed that it should always be seen at the entrance to his temples.

The visage of Keertimukha is sometimes worshipped as Kala, the god of time. Even more than in India, it is an important symbol in ancient temple art from Cambodia, Thailand, and Indonesia.

Ref: 507

KEIMI

Keimi are weretigers, a race of shapeshifters known from the folk stories of the Mizo, Gangte, and other Kuki tribes of Northeast India. They live in their own villages, where everyone is a weretiger; but during the day they go about in human form. They only change into man-eating cats when they go into the jungle at night to hunt.

There are many stories about Keimi who take human spouses. This sort of marriage almost always turns out badly.

One tale tells of a man who married a Keimi woman without knowing her true nature. When she got pregnant, she craved human meat. She told her husband to go and pick up a special preparation from her parents. Her husband did as he was asked, only to discover on the way home that the package contained the body of a human child.

Another famous story involving Keimi shows that they have some other magic powers besides the ability to transform. This is the tale of Kungawhri, a girl who was magically born from a blister on her father's thumb. Though she started out no bigger than a grain of rice, she quickly grew into one of the most beautiful young women anyone had ever seen. Men from all around fell in love with Kungawhri and wanted to marry her.

One of these men was a brave Keimi. He secretly stalked her in the jungle, and found a place where she had left a footprint in the mud. He carefully excavated the footprint, wrapped it up in cloth, took it home, and hung it above a fire, where it began to smoke.

This spell made Kungawhri fall seriously ill. Her distraught father announced that any man who could cure her would marry her. Many of the suitors tried, but failed.

Then the Keimi arrived and pretended to save her—when all he had really done was to remove the footprint from the fire.

Afterwards, the Keimi took Kungawrhi back home with him to the village of the weretigers.*

Garo folklore has a similar race of weretigers, called the Matchadus, who live in their own villages. They are stupider than the Keimi and more easily outwitted. Several caves and waterfalls in Meghalaya are said to have formerly been home to the Matchadus.

Ref: 6, 52, 192, 206, 306, 508

⟩⤞ KENGLONG-PO ⤛⟨

Kenglong-po is an ape-like being said to inhabit the forests of Karbi Anglong in Assam.

It is a furry creature, at least six feet tall and massive. Its limbs lack elbows and knees, so it either walks stiffly or goes about on all fours with an awkward gait. Its mouth is located at the top of its forehead. Unlike the **Yeti**, to which it is often compared, Kenglong-po is thought to be intelligent.

According to those who claim to have encountered the creature, it sleeps standing up, leaning against a tree.

Kenglong-po is terribly strong and fearsome. It is a generalist omnivore, feeding on many varieties of plants as well as prey animals ranging from small rodents up to and including elephants.

If a person travelling through the forest hears the eerie sound of a Kenglong-po, he should turn around at once and walk in the opposite direction from the voice in an absolutely straight line. If instead he delays or deviates from the path, he is liable to disappear.

Kenglong-po is a favourite subject of Karbi-language songs, ranging from traditional lullabies to psychedelic rock anthems.

Ref: 81, 193, 509

....

* There is more to this story, though the Keimi are not part of it. Kungawrhi was later kidnapped from the weretiger by the **Khauvang**, and lived for a time in their underground lair.

⤬ KETU ⤬

In Hindu mythology, Ketu is the demon responsible for the lunar eclipse. He is headless, being one-half of the serpent-demon **Svarbhanu**, whose head was sliced off by Vishnu. Svarbhanu's head became **Rahu**, the demon of the solar eclipse.

Ketu represents the descending lunar node, the southern intersection point of the celestial paths of the sun and moon. It is one of the *Navagraha*, or nine "planets" of Hindu astrology.

While Rahu is associated with sinfulness and terrible accidents, Ketu's influence in astrology is somewhat less pernicious. He brings loss, misfortunate, and failure, but primarily with regards to material things—the sort of failures that build character.

Ref: 510

⤬ KHABISH ⤬

Khabish is a ghost from Kumaon. He appears as a dark-skinned, middle-aged man who is missing his left arm. This spirit has many afflictions: he suffers from seizures, severe rashes and boils on his skin, chest pain, and extremely poor eyesight. Forever in a wicked temper, he wanders around cursing at people, shouting foul abuse at anyone who crosses his path.

Khabish is said to have once been a trusted servant of Lord Vishnu, but he fell from favour after plotting to abduct the daughter of Karthikeya, the god of war. Since then he causes sickness and trouble for dishonest people or those who try to rise above their station.

He is an assistant to **Masaan**, and the two ghosts are often seen together.

As with the **Khais** and **Khavees** of Western India, the name of this spirit probably derives from the Arabic and Persian word *khabis*, meaning "evil" or "malignant". In India, the word is used in different regions for very different ghosts.

Ref: 165, 511

⟩⟩⟨⟩ KHAIS ⟩⟨⟩⟨

In the folktales of the Thakur tribe of Maharashtra, a Khais is an evil spirit that appears as a tall and muscular man with blue-black skin. The Khais goes bare-chested, wearing only a loincloth; but he can also turn himself invisible. He is a powerful wrestler, and likes to challenge strong men to contests.

The Khais is fond of tobacco, liquor, meat, and blood.

Like the **Barambha**, the albino spirit of Thakur lore, Khais try to kindle romantic relationships with human women. Since Khais are strong, suave, handsome, and bold, they are very often successful in their pursuits. However, it is extremely dangerous for a woman to conceive by a Khais. A child resulting from this union is likely to be born sickly or suffer from deformities.

Khais can also possess people and cause illnesses.

Ref: 485

⟩⟩⟨⟩ KHAVEES ⟩⟨⟩⟨

A Khavees is a ghost from Gujarat, Maharashtra, and the Konkan coast. He is known especially from Muslim folklore, but belief in the Khavees is found in other communities as well. Some say the Khavees is the ghost of a Pathan warrior from Afghanistan. Others say he is the ghost of a Siddi, one of the African soldiers that came to India centuries ago along with Muslim armies.

In stories from Maharashtra, he appears as a tall, muscular man with fiery red eyes. The sight of a Khavees is said to be a portent of imminent doom. A person may see the Khavees quite clearly—even standing in a crowded market in broad daylight—but the ghost will be invisible to everyone else around.

The Khavees might just give you a long, piercing look, and then walk away, melting into the crowd. Or it might approach you to ask for a cigarette and a matchbox. The interaction may seem a little strange and uncanny, but not especially remarkable or threatening. However, should you happen to see or speak to this spirit, you are destined to have a fatal accident or be murdered within a few days.

In Gujarati folklore, the Khavees is often described as headless.

Ref: 115, 512

❧ KHAWHRING ❧

In the folklore of the Lushai of Mizoram, Khawhring is a greedy, gluttonous, and jealous spirit that covets things. It is especially fond of gongs and eggs. Typically, it inhabits young women.

Khawhring is similar to the evil eye (see **Nazar**), but it doesn't operate in exactly the same way. People who have it within them can cause illness and death to those they envy. In pre-Christian times, women accused of having Khawhring would be ostracized from society, or even hunted down and killed by mobs.

It is said that Khawhring originated from the wild boar. Long ago, a hunter killed one, and butchered it and cooked it. Then he sat down with his sister and served her some of the meat. While she was eating, a bit of fat got on her hand, and she happened to rub her head with it. In this way the Khawhring passed into her.

A few days later the spirit spoke through her, claiming that it was the spirit of the wild boar her brother had killed, and demanding eggs. This is how Khawhring came to reside in humans.

A woman with Khawhring can send it to temporarily attack someone else. That person then comes down with a violent stomach ache. Sometimes, the spirit speaks through this person, thereby letting its demands be known without revealing the identity of the woman in whom the Khawhring resides. Unless it is given what it wants, the victim may waste away and die.

Khawhring is thought to be passed down from mother to daughter. It can also be passed around through shared headgear, for instance through a *hnam*, the woven-cane head strap attached to a basket.

Ref: 6, 150

❧ KHETOR ❧

In Assam, people of many ethnicities believe in a demon called Khetor and a demoness called Khetori; but descriptions vary widely from group to group.*

----

* This word is thought to derive from the Sanskrit term *kshetrapala*, the presiding deity of the field.

Perhaps this variation is to be expected, for in Benudhar Rajkhowa's classic 1905 text *Assamese Demonology*, they are identified as the most skilled shapeshifters among all the spirits.

Among the Bodo people, Khetors are believed to trouble little children by appearing in recurring nightmares as ferocious animals. These dreams result in epileptic fits, blood loss, and other ailments, which can be fatal if not treated with ritual offerings and mantras. Sometimes the Khetors abduct babies in the night.

Another type of Khetor likes to steal newborn calves. This can be prevented by taking a portion of the cow's milk, heating it, and daubing a bit of the cream on the ears, neck, and loins of both the calf and its mother. The Khetor comes in the night and eats these bits, and leaves satisfied.

In the Karbi tribe, Khetor is a near-synonym for the **Chekama**. In addition to the terrifying traits of that demon, the Karbi version of the Khetor also has an extremely long and flexible tongue, and in the centre of its forehead is a sort of headlamp that glows with an eerie light.

In the Rabha tribe, it is believed that there are five types of Khetors: Chamen, Puwati, Duwari, Sesha and Kalkhetor. These godlings are appeased with effigies of hay built on the roadsides.

For the Khamyang, the Mota Khetor is a demon that causes miscarriage in the second or third month of pregnancy. The exorcism of a Mota Khetor must be performed by an ojha who already has children, or else the demon's next target will be the ojha's wife. The ritual involves feeding the victim a bit of green gram cooked with chopped earthworms.

The Tiwa people believe that Khetors are the ghosts of dead people who return to harm the living.

Some Khetors and Khetoris are lascivious spirits who visit sleeping adults in their dreams and proposition them for sex. If the dreamer accepts, they experience night after night of nocturnal emissions; but the demon slowly drains them of their life-force, until they waste away and die.

Ref: 23, 93, 294

KHOND

The Khond or Khondmura is a monster from Assamese folklore. It has a short, stout body with gnarled limbs and no head. Instead its giant mouth is set in its belly, with its eyes just above it on the chest. These eyes are said to have a wicked

sparkle, like those of a man-eating tiger. There are reports of Khonds that have more than two of them.

Khonds live in dense jungles near the seashore. They sometimes venture into overgrown backyards.

A weird and unpredictable creature, the Khond wanders around at night doing a hideous dance, emitting unearthly shrieks. It may try to kill any human it encounters; or it may run off at full speed for no apparent reason, screaming and laughing horribly.

Ref: 294, 448

⋙ KHUAVANG ⋘

In the folklore of Mizoram, the Khuavang are a type of protean spirit inhabiting hills, rocks, and caves. They go by many other names—Lungzai, Nungzai, Nuaizinmang. They are usually invisible, but sometimes manifest as fireflies, reptiles, or old women. They live in human-like family structures, with couples marrying and rearing their young. Some people believe the Khuavang have been around since the days long before humans, and that they played a role in shaping the landscape itself.

There are a few stories in which Khuavang kidnap humans and carry them into their caves. More often, though, they act as benevolent and even playful guardian spirits, blessing people with long life and many children. Moles or other birthmarks are seen as protective "Khuavang marks". Khuavang are thought to control people's fates.

Certain people—usually women—are said to have the power to communicate with the Khuavang. Such women, called *zawlnei*, are privy to many arcane secrets, particularly in the art of healing. Through the Khuavang, they can learn what sort of sacrifices are necessary to cure any given illness.

When an invisible Khuavang comes close to a group of humans, it can cause people to forget what they were about to say. So when there is a sudden lull in conversation, people hold the Khuavang responsible.

When humans meet a Khuavang in material form and don't realize its true nature, the Khuavang may judge their behaviour. If they show kindness and charity, they will be blessed with riches and good fortune; but if they treat the Khuavang rudely, they will be cursed with degradation and ruin.

One story tells of an orphan named Liandova and his brother. The two boys were playing in a field when they saw a crow swoop down to catch a small snake. They shouted and chased the bird away until it dropped the snake. Then the two boys picked it up and kept it in a basket.

It turned out that the snake was really a baby Khuavang that had wandered away from its mother. Its mother appeared to the two boys, thanked them for saving her child, and blessed them with a bountiful paddy crop for years to come.

Ref: 6, 150, 192

KHUBA AND KHUBI

The following story comes from the folklore of Assam.

Lord Shiva once decided to come down from his mountain hermitage and try to live the life of a farmer for a while. He soon got so busy tending his crops that he forgot to return to his wife Parvati. Parvati sent gadflies to try to get him to come back. When this didn't work, she sent a tiger. And when that didn't work, she travelled down to the field herself.

When she found her husband, she cried out "Ah!" and "Ih!" Each of these sounds emerged from her mouth as a tiny puff of flame. The two fires landed on the crops, and quickly began to burn through Lord Shiva's field.

Shiva rushed at them to force them to stop. The fires shrank back from him, and turned into two demons. They looked up at his divine face and then fell prostrate at his feet.

Ever since then, the flame-demons Khub-"ah" and Khub-"ih" lie in wait at junctions where three roads meet. Whenever people get married, they possess the newlyweds, and begin to cause disagreements and strife. It is crucial that on the third day after a wedding, a special ceremony is performed to propitiate the two demons; otherwise, the flames of discord will burn out of control, and the marriage is doomed to be an unhappy one.

Ref: 167

KIMIDIN

Kimidins are a class of evil spirits who appear in the *Rig Veda* and the *Atharva Veda*, two of the very oldest Hindu texts, where they are often mentioned in conjunction with the **Yatudhanas**. They are described as greedy eaters of human flesh with wicked souls. They usually travel in pairs.

Not much is known about this class of spirits. One guess is that the word Kimidins is of Mesopotamian origin, and derives from Ekimmu-Dimme. In ancient Sumer, an Ekimmu was a type of wrathful ghost, a wind spirit that attacked people in their sleep. Dimme was a demon-goddess who fed on infants and unborn children. Both these legends are very ancient, dating back to around 4000 BCE.

Atharva Veda Book 2, Hymn 24 is a chant of protection against demonic forces, in which several Kimidins are named.

Serabhaka, Serabha! Back fall your arts of witchery! Back, Kimidins!
　　Let your weapon fall.
Eat the one you belong to; eat the one who sent you; eat your own
　　flesh itself.
Srvridhaka, Sevridha! Back fall your arts of witchery! Back, Kimidins!
　　Let your weapon fall.
Eat the one you belong to; eat the one who sent you; eat your own
　　flesh itself.
Mroka, Anumroka! Back fall your arts of witchery! Back, Kimidins!
　　Let your weapon fall.
Eat the one you belong to; eat the one who sent you; eat your own
　　flesh itself.
Sarpa, Anusarpa! Back fall your arts of witchery! Back, Kimidins!
　　Let your weapon fall.
Eat the one you belong to; eat the one who sent you; eat your own
　　flesh itself.
Joorni! Back fall your arts of witchery! Back, Kimidins! Let your
　　weapon fall.
Eat the one you belong to; eat the one who sent you; eat your own
　　flesh itself.
Upabdi! Back fall your arts of witchery! Back, Kimidins! Let your
　　weapon fall.
Eat the one you belong to; eat the one who sent you; eat your own
　　flesh itself.
Arjuni! Back fall your arts of witchery! Back, Kimidins! Let your
　　weapon fall.
Eat the one you belong to; eat the one who sent you; eat your own
　　flesh itself.
Bharooji! Back fall your arts of witchery! Back, Kimidins! Let your
　　weapon fall.
Eat the one you belong to; eat the one who sent you; eat your own
　　flesh itself.*

The meanings of most of the names invoked here are unclear. Serabhaka
and Serabha are thought to be serpent-like demons—perhaps chiefs among the
Yatudhanas. Sarpa and Anusarpa are also thought to be serpents. The words

---

* Translation: Griffith,[119] with minor edits.

Srvridhaka and Sevridha, confusingly, mean "auspicious" and "blissful"; it's possible the names are meant to be ironic. Mroka and Anumroka are associated with fire, perhaps indicating that they cause their victims to burn with fever. Upabdi is a noisy demon that makes a clattering sound. Arjuni means "white", and may refer to a silvery snake, or possibly to leprosy. Bharooji may be some sort of ferocious beast, or it may mean "to roast"—as in, with fever.

Ref: 119

KINNARA

Kinnaras are mythological creatures mentioned in ancient Sanskrit and Pali literature. In the *Mahabharata*, they are described as half-human and half-horse; but in Buddhist texts, they have human torsos with wings and bird-like legs.

Kinnaras have great affection for music. Male Kinnaras typically play drums; female Kinnaris favour the lute. Kinnara couples are considered ideal romantic lovers, blissfully happy and inseparable, though they are eternally childless. (There are also legends in which Kinnaris marry human men. The Buddhist Jataka tale about the Kinnari princess Manohara and her husband Prince Sudhana, popular throughout Southeast Asia, provides one example.)

Kinnaras are benevolent towards humans, especially children. However, they were not always treated well by humans in return. The Jataka tales, which date to about the 4th century CE, tell of Kinnaras that were cruelly captured and kept in cages for the amusement of kings.

In Buddhist mythology, Kinnaras are counted as one of the *astagatyah*, the eight supernatural races in Buddhism.

Ref: 513

KOKAACHI

The Kokaachi is a small monster from central Kerala who likes to steal people's food. It is most often invoked by Malayali parents trying to coax small children to finish their meals.

The name has been adopted by the Kochi-based indie comics company Studio Kokaachi, whose network of artists has invented a wide variety of different Kokaachi characters. There is Amminikutty, who raids the fridge when

everyone is sleeping; Aagolu, a sort of living hairball; and the pelagic, tentacled species Kokadelmar.

The rare, unnamed Kokaachi pictured here is from the Western Ghats. It roams the forest floor on new-moon nights, looking for scraps of food left behind by other Kokaachis.

Ref: 514

⤛ KOLAVO ⤜

The folklore of many tribes in the northeast feature a soul-stealing demon who lives on a narrow stretch of the path that leads to the village of the dead. He sits there in wait for the souls of the freshly deceased who come travelling by that path, hoping to catch them and eat them. In Garo lore he is called **Nawang**; for the Angami Naga he is Metsimo, one of the **Terhoma**; the Lhota Naga call him Echlivanthano, one of the **Tsungrem**; the Zumomi Naga call him Litwoso; and the Chang Naga call him Ujingkaklak. In some stories of the Ao Naga, the female spirit Aonglemla (see **Aonglamla**) performs this role. The gate-guardians **Pu Pâwla** and **Sanu** of Mizo lore, Ramcharipu of the Aimol, and the **Chhongchhongpipa** of the Mara serve a similar function.

Kolavo is the Sümi Naga version of this spirit. When a ghost on its way to the village of the dead first encounters him, he doesn't attack it right away. First he says, "My hair is full of lice." The ghost is expected to offer to pick these monstrously engorged insects out of Kolavo's hair.

In Sümi Naga tradition, women are buried along with a swordbean seed and a small flat piece of bamboo to carry with them on their journey. When they bend over Kolavo's head, they use the bamboo to make little clicking sounds, pretending to be killing the fat lice. Then they suddenly throw the swordbean seed off to the side. As it rolls away, Kolavo runs to fetch it, thus leaving the path clear for the soul to run onwards towards the village of the dead and avoid being eaten.

Men are buried with a spear, a shield, and a spinning top. The top is used to distract Kolavao, just as women use the swordbean seed, but the bamboo is not part of the man's equipment. Perhaps men are expected to go through with the lice-killing—or perhaps Kolavo sees the spear and shield, and doesn't ask to be groomed.

Ref: 140

⤛ KOLLIVAY PEY ⤜

The Kollivay **Pey**—also called Kolli Pisaasu or Kolli Deva—is observed as a strange, unexplained fiery light. When it occurs over a marshy area, it is the South Indian version of the will-o-the-wisp or *ignis fatuus*, explained as the result of luminous pockets of methane gas (see **Aleya**). But the mysterious torch

fires are also commonly reported from the mountains, and from agricultural areas. The lights often appear in groups, dancing together near temples devoted to the village guardian deity.

In folklore, the Kollivay Pey is a small, goblin-like demon that breathes fire. Some say that it is the ghost of a person who was burnt to death.

Kollivay Peys that live at higher elevations like to lure people into the jungle. When those who witness the unexplained lights get curious and go to investigate the source, they find that the fires keep winking out and reappearing further and further away. The observers become gripped with a sort of madness, running after the light without looking where they're going. The Kollivay Pey leads its hapless victims to the top of a hill, hovers in mid air just past a cliff edge, and breathes its fiery breath once again, causing the chasers to jump to their deaths.

Unprincipled *manthiravadis* (tantric sorcerers) can employ Kollivay Peys for wicked deeds of black magic. But these spirits are not always portrayed as hostile. In Kalki Krishnamurthy's classic Tamil historical novel *Ponniyin Selvan*, the heroine Poonkuzhali introduces the Kolli Pisaasus of the marshes of Kodikkarai as her lovers.

Ref: 170

⤐ KONDHOKATA ⤐

In some Bengali stories, this name is a synonym of **Skondhokata**, the headless ghost that haunts railway lines.

In other tales, though, the Kondhokata has a very large head and a correspondingly huge mouth—so big that it is capable of gobbling up a human being in one gulp. An ambush predator, it digs a hole on the side of a road, or lies in wait in a drain. It bides its time until it is dark and the area is nearly deserted, so that no one will notice it silently crawl out of the mud and swallow you up.

Ref: 277, 418

⤐ KRONI ⤐

The Ayyavazhi faith, practised by nearly ten million people in South India, is sometimes considered a branch of Hinduism; but some of its adherents prefer to call it a separate religion. It is founded on the teachings of Ayya Vaikundar (1809–1851), a social reformer born in Kanyakumari, who is venerated as a prophet by his followers.

In Ayyavazhi mythology, Kroni represents primordial evil.

According to the Ayyavazhi holy book, the *Akilam*, there are eight great ages, or *yugams*, each lasting around one million years. Kroni was born in the first yugam (Neethi Yugam); he was the first evil to exist in the world. In his first form, he had hundreds of limbs, each one the size of a mountain. As soon as he was born he felt extremely thirsty and ravenously hungry. He started off by drinking all the water in the sea, and proceeded to try to eat the entire universe.

Luckily, the universe was saved by the god Mayon, who sliced Kroni into six pieces before he could consume all of creation.

In each of the next six yugams, one of the Six Fragments of Kroni came to plague humankind and to battle Mayon.

The first fragment of Kroni, which appeared during the second yugam, incarnated as Kuntomasali, a monstrous, gigantic leech hundreds of feet high and thousands long.

The second fragment of Kroni became a pair of wicked rulers named Thillaiamallalan and Mallosivahanan, who squeezed their subjects with exorbitant taxes.

The third fragment took the form of a pair of brothers, Suraparppan and Sinkamuka. These, too, reigned as wicked and oppressive kings until Mayon defeated them. During the same age Suraparppan was reincarnated as yet another evil tyrant named Iraniyan (associated with the **Asura** king Hiranyakshipu of mainstream Hindu myth.)

The fourth fragment of Kroni was Ravanan, king of Lanka.

The fifth fragment became Duryodhanan, the primary antagonist of the *Mahabharata*.

The sixth and final fragment—the one who rules the current yugam, the seventh age—is Kaliyan, the Tamil name of **Kali**.

At the end of the seventh yugam, Kroni will be defeated once and for all. This will usher in the blissful era of Dharma Yugam, the eighth and final age.

Ref: 516, 517

⟞⟝ KSUID ⟞⟝

In Khasi lore of Meghalaya, the Pariksuid (or simply Ksuid) are evil spirits. The word is used for a broad category of noxious and pestiferous beings. There are the Ksuid-Lum, the devils of the hills and woods, who reside in trees or in caves. There are the Ksuid-Lah, or water devils, who reside in streams and ponds. And there are the Ksuid-Suin, or air devils, who live in the clouds and in the wind.

The Ksuid are constantly on the lookout, trying to find people to attack and possess. They prey especially upon people who are weak in spirit and low in confidence.

A person who is secure and comfortable in his faith can easily shake the spirits off. If a confident man is followed home by a Ksuid after he takes a walk through the jungle, he can simply offer it a betel-leaf or a plate of rice, and then command the spirit to go back to its home.

A weak-willed person, on the other hand, may wind up worshipping the Ksuid, giving in to all its demands, and even offering it sacrifices.

Some of the most notorious of these demons are listed below.

The queen of all the Pariksuid is **Ka Tyrut**, a malevolent force which causes violent death. Ka Tyrut is associated with specific locations where a suicide, murder, or deadly accident has occurred. Because blood has soaked into the ground, it is thought that some portion of the deceased person's spirit lingers there as a *raibi*, which can be translated as "curse" or "taint". A special ceremony called *mait tyrut* must be performed three times to remove the curse, and allow the dead to rest in peace.

Ka Lasam is a minor Ksuid who has the power to make people break out in hives. People who "keep" Ka Lasam—that is, who worship her at home—can send her to punish their enemies.

Ka Ñiangriang or **Ka Kyian** is a Ksuid embodied in a water beetle. It is believed that this spirit causes ear infections in little children who play in streams or lakes, and that she can eventually make the child go deaf if she is not propitiated. A rooster or a piglet should be sacrificed to get Ka Ñiangriang to leave the child alone.

Ka Thapbalong is a Ksuid that lives underwater in the streams and lakes of the Khasi Hills. She is said to cause deafness and arthritis.

She is propitiated with a conical cane basket called a *ka khoh*, a head strap for carrying the basket, a little bit of rice, and sometimes a chicken.

The name Thapbalong also refers to a species of black moth associated with drunkenness and alcoholism. The Thapbalong is said to play a *mieng*—a stringed instrument—which muddles the thoughts of the drunkard and makes them talk nonsense.

Ka Bih, also called **Kymbad**, is the demon of poison. Those who worship this evil spirit in their homes make a deadly contract (called a *jingiatang*) which brings them great riches, but requires them to use poison to kill. Different types of poisons are used, including some which are slow-acting and others whose effect is immediate.

Throat and mouth cancers are often blamed on this demon, as well as less serious ailments like neck pain and rotten teeth.

If a family is suspected of keeping Ka Bih, people avoid visiting them or eating their food.

Ka Lei Khuri is a guardian spirit, the goddess of the hearth and protector of the home among the Khasis. She wards away thieves and increases the family's prosperity. She is worshipped at home in the form of three hearthstones; a few grains of rice are always left in the bottom of the boiling pot, so that she may not be offended by an empty vessel.

But some accounts describe Ka Lei Khuri as a minor demon, rather than a goddess, who can cause stomach illnesses to the family's enemies.

Ka Raliang is a Ksuid that is similar to the evil eye (see **Nazar**). If someone who worships Ka Raliang gives someone else a compliment—"That's a nice new motorcycle", for example—it's likely that Ka Raliang will show up soon afterwards to cause engine trouble or a smashed headlight.

The Ka Raliang curse can be applied to any sort of possession, such as livestock, or a house.

If anyone should become the victim of a Ka Raliang curse three times, that person will themselves gain the power of Ka Raliang. This means that if they give a compliment or speak any word of praise about a third party's possession, that thing will be ruined or destroyed. And yet the person who caused the curse may remain totally unaware of their power.

Ka Raliang is said to be worshipped at home by some jealous and unscrupulous people.

Ka Sabuit ka Sakai is the demon of stomach ache and intestinal pain. It is thought to enter the body through fruits and other raw food. When eating such items, Khasis used to rub a little slaked lime (calcium hydroxide) on the food to drive out the demon, while uttering a short incantation:

Flee away thou Ka Sabuit ka Sakai, go to thine own habitation;
God has not ordained thee to exercise thy power over mankind.*

---

* Translation: H. Oderson Mawrie.[221]

If someone does get possessed by Ka Sabuit ka Sakai, a ritual is performed in which a betel-leaf or a red chilli is burnt on a fire, and slaked lime is rubbed on the victim's belly. Meanwhile, an incantation is spoken, banishing the demon back to its home.

Ka Shwar is a witch-spirit who kills by strangulation. When she strikes a victim, they may suffer from convulsive fits, or their neck may be twisted around until they are facing backwards.

Ka Shwar is supposedly worshipped at home by greedy, unscrupulous people who are overly protective of their property. If anyone steals from them, trespasses upon their land, or infringes their rights, the keepers of Ka Shwar will send the demon's power against their enemies. Ka Shwar may also cause thieves to confess their crimes by talking in their sleep, or falling into an unconscious state and speaking.

Ka Taro is a demon goddess of wealth, known especially among the Pnar or Jaiñtia people. Families that worship Ka Taro are said to possess a secret wooden box that is passed down through generations without ever being opened.

It is considered very dangerous to borrow money from anyone suspected of worshipping Ka Taro. It is unlucky even to eat their food or accept a gift from them, because afterwards the demon believes that a debt is owed to her, and she may come to collect it—possessing the debtor, causing them to fall ill and suffer from fits. When leaving the house of someone suspected of keeping Ka Taro, people used to whisper a prayer, and throw a coin or two over their shoulder to placate the demon.

Ka Taro also punishes anyone who misuses property that was earned by her keepers.

If someone falls sick with fever, and it is believed that Ka Taro is causing the illness through the agency of another, the sick person's friends will break eggs in order to try to get them to say the name of the keeper in their delirium. Then they will take the sick person to the house of the man believed to be casting the spell and throw ashes and shards of broken clay pots over the wall of his compound. If the sick person recovers, it is believed that the accusation was correct. The guilty party will be excommunicated from society, unless he destroys his house, burns all his clothes and furniture, sells everything he owns, and throws away the money from the sale. The money is considered cursed by Ka Taro and should not be touched.

Ka Lei Kupli is the demon goddess of the Kupli (or Kopili) River. She is said to have once been the beneficiary of human sacrifice.

In the early 1800s the Jaiñtia Kingdom occupied parts of what is now Meghalaya and part of what is now Bangladesh. The citizens of the kingdom, who were mostly Pnar (a sub-tribe of the Khasi), followed their indigenous faith, called Ka Niamtre. But the rajas professed Hinduism, and they conducted periodic human sacrifices to the goddess Kali.

Volunteers were sought. Those who came forward were called *bhoge khaora*. The raja would present them with a golden anklet, and for a few days they were allowed to do absolutely anything they wanted, with the royal treasury covering any costs. Then, when the last day of the Navaratri festival arrived, the victim would be bathed, garlanded, daubed with kumkum and sandal paste, seated on a dais in front of the idol, and beheaded.

The head would be placed on a golden plate before the goddess; the lungs would be cooked and eaten by attendant yogis; and rice cooked in a bit of the victim's blood would be served to the royal family.

According to the British officer P.R.T. Gurdon, writing in 1914, these *bhoge khaora* sacrifices to Kali had merely replaced a pre-existing tradition of sacrifice to Ka Lei Kupli, which was conducted twice a year on the banks of the river. This is disputed by some Pnar people, however, who say there was no human sacrifice before the arrival of Hinduism.

In any case, in the year 1832, volunteers ran short, and the Jaiñtias captured and sacrificed three British subjects. This prompted (or was used by the British as a pretext for) the annexation of the Jaiñtia Kingdom.

Ka Ron is a demon goddess of accidents; in the Ka Niamtre faith, she is the most dangerous of all the demons.

U Ksuid Lam Iap is God's servant who takes souls to the afterlife. He is an enormous giant of hideous appearance with long tangled hair and teeth the size of axes.

Ka Smer is a demoness who brings violent death.

Ka Duba is a demon who caused a fever local to the town of Therriagat, where there are many caves.

Ka Khlam is the demoness of cholera and plague. In June, during the Beh-Dieng-Khlam festival, this demon is driven out of the houses with sticks of oak.

Ka Byrdaw is the demoness of epilepsy.

Ka Tihar is the demoness of severe colic.

U Jingbih-U Lasam is the demon who causes tooth-rot.

U Rih is the demon of malaria.

U Kyrtep is the demon of blindness.

U Thynrai is a demon who makes existing diseases worse.

U Trang and *U Rwaibah* are demons who cause heartache.

U Lasamdoh is a demon who causes hoarseness and a swelling of the joints.

Ka Syri is a demoness who saws, files, scratches, and cuts. She causes bowel pain.

Ka Jumai is the demoness of earthquakes.

U Ksuid Briew, also called U Ksuid Ngon, is responsible for early-morning attacks of frailty or laryngitis.

U Ksuid Kynta Maram is the demon of headaches.

U Synkai Bamon is an evil spirit.

U Ksuid Kynta Maram causes sterility and miscarriage.

Ka Ramshandi is a bloodthirsty demoness associated with headhunting; there is also a masculine version, U Ramshandi.

Most of the Ksuid are not thought to be the ghosts of humans, but *Ki Ksuid Mynsaw* is an exception. This is the spirit of a person who died an unnatural death—in particular, the ghost of a criminal who was murdered in the forest by a treacherous partner-in-crime.

Ref: 112, 176, 204, 205, 221, 232, 254, 287, 334, 349, 431, 518, 573

KULI

A malignant spirit called Kuli or Kule is found in the folklore of various parts of South India. Some regard it as equivalent to the **Preta**.

In the Tulu language, Kule signifies a troublesome ghost that has not completed its journey to join the ancestor spirits. A ceremony known as *Kule madime* ("ghost marriage") used to be practised, in which the spirits of two unmarried deceased individuals would be joined in matrimony, in the hope that this would satisfy the ghosts and they would stop bothering the living.

In the older traditions—now largely forgotten—of the Kodava people (also known as the Coorgis), Kuli was an invisible demon who carried off the spirit of a deceased person before the funeral rites were complete. When a Kuli haunted a house, it caused repeated misfortune and accidents.

To put an end to a haunting, a ceremony called a Kuli-Kola was performed: a costumed dance bearing close similarities to the **Bhoota** Kola of Tulu tradition. Some of the named Coorgi Kulis coincided with the Tulu Bhootas, too, including Panjurli, the boar; Kalluruti, the stone-roller; her brother Kallugutti, the stone-thrower; Gulika, the shadow of Saturn; and the tantric goddess Chamundi.

In Tamil, a Kuli is a malevolent imp, an enemy of God who causes diseases.

In the folklore of the Paniya tribe of Kerala, Kuli is a fearsome sexless spirit. It appears pitch black in colour and wears a black cloak. This Kuli is worshipped in the form of a rock at the base of a tree.

Ref: 301, 519, 520, 521, 522

KUNDRA

Kundras or Kudras are spirits known from the folklore of the Bauri, Bhumij, Kurukh, Lodha, Munda, and other tribes of Jharkhand and West Bengal. There are various types of Kundras.

Kal Kundras are tall, lean, jet-black beings. They can be heard climbing over the thatched roofs of huts late at night, making strange and incomprehensible noises. They like to eat people.

Bisai Kundras are mischievous spirits which can cause outbreaks of disease in a village.

Dhan Kundras (also called Gudro Bongas, Dhankudras, or simply DK) are smaller spirits, appearing as monkey-like goblins with pasty white faces and straggly hair that hangs down to their shoulders. They stand one or two feet tall, but can shrink themselves to fit into tiny, compact spaces to hide or sleep. They are extremely fast, perhaps even capable of instant teleportation.

Dhan Kundras are believed to reside in thick groves of trees, where they have their own society with a clan structure. They sometimes abduct newborn humans and raise them to become Kundras. Such abductees will never grow more than about two feet tall.

Dhan Kundras are attracted to human habitations. If one offers the spirit the right sorts of sweets and snacks, the Dhan Kundra may pledge its services as a familiar. Once a person has successfully tamed the Dhan Kundra, he keeps it at the side of his hearth in a small brass kalash.

Though they are powerful spirits, Dhan Kundras seem to enjoy playing the role of a pet—at least as long as they are well fed. They typically eat bananas and coconuts. It is said that a Dhan Kundra can eat the fruit of a banana without removing the peel and the flesh of a coconut without removing the shell. It should be noted that even if these offerings are made regularly, Dhan Kundras are not always entirely obedient.

Dhan Kundras were traditionally used to steal paddy or grain stores. But they are capable of performing other magic too. They can make a person very wealthy, for they possess knowledge of treasure buried within the earth, as well as other secrets.

The downside is that if a male child is born into a house where a Dhan Kundra lives, the Dhan Kundra may become jealous and try to kill the child.

Luckily, Dhan Kundras can be sold or transferred from one owner to another. They are sometimes even traded over the internet.

The ritual to ward off a Dhan Kundra that is repeatedly invading one's house involves the sacrifice of a black rooster with inverted wing feathers.

Other, lesser-known types of Kundra spirits include the **Lalpat Kundra**, **Desai Chandi Kundra**, **Sonamukhi Kundra**, and **Kalipat Kundra**.

Ref: 30, 84, 258, 418

KUNGUMI

The Kungumi are a race of sky-spirits in the pre-Christian lore of the Sümi Naga people of Nagaland. Kungulimi is the feminine form. Other Naga peoples recognize these spirits too, but they call them by different names.

Kungumi live high above the atmosphere. Celestial events such as meteor showers, comets, and supernovas were interpreted as taking place in the realm of the Kungumi.

The sky-spirits visit Earth occasionally. Sometimes they take human lovers. In most stories Kungumi appear as beautiful angels, and they are benevolent. There are exceptions, though: not all unions between Kungumi and human beings end happily.

One Chang Naga folktale tells of a sky-spirit named Shambili, who used to come down from the heavens at night to pluck flowers from a lovely garden. The man who tended this garden was a lonely bachelor; he was cultivating the flowers in the hope that they would catch some woman's eye. He noticed that his flowers kept disappearing, and one night he stayed up late to see who was taking them.

He watched as the beautiful Shambili descended and strolled among his plants, singing softly to herself as she smelled the blossoms. He saw her pluck all the loveliest ones she could find.

The man was instantly smitten by her. He ran outside, grabbed her, and refused to let her go. She protested at first, saying that because she was a Kungulimi she shouldn't marry him. But he insisted, and soon they became man and wife.

For months, they lived together happily. Then Shambili announced that she had to leave for a few days, as it was time for the spring festival up in the sky. Her husband let her go.

The day after she left, the man's next-door neighbour died suddenly. He was a disabled man who had been born with a deformed leg.

A few days later, Shambili's husband saw her walking down the path towards the house carrying a basket. As she approached, he realized with a shock what was in the basket. It was the deformed leg of the neighbour who had died!

He blinked in disbelief, and when he looked again, the thing in the basket had transformed into a leg of beef. Shambili greeted her husband as if everything was normal, and set to work cooking the beef. But her husband refused to eat it.

The next morning, their other neighbours noticed that Shambili and her husband did not come outside. As they day wore on, they got curious, and tried the door of their house, but it was locked. When they peered in the window, they saw Shambili's husband lying dead on the floor. Shambili was sitting on top of him, tearing his organs out of his belly and contentedly chewing them up.

The villagers gathered around, planning to break into the house and catch Shambili. But just as they moved forward, a huge dark storm cloud formed around the house. There was a deafening rumble of thunder.

When the air cleared, Shambili was gone, returned to her home in the sky.

Half-Kungumi

In most tales, children born of unions between Kungumi and humans seem to favour the Kungumi parent, in that they are more comfortable living in the sky than on Earth. In fact it may be hazardous to the health of a Half-Kungumi child to mingle in human society. One story tells of a human woman who married a Kungumi and bore him a son; but when she brought the baby down to Earth and let several of her relatives hold him, the child promptly died.

Ref: 140, 523

⊱⊷ KURALI PEY ⊶⊰

A Kurali or Kuralai Pey, known from the folklore of Tamil Nadu, is a small female spirit that lives at the tops of palmyra trees.

When a human passes alone below the Kurali Pey's tree, she steals their voice, and the person can no longer use it. The Kurali Pey then gains the ability to sound exactly like the person when she speaks.

Kurali Peys consider human children a delicacy. They lure them into lonely areas by stealing their parents' voices and calling to them.

It is possible to catch a Kurali Pey by tempting her with sweets and sneaking up on her from behind. By driving a nail into her head, she will become the captor's servant. A Kurali Pey is strong and hardworking. She can complete most tasks easily. But she goes all to pieces when tasked with a mathematics problem, even a very simple one.

When a Kurali Pey works hard, she does so simply to show off her power, rather than out of any sense of duty. She has a strong tendency towards disobedience. What's more, she holds grudges. It usually doesn't take her long to persuade someone to remove the nail from her head so that she can make her escape. And if her master abused her while she was in his service, the Kurali Pey will make sure he gets his due punishment.

Once a Kurali Pey is no longer bound, she has the power to shapeshift. One trick she uses is to assume the guise of her former master, do something outrageously criminal, and then quickly disappear, letting him catch all the blame for the act. Worse still, she leaves him mute, unable to speak in his own defence.

When a Kurali Pey is in a rage, she also delights in arson, and hops from house to house lighting thatched roofs on fire.

Ref: 107

~~ KUTTICHATHAN ~~

Kuttichathan is known throughout Tamil Nadu and Kerala as a mischievous, child-like spirit. However, there are several very different stories of his origin.

One legend tells of a god named Chathan, whose mother was a beautiful tribal woman named Koolivakka and whose father was Lord Shiva. Chathan also had an older brother, Karimkutty, who was Koolivakka's son by a different father.

One day, an **Asura** named Briga tried to assault Koolivakka. Chathan and Karimkutty fought to defend their mother's honour. In this battle, Chathan was injured—but from his blood that fell on the ground, 400 "Kuttichathans" sprang up. (*Kutti* means "little".) Each of these small spirits began fighting as a soldier. Ten were killed in the battle, but the other 390 survived, and helped defeat Briga.

These small Kuttichathans still exist in the spirit realm today. They appear as pitch-black, child-sized figures, sometimes with tails, sometimes with a single eye.

According to another legend, Kuttichathan was the son of Shiva and Parvati. The divine couple had two childless devotees, a woman named Kalakkattamma and her husband Kalakkattachan, who had been praying for years for a son; so they gave them Kuttichathan to raise as their own.

Kuttichathan was not a well-behaved child. In fact he was so unruly and violent that he once cut off his own schoolteacher's head. When his adoptive mother Kalakkattamma chastised him for this act, he raised his hand against her. This insolence angered his adoptive father Kalakkattachan so much that he ripped Kuttichathan into 396 pieces and threw him into the fire.

But the fire did not kill him. Instead, 396 fully-formed Kuttichathans poured out of the flames and went on a rampage.

(This story is enacted annually by elaborately-costumed performers in northern Kerala and southern Karnataka, as part of the ritual worship known as *Theyyam*.)

Today, neither of these origin stories are nearly as well known as the 1984 Malayalam film *My Dear Kuttichathan*, in which Kuttichathan is a child-spirit who has been enslaved by a magician. The dubbed Hindi version, *Chhota Chetan*, was released in 1997, and was a superhit in that language as well.

The Kuttichathan in the movie is a mischievous but good-hearted ghost. He gets rescued from the magician's clutches by three other children, after which he proceeds to treat them to limitless ice cream and pull pranks on the bully at

their school. Despite having the appearance of an eight-year-old boy, he has a high tolerance for alcohol, and goes around guzzling the stuff. He also has the power to turn into a bat.

As depicted in the film, it is believed that Kuttichathans can be summoned by powerful *mantravadis*, or black magicians, to act as their familiars. The summoning ritual is said to require some lion's milk, some tiger's milk, and some elephant's milk. In order to keep a Kuttichathan loyal the mantravadi must ensure it is well fed with meat and liquor, for these spirits have superhuman appetites. If a Kuttichathan is starved, it may rebel, and this can be very dangerous for the mantravadi.

In 1901, a Travancore census commissioner wrote that a man in Changanacherry had more than 100 Kuttichathans under his control, guarding his house and running errands for him.

Today Chathan shrines do a roaring business in many parts of Kerala, in particular the town of Peringottukara, near Thrissur. For the price of 20,000 rupees, a hen, and a bottle of liquor, you can get a consultation with the spirit, who possesses a medium and gives advice—and, if you are lucky, agrees to run a supernatural errand for you.

While they don't often cause serious injury, Kuttichathans can possess people and make plenty of mischief. Those who are attacked by a Kuttichathan may find stones raining down around them whenever they step outside. Fruit will wither as soon as they approach it, and the water they're drinking will suddenly turn to mud.

Ref: 190, 197

LAI-KHUTSANGBI

Lai-Khutsangbi is a demoness who used to terrorize the Meitei people of Manipur. Her name means "demon with long arms"; for when she stood erect, her arms hung all the way down to the ground. When she wanted to, she could stretch them out even longer.

During the day, Lai-Khutsangbi lurked hidden in the woods, spying on little boys and girls as they played. But late at night, she would wander about the villages, visiting the homes where the children lived. She would knock on the door and ask if the man of the house was at home. If the answer was yes, Lai-Khutsangbi would go away. But if the answer was no—if the women and children were home alone—then Lai-Khutsangbi would extend one of her arms through a window or a gap in the walls. She would feel around inside the house until she caught hold of a child. Then she would pull him out, carry him into the forest, and eat him.

Everyone in the area lived in fear of Lai-Khutsangbi. No one let their children play outside after dark. At night, they did their best to keep them from making noise, so the demon would pass by their house.

None of the people who lived in the area were rich. One family in particular was going through very hard times. The man of the house, whose name was Kaliyong, had not been able to find work for weeks. One day, he finally got wind of a chance to earn some money; but it meant he would have to leave

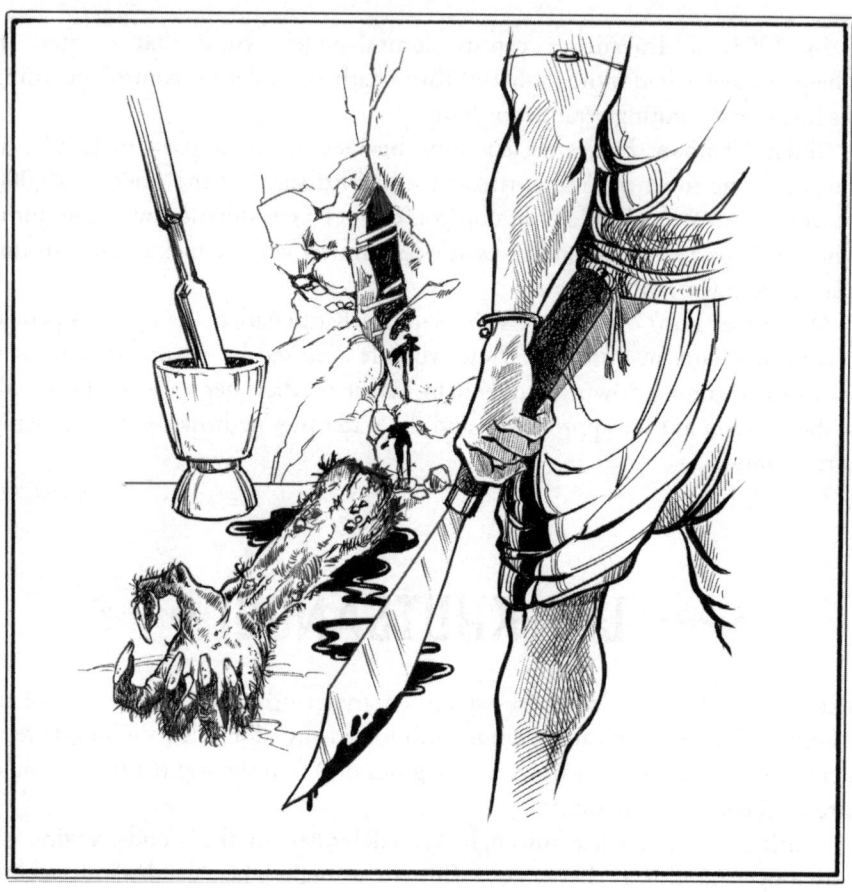

the village for four days. His wife and son were worried about being left alone, for they had heard rumours about the demon. But they also knew that unless someone earned some money, they might all starve. So they bid him farewell.

The night after Kaliyong left, his wife Roopa prepared dinner. But there wasn't much food, and her son began wailing from hunger. Roopa tried everything she could to get him to quiet down, but it was no use: the demoness heard his cries.

Lai-Khutsangbi came to their door, knocked, and asked in a creepy, high-pitched voice if the man of the house was at home. The boy and his mother both knew who it must be standing outside, and the boy, terrified, stopped crying immediately.

Bravely, doing her best not to sound afraid, Roopa lied, "Yes, my husband is here."

Hearing this, Lai-Khutsangbi slunk away into the night. She never tried to snatch a child while the father was at home.

The next night, the boy was far too scared to cry, even though his stomach rumbled. Despite his silence, Lai-Khutsangbi now knew that a child lived in the house. She knocked on the door again, and asked if the man of the house was in.

Again, Roopa lied, "Yes, my husband is here." And again the Lai-Khutsangbi slunk away.

The next night, the same thing happened again. And the next.

Finally, on the fifth day, Kaliyong returned, bearing lots of food and some extra money besides. His wife told him about the demon's nightly visits. They made a plan that when Lai-Khutsangbi came again, Roopa would answer that her husband was out.

For the first time in many days, the family ate a hearty meal together, though they were too nervous to enjoy it as much as they should have. After dinner, Kaliyong spent some time sharpening his sword. Then darkness fell, and they all sat quietly, waiting.

Finally they heard the knock on the door that they had been expecting. Lai-Khutsangbi asked again if the man of the house was at home. Her voice sounded even more evil than usual; she hadn't been able to catch a child for a few days, and she was ravenous.

"No," said Roopa, "my husband has gone out. Who is it?"

On the other side of the closed door, Lai-Khutsangbi grinned a hideous grin. She looked closely at the mud walls of the house until she found a gap, and stretched her arm through it. Then she began to grope around inside the house.

But Kaliyong was standing just to the side of the gap. With one swing of his sword, he chopped off Lai-Khutsangbi's arm.

"You lied! You lied to me!" the demon screamed. She ran off into the forest, howling with pain, blood pouring from her arm.

Some of Lai-Khutsangbi's blood fell on the *ee-ka* bushes, which is why the leaves of that plant are stained with red streaks even today.

Some versions of the story say that Lai-Khutsangbi bled out and died that night. Others say that she survived, and lurks in the forest even today. Mothers warn their children not to cry too loudly at night—for if Lai-Khutsangbi is indeed still out there, then she still has one arm remaining.

Ref: 42, 132, 203, 256, 333

⤙ LAQA ⤚

Laqa is a character who appears in *Hoshruba: The Land and the Tilism*, an Urdu epic fantasy first published in the late 19th century in Lucknow. The authors, Syed Muhammad Husain Jah and Ahmed Husain Qamar, claimed that the story was based on a much older oral tradition.

Laqa, whose real name is Zamurrad Shah Bakhtri, is one of the important adversaries of Amir Hamza, the hero of the epic. He is a megalomaniac who proclaims himself god-king-prophet and surrounds himself with an army of powerful sorcerers. Unfortunately for him, his prophecies don't often come true.

He is described as an eighty-five-foot-tall pitch black giant with long, flowing hair. His arms are the size of tree trunks, and his head resembles the half-crumbled dome of a ruined palace. He rides a giant rhinoceros.

Ref: 147

⤙ LASI ⤚

In the folklore of Mizoram and the Kuki tribes of Manipur, the Lasi are a race of hidden folk that live in the hills. Their capital lies between the Lurh and Tan mountains on the border of Mizoram and Myanmar.

Lasi bear some similarity to the elves or fairies of European tales. They are normally invisible, but can show themselves to humans in dreams. They appear as beautiful, ethereal humanoid beings with eyes turned vertically in their heads, so the corners of each eye point up and down.

Lasi have power over the animals, and they enjoy assisting humans in their hunting. They sometimes choose to bless certain humans with superior skills. These people are called *Lasi zawl*, and they gain the ability to see the Lasi when they are awake.

One such legendary character was Buizova, a man who is supposed to have been unusually ugly. Nevertheless, he confidently wooed and won a Lasi maiden, who taught him the art of singing. He became a famous bard: the man with the supernatural voice.

Another Lasi zawl was Thasiama, who asked the Lasi for a long life and was granted it. Thasiama is said to have lived so many years that he lost and regrew more than a dozen sets of teeth, before finally dying in disgust at the ways of the modern world.

Once one enters the world of the Lasi—either in a dream, or through some magical enchantment—one finds that the moon appears a thousand times brighter.

The king of the Lasi is named Lalchungnunga, and his wife is named Tantinchhingi.

Lasi sometimes fall in love with humans. One of the best-known folktales of Mizoram involves a Lasi prince (in some versions, it is Lalchungnunga's son Thangchina; in other versions, it is King Lalchungnunga himself) who falls in love with a human woman named Chawngtinleri.

Chawngtinleri, who had been orphaned at a young age, was not interested in getting married. She grew up very close to her older brother Liana, and didn't want to leave his side. But the Lasi appeared again and again in Liana's dreams, tempting him with wealth, good fortune, fame—even a gun and

a basketful of ammunition—if only he would agree to marriage. Finally, in a weak moment, he accepted this bride price, and promised his sister to Lalchungnunga in his dream.

When he woke up, Chawngtinleri was nowhere to be found. She had been taken to the world of the hidden folk, and he could no longer see her. However, he could still hear his sister's voice singing to him in the hills sometimes.

Later, Chawngtinleri was allowed to visit home along with her half-human, half-Lasi infant child. She kept the baby covered and hidden from sight, warning everyone not to look at it. But when Chawngtinleri stepped out to go to the bathroom, someone snuck a peek. To their shock and horror, they found that the baby had the body of a human, but the head of a goat!

As punishment for allowing humans to see her child, Chawngtinleri was forbidden from ever visiting the human realm again. Even though she was the Lasi queen, she still felt despondent and miserable all the time.

The Lasi eventually turned her eyes in her head so the corners pointed up and down. Only then did she forget her human attachments.

Half-Lasi

Chawngtinleri's goat-headed baby is not the only half-Lasi to be mentioned in Mizo folktales.

According to a creation myth common to the Lushai and other Zo tribes, there was a time when the progenitors of the clans were trapped in a cave under a massive rock called Chhinlung. The Lasi were imprisoned there along with the humans, and it wasn't uncommon for the two races to interbreed. The children born from these unions were said to be bigger and stronger than normal people. (There is no mention of them having goat heads.)

One such half-Lasi was a man named Thlanrawkpa, who plays a central role in the Mizo creation myth. It was at his *kuangchawi* ceremony—a ritual feast celebrating the prowess of a hunter—that many of the animals were given their names, and acquired the characteristics by which we recognize them.

Ref: 192, 214, 508

LAVSAT

In the folklore of the Konkan coast, a Lavsat is the ghost of a woman who was a widow at the time of her death. Lavsats live in trees near cemeteries or cremation grounds. They feed on livestock, attacking cattle and their calves. They also eat human corpses.

A Lavsat will rarely bother living humans. Sometimes, though, the sight of a happy family, recently married or with young children, will make her so jealous for life that she will begin to haunt them. Even then, she is usually limited to poltergeist-type pranks such as ripping clothes and breaking glass.

Ref: 115, 219

LHA

Lha is a Tibetan word meaning deity, spirit, ghost, or other supernatural entity.

Words derived from the same root occur in many Tibeto-Burman languages, for example **Thla** in Mizo Tawng and **Lai** in Meitei-lon. This family includes languages spoken by over ten million Indians in the states of Ladakh, Himachal Pradesh, Uttarakhand, Sikkim, Assam, Nagaland, Mizoram, Tripura, Arunachal Pradesh, Meghalaya, and Manipur, as well as in Tibetan refugee communities and other pockets around the country. Perhaps most familiarly, it occurs in the name of Tibet's capital city, Lha-sa, the place of the gods.

Lha is roughly equivalent to the Indo-Aryan root **Dev**, with a similar amount of variation in the entities it describes. In Tibet, Ladakh, and Bhutan it is most often used for benevolent spirits; but in other traditions there are evil Lha that can possess a person, causing the same sort of trouble as a **Bhoot**.

Ref: 524

LHADAM

Among the Kuki tribes of Northeast India, a Lhadam is the lingering ghost of a human for whom the proper burial rights have not been performed. Lhadams can haunt a village or forest with strange sounds and threatening cries, but they rarely cause serious harm.

See also the Mizo **Thlarau**.

Ref: 123

⤙⤚ LHANGNEL ⤙⤚

A Lhangnel is a powerful shapeshifting spirit that can cause landslides and flash floods. It is known from the folklore of the Thado Kuki tribe of Manipur.

In its natural form, a Lhangnel is a huge water-dwelling serpent with seven nostrils, a crest of spines on top of its head, and a pattern of reddish diamonds on its back. Its head may appear to have a glowing halo around it.

Lhangnels hunt wild animals, and sometimes humans as well.

A Lhangnel has the power to create a magical vibration which affects all creatures around it, blurring their vision and clouding their thoughts. Once its prey is mesmerized in this way, the Lhangnel constricts it and eats it. It may also carry it down to its home deep under the water, where it uses its body as a cushion.

Lhangnels can appear in the form of various non-magical snakes, including a rock python or a watersnake. It may also take the shape of other animals, such as a jungle fowl, or a deer with two straight, unbranched antlers. (Hunters who try to shoot this deer will never be successful.)

A Lhangnel may also take the form of a human. This is the most dangerous manifestation of all, as it augurs mortality in large numbers. If a Lhangnel appears near a village in the form of a boy, it means that many men of the village will die; if it takes the form of a girl, many women will die. For example, during a heavy rain when a river is in spate, if a strange boy should be seen swimming upstream, this is a portent of a flood that will drown many men.

Today many Kukis have converted to Christianity. But for those who strictly follow the tenets of the old religion, it is forbidden to speak the name Lhangnel. When priests propitiate this spirit they use the words *Noiningnu* and *Noiningpa* instead.

Rarely, a Lhangnel may take a human lover. It is said that the patterns used in the weavings of the Thado tribe were originally designed by a woman who was in love with a Lhangnel. The Lhangnel modelled for her in the guise of different snakes, and she imitated the patterns of its scales on her loom.

Another legend about the Lhangnel is the story of Manmasi.* He was a strong and handsome man, as well as a gifted musician, who often sat on the banks of the river near his village and played the *gosem* (a kind of gourd flute, which is said to have been stolen by the Kuki people from the **Nelhaoloi**.)

....

* In some versions, he is called Vanthang.

One day while Manmasi was playing, a beautiful young woman rose from the water. She asked him to stop playing, for the music made her too emotional. Manmasi refused, saying that playing music was the only way he could keep from feeling sad himself. The Lhangnel then said that if she ever heard him playing the pipe again, she would have to marry him. And with that, she went back into the river.

Manmasi returned to his village, but he was unable to get the beautiful woman out of his mind. The elders learned about what had happened and, realizing that the creature Manmasi had seen was a Lhangnel, grew very concerned. They started explaining to Manmasi that they would have to immediately perform rituals to break the bond between him and the magical being.

Once all the preparations were done, the elders summoned the Lhangnel for the ceremony. She appeared in the form of a gigantic python, and she looked so fearsome that all the villagers fled in terror, even the elders. To Manmasi, though, she appeared just as beautiful as before. She caught hold of him and took him down into the river with her.

For several years, Manmasi's friends and family thought he was dead. But one day he reappeared, along with three sons he had fathered by the Lhangnel. Their names were Shongthu, Shongja, and Jahong.

Though his sons appeared human, the villagers considered them half-demons, and refused to allow them to live nearby. Manmasi had to raise his family as an outcast in the forest. Life was difficult, and he and his sons faced great hardship. Finally, Manmasi went back to the Lhangnel's river to plead for help.

The Lhangnel heard his story and pitied him. She decided to bestow upon his sons three great treasures: a huge white gong for Shongthu, a sword for Shongja, and a household charm or *indoi* for Jahong. Once these gifts were given, the Lhangnel said that her part in the matter was done, and the bond between her and her husband should be broken. With this, she returned to the river.

The three gifted artifacts contained immense magical power, and their owners used them to perform mighty deeds for which they won great respect and honour. Manmasi and his sons were soon welcomed back into the village, where Manmasi married again—to a human woman this time—and bore more children.

Manmasi is sometimes regarded as the forefather of the Kuki tribe. If this is true, then there are many people alive today who can claim some Lhangnel ancestry.

Ref: 148, 525

❧ MAADAN ❧

Maadan is a name given to several gods from southern Tamil Nadu and Kerala. Sudalai Maadan, perhaps the best known, watches over cemeteries. There is also Chula Maadan, Poruthu Maadan, Kumili Maadan, and Neesa Maadan.

One story of the origin of Maadan says that he was Shiva's son by Parvati, but that he was born as a deformed blob with no limbs or head. Distraught, Parvati begged Shiva to give him arms and legs and a face. Shiva did as she asked, and for some time Parvati was happy. But soon afterwards she discovered that the boy was sneaking off to the graveyard at night to dig up dead bodies and feast on them. She chastised him, but he proved to be incorrigible, and in the end she banished him to Earth.

Maadan demands offerings of toddy, liquor, and fresh meat at his festivals. His wife is Karimkali, another bloodthirsty goddess.

In the folklore of non-devotees, Maadan is a ghostly watchman who patrols around graveyards late at night holding a club. He detests whistling, and will kill any trespassers who make this sound.

Ref: 212, 341

❧ MAHORAGA ❧

In Hindu, Buddhist, and Jain mythology, the Mahoragas are a race of giant supernatural serpent-like creatures that live deep underground. They are sometimes described as having broad-shouldered human bodies with snake heads; other times, as having snake bodies with human heads. They are thought to be responsible for earthquakes.

The non-venomous Mahoragas are associated with pythons and other giant constrictor snakes, whereas the **Nagas**—a distinct race of mythical serpent-men—are associated with cobras. Both Mahoragas and Nagas are counted among the *astagatyah*, the eight classes of mythical beings in Buddhism.

Like the **Gandharvas** and **Kinnaras**, the Mahoragas are said to be great musicians.

In Tibetan tradition, Lto 'Phye is a giant Mahoraga that lives beneath the earth, slowly rotating over the course of the year, so that at the solstices and equinoxes he is aligned with the north–south or east–west axis.

Ref: 361

ᐳ━ MAKARA ━ᐸ

The Makara is a mythical sea monster of Hindu and Buddhist lore. It is a hybrid creature, part mammal, part fish, part crocodile, and part elephant. It is also a zodiac sign in Hindu astrology, corresponding to the Western constellation of Capricorn. Makaras are common elements in temple architecture throughout South and Southeast Asia.

The Makara serves as the mount of Varuna, the Vedic Hindu god of water, and of Ganga, the goddess of the river.

There has been speculation as to whether the Makara legend is based on a real cryptid animal, as yet unknown to zoologists. Another possibility is that the Makara represents a recently extinct creature that was encountered by early Indians. Perhaps it was a giant crocodilian: *Magar* and related words mean "crocodile" in many Indian languages. Or perhaps it was an aquatic proboscidean, related to elephants. Or a cetacean—some sort of outsized relative of the Ganges river dolphin.

Connections have also been drawn to Trunko, a mysterious marine creature that was sighted off the coast of South Africa in 1924, doing battle with two killer whales. The creature finally succumbed to its injuries and the carcass later washed up on the beach. Trunko reportedly had thick white fur and the trunk of an elephant.

Ref: 416

ᐳ━ MALTONG ━ᐸ

A Maltong is a type of **Thilha** in the Kuki folklore of Manipur. It is encountered as an old woman hobbling through the forest with a deformed or amputated leg. Sometimes, the demon leaves a trail of blood behind it.

A Maltong is fond of tasty snacks, and she is always hungry. If she is offered something to eat, she may repay the kindness by offering to grant a wish, or to bestow great wealth upon the giver.

However, these riches may not last long. Some say that one who becomes very rich through the gifts of a Maltong is destined to eventually end up destitute and childless.

The legend of the Maltong overlaps with the Lushai story of the **Pheichham**, and some tribes consider them to be the same creature.

Ref: 18, 123

⤙⤙ MAMADEV ⤚⤚

Mamadev is a *pretatma* or ghost-spirit with a serious tobacco habit, who has been evelated to the status of a minor deity. He is worshipped in the Saurashtra region of Gujarat, particularly in Junagadh.

This ghost is ecountered on dark nights, wandering on lonely roads. If you should happen to meet him, he will ask you for a cigarette. If you have one, you should give it to him at once, without saying a word. If you *don't* have one, you should indicate so; again, without saying a word, but using only hand motions. In the latter case, though, you must go to his shrine the next day without fail and offer him not one but two cigarettes. Mamadev is generally considered friendly, but he can bring bad luck if you neglect this tribute.

Mamadev is said to have the power to grant wishes and help devotees achieve the impossible. His powers are greatest during the new moon. On these days, at his temple in Surat, hundreds of packets of cigarettes are offered; wealthy devotees even purchase cartons of Dunhills and other expensive foreign brands at nearby shops to offer at the shrine. The priests will light one of the cigarettes, take a few drags, and place the rest to burn on the altar.

Mamadev is said to hang around lumber and timber yards, and guard them against robbers. He also protects those who travel late at night.

Ref: 579, 580

⤙⤙ MAN-EATING BOULDER ⤚⤚

Man-eating boulders occur in stories from the Khasi hills of Meghalaya.

In one famous tale, a widow who was working in the fields gave her two sons some bananas to eat and left them to play by themselves.

The younger boy was climbing rocks when suddenly he found that he could not lift his foot. The older boy came over and tried to pull his brother free, but found that his feet were only sinking deeper into the rock.

The older boy shouted to his mother, "Mother, come quick, my brother's feet have been swallowed by a boulder!" But the mother was too busy ploughing to turn around. She assumed they were just playing some silly game.

By the time she was finished with her work, not only had the younger boy been completely swallowed, but the older boy had been captured as well. He

had almost disappeared into the stone. Only his outstretched hand, holding a banana, was still visible.

The woman brought all the men from the village to try to free her son. They tried to break the stone with their hammers and chisels. But every time they hit the boulder, they found that it only grew larger.

Finally they gave up, fearing that they might be captured themselves.

Ref: 254

MANDE BURUNG

The Mande Burung is a giant, hairy, bipedal ape-like creature with black fur that is believed to live in the jungles of the Garo Hills of Meghalaya. It has been called the "Indian Bigfoot", and is considered by some to be a type of **Yeti**.

Cryptozoologists have speculated that the Mande Burung may in fact be the giant prehistoric ape *Gigantopithecus blacki*, a nine-foot-tall primate that was once common from India to Indonesia. This species disappeared from the fossil record about 100,000 years ago, around the same time that modern humans migrated to Asia.

Expeditions to find the Mande Burung in the Nokrek National Park in Meghalaya and surrounding areas have turned up some mysterious clues, such as footprints and hair samples, but the evidence is inconclusive.

Mande Burungs are thought to eat freshwater shellfish, bananas, roots, and berries. They are phenomenally strong. Unlike other Yetis, they do not fear fire.

While there have been dozens of sightings over the past few decades, there are no reports of a Mande Burung ever harming or attacking a person. However, in 1999, a Garo Hills resident claimed that a female Mande Burung abducted him and forced him to live in her nest for three days. During this time, she forcibly suckled him from her breast.

The Mande Burung's milk reportedly tasted awful.

Ref: 35, 138

MANGERMACHH

Mangermachh means "crocodile" in Sindhi. But the word is also used for a legendary giant sea monster.

The story of the Mangermachh is over seven hundred years old, from back when the teeming metropolis of Karachi was only a small fishing village called Kalachi. Just off the coast of this village was a deadly whirlpool known as the Kalachi Vortex. All the local fishermen were careful to avoid this part of the sea; for inside the vortex, at the bottom, lived the Mangermachh.

This monster was as large as the largest whales; its wide mouth was full of rows and rows of shark-like teeth, and one blow from its powerful reptilian tail could capsize a fishing boat. The Mangermachh was always hungry. Any boats that got caught in the swirling maelstrom would be sunk and smashed to pieces, and the hapless sailors would be tossed into the sea and gobbled up alive.

In the village there lived a man by the name of Moriro Meerbahar. He was handicapped, the youngest and weakest of a family of seven brothers. He wasn't much use on a boat, so he usually stayed home while his brothers went fishing.

But one day their boat did not return, and everyone knew that the Mangermachh had devoured them.

Moriro decided to avenge his brothers. He built an iron cage for himself, covered with long spikes on the outside. Then he got his friends to take him out to sea in the cage and lower him into the water by means of strong ropes.

When the Mangermachh saw Moriro, it rushed towards the cage at full speed, intending to swallow him. Instead, the monster was impaled on the spikes and died.

Moriro got his friends to pull him up out of the water. Then he cut open the belly of the Mangermachh and retrieved the bodies of his brothers. He buried them in a place which, for centuries afterwards, was called Moriro's Graveyard.

It remained a landmark in Karachi until 2006 when it was bulldozed to make way for a road, over the protests of many local residents.

Ref: 19, 526, 527

MANTICORE

The *Martichora* is a legendary Indian beast that was described by the Greek writer Ctesias in the 5th century BCE. The word eventually passed into English as "Manticore".

Ctesias wrote about the Manticore in his book *Indica*. He claimed to have seen a live, caged specimen that was brought by an Indian dignitary from his homeland and displayed at court in Persepolis, the capital of ancient Persia.

The Martichora had a face somewhat like a man's, with blue human-like eyes and large and hairy ears, but with three rows of sharp teeth in each jaw. It had the feet and claws of a lion and the stinger of a scorpion attached to the tip of its tail. This stinger was half a metre long and as thick as a rope, and Ctesias was told that the venom from it could kill a man instantly. The creature could fire these stingers like harpoons. It could aim either in front or behind it to hit targets at long range. Once a stinger had been discharged, it would quickly grow back.

Manticores ate human flesh, and were reportedly responsible for many deaths. Ctesias wrote that ancient Indians used to hunt young animals that had not yet developed stingers in order to smash their tails with rocks, so that they would never develop into the deadly harpoons.

The Manticore made a sound like a giant trumpet.

Ref: 251, 417

 MARU

Maru is a demon-god of the Konkan coast who lives on hilltops and in banyan trees. He is sometimes associated with **Devchar**, and also with the deity Kshetrapala, the guardian of the farmland (see **Khetor**). If worshipped properly, he can be a village protector; if insulted, he can be very dangerous.

He is propitiated with small clay horses.

Among the Kumbri Marathi people of Karnataka, Maru (plural: Marava) has the more general meaning of "spirit". In this belief, there are many kinds of Marava, including Barochemarava or benevolent spirits, **Padosomarava**, and **Balishtamarava**.

Ref: 161, 528

MARUDYL

Marudyl is a species of liana, or climbing vine. When you cut it, a red liquid spurts out that resembles blood.

There is a belief in the Garo Hills of Meghalaya, especially among speakers of the Atong language, that this creeper turns into a ghost at night and goes crashing through the foliage. It breaks branches and snaps tree trunks, making a deafening racket—so loud that anyone sleeping within a hundred metres is sure to be startled awake.

However, in the morning, if you go and look, you will find no damaged plants, nor any other sign to explain the unearthly noise.

Ref: 51

❧— MASAAN —❧

Stories of an evil spirit or demon called Masaan are common across large parts of Northern and Eastern India. The name means "cremation ground" in many North Indian languages, and is derived from the Sanskrit *smashaan*.

Masaan is usually said to be the ghost of a pre-teenage boy who used to work in a traditional bullock-powered oil press. This child has a hideous face and appears covered with oil and/or the ash of dead bodies. He is fleet of foot, and rarely stays in one place for very long.

Masaan likes to possess children, causing fever and delirium. This possession can be caused by throwing cremation ash at someone. To exorcize Masaan, the child's weight should be matched in salt, and then the salt given away as charity.

A female version of the spirit is called Masaani. She is worshipped as one of the sisters of Shitala, the smallpox goddess (see **Seven Sister Spirits**).

E. Sherman Oakley, a British missionary who worked in Kumaon and Garhwal at the end of the 19th century, reported a common belief that:

> wicked people, or those who die by accidents, such as falling from a tree or precipice, by drowning, snake-bite, or wild beasts, women who die in childbirth, suicides, and all who die a violent or wilful death, or those whose funeral rites have been neglected, after death become ghosts for a time. When the term of a thousand such ghosts expires, that is, when they have expiated their sins by a ghostly existence for a period, the souls of all the thousand are concentrated and transformed into one body, and the being thus formed is called Masaan.[511]

The following quite different legend of Masaan comes from Kumaon as well.

In life, this Masaan was said to be an ascetic who lived in a cave. At night, in a quest for spiritual power, he would visit the cremation ground at Bhimandeshwar and worship Lord Shiva while lying on the back of a unburnt corpse.

Shiva, disapproving of this, appeared to Masaan and warned him to stop. He told him that he must never come back to the cremation ground, or he would suffer terrible misfortune.

Masaan went away. But on the way back to his cave, he met a young woman who told him that Shiva was only jealous of his increasing power. If he would only continue his meditations for a while longer, she said, Masaan would himself become a god.

So Masaan returned to the cremation ground and began his meditation anew. However, he went into such a deep trance that the next morning when people arrived, they thought he was dead, and they cremated him. When he awoke from his meditation, he was surprised to find himself in a charred, dead body. Shiva and Parvati appeared before him, and told him that because he had disobeyed a divine order, he would be cursed to stand guard over the cremation ground for many ages.

It is said that even now, Masaan is not entirely obedient. His charred, half-burnt form is sometimes seen straying from the cremation ground, haunting lonely ravines or pools in the forest. A strong smell of burnt flesh accompanies him wherever he goes.

Masaan is often venerated as a god and protector, propitiated with offerings of liquor, tobacco, and meat. However, he can also afflict people with headaches, goitre, and other more serious diseases.

Whenever someone dies, a goat is always supposed to follow the funeral procession. This is so that in case Masaan feels hungry, he can eat the goat instead of the person's corpse.

*

In parts of Assam, there are different Masaans, each responsible for a different malady. Some communities say there are sixteen types of Masaan; others say there are 126. Some of their names are Ghora Masaan, Garkata Masaan, Gohelideo, Shol Masaan, Kishkindhya Masaan, Baarikaa, Jalaa, Poraa, Chuchiyaa, Naariyaa, Haatiyaa, Amaataa, Bhengraa, and Buraa Roug.

Among the Rajbongshi people of Bengal and Assam, Masaan is associated with water as well as with the cremation ground. He is at once an evil demon and a minor deity, believed to be the son of the goddess Kali and the god Dharma, conceived and born underwater. This Masaan can manifest in the form of a leech.

Anyone who fouls a source of clean drinking water by urinating in it, defecting in it, or bathing in it while menstruating runs the risk of being possessed by Masaan. The first sign of such possession is that the afflicted person starts dreaming about fish. Soon afterwards, they begin to act strangely; their tempers flare easily, and they stop speaking to their friends and family. They also develop cravings to eat charcoal, burnt earth, and clay.

Ref: 21, 83, 165, 194, 511

 MATIYA

Matiyas—also called Chatiya-Matiyas when they come in pairs—are small, mischievous goblins in the folklore of Chhattisgarh and Odisha. They generally haunt ponds and wells. They are friendly towards children.

Some consider Matiya to be synonymous with **Dhan Kundra**; but a Matiya is usually described as a jovial thief and mischief-maker, without the Dhan Kundra's streak of violent jealousy. They can make themselves invisible, and they can emit an eerie, heatless blue flame.

They can be coaxed into service if given regular offerings and a place to stay in the house. Afterwards they must be trained. A typical first training exercise is to rip a five-rupee note in half. Then, while walking along a path, one should close one's eyes and drop half of the note somewhere in the foliage, sight unseen. The Matiya is then asked to retrieve the second half of the note.

For a more advanced exercise, a gold ring or mobile phone is locked in a small box, and the Matiya is asked to get it out.

A Matiya is generally employed to steal money or valuables from the home of an enemy. While on the job, it won't miss a chance to rob food from the kitchen as well. It will wait until the cook has finished preparing a meal, and all the vessels are full of steaming food; then, when the cook turns her back for a few seconds, it will gobble up everything, licking the pots so clean that they appear to have been freshly washed.

Matiyas also make good assistants for treasure hunters.

Ref: 21, 311, 330

MAYEL

Among the Lepcha people of Sikkim there is a belief that somewhere halfway up the slopes of the great mountain Kanchenjunga lies a hidden valley, and in that valley there is a village called Mayel Kyung. This is said to be the ancestral village of the Lepcha. In this place the Mother-Creator Itbumoo created the 108 Lepcha clans from the snows of the great mountain, and then gifted to each clan one lake, one cave, and one mountain peak.

The Lepchas believe that the village of Mayel Kyung is still inhabited by ancestral beings called the Mayel. The Mayel are immortal, somewhere between human and divine—neither Rum (good spirits) nor **Mung** (evil ones). There

are said to be seven families of Mayel; in some tellings, it only seven individuals, all men. The eldest two Mayel are named Adoo Yook and Alau Yook, and their wives are Talyeu Nimu and Sangvo Nimu, spirits of the earth and soil.

By most accounts, the Mayel are small and hairy people, somewhat like hobbits. They have large goitres at their throats, which are thought to be signs of prosperity. They appear as infants in the morning, as adults in the afternoon, and as elders in the evening; then at the sunrise of the next day, they become infants again.

Mayel Kyung is a paradise. The land around the village is extremely fertile and the crops brought forth by Talyeu Nimu and Sangvo Nimu are fantastically bountiful, never affected by any blight or infestation. It was the seeds of these plants that were brought to the Lepcha in the earliest times by the legendary hero Thekung Mensalong, and even today, after every harvest, the Mayel are honoured.

In ancient times, Mayel and humans used to intermingle. But today it is very difficult to get to Mayel Kyung. Only a person with Lepcha ancestry who speaks the Lepcha language and follows Lepcha customs may be granted access, and even then, the way is hard to find. The path is said to be as narrow as the edge of a razor. There are tales of explorers who found a pass which seemed to lead to Mayel Kyung, only to have it blocked by a sudden blizzard.

Despite their failure, when they came back to civilization, these adventurers found they had somehow magically acquired arcane knowledge—an effect of having got so close to the mystical land.

Some Lepchas believe that the souls of people who have lived exemplary lives go to reside in Mayel Kyung after death.

Ref: 274, 364, 529

✎❧~ MEMANG ~❧✎

Memang is a general term for ghost among the Garo people of Meghalaya. The terms *Memong* in the language of the Rabha tribe and *Meme* in Kokborok are used with a similar meaning.

Some Memangs are the spirits of dead humans whose funeral rites were not properly completed, while others (*Memang Gitting*: see **Tsine Nat**) are ghouls or cannibal spirits that were never human.

It is said that long ago, Memang would sometimes hire themselves out to work for the living. They would help with weeding and with the harvest. They charged very little for these services—just a few grains of rice, a tiny piece of fish, or a small wad of tobacco. Any attempt at paying them with large quantities of anything would only leave them feeling insulted. These shades were invisible, and one had to take care not to disturb them.

The story goes that once, a rich landlord had a son who was incredibly spoiled. He would wander around his fields spitting wherever he pleased and throwing his spear at tree stumps for target practice, wholly ignoring the presence of ghosts labouring in the area. This rude boy offended the Memang so much that they stopped working for human employers, and have never returned since.

Like many other ghosts, Memangs have a great fear of mustard seeds, and they will not harm anyone who carries them.

Ref: 51, 306

⟩⥱ MERCHING ⥲⟨

This ghost comes from the folklore of the Parangi Porja tribe of Andhra Pradesh.

When a graveyard starts to fill up, the Parangi Porja don't just go ahead and start a new one. They must wait for the death of a child in its first year of life. This dead baby becomes the first to be interred in the new chosen place, and its ghost, the Merching Dumma, becomes the lord of the graveyard, presiding over the spirits of everyone who is subsequently buried there.

It is sometimes heard crying out for its parents.

A Merching often attacks the parents of infants, presumably out of jealousy, causing headaches, stomach problems, and throat infections.

Ref: 345

⟩⥱ MIRCHUK ⥲⟨

Among the Muria tribe of Chhattisgarh, a Mirchuk is the ghost of an unmarried girl. Mirchuks usually live in peepal trees. They can be dangerous, and various precautions are usually taken to prevent them from harassing the living. This is why, when an unmarried girl dies, four nails are hammered into the ground at the corners of the grave.

A Mirchuk may become jealous of the next girl in the family to get married. To avoid this, the village headman goes and ties a string round and round a date palm trunk at the boundary of the village, forbidding the spirit to enter. After the wedding, he removes the string.

This doesn't always work. The Mirchuk may still trouble the bride with illness or madness. If this occurs, and if a *siraha* (diviner/healer) diagnoses the condition correctly, he will recommend that a doll be made out of straw. The spirit is then coaxed to possess the doll instead of the girl. Afterwards, the doll is thrown outside the boundary of the village.

Premarital sex is encouraged in traditional Muria society, so even though the Mirchuk is the spirit of an unmarried girl, she is likely to have had a few lovers already. While Mirchuks are unable to enter houses, they may come back to bother their former lovers whenever they sleep outside, coming to them in the night and trying to arouse their passions.

Another reason Mirchuks are dangerous is that if a witch gets hold of the spirit, she can bend it to her will, persuading it to take the shape of a beautiful young woman and go out to rob men of their vital force.

The male equivalent of this ghost is called a **Matiya**. In Muria belief, these ghosts also like to trouble their former lovers, but they are less dangerous than the Mirchuk.

Ref: 99, 530

 **MISHING**

In the folklore of the Sherdukpen tribe of Arunachal Pradesh, a Mishing is an apparition of foreboding. It is the ghost of someone who has not yet died, but is about to.

For example, one story tells of a driver driving on a lonely mountain road at night who came upon a woman standing in the middle of the pavement, facing away from him. When he stopped his vehicle, she turned to face him; half her face was missing, and her dress was smeared with blood. Then she disappeared.

The driver was terrified, but as nothing else strange happened, he eventually decided it must just have been some strange hallucination, and continued on his way.

One month later, the same driver was carrying passengers on the same road when he lost control and met with an accident. The back of the car collided with a tree, and a woman in the back seat died, her face smashed in. The driver realized that he was in exactly the same spot where he first saw the Mishing, and that the dead woman was wearing the same clothes that the Mishing was wearing.

A Mishing can choose who it shows itself to. In a group of people standing together, only one of them might see the Mishing. However, the still-living person whose ghost it is will not be aware of it.

A Mishing is not always visibly disfigured. It might appear to be a normal person, even befriending the living, having conversations, and persisting for days before it is revealed as an apparition.

Ref: 316

MOHINI PEY

In the folk belief of Tamil Nadu and Kerala, a Mohini **Pey** or Mohini Pisaasu is the ghost of a woman who died a virgin. These succubi lurk on lonely roads and paths at night, waiting for men to pass by.

Mohini Peys appear ravishingly beautiful, dressed in white saris with jasmine flowers in their hair. The scent of these jasmine flowers is bewitching; once the victim smells them and catches sight of the ghost, he will follow her in a trance. The Mohini Pey then lures him to a secluded place and sucks out his life.

The Mohini Pey doesn't always kill her lover on the first date. Sometimes she toys with him. When a man is visited at night by a Mohini Pey he has vivid hallucinations of sexual intercourse, often waking up in the morning believing the encounter was real, and hungering for more. If he keeps sleeping in the same spot, the Mohini Pey will consume more and more of him until he wastes away.

Mohini Peys can set their legs on fire, and thus use them for cooking.

The Mohini ghost is found in other parts of India, and has become common in tales from Malaysia and Singapore as well. Outside South India, the ghost of a married woman who was killed by her husband is called Mohini; she may prey upon happily married couples as well as bachelors.

The Buttamboj is a similar spirit from the folklore of the Sora tribe of Central India. This is the ghost of a beautiful girl who died just after she began menstruating. She lives in a cotton tree (*Bombax ceiba*), but at night she invades the dreams of young men.

Ref: 11, 351

MOILA DEO

Among the Hajong tribe of Meghalaya, Moila Deo is a spirit of jealousy. The term refers both to an invisible spirit which can possess a man and make him full of envy, and to that man's ghost after he dies.

The spirit looks like a ugly dwarf with long unkempt hair and skin the colour of ash. He wanders through the forest, catching lonely travellers, killing them and eating them. He can also afflict infants; when this happens, he is propitiated with wild bananas, molasses, and pounded rice.

One story tells of a man whose livestock were killed and eaten by a pair of leopards in the night. When he awoke to find his animals missing, he was very annoyed; and when he saw that his neighbour's pen was still full of snorting and bleating animals, he was enraged that his neighbour should have such good fortune while his own should be so bad.

At this moment the Moila Deo possessed him, and the man turned very dangerous.

He took his gun, went to the forest, stalked the leopards and finally shot one. Then he slit open its belly and removed the bile from its liver. He took the bile home, rubbed some of it into a drinking-pot, and poured some beer in it. Then he asked his neighbour to join him for a drink.

Just a few hours later, the neighbour fell sick with excruciating stomach pain and expired.

The dead man's wife called in the *kaviraj*, or diviner, who prepared a potion of trial. This potion would be deadly to a person possessed by Moila Deo; but an innocent man would be able to drink the potion without any ill effect.

The guilty man drank the potion and quickly died. His ghost was rejected by the ghosts of his clan in the underworld, so he was doomed to wander the jungle as a Moila Deo.

Ref: 582

MOMIYAIWALA SAHIB

The Hindi word *momiyai* derives from the Greek word *momijo*. It is commonly used as another term for *shilajit*—a black, tarry substance formed from compressed plant matter that can be found exuding from the rocks of the Himalayas (and a few other mountain ranges). Momijo is mentioned in Aristotle's writings as having healing properties; it has a long history of use in Indian traditional medicine.

During British rule in the 19th and early 20th centuries, a conspiracy theory gained widespread currency in northern India. This theory held that the colonial administrators were involved in the production and sale of a more macabre sort of momiyai—a mixture of shilajit with a powerful magical substance produced from human fat. It was believed that this grisly medicine was obtained by drilling a small hole in the top of a person's head, hanging them up by their feet, and then roasting them alive over a fire until their life force dripped out.

When ingested, the momiyai imbued a person with great vigour and energy—especially if it had been extracted from a child. Momiyai was even rumoured to have the power to transmute base metals to gold and silver. It was believed by many to be the dark secret behind the economic success of the British.

A Momiyaiwala Sahib was a foreigner who roamed around looking for chubby little dark-skinned native boys to abduct and roast in order to procure this substance. He carried a magical device to hypnotize children. In some tellings it was a bent and shrivelled stick, pointed at a victim like a magic wand; in others it was a small, shining mirror. Entranced by the charm, the boys would follow the man blindly. The Momiyaiwala would lure them into a wagon and then pack them off to a momiyai production facility.

Every major city was rumoured to have one of these production centres. British-run hospitals were accused of being involved in the trade as well; it was thought that the doctors extracted momiyai from terminally ill patients. This led many Indians to insist on bringing their loved ones home to die.

Momiyaiwala Sahibs were said to be especially active in hill stations, where foreigners were more common and population densities were lower, so that their nefarious activities could escape detection. However, reports of attempted Momiyaiwala abductions were common in crowded cities like Meerut as well.

During the time the rumour was current, young boys across North India lived in terrible fear of the Momiyaiwala Sahib.

Ref: 74, 532

❧— MONKEY MAN —❧

In the summer of 2001, there was a rash of reports from East Delhi about a four-foot-tall black langur invading people's homes in the middle of the night. The beast reportedly wore a metal helmet and steel claw extensions. Its eyes were flaming orange. Some eyewitnesses claimed it wore roller-skates on its feet; others said there were green lights blinking on its chest.

The news channels dubbed him Kala Bhandar—the Monkey Man. His *modus operandi* was to burst suddenly into a dark room where a victim was sleeping, grab hold of them, and scratch them viciously with its metal claws. Then, just as suddenly, it would make a fleet-footed escape into the darkness, nimbly leaping from building to building over balconies and terraces.

Over 350 sightings of the Kala Bhandar were reported, and sixty injuries. Two or three people died. The deaths occurred when people fell down stairwells or from building tops while trying to escape from the Monkey Man.

Seventeen years later, in 2018, nocturnal attacks by a similar creature were reported from several districts of Manipur. Victims said their assailant had torchlight-like eyes and metal claws. Local press termed it a "Monkeyoid"—a robot or mutant monkey. The creature was said to be able to deflect bullets.

The Manipuri Monkeyoid was also blamed for a rash of unexplained livestock killings that year in Manipur. Connections were drawn to the **Sheep-Killer of Niali**.

Ref: 124, 347

ᵗ᠆ MONOCOLI ᠆ᵗ

According to ancient Greek geographers, the Monocoli were a race of one-legged people who lived in the "furthest east reaches of India". They were said to be able to hop very fast.

Their feet were so big that on hot days, they would lie down on their backs, put their feet up, and lie under them for shade.

There are many legends of one-footed beings in Asia, any of which is a possible source of the Greek belief in Monocoli. These include the Bengali *Ekanore*, a one-legged ghost that haunts palm trees; the Northeastern **Pheichham** and **Maltong**; the *Phi Kong Koi* of Thailand; the Chinese one-footed demon called *Shanxiao*; and the deity *Ekapada*, a one-legged aspect of Shiva.

Ref: 251

ᵗ᠆ MORAKON ᠆ᵗ

A Morakon is a spirit familiar kept by Assamese ojhas (sorcerers) as a pet or assistant. It is the size and shape of a gourd, with two big eyes on opposite sides. It scurries around doing errands.

Sometimes, an ojha will send a Morakon into someone's house to give them a scare. But these spirits are not really capable of doing much harm.

Ref: 448

MORUA

In the tribal folklore of South Andaman (whose indigenous languages are now mostly extinct), Morua are sky-spirits.

Unlike the **Bido Tech Lau** or the **Jurua**, which are ghosts of dead humans, Morua are thought to be the children of Biliku, the goddess of lightning. These spirits sometimes reside at the tops of big *Sterculia* trees, but mostly they live in the sky.

They eat nothing but pork.

Ref: 54

MUDMUDIYA-GUDGUDIYA BHOOT

A Mudmudiya-Gudgudiya Bhoot, also called a Luli Bhoot, is a ghost that has no arms or legs, and moves by rolling along the ground. They are known from the folklore of the Tea Tribes of Assam.

When Mudmudiya-Gudgudiya Bhoots speak, they do so in gobbledygook, a language that has no meaning even to other ghosts.

These spirits are typically included in ghost stories for comedic relief. However, in some stories, they can possess people and cause disability. They are most active at midnight, twilight, and high noon.

Ref: 258

MUGHAL GHOSTS

No dynasty can hope to rule over an entire subcontinent for two centuries and then fade quietly into a peaceful afterlife. The history of the Mughal emperors is so soaked with blood and riven by treachery that it's only natural to find several members of the family lingering on in spectral torment.

Khooni Darwaza

The Khooni Darwaza, or the "Bloody Gate", was built by the Mughal emperor Sher Shah Suri in 1540. At that time it was known simply as Lal Darwaza, the "Red Gate".

Throughout the history of the Mughal Empire and even afterwards, the Khooni Darwaza has been a site of several high-profile killings:

- After Akbar's death in 1605, Emperor Jahangir had two of his step-brother's nephews executed because they opposed his ascension to the throne. Their bodies were hung at the gate to be eaten by birds.

- In 1659, Emperor Aurangzeb cut off the head of his brother, Dara Shukoh, and displayed it on top of the Khooni Darwaza.

- During the Indian Rebellion of 1857, a British officer named Major William Hodson arrested two sons and a grandson of Emperor Bahadur Shah Zafar. He and his men were marching the royals back to the Red Fort when they were surrounded by a huge mob at the Khooni Darwaza. In response, Hodson stripped off the princes' shirts and then shot all three of them in the head at point-blank range in front of thousands of onlookers. The princes' bodies were hung in front of the Chandni Chowk police station and displayed there for days.

- During the 1947 partition of India, there was a riot at the gate where many refugees on their way to a camp at Purana Qila were killed.

Inevitably, given its long history of violence, there are many stories of hauntings at the Khooni Darwaza. Blood is said to drip from the ceiling during monsoons. There is a legend of a headless ghost—presumably that of Dara Shukoh, the murdered brother of Aurangzeb—who haunts the stairways. (These are currently closed to all visitors). There are reports of an invisible force that slaps people's faces, knocks them over, rips their clothes, or whisks away their bags. It is thought that British tourists are particularly at risk of this, since the ones doing the slapping are the ghosts of Bahadur Shah Zafar's sons, out for revenge.

Ghost Funeral

Another legend says that the ghosts of Bahadur Shah Zafar and his wife Begum Zeenat Mahal hold a weekly funeral procession in grief for their sons who were killed at the Khooni Darwaza. This is said to happen every Thursday; they emerge from the Lahore Gate, walk slowly around the perimeter of the Red Fort, and then go back inside. (Both of these rulers actually died and were buried in Yangon, Myanmar, not in Delhi.)

Salimgarh Fort

Zeb-un-nissa was Emperor Aurangzeb's first daughter, and for many years his favourite. Born in 1638, she was said to have become a *hafiza* (a person who can recite the Quran from memory) at age seven. She went on to be a poet and musician of some renown, and wrote many famous ghazals, using the name Makhfi—the "hidden one".

However, in 1682, her father imprisoned her in Salimgarh Fort. There are various theories as to why he did this. Aurangzeb may have been punishing her for an illicit affair, or for indulging in what he saw as blasphemous arts.

Whatever the reason, she spent the last two decades of her life in the fort, finally dying in 1702 due to an illness while her father was away in the south. It is said that her ghost haunts the fort, appearing on moonlit nights wearing a black veil, singing her ghazals.

Zeb-un-Nissa's ghost is not the only one that haunts the fort. Members of Subhash Chandra Bose's Indian National Army were imprisoned and tortured here by the British in 1945, and some of them died in captivity. Their ghosts can sometimes be heard laughing, groaning, or clanking iron shackles.

Ref: 533, 534, 535

MUHNOCHWA

Muhnochwa, which means "face scratcher" in Hindi, was the name given to a mysterious object or creature reported from villages and towns around Lucknow, Uttar Pradesh, in 2002. Police received a rash of reports of late-night home invasions. Several people were assaulted in the dark by something that left bloody claw marks on the victims' faces, necks, and arms. One man was rumoured to have died after his stomach was clawed open by the Muhnochwa.

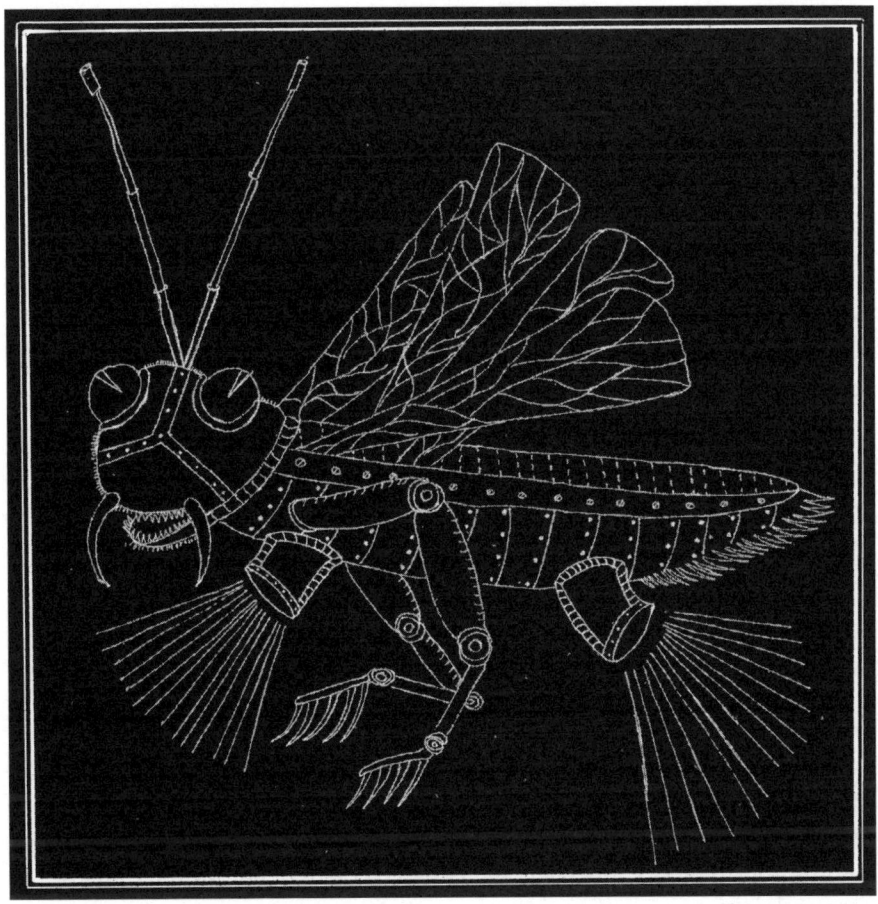

The thing was said to be roughly spherical in shape, about ten inches long. Some said it had wings like a bat, and emitted bright red and blue lights from both front and behind; however, it always flew away too quickly for anyone to get a good look at it. Some people claimed that it gave a powerful electric shock.

A wave of paranoia and panic gripped the region for several weeks. One Barabanki housewife woke up in the middle of the night to the sound of what she believed was the Muhnochwa breaking into her house. She had thrashed it within an inch of its life before the lights came on and she realized she had been beating her hapless husband, who had returned home late.

Another man shot his dog to death after it licked his face in his sleep.

At one point, a 10,000-strong mob formed and demanded that the authorities take action against the Muhnochwa. The protesters dispersed only when the police began firing gunshots in the air.

Various theories for the true identity of the Muhnochwa were put forward. Some people thought they were tiny alien spaceships. Others blamed evil spirits. Scientists ascribed the sightings to ball lightning, an unexplained phenomenon usually reported during thunderstorms. The police claimed the creatures were giant metallic insects—possibly related to the nocturnal, carnivorous cricket *Schizodactylus monstrosus*. One deputy inspector general went on record with speculation that genetically modified bugs had been released in the area by Pakistani infiltrators with the aim of destabilizing the country.

After a few months, the attacks stopped.

Ref: 280, 320, 433

MUNG

In the mythology of the Lepcha people of Sikkim, the Mung are a diverse class of malignant devils. They are the enemies of the Rum, the good spirits and deities.

In the earliest times, after the goddess Itbu Debu Rum created the world, she took the snow of the mighty mountain Kanchenjunga and shaped it into two beings. She named them Nazong Nyu and Fadrong Thing. While they had the appearance of a woman and a man, they were not mortal humans but powerful deities.

Itbu Debu Rum wanted her two creations to live separately, as brother and sister. So she made Fadrong Thing's home on the top of a tall mountain, and Nazong Nyu's in the foothills.

But as Nazong Nyu and Fadrong Thing grew up, they began to desire each other. Defying her mother, Nazong Nyu built a staircase so she could secretly visit Fadrong Thing at night.

Nazong Nyu soon became pregnant by Fadrong Thing. But when her first child was born, Nazong Nyu became terrified of what her creator-goddess-mother would do to her for breaking the incest taboo. So she asked Fadrong Thing to go and abandon it in a cave in the jungle, which he did.

Nazong Nyu and Fadrong Thing kept up their clandestine meetings, and she became pregnant again and again. She bore six more children. After each delivery, Fadrong Thing took the squalling infant to the jungle cave and left it there.

Finally, when her eighth child was born, Nazong Nyu's maternal instincts became too powerful to deny. She nursed this child from her breast, and cared for him tenderly. This became the first human, named Ralbusingu.*

After that Nazong Nyu bore many more human children, and nursed them all. These humans had children of their own. Soon they went out into the world and became the Lepchas.

Meanwhile, the seven children whom Nazong Nyu had discarded had somehow managed to survive. These beings grew up on their own, and became the first Mung.

The King of the Mung

The first-born son of Nazong Nyu, and the first to be abandoned, was *Laso Mung Pano*. As the eldest and strongest of the Mung, he soon became their leader.

Laso Mung Pano hated his human siblings with a passion. He was bitterly jealous of the way his parents treated them with so much love and affection while completely ignoring him and the other Mung. He spoke his mind forcefully to his Mung brothers and sisters, preaching hatred and violence against the Lepcha. It didn't take long before he had rallied all the other Mung to the cause of wiping them from the Earth.

The names of the other original six Mung vary in different versions of the myth. In one telling, they are:

Arot Mung, the demon of violent death, who has a long, hooked beak. He haunts Mount Tendon in South Sikkim, and takes exactly two lives every year. He appears in dreams as a red butterfly.

Sor Mung appears as a woman with long dishevelled hair. She is the demon of lust and wantonness. She also causes miscarriages, and less serious afflications like coughs and colds. Her coming is foretold by dreams of a kite flying in the sky.

Dom Mung, the demon of leprosy.

---

* In some versions, it was two twins who were the first humans, and their names were Ralbu and Singu.

Khung Mung, the demon of youthful lust, who tempts young Lepchas into premarital sex.

Soomu Mung, the demoness who appears in the night as an ugly, dirty woman to harass lonely travellers.

Chen Mung, the demon who causes rheumatism, body aches, and fever. He lives in rocks and caves in the deepest, thickest part of the forest.

As for Laso Mung Pano, he was a powerful illusionist, capable of changing his shape into many forms.

Laso Mung Pano began killing many Lepcha people, and soon the Rum—the benevolent deities—decided they needed to put a stop to it. They came after him, but Laso Mung Pano hid in Sanyol Kung, a giant sago palm tree at the top of a mountain. The Rum tried to chop the tree down, but whatever progress they made during the day would be undone during the night, as the tree magically regenerated itself. Finally, they enlisted the help of a hairy caterpillar named Patyok Bu, who ate through the tree's trunk and sent it toppling over.

But this only prompted Laso Mung Pano to unleash his rage in full effect. Taking the form of a gargantuan black bird with eyes of fire, he spread his wings and flew from the tree as it crashed to the ground. Then he went on a lethal rampage through the villages of Dzongu Valley, gobbling up the inhabitants or massacring them in gruesome ways. In some villages he simply liquidated the entire population; in others, he exterminated everyone by means of a deadly blast of sound, like the cawing of an infernal crow. No one was safe from the demon. He murdered and ate men, women, and children alike. He would even dig people out of their hiding places and torture them before killing them.

The creator goddess Itbu Debu Rum decided she needed to create a hero to combat Laso Mung Pano. From the snows of Mount Pandim, she made the demigod Tamsang Thing. This Tamsang Thing was the hero who brought magic to the Lepchas; he taught the two types of Lepcha shamans, the *mun* and *bongthing*, how to perform their ritual arts. He and the humans began a long war against Laso Mung Pano, one which lasted many years.

As Tamsang Thing and the Lepcha warriors pursued Laso Mung Pano, the demon tried changing his shape. First he became a mouse; then an ox; then a tiger, an eagle, a dragon, a snake, a horse, a sheep, a monkey, a bird, a dog, and a pig, spending one year in the form of each animal. These are now the animals associated with the twelve-year cycle of the Lepcha calendar.

Finally, on the twenty-ninth day of the last month of the twelfth year of the war, the demon was chased to a high valley, and there he was slain by Jor Bongthing, the first Lepcha shaman.

After Laso Mung Pano was killed, his gigantic corpse was mutilated to make sure he didn't come back to life. His eyeballs were punctured, his limbs and head were cut off, and his still-warm muscles were removed, shredded, pulverized to dust, and blown into the air.

Some say that parts of the demon's body turned to stone after he died, and can still be seen in the rocks.

And yet even then, vitality remained in the marrow of the monster's bones, and new demons sprang forth from them.

Today, there are ten clans (called *moo*) in Lepcha society, and each clan is named for their ancestors who fought in the war against Laso Mung Pano and the role they played in it. For example, Kurwo Moo are the descendants of those who made the swords and axes to fight the demon; Joriboo Moo are the descendants of those who provided food and water to Tamsang Thing and the human soldiers on the front lines; and Simik Moo are the descendants of those who went forward to poke out his eyes after he was dead.

Though their king had been vanquished, the Mung did not stop harassing the Lepcha. There were still Laso Mung Pano's six Mung siblings and their children to contend with, along with the new Mung born from Laso Mung Pano's bone marrow.

The cruel depredations of these demons went on and on until it became too much for even the gods to bear. Finally, the creator goddess Itbu Debu Rum asked Kumya Kumshi Thing, the mediator of the deities, to come and intercede.

Kumya Kumshi Thing called a general meeting for the Rum and Mung. It was attended by all the Mung—except Dom Mung, who somehow missed the message. Kumya Kumshi Thing gave an impassioned speech, imploring the evil spirits to stop bothering the humans. Despite his best efforts, he could not convince them to give up their hatred for humans entirely. But he did get them to promise that, as long as the humans propitiated them with some grain or an animal sacrifice, they would leave them alone.

So from that time onwards, by means of various rituals and offerings, the Lepchas were able to keep the demonic attacks to a manageable level. They were able to find cures for most of the illnesses the Mung caused. However, since Dom Mung missed the meeting and never made the promise, there was (for many years) no cure for leprosy.

Afterward, both the Lepcha and the Mung prospered and multiplied, but the Mung were even more fruitful than the Lepcha. Today they occupy nearly every corner of the Earth. There are Mung who reside in strangely shaped rocks, in old trees, in swamps, and in marshes. They are especially abundant in virgin forest. It has been said that there are more demons and spirits and other supernatural entities inhabiting the environment of Sikkim than there are human beings,* and if there were to be a census, the vast majority would be Mung.

Some Lepchas say that there is also a separate realm called Mung Lyang, a country wholly populated by devils; another source gives the name of this land as Mashyok Matel. The term Mung Lyang is sometimes translated into English as "hell"; but the original concept is different, in that it is neither a land of suffering, nor a destination for human souls. There is a mango tree in this world which has hanging from its branches, instead of mangos, the hearts of the dead, and the Mung feed greedily on this macabre fruit.

Most Mung, though not all, are humanoid in appearance. Many of those who do have a human shape are described as having huge goitres. Most of them wear clothes, but a few go naked. Female Mung have extremely long, bushy pubic hair.†

Mung can keep their spirits outside their bodies, making it impossible to kill them unless the secret hiding places are known. For example, a Mung might keep his spirit in a tree, in a school of fish in a stream, and in a honeybee. When the tree is chopped and the fish are caught and the honeybee is burnt in a fire, the demon falls sick and dies.

Mung typically live in families, with social structures similar to those of humans. Female Mung are more open to having extramarital relations with humans than male Mung are, though they usually kill and eat their lovers in the end. In one folktale, a female Mung even helps her human lover murder her Mung husband. But the relationship is still an abusive one. After her husband is dead, the Mung feeds the man poisoned rice beer which puts him to sleep for three years—during which time she covers him with mud, puts three stones on his chest, and uses him as a hearth for cooking.

There are also stories about adventurers who encountered monasteries full of Mung. In these institutions, the demon-monks busied themselves by piling up mutilated bodies.

Mung are ravenous carnivores, and a typical meal might include a few human corpses, a few whole cows, and a horse or two, all stewed in separate pots. When

---

* Attributed to the Buddhist lama Lopen Dogyal.
† One tale features a female Mung in pursuit of a human. Her quarry keeps hiding, but her bush always magically points in his direction, so she keeps looking at her crotch to guide her.

meat is not available, they eat charcoal with earthworm relish, and a few varieties of bitter fruit that humans consider inedible. Most Mung are nocturnal: they are at their most powerful in the wee hours of the night, and weakest in the late afternoon. They speak in a shrill, high-pitched whine, with broken syllables and strange grammar. When Lepcha storytellers tell tales about the Mung, they often imitate this "devil language"—either to enhance the creepiness, or for comedic effect, depending on what sort of story it is.

Lepcha traditional religion has been described as "a permanent hand-to-hand fight with the Mung". There are an astounding number of these demons, and an incredible variety of rituals for propitiating them, placating them, warding them away, or killing them. The list that follows is merely an incomplete list of the Mung that have been named in published English-language literature.*

Ginoo Mung Pandi is the Queen of the Mung; her descendents are also called Ginoo Mung.

The origin of these spirits dates back to a human family by the name of Ginoo, from a place called Lingthem in North Sikkim. The family consisted of seven brothers and one sister. The seven brothers all lived together, and each had a wife and a son and a daughter and a son-in-law and a daughter-in-law who lived with them. They were struggling to feed all these mouths, just barely managing to make ends meet; they possessed no jewels or oxen or land of their own.

Their sister, on the other hand, was a widow who lived alone, with only one daughter, and she had plenty of wealth. She was also a powerful *mun*, or shaman.

The brothers, covetous of their sister's riches, conspired to murder her. They snuck into her house one night, hacked her to bits, and stole her jewellery and cattle.

But so great were the woman's magical powers that the pieces of her body joined back together, and she lived once more. The next day, the brothers found a trail of blood leading to a tall rock wall with a door in it which they could not open. Behind that door, their sister had gone into *munthen*, a religious meditation.

At the end of the seven days she succeeded in summoning a vicious, powerful she-demon. She unleashed this Mung to wreak vengeance upon her brothers.

---

* Due to different transliteration schemes and variations in dialects, it is possible that some of the same demons are listed under two different names.

Within a year, every member of that large family—save the woman's own daughter—was dead.

This demoness was given the name Ginoo Mung Pandi, "Ginoo Demon Queen", after the murderous brothers she was summoned to destroy. She is also sometimes called Lingthem Anyou, "Lady of Lingthem," after the place where the killings occurred. From that time she went forth to prey upon others, attacking and destroying anyone who amassed too much wealth or who had too many children.

To this day, Lepchas say that it is dangerous to speak too loudly about your possessions, lest the Ginoo Mung overhear and decide to cut you down.

Mara Mung is Laso Mung Pano's afterbirth. He lives high on a mountain in the hollow of a tree. He sometimes manifests as strange lights in the sky, such as comets and auroras.

Num-een Mung, also called **Chumje Mung**, is a demon which comes into existence after the death of a child under the age of ten. Such children are not considered fully developed people yet, and receive only cursory burial rituals. The demon-ghosts of these children haunt their families for about three years after their deaths. A Num-een Mung becomes active during storms, when it can be heard howling ominously in the wind. It mostly haunts other children, especially its siblings and cousins, trying to make them fall prey to fatal illnesses so that they too will turn into Num-een Mung. The ritual for driving out Num-een involves the *mun* shaman building a gateway over a narrow stream. A bamboo vessel should be filled with a mixture of blood and rice beer, and some fried rice and meat should be wrapped in a banana leaf; the *mun* must pass both of these things over the victim's body, and then throw them through the gateway as offerings to the demon. Then the *mun* should fill the gateway up with nettles and wild raspberries and other thorny plants. He then proceeds to build two more gateways like this, one upstream and one downstream, and fill them up with nettles. Finally he has to run home without meeting anyone. (If he sees someone on the way, the Num-een Mung will possess that person.)

Ingbong Mung is the demon ghost of a stillborn child. This type of spirit searches for other children to afflict with infantile diarrhoea. Ingbong Mungs manifest as small dust devils; they make cooing or crying sounds as they whirl about. It is easier to get rid of an Ingbong Mung than a Num-een Mung. To kill an Ingbong Mung, one person should chase it towards another person who waits with a knife. Then that person should slice it through with his blade. The next day, if a dead insect is found at the spot, this means that the demon has been vanquished. (All sorts of Mung can take the shape of insects, especially in rituals devised to control and kill them.)

Rot Mung is the demon which causes people to commit suicide. Suicide and other forms of violent deaths are thought to be hereditary, with Rot Mung or Arot Mung attaching themselves to families. The relatives of suicide victims used to perform an annual ritual called *Mung Sot*, "killing the Mung", to ensure that the demon would not return for their friends or relatives. A goat would be killed and skinned (though not completely; the skin would be kept attached to the feet), and laid on its back next to a pit, and a bamboo structure would be built over it. Next to the goat, a post would be stuck in the ground, with the goat's heart on top of the post, and a banana flower stuck in the ground next to the post, so that the blood from the heart would drip onto it. A man with a bow would stand facing the goat's rear, and several other men would stand about with knives drawn, while the *mun* stood facing in the opposite direction. Then the *mun* would summon Rot Mung in the shape of an insect, which would start climbing up the post towards the goat heart. It was the job of the man with the bow to shoot the insect with an arrow; if he missed, the demon had to be summoned again. After the insect was killed, the men with knives would chop the goat to bits and bury it with the insect in the pit.

Chyom Mung is a demon that pushes people off cliffs, or makes them fall to their deaths from tall trees. The ritual to ward away this demon is similar to the one used for Rot Mung. It is associated with the colour green.

Shom Mung is a demon who creeps up behind people and whispers a suicidal or murderous suggestion in their ear. *Jump into that ravine*, it says, or *Push your friend over the edge*. When Shom Mung kills a person, it possesses their soul, and will not allow it to travel to the afterlife. In order to release the soul, a different Mung Sot ritual is performed the night after the funeral, in which a wide, shallow vessel is filled with the blood of a sacrificed goat. The *mun*, this time dressed in red, goes into a trance, and summons Shom Mung into the blood; when the spirit arrives, the *mun* throws a grass whisk into the vessel, and begins to beat the blood with a flat wooden stick. Other relatives join in in beating the blood with various knives and weapons. Finally, the blood is poured into a pit outside, and buried there along with all the weapons used in the ritual. If this is not done, Shom Mung will return and kill the other members of the family.

Mamoo Mung is a demoness of sickness. She is depicted as a black or indigo-skinned naked woman with snakes for hair, either seated on a tiger, or sitting with her legs splayed. She lives in caves whose entrances point north or west, and she has the power to call thunderstorms. She is propitiated with offerings of copper pots and clothes.

Jyamphi Mung is the Lepcha **Yeti**, a huge, ferocious, and hairy beast. It has its feet pointing backwards. Jyamphi Mungs love music and are attracted by flutes or whistling. For this reason, whistling is taboo among the Lepchas, especially in the nighttime or at dawn, or when walking high in the mountains. The Jyamphi Mung itself makes a long, spooky whistle as it roams around in the dark in search of food.

Though fierce, these creatures are not very intelligent.

Male and female Jyamphi Mungs do not live together. They meet just once a year to mate, and then go their separate ways. The female of the species is much larger and more aggressive than the male, but a bit slower, as her gigantic pendulous breasts weigh her down somewhat. It is said that in order to escape from a female Jyamphi Mung, one should always run downhill, for her breasts will get in her way and make it hard for her to give chase. While running uphill, she simply throws them over her shoulders onto her back, so she can outrun most humans.

Jyamphi Mungs live on the highest peaks of the Himalayas. But it was not always so. The story goes that a herdsman named Aatek, who lived in a remote place in the foothills, used to sit by his fire playing his bamboo flute in the evenings after work and dinner were done. One day, by playing his music, he accidentally attracted a female Jyamphi Mung, who sat down near him to listen. When Aatek put down his flute, the Jyamphi Mung picked it up and tried to imitate his actions, but could not produce a sound. So she gave the flute back to him and motioned for him to continue. Aatek had to play all night; if he stopped, the creature would become angry and threaten to kill him.

At dawn, the Jyamphi Mung left. But she came back that night, and every night afterwards, to force Aatek to play his flute for her. Aatek could hardly get any sleep.

Finally, remembering how the Jyamphi Mung had tried to imitate his flute-playing, Aatek had an idea. That night, when the creature arrived, he began doing a little dance as he played. He would stop now and then to smear butter all over his body. The monster, entranced by the music, started to copy his actions, and began smearing butter all over her own body too. Then Aatek took a log from the fire and pretended to rub it on himself. The Jyamphi Mung imitated this action as well—but in the process, she set her long buttered hair ablaze! Screaming in pain, she ran towards the cold snowy peaks to put out the fire, and disappeared into the night.

It is said that ever since this incident, Jyamphi Mungs avoid the foothills, and live only at very high altitudes.

Chu Mung is the demon who lives on the glaciers, and **Lho Mung** is the demon of the highest mountains. Both of these beings are described as ape-like, and they may both be conspecific with the Jyamphi Mung, with *chu* ("glacier") and *lho* ("mountain peak") simply indicating places where the creature can be found. Another name is **Mi Gat Mung**, a demon who lives so high in the mountains that only its footprints are ever seen. There are both male and female varieties. These Mung have a somewhat more positive aspect than the others, as they are considered the lords of wild beasts; hunters make offerings to them and are blessed with good luck in return.

Chu Mung is sometimes encountered in the form of an abandoned, apparently human baby. When the infant is taken home, it starts growing freakishly fast and sprouting hair all over its body. When this happens the Mung-child should be returned to the mountain wilderness as soon as possible.

Thloh Mung is another ape-like creature that was said to live in the mountainous forests long ago. It was the size and shape of a man—much smaller than the Jyamphi Mung—and had thick black hair all over its body. It could climb through trees as nimbly as it could walk on the ground. It lived alone or in small family groups. It was said to be both ferocious and very clever, and Lepcha hunters could never catch it.

Some say that human encroachment into the forest drove the Thloh Mung to extinction. Others believe that the creature simply moved to other regions, and is synonymous with the **Mande Burung** of Meghalaya.

Soo Mung, **Ge Mung**, and **Thor Mung** are demons who cause disputes and quarrels. Soo Mung is the demoness of hateful speech; Ge Mung is the demon of hateful thought; Thor Mung is the demon of hateful action. They combine to form the evil trinity **Soo-Ge-Thor**. There is an annual ritual to exorcize Soo-Ge-Thor from the community, in which an effigy of the demon is shot by an archer and then hacked to pieces by the crowd. Finally the pieces of the images are collected, stuffed into tubes of bamboo along with strips of paper inscribed with the demon's name, and burnt.

Soo Mung seems to be the same demon referred to in older accounts as *Tssu Mung*, who was represented by a dog's skull covered with paper, placed in a prison of sticks of bamboo, and surrounded with bladed weapons. Flowers were offered to Tssu Mung to entice her into the prison so that she couldn't stir up trouble.

Tamsi Mung is another demon who causes arguments, but he is associated with more serious ones, including outbreaks of war. He is exorcized by a ceremony in which his image is stamped on a piece of paper; the paper is surrounded by thirteen crossed sticks; then the demon is summoned onto the paper in the form of an insect, and a group of lamas stab it to death with a ceremonial dagger. Finally the paper and the dead insect are stuffed into the skull of a rat.

Hlamen Djeme is an interesting case; he is considered a Rum when appeased, but a Mung when angry. He comes from a separate, Lamaist spiritual tradition practised by the Lepcha, and is somewhat of a guest in the Mung pantheon.

Dut Mung are fever-demons who appear as men with long hair growing all over their bodies. There are seven of them, and each may appear with any number of heads between one and five. In ancient times they were the first blacksmiths, and the first possessors of fire. These spirits live in large, isolated trees, or sometimes under small waterfalls. They can also reside in objects made of gold or in animal skins. If such a possessed object is brought into a house it can bring sickness and death to the occupants until it is disposed of.

When Lepchas choose sites to build their houses, it is important that the road to the house does not come from the south or west, as these roads are used by Dut Mung.

Dut Mung can attack people with an invisible chain, which causes them to die a few days later. They are eaters of souls; sometimes the soul of a victim is devoured a few weeks or months prior to the person's actual death. A Dut Mung sometimes joins forces with Tshen Mung to cause rheumatism or body aches; or he forms a trinity with Mamoo Mung and Tshen Mung—"Mamoo Dut Tshen"—which causes a swollen stomach.

One of the Dut Mung is married to Soomu Mung, one of the original Mung siblings from the creation myth. They live in a house in the jungle, like normal humans, along with their children and a servant named Su Mo Thor. In her true form, Soomu Mung is a haggard ogress with large flaccid breasts and matted hair; but she has the power to transform her appearance by brushing her hair back and running her palms over her body so that she looks like a voluptuous young woman. In this way she seduces young travellers to come back to her house. If she likes them, she toys with them for a while before torturing and killing and eating them. Sometimes her husband joins in the fun.

Ma Zom Mung is a demon who appears as a huge black fire-breathing dog with blazing eyes. He often tries to haunt houses where a death has just occurred. For this reason, people coming back from a funeral are advised to set up thorny bracken along the path to bar the demon's way. The night after the funeral, the relatives of the deceased heat three stones on the hearth. Then they place them outside, and call Ma Zom Mung's name, telling him to come and eat some meat. The greedy demon comes to swallow the stones, gets burnt, and runs away.

Sande Mung is a death demon. If Sande Mung is determined to have been responsible for a person's (non-violent) death, then after the disposal of the corpse, a ritual is performed immediately in which an effigy is built from powdered grain: a cat with a long tail and a horse saddle, upon which sits a small rider, with two more figures in front ahead and behind. This effigy is then led out of the village, while people beat all corners of the house and neighbouring houses with weapons to ensure that the Mung does not return.

Shidook Mung is another death demon; like Sande Mung, it is responsible for non-violent deaths. (Violent deaths are caused by Arot Mung.) If Shidook Mung is responsible for a death, the ritual for expurgating the demon takes place two months after the death. It involves animal sacrifice and the construction of a "demon's palace", a tower of polyhedra fashioned from black thread, with weapons placed in sets of thirteen at the base, and a ceramic cup with nine handles.

While Sande Mung, Shidook Mung, and Arot Mung are the demons who *cause* deaths, **Maknyam Mung** is the demon of death itself—the state into which every human must pass at the end of life.

Karo Mung is a troublesome but non-lethal demon summoned by evil thoughts, such as being unreasonably annoyed with someone, or jealous of their possessions. If the person who unleashes Karo Mung is remorseful and wishes to withdraw it, they can do so by means of a ritual involving chanting and beating drums in the dark.

Chumen Mung is a demon who troubles couples who have clashing horoscopes—e.g. incompatible year signs. The dream-sign of this Mung is a broken-down house near a stream. Those afflicted by Chumen Mung should not wear black.

Rumdu Mung is the demon of smallpox, sometimes said to be one of the original six brothers of Laso Mung Pano.

Namjet Mung is a fever-demon sent by an enemy to trouble another person.

Sabdok Mung and his wife *Loo Mung* reside in outcroppings of rock. They cause rashes and other skin problems. An angry Sabdok Mung can also prevent a man from having any sons.

Cherko Mung causes whooping cough. Curiously, he is a "foreign" Mung; when he possesses a shaman, he speaks only in Nepali, rather than Lepcha.

Rung Si Mung is a demoness who causes nightmares in children. She always carries an umbrella.

Sang Rong Mung is a tiny, baby-sized demon, used by parents as a bogeyman to keep their older children from playing with infants. ("Don't go near the baby, it's a Sang Rong Mung and it will eat you.")

Sung Grong Mung is a demon who steals children. She comes in the form of a girl with very long hair.

Sang Grong Mung is a half-man half-ape who lives in deep caves in the mountains with his wife. This couple are always hungry for human flesh, and offer gifts of food to entice travellers into their lair. If a person refuses the gift, he is lost. The only way to survive is to accept it, but on the back of the hand, instead of in the palm.

Meloan Mung are a family of man-eating Mung who live in a cave set in the face of a cliff.

Num Shang Mung is the spirit of barrenness.

Num 'Ayeen Mung is the spirit of chronic diseases.

'Ayon Mung is a demon who comes in the form of wild animals.

'Ayot Mung is the demon of jaundice.

Ta-an Mung is the demon of œdema.

Nyi Dyop Mung is the demon that causes the common cold.

Apal Mung is a demon who frightens little children.

Tong Mung is the white-haired demon of old age.

Tyak Glot Mung is a ravenous, devouring demon.

Na Ru Mung is the demon of wasting diseases and tuberculosis.

Na Vyar Mung is the demon of impatience, excitableness, and hastiness.

Tuk Prap Mung is the demon of gout.

Fon Mung is a demon who encourages infidelity and adultery.

Bun Shu Mung is the demon of indigestion.

Bong Mung is the demon of stupidity.

Nat Mung is a mischief-making demon and noxious spirit.

Mang Mung is the demon of sorrow and depression.

Payon Mung is the demon that causes dysentery; he is called by the positive name *Payon Rum* so as not to antagonize him.

Da Bru Mung is a demon that screeches in the night, associated with owls.

Pazok Mung is a demon who lives in the forest.

Ta-lyang Mung is the demon of the heavens, who causes sunstroke and moonstroke.

Tong-ryong Mung is a demon who takes the shape of a tiger and chases people down and kills them in the forest.

Sa Kyar Mung is a demon who bothers people sleeping outside at night by throwing dirt on them.

Thing Mung and his wife ***Nyo Mung*** can kill a person by cutting the cord of their fate.

Sa Tim Mung is the demon of cholera.

Sungi Mung is the demon of venereal disease.

Mung-Shin Mung is the demon of foul smells.

Yeng Dor Mung is the demon of sloth.

Rung-Mang Mung is the demon of delirium.

Pa Hu Mung is the demon of plague and contagion.

Mi-toor is an unkillable dog.

Ref: 28, 31, 60, 61, 116, 199, 213, 235, 236, 274, 350, 351, 430, 529

MUNI

Muni is a short form of Muniyandi, Muniappan, or Muneeshwaran. All three of these are names for village gods from South India.

Munis appear as handsome, virile men with large moustaches. Some are more ferocious than others. There is something of a continuum: at one extreme are the benevolent protector deities who preside over village festivals, such as the bull-wrestling event known as *jallikattu*. At the opposite extreme are voracious evil spirits who abduct human women and eat their babies. Somewhere in the middle is another type of vengeful-ghost Muni, the spirit of someone who was murdered or wronged in life. These Munis come back from the dead to punish the guilty and restore justice to towns overrun by corruption and criminal enterprise.

Malevolent Munis, though frightening, are also fairly easy to fool. One story tells of a woman who was abducted by one of these fiends and forced to marry him. The day after she came to live in his house, her husband went out hunting, but didn't catch anything. The woman had guessed that this would happen, and she knew it meant he would come home so ravenously hungry that he would probably eat her up. So she made an effigy of herself out of jaggery and rice flour and placed it at the door. When the Muni came home intending to eat his bride, he ate the effigy instead, and the woman escaped before he discovered the deception.

The weapon of Muniyandi is the trident, and outside any of his shrines a trident will be found stuck in the ground with limes skewered on its prongs.

The Muneeshwara of Chengalpattu

Edgar Thurston, the former superintendent of the Madras Government Museum, recounted in his 1912 book *Omens and Superstitions of Southern India* an incident that had occurred many years before in Chengalpattu, in what is now Tamil Nadu.

Some members of a nomadic tribe had set up camp on a hill with a large herd of cattle. Villagers used to come and take the cow dung for fertilizer. The tribespeople singled out one of the villagers and put him in charge of this commodity, giving him all the fertilizer he wanted for himself and letting him apportion the rest to his neighbours.

A week or so later, the tribe invited this man for a festival to honour their goddess. When the man arrived, they fed him a great feast, and plied him with tremendous quantities of liquor. At midnight, when he was good and drunk, they took him to a pit in the ground which had been prepared for him and buried him up to his neck. Then they covered his head with cow dung, lit a diya on top of it, and finally drove their whole herd of cattle over his head.

The man's body and crushed skull were found by the villagers the next morning. The tribespeople had all cleared out of the area with their animals and belongings in the night.

The ritual was said to have been conducted to insure the tribe's cattle against death from disease.

It was believed that the victim of this particular sacrifice became a Muni. For many years afterward, his spirit troubled anyone who ventured too close to the spot where he died, especially at noon or midnight.

Ref: 291, 292, 379

⤜᠃⤛ MUNJYA ⤛᠃⤜

Some Hindu and Jain communities hold a ceremony for their boy children just before they start their formal education. This is called the *upanayana* ceremony, during which a sacred thread is tied around the torso, over the left shoulder and under the right. A girdle made of *munja* grass is also tied around the waist. This ceremony is usually done around the age of seven.

In the folklore of Maharashtra and the Konkan coast, a Munjya is the ghost of a boy who dies after his upanayana ceremony but before getting married.

Munjyas inhabit peepal trees. These bachelor ghosts are very restless, spending the whole night jumping from branch to branch and tree to tree. They are said to be very clever, and to have the ability to speak in many languages—even the languages of animals.

Most Munjyas are not particularly menacing. They can even be helpful and friendly, especially to children. But they can still give a good scare. They react violently if anyone defiles the tree in which they live—whether by drinking alcohol beneath it, throwing garbage at its base, or urinating on it. In such cases the Munjya may retaliate by pelting the offender with stones or scorching him with fire.

A few Munjya stories describe more vicious spirits. One tells of a ghost that caused multiple deaths by jumping out in front of a group of horse-drawn tongas as they passed his tree. The terrified animals went into a panicked gallop that ended with the human passengers lying crushed in a ditch.

Munjyas sometimes possess living humans with the aim of dying inside their bodies, so as to free the soul for reincarnation. A ghost in search of a host body will hover invisibly near a tired person on a sweltering afternoon. Then, when the person opens his or her mouth too wide to yawn and fails to cover it with a hand, the Munjya swoops inside. This type of Munjya is extremely dangerous, for they consider murder a less grievous sin than suicide; therefore, instead of having the occupied body kill itself, they force it to kill as many other people as possible, in the hopes of attracting a death penalty.

Ref: 74

⟩⤙ MURA ⤚⟨

In Mizo mythology, the Mura was a gigantic predatory bird that lived in the times of the earliest men. It was like a huge eagle, so big that it could feed on human children and sometimes even adults.

The Mura had a wicked tactic for hunting people. It would perch on the roof of a hut, and then stick its monstrous tail in through the back door. The people in the house would become terrified and try to flee through the front door... where the Mura's head would be, waiting to snatch them up and eat them.

There is a legend about a Great War of Animals that took place in ancient times, in which the creatures of the air were pitted against the creatures of the land. The war initially broke out because of a dispute between the Mura and a giant python. The Mura was the leader of the army of the flying creatures. Humans, being unable to fly, fought alongside the creatures of the land.

The Mura was finally killed by a human named Mualbueva.

Ref: 508

⟩⤙ NAALE BA BHOOTA ⤚⟨

The Naale Ba Bhoota is a female ghost that knocks on the doors of houses late at night. In some tales she comes begging for alms with dishevelled hair and tattered clothes. In others, she is dressed in a bridal sari and draped with jewellery; she arrives in search of a man to steal away to be her groom, calling his name in a voice that he finds eerily familiar, but unplaceable.

Either way, if you open the door to this ghost, you won't live to see the morning.

Luckily, it is easy to protect yourself against her. All you have to do is write *Naale Baa* or *Naale Baa, Bhoota* on the outside of your door with turmeric paste or charcoal. This means "Come back tomorrow, ghost" in Kannada. After reading this message, the ghost leaves, and returns the next night—only to be turned away again, *ad infinitum*.

Sometimes, a *naamam* of three horizontal lines is added below the slogan. This is interpreted by the ghost as "You get nothing."

The story of the Naale Ba Bhoota was especially popular as an urban legend in Bangalore in the 1990s. The phrase was written on the doors of hundreds of thousands of flats throughout the city.

The same method of turning away a ghost or evil spirit is known in Andhra Pradesh (the Telugu phrase is *O Sthree repu raa*) and in Tamil Nadu (*Indru poi, naale va*).

Ref: 407

NAAR MOKAL

In Kashmiri folklore, the Naar Mokal is a spirit made of fire. Wherever it steps, it starts a blaze. It can jump quickly from house to house, burning down whole villages.

Ref: 94

⤙ NAGA ⤚

The mythological race of Nagas is common to Hindu, Buddhist, and Jain tradition. Their cult of worship in South Asia is so ancient that it may in fact predate all of these religions. They feature in folktales from Afghanistan all the way to the Philippines, but are perhaps most closely associated with Jammu and Kashmir.

These beings can manifest either as cobras, as humans, or as hybrid creatures with human torsos and snake-like tails. They breathe fire. Sometimes they are described as having a flaming halo flickering around their heads and shoulders. They are the traditional enemies of the bird-like **Garudas**.

The realm of the Nagas is Naga Lok, a magical underworld filled with jewels. It is sometimes identified with Paataal Lok, home of the **Yakshas**. Pools, lakes, springs and rivers are the portals through which Nagas enter the human realm: in the Kashmiri language, such a lake is called a Nag.

One famous passage to Naga Lok is supposed to lie at the bottom of a well located in Varanasi.

Some Nagas reside in the forest at the base of Mount Meru, the five-peaked mountain at the centre of the worlds.

Several works of ancient Sanskrit and Tamil literature describe semi-historical Naga tribes that inhabited the surface world. Some texts place these tribes in Northwest India; others, like the Tamil epic *Manimegalai*, place them on the Jaffna peninsula of Sri Lanka. Though these Nagas are described as having supernatural powers and the ability to change into snakes, scholars think the legends may be based on real tribes whose religions involved snake-worship.*

Some Nagas are worshipped as Hindu demigods, especially on Nag Panchami, a festival falling in the month of Shravana (July or August). Perhaps the most familiar is Adisesha, the thousand-headed cobra, the primordial serpent in Hindu mythology. He is a cosmic entity who floats coiled up on the Ocean of Milk and holds all the planets in his hoods. He will continue to exist when all else is destroyed at the end of the *kalpa* (the current æon, one day in the life of Brahma, lasting 4.32 billion years).

Another well known Naga, Vasuki, is most often seen coiled around Lord Shiva's neck; in the centre of his forehead is a sacred jewel called a *naga mani*. Vasuki was used by the gods as a rope to wrap around Mount Meru during the

---

* Not to be confused with the Naga tribes of Nagaland and Manipur. That ethnonym "Naga" is apparently unrelated, and has nothing to do with snakes.

Churning of the Ocean of Milk. His sister Padmavati, also known as Manasa or Nagalakshmi, is worshipped as the goddess of snakes.

In the *Mahabharata*, a clan of Nagas under King Takshaka lives in the Khandava Forest before being banished by the hero Arjuna. There is also a kingdom of Nagas beneath the river Ganga; Ulupi, the warrior-princess of this kingdom, became one of Arjuna's wives.

The term "Nagaraja", King of the Nagas, usually refers to one of Adisesha, Vasuki, or Takshaka.

Among the inimical Nagas of Hindu mythology, probably the best known is Kaliya, a foul cobra-demon with 101 heads. Kaliya's venom was so powerful that the lake in which he lived—a widening of the Yamuna River near Vrindavan—had become extremely toxic. The waters bubbled and boiled with poisonous gases. If a bird made the mistake of flying over the lake, it would instantly asphyxiate and fall dead into the water. No plants could grow near the shore.

One day the fearsome serpent frightened Lord Krishna's consort Radha, and Krishna decided to teach him a lesson. He climbed a tall kadamba* tree—the only tree that managed to grow somewhat close to the water—and jumped in. He started splashing as loudly as he could.

The Naga immediately rose from the depths, bit the intruder on the chest, wrapped his mighty coils around him, and began to constrict. For a long time, Krishna stayed motionless, and all the people of Vrindavan began to fear he had been squeezed to death.

But finally Krishna extricated himself. Shaking off the giant coils, he climbed up Kaliya's neck and onto the top of his heads. Then he started dancing there, right on the jewelled backs of the Naga's many hoods.

This dance is one of Hinduism's most enduring images, found in paintings and temple sculptures in many parts of the country.

With each step of Krishna's divine heels, one of the snake's heads bowed down, and finally, the Naga submitted completely.

Kaliya renounced his evil ways, and Krishna banished him to Ramanaka Dweep, an island far out in the ocean.

The Hindu descendents of the indentured labourers who travelled to Fiji in the 19th century believe that Ramanaka Dweep is, in fact, Fiji. For them, Kaliya is just another name for the creator god of the native Fijians, a giant serpent named Degei.

---

* *Neolamarckia cadamba.*

In Buddhist lore, the Nagas are one of the *astagatyah*, the eight classes of supernatural beings.

Muchalinda is the Naga who sheltered the Buddha from the rain as he meditated under the bodhi tree. This role of Nagas as protectors is common throughout Southeast Asia: in Laos, for example, they are believed to be the guardians of the capital city Ventiane. In Thailand, it is said that giant Phaya Nagas inhabit the Mekong River.

Apalala was a fearsome Naga who terrorized the region of Swat, in what is now Pakistan. Legend says he was subdued and converted by the Buddha.

Nagas were often appointed as the guardians of the Buddha's relics. For instance, in one stupa near Pataliputra which contained parts of the Enlightened One's body, a powerful Naga was said to stand as the second line of defence behind a legion of Roman-engineered killer robots, the **Bhoota Vahana Yanta**.

In the folklore of Tibet, Nagas—which are known there as *Klu*—can possess people. A person thus possessed will tend to slither around the floor, lick the corners of his mouth incessantly, and constantly crave sweet things like candy or honey. His eyes will bulge out and go bloodshot.

As an illustration of how prevalent belief in Nagas once was in India, consider the *Arthashastra*, a two-thousand-year-old work on governance and warfare written by the Mauryan statesman Kautilya. In the section of this book entitled "Strategic Means to Capture a Fortress," the author gives detailed instructions on how to impersonate Nagas. Various strategies are provided for spies to infiltrate an enemy fort, and then to hide, in Naga costume, near a temple tank or other water body. At an opportune moment, the fake Naga was supposed to emerge from the water along with a pyrotechnic display and a flash of shiny weaponry. In a booming voice, he would then issue a dire prophecy: "We are going to eat the flesh of the king or of his ministers; let the worship of the gods go on." This would apparently convince the gullible enemies to surrender.

Nagas still abound in television, film, and fiction. In 1986, Delhi-based Raj Comics created Nagraj, a green-skinned Naga superhero who fights terrorists by shooting magical snakes out of his wrists. The same year saw the release of the blockbuster Hindi film *Nagina*, with Sridevi in the role of the shapeshifting serpent. But these are just a couple of examples. New Naga-themed television serials, films, and pulp novels come out every year, in dozens of Indian languages.

Myths of Nagas and Naginis have travelled to foreign shores, too, where they have been incorporated into franchises such as *World of Warcraft*, *Magic: The Gathering*, and—most famously of all—J.K. Rowling's *Harry Potter*.

Ref: 325, 435

NAKSHATRA MEENU

Nakshatra Meenu means "starfish" or "brittle star" in Kannada. Brittle stars are echinoderms: they are related to starfish and look somewhat similar, but they tend to be longer-limbed, faster-moving, and more flexible.

According to a legend from Karnataka, a horde of giant brittle stars crawled out of the sea onto land in the early 16th century and waged war against the Vijayanagara Empire.

The largest of these beasts were said to have arms up to four metres long (much larger than any echinoderm known to modern science). They attacked people by wrapping one arm around the neck and another around the feet, and then ripping them in half. They could also detach their arms and send them crawling into buildings and forts, where they would strangle people. The detached arms would be quickly regenerated.

The story goes that the armies of the great Vijayanagara emperor, Krishna Deva Raya, finally defeated the sea monsters and drove them back into the ocean in 1514 by shooting flaming arrows at them.

Ref: 143, 171, 240

NASU

Far in the north and deep underground, in darkness so dark it can be grasped by the handful, lies Duzak, the Zoroastrian hell. Here there is a narrow, stinking pit, at once colder than the coldest ice and hotter than the hottest blaze. At the bottom of this pit is the place where wicked souls are condemned to spend an eternity of torment and loneliness. They are crammed together as close as the hairs on a horse's mane, and yet none of them can see or speak to any other.

Living there with them in the pit are the Xrafstar—monsters as tall as mountains, combining the most terrifying aspects of snakes, scorpions and wolves—who torture and devour the souls.

Next to this pit lies the abode of the Druj, the demons of falsehood. Chief among them is Nasu, the demon of decomposition and decay. She attacks through any form of dead matter, including nail trimmings, hair, urine, menstrual blood, and human corpses.

When a person dies, Druj Nasu comes out of the north in the shape of a wrathful fly, with her moist proboscis extended in front, her knees bent outwards, and her ovipositor protruding behind, making a relentless droning noise as she flies through the air.

During Zoroastrian funeral rites, it is crucially important that the bodies of the dead be protected from Nasu's depredations. During processions, corpses are to be exposed naked and carried by two people, since a single person will not be strong enough to withstand Nasu's attack. Furthermore, to counteract Nasu's influence, the corpse must be gazed upon by a dog, or eaten by a dog or a vulture; the arrival of these carrion-feeders is enough to send Nasu flying back to Duzak.

Nasu is a fecund progenitor of many other evil Druj. She is impregnated whenever a man is greedy; whenever he urinates on his feet; whenever he has a nocturnal emission; or whenever he goes outside without wearing the sacred undergarments, the *kushti* and *sedre*.

On the other hand, Nasu's children can be destroyed in the womb by means of good deeds and prayer.

Ref: 230, 538

⟩⟩⟩⟩⟨ NAWANG ⟩⟩⟨⟨⟨

In the pre-Christian Songsarek religion of the Garo people of Northeast India, when a person dies, their ghost (or **Memang**) must make a journey to Mangru-Mangram, the ghost world. Here it waits for some time before being reincarnated. The path to Mangru-Mangram wends through Balphakram, now a national park in Meghalaya.

Along this path is a cave, and in the cave lurks a hungry, wide-mouthed ogre. His name is Nawang. He jumps out to accost the travelling ghost, demanding to know what it has accomplished in its life. He also asks what valuables the ghost is carrying.

If the last rites and cremation have been done properly and the ghost has been prepared for the journey, he should be carrying some brass rings or coins. At this point he should scatter them on the ground. Nawang, who is crazy for shiny things, immediately forgets about the ghost and runs about trying to collect the trinkets. Meanwhile, the ghost should run onwards to Mangru-Mangram. Nawang does not follow; he always stays close by his cave, waiting for the next ghost to arrive.

Another way for a man to get past Nawang is to reply to his question, "What have you accomplished in your life?" with the answer "I've married a thousand wives!" Nawang gets so shocked at this impropriety that he simply gives an awkward laugh and runs away.

If Nawang is not satisfied with the ghost's answers and gifts, he can devour the soul, preventing it from ever being reincarnated. Thus, in a traditional Songsarek funeral, the *kamal* conducting the ceremony gives careful instructions to the deceased about what tricks to use to get past Nawang.

Nawang is also thought to be responsible for eclipses. When he begins to eat the moon or the sun, horns should be blasted and drums beaten loudly to scare the evil spirit away.

Ref: 173, 275, 314

⊱⊱⊶ NAZAR ⊷⊰⊰

Nazar is the Urdu word for "sight". It is one of many different words in India used to refer to the Evil Eye.

Nazar or Buri Nazar is not exactly a ghost or spirit, but rather a malignant aura arising from feelings of jealousy. Those who are by nature always envious cast the evil eye upon practically everything they look at; but it is thought that good-hearted people, too, can unwittingly put Nazar on a thing or on a person, if they allow even the slightest insincerity to creep into a compliment.

Belief in the evil eye is probably the most common superstition in India, if not the entire world. There are innumerable types of talismans to ward it away, including scary faces drawn on the axles of trucks; dots of kohl on babies' cheeks; eye-like disks of blue glass; painted terracotta heads placed on the terraces of buildings; chillis and limes threaded together and pinned above door frames; and crystals, shells, dried sea stars, and aloe leaves tied up in human hair and hung above shop entrances.

Among some communities, the "evil eye" is thought to be cast more by the mouth than by the eye. In Assam, amongst the Bodo and related tribes, it is called *Mukhloga* or *Khuga Nangai*. In Central India, Oraon people consider the "evil mouth" *Baibakh* as a spirit or force separate from Nazar. Similar beliefs are common among Santals and other Munda tribes as well.

Ref: 85, 536

⇒⇒ NEELI ⇐⇐

There are many versions of the story of Neeli, some of them very ancient. The earliest ones appear in Tamil Jain and Buddhist texts dating from the 6th century; but the version that is best-known today is quite different.

The story of Pazhayanur Neeli begins with a wayward husband who had become ensnared in the charms of a money-hungry temptress. So consumed was he with a desire to please her that he killed his pregnant wife—luring her into a cactus patch, bashing her head in with a rock, and then stealing the jewels from her corpse.

In his next birth this man was reborn as a merchant. One day he went travelling, carrying his wares to Pazhayanur to trade. On the way he met a woman with an infant child. She called herself Neeli, and claimed to be his wife. In actuality, this woman was a vengeful **Pey**—the ghost of the woman he had murdered in his former life.

The merchant protested, but she hounded him. At Pazhayanur she went before the village council—made up of seventy Vellala elders—and made a big show of piteous weeping, begging them to restore her rights as the man's wedded wife.

The ploy worked, and the Vellalas ruled that the couple would have to stay together. The man protested vehemently that he would be in danger, but the Vellalas swore on their lives that no harm would come to him.

That very night, Neeli murdered the man in the most gruesome possible fashion, and then she and her child promptly disappeared.

The legend tells that sixty-nine of the seventy Vellalas, when they heard the next morning what had happened, honoured their vow by committing mass suicide in a bonfire. The seventieth Vellala, who had already gone off to the field, impaled himself on a plough blade as soon as he heard.

Neeli went on to haunt the area, transforming into the fearsome goddess Kali of Tiruvalangadu, a hideous, skeletal demoness who sits in the cremation ground, eternally watching Lord Shiva's cosmic dance.

Even today in Tamil, the expression *Neeli kannir*, or "Neeli tears", is equivalent to the English "crocodile tears": a counterfeit outpouring of emotion calculated to serve an ulterior motive.

Ref: 5, 387

❧ NELHAO ❧

A Nelhao is a **Thilha**—that is, one of the evil spirits of Kuki folklore. In fact, there are exactly seven Nelhao brothers; together they are called the Nelhaoloi. They live high in the hills and mountains, away from people, but they sometimes visit human villages to play jokes and pranks. If humans trespass in their territory, they can be more malign, causing serious illness or bad luck.

The Nelhaoloi can manifest as strong winds and storms. In particular, they come every year in the form of a cyclone at the end of May, after which many mushrooms spring up from the earth.

The *gosem*, a kind of gourd flute, is said to have been invented by the Nelhaoloi. We humans stole it from them. For this reason it is considered unwise to play the gosem in hilly forests; if the Nelhaoloi hear the sound, they will come to take back their instrument—and the foolish musician may not live to tell the tale.

Ref: 59, 537

❧ NEWAND DOKKA ❧

Newand Dokka means "chameleon" in the language of the Durwa tribe of Chhattisgarh and Odisha. There is a belief among the Durwa that the spirit of a chameleon can possess a person, causing them to feel unsteady and off-balance. Anyone possessed by a Newand Dokka will be accident-prone and clumsy with blades.

To drive out the spirit, an effigy of a chameleon should be woven from bamboo and placed at a fork in a path leading away from the village. Also, two chickens and a goat should be sacrificed.

In parts of Tamil Nadu and Karnataka, too, chameleons were once believed to be hosts of evil spirits. If they ventured near human habitations, the poor reptiles would be attacked and killed, and then buried under piles of pebbles. In Tripura, they are associated with the **Swkal**.

Ref: 113, 296

[Full-page illustration]

NILA

In the folklore of the Pucikwar—a tribe from the Andaman Islands whose members died out or were absorbed into other groups around 1931—Nila was a demon who lives in hollow *Pterocarpus* trees or in termite mounds. He was described as a loner, without any sort of family, who is always armed with a knife. He eats nothing but dirt.

When humans come too close to Nila's dwelling place, he comes out and kills them with his knife.

Unexplained murders were sometimes blamed on Nila.

Ref: 54

⤛ NIM-TAN ⤜

Nim-Tans or Nim-Chehras are a race of supernatural creatures that appear in Urdu fantasy literature, as well as in older Persian and Arabic legends, where they are called *Nasnas*. According to some, they are the offspring of one human parent and one Shiqq **Jinn** parent.

Each Nim-Tan is a half-person, split down the middle, having just one leg, one arm, one eye, etc.

Male Nim-Tans appear as the right side of a body, having only a right foot and a right leg. Female Nim-Tans appear as the left side. When a male and female join together, they look and act like a normal human being. When they are separate, however, they are dangerous and ferociously cruel.

Nim-Tans can hop at tremendous speeds.

Ref: 104, 191, 283

⤛ NIPONG ⤜

Among the Adi, Mising, and several other tribes of Arunachal Pradesh, Nipong is a female spirit that causes miscarriage, labour trouble, and painful periods. She is also called Niji-Nipong. She is a descendant of the sylvan demon Robo (see **Wiyu**).

Nipong usually targets women, but can also cause illness or bad luck for men. She is one of the most feared of all evil spirits—so much so that whenever a different malevolent spirit is being propitiated, an additional offering is made to Nipong, as well. Whenever a woman is having a difficult pregnancy or labour, her husband or relatives sacrifice animals to Nipong.

When Nipong possesses a woman, she will raise both hands to her hair, clutch it tightly, and begin to scream incessantly.

The spirit of any woman who dies while pregnant or in childbirth travels to the realm of Nipong, a world which lies parallel to the world of the living. There she becomes a Niji-Nipong. These female ghosts manifest themselves in marshes, along the banks of streams, or wherever wild plantains grow. A Niji-Nipong can take the form of a small animal, such as a mole shrew, gecko, frog, bat, or small bird.

The spotted owlet in particular is feared as an embodiment of Nipong. It is said to be very unlucky to hear its screech. When travellers in the forest hear this sound, they are supposed to remove some article of clothing or ornament that they have received as a gift, and get rid of it.

Another legend tells us that there are many Nipongs, both male and female. They once lived together in a village in the human realm, farming and raising families, but also attacking and eating human beings whenever they could find them.

The story begins with two human brothers, Tani and Taro. Tani married many beautiful wives, while Taro married only one; what's more, while Tani's wives were healthy and curvaceous, Taro's wife was lean and sickly. When the jealous Taro asked Tani how he kept his wives so healthy, Tani told him that he should keep his wife in a giant pot for five days, and pour boiling hot water over her every day. Ignoring the cries and screams of his wife, Taro did as instructed; but when he opened up the pot after five days, instead of finding a fat healthy wife, he found a mass of writhing worms.

Enraged, Taro decided to get back at his brother. He split a large log in two lengthwise and carved it out to make a trough. He told Tani that he planned to use it as a bed; after all, now that his wife was dead, he would be sleeping alone. Taro asked Tani if he would like to get into the trough and try it out. As soon as Tani obliged, Taro slammed the other half of the log on top of him, imprisoning him inside. He then tied the log shut with strong ropes, threw it into a lake, went to his brother's house, and began living with his wives.

From within his log-prison, Tani was screaming for help. He shouted so loud that the plants heard him. A creeper grew towards him and slowly pried apart the two halves of the log, eventually allowing him to wrench his way out of his prison. When Tani got back to his home and found Taro making love to his wives, he got wild, and beat him until he ran away.

Soon, Tani began to regret his behaviour. After all, Taro was his brother, and Tani had been responsible for his wife's death in the first place. He decided to go and find Taro.

He hunted for his brother high and low, day and night. Finally he found him—in the village of the Nipong. Taro was watching over the Nipongs' children while the spirits worked in the fields. Though he wasn't bound or tied, he told Tani that he couldn't leave: the Nipong were keeping him captive there. What is more, he said that he had overheard the Nipong whispering that soon, they meant to kill him and eat him.

Tani and Taro managed to preempt this by killing all the Nipongs—except for one, by the name of Poyi Pomar, who escaped into the forest.

After killing all the Nipongs, Tani and Taro chopped them up into bits and set off back to their own village, carrying the pieces with them as trophies. On their way home, though, Taro became upset that he didn't have as many trophies as Tani, and began fighting over them. Frustrated, Tani threw all the Nipong bits into a bush of stinging nettles, and said, "Go and get them if you want them so bad!" Taro rashly jumped in after them, but the stinging spines of the nettles tore at his flesh all over. The plants injected so much toxin into him that his heart stopped, and he died.

Afterwards, the stinging nettles copulated with the discarded Nipong bits, and soon gave birth to a new race of Nipongs, who still live today among the thorny plants in the jungle. These Nipongs are the ones responsible for causing labour trouble.

There is also a second, separate lineage of Nipongs, the descendants of Poyi Pomar, the sole escapee from the village. These Nipongs are content to catch a human once in a while to eat.

Both sorts of Nipong hate the smell of ginger, and they will avoid anyone who carries a piece of the root on their person.

Ref: 241

NIRRTI

Nirrti is the ancient Vedic goddess of doom, death, and destruction: the personification of evil. She is described as being dark-skinned and dressed all in black, with long golden hair.

In later Hindu tradition, Nirrti became associated with various forms of the Divine Mother—especially Dhumavati, the widow seated upon a crow, goddess of dissolution and the void. But in the oldest hymns, Nirrti's character is unequivocally demonic. When she is invoked, it is to banish her from the prayer site, or else to unleash her on the supplicant's enemies. She is propitiated at a crossroads, and offered blackened husks of grain.

Other texts prescribe sacrificial offerings of owls, pigeons, and hares to Nirrti. Owls are said to be her messengers.

While most Hindu deities have an animal for a mount, Nirrti rides on the back of a pitifully hunched-over hungry ghost (see **Preta**).

Ref: 299

᚛ NISHI ᚜

The Nishi or night spirit is one of the most feared ghosts of Bihar and Bengal. She manifests simply as a voice—*Nishir Daak*—that calls a person's name in the night when they are sleeping. If the person follows the voice, it leads them to a secluded place outside the house... and then the person disappears forever.

The Nishi can only call someone's name twice while they are inside. This is why you should never answer a call at night unless you hear your name called three times.

In some stories, the Nishi is a ghost of a dead mother who loves her child so much that she cannot bear the afterlife without them. So she calls them at night and leads them out to their deaths, either drowning them in a pond or hanging them by their neck from a tree.

Nishis are believed to be responsible for the phenomenon of sleepwalking.

Ref: 34, 418

᚛ NOERI SIMERI JAHPRAMMA ᚜

In Garo folklore, Noeri Simeri Jahpramma is a giant ogress who lives in a house at one of the farthest corners of the Earth.

Noeri Simeri has an extensive collection of hammers. They come in a wide range of sizes, and with differently shaped heads. She has the power to turn invisible, and this is how she sneaks up on her prey before smashing them with one of her hammers. Sometimes, she chooses a small hammer, and attacks the joints, causing afflictions like rheumatism, arthritis, and gout. Other times, she chooses a large hammer, and—wham!—crushes a person to death.

She also hunts animals of various sizes.

Goera, the Garo god of thunder and strength, once crept up on Noeri Simeri in her sleep. He took down her biggest hammer—the one that she kept for killing elephants—and whomped her over the head with it. But this only enraged her, and Goera had to run for it.

Ref: 306

NONGSHOHNOH

In Khasi lore of Meghalaya, Nongshohnoh are zombie-like mercenary killers who have been drugged by worshippers of the serpent-demon **U Thlen**.

When a *nong-ri-Thlen* ("keeper of Thlen", i.e. someone who worships the demon at home) wants to conscript a person into service as a Nongshohnoh, he must feed him *kyiad tangsnem*—a triple-distilled rice liquor that has been aged for a year and mixed with drops of the demon's sweat. This brew gives the Nongshohnoh the courage to kill, and the ability to identify appropriate victims.

When the nong-ri-Thlen sends Nongshohnoh to attack his enemies, the Nongshohnoh act as wild berserk killers, completely fearless and unmindful of injury. At other times, when the nong-ri-Thlen needs to collect blood for sacrifice, the Nongshohnoh act in a more premeditated way.

The Nongshohnoh is given some uncooked rice mixed with a little turmeric that has been enchanted by Thlen. The Nongshohnoh then goes out and lies in wait for his victim. When the victim appears, the Nongshohnoh throws a few grains of enchanted rice at him, while chanting a spell absolving himself of responsibility and blaming the victim for being in the wrong place at the wrong time. When the victim is hit by the enchanted rice, he becomes numb and paralyzed. Now it's easy for the Nongshohnoh to murder him.

After the job is done, the Nongshohnoh uses a pair of silver scissors to take a cutting of the victim's hair and a few of the victim's fingernails. (Steel or iron implements may not be used, as iron is poison to Thlen.) Then the Nongshohnoh uses a small silver knife to cut the victim's nostrils, fills a bamboo container with some of the person's blood, and returns these items to the keeper. By offering this blood to Thlen, the nong-ri-Thlen becomes rich and prosperous.

There are a few different ways to defend oneself against Nongshohnoh.

The first and simplest defence is to have a strong *rngiew*, or spirit essence. Thlen's power is weaker against those who are good-hearted, confident, and firm. When a person has a strong rngiew, the tassels of that person's clothing will appear to the intoxicated Nongshohnoh as thick whips swinging powerfully through the air, and the Nongshohnoh will be scared away.

The second defence is to be quick-minded when one is attacked with the enchanted rice. If the victim is able to figure out what is happening, then before the paralysis takes effect, he should quickly place a clod of dirt in his mouth. This gives the victim a connection to Mother Earth and breaks the spell.

The third defence is to carry some rice grains of one's own, and to mount a counterattack. If a man sees Nongshohnoh in his path, he may throw this rice at them while chanting a counter-spell. In this way the Nongshohnoh will be struck senseless.

Witch Hunts and Lynchings of Suspected Nongshohnoh

Belief in Thlen and Nongshohnoh remains common in modern times, with consequences that can sometimes be deadly.

In 2013, there was a much-publicized incident in which a man was found half-drowned on the banks of a stream near the village of Smit. The man's relatives accused a wealthy local family, who were rumoured to be keepers of Thlen, of attempting to murder him. An angry mob formed, rallying around cries of "They are Nongshohnoh!" The group attacked the family's house and hacked three members to death before the police arrived.

People with deformities or intellectual disabilities have sometimes been targeted by these witch hunts. More commonly, though, it is people who have amassed wealth.

Ref: 254, 272

NYALMO

Nyalmo are the largest and strongest variety of **Yeti**. They are carnivorous, bipedal, bear-like creatures that stand fifteen to twenty feet tall and are covered with black fur. They have long arms and huge hands, with legs that are rather short by comparison. They live at a higher altitude than other Yetis, way up near the Himalayan peaks where the snow never melts.

Nyalmo feed on yaks and other large mammals. To kill their prey, they grab them by their horns and twist their necks. When large game is scarce, they subsist on frogs and moss. They are also man-eaters.

Female Nyalmo are bigger and fiercer than males. The creatures live in small matriarchal groups. Female Nyalmo have been reported to capture human males and mate with them. If the captive is submissive, she may keep him in her lair for a long period of time, and even raise a family with him. On the other hand, if the Nyalmo becomes displeased with her captive, she may crack open his skull and eat his brain.

The lair of Nyalmo is foul-smelling, and the creatures' bodies reek of garlic.

Like other types of Yeti, the Nyalmo have excellent hearing and can see in the dark. In some tales, they have two extra eyes on the backs of their heads. Nyalmo do not wear clothes; neither do they use weapons nor fire. Though they have subhuman intelligence, they are emotional creatures, capable of love and affection as well as frustration and anger. In one well-known story, a female Yeti become so despondent after her human spouse escaped with their children that she committed suicide.

The Nyalmo have some elements of culture. For example, they are known to practise haruspication—the inspection of the internal organs of the animals they kill as a means of foretelling the future. There are also reports of groups of Nyalmo making music by drumming on hollow logs while chanting.

Ref: 269, 294

➤— ODIYAN —➤

The Odiyan myth, which must count as one of the country's creepiest and most twisted folkloric traditions, comes from northern Kerala.

An Odiyan is not a ghost. Rather, he is a human practitioner of black magic who has the ability to shapeshift. The Odiyan usually transforms into a bull or a black dog, but sometimes into other animals, or even inanimate forms. Odiyans work as hired assassins for wealthy landlords.

The secret ingredient that an Odiyan uses to change his shape can only be obtained from an unborn child. To this end, the Odiyan selects a pregnant mother as his first victim. By means of a magic spell, he causes her to sleepwalk to a lonely place in the jungle. Then he cuts her open and takes what he needs. The woman, still in a trance, walks back to her home to bleed out and die.

The secret ingredient obtained from the fœtus (some say it is the amniotic fluid; others describe it as a sort of oil) can be stored and used for a few transformations. When it is time for the Odiyan to commit his next murder, he goes to a dark place in the jungle and rubs a few drops of the fluid on the backs of his earlobes. This fluid is supposed to have a hideous stench that can be smelled some distance away. Once it has been applied, the Odiyan must sit for some hours meditating in silence until, gradually, he takes the shape of an animal.

During this period of transition the Odiyan is quite vulnerable. He is not completely conscious, and thus unable to fend off an attack should any enemy discover his hiding place. For this reason, the Odiyan generally works with an assistant, called a *shinkidi*, who guards him when he is helpless.

The beast into which the Odiyan transforms always appears disfigured in some way. It might be missing a leg, or it might bear a gruesome scar in place of an eye. The foul smell from the magic oil clings to the Odiyan in its animal form, too.

In this shape, the Odiyan chooses a path where he knows his target will travel alone, and lies in wait.

The target walks along unawares. He may not be too surprised to see a lame bull standing at the side of the path. When he comes within range, the Odiyan moves forward. A hoof or paw transforms into a hand. Suddenly there is a knife in it—and a second later the knife has slit the victim's throat.

Ref: 379, 539

ODONTOTYRANNOS

The Odontotyrannos is a monster said to have lived in the region of the Indus River in ancient times. It is described in a letter supposedly written by Alexander the Great to his former tutor Aristotle when Alexander's army invaded India in 326 BCE. The original version of this letter has been lost, but translations into several other languages exist. All contain slightly different accounts of the encounter with the monster.

Alexander described it as bigger than an elephant (some translations of the letter say that it was big enough to eat elephants). It had a horse-like black head, three long horns growing out of its skull, and long sharp teeth.

The Odontotyrannos gored 26 of Alexander's men to death and wounded another 52 before the soldiers were finally able to kill it with spears.

The Odontotyrannos was so enormous that it took hundreds of men to move its dead body. When they cut open its belly, man-sized scorpions and giant fish spilled out.

Ref: 10, 223, 410

ONIDA DEVIL

For a generation of Indians who spent the 1980s and 1990s glued to their television sets—first on public service broadcaster Doordarshan, then on a steadily growing number of cable channels—the Onida Devil is probably the most instantly recognizable of all demons in this book.

Invented by Advertising Avenues (a firm founded by Goutam Rakshit, Ashok Roy, and Gopi Kukde) for the Onida television brand in 1984, the character had all the attributes of a typical Western devil: horned head, pointy ears, claw-like nails, and a long pointy tail. There was just one exception: he was usually clad in green, instead of red. The colour was chosen to go with the slogan: "Neighbour's Envy. Owner's Pride".

In a series of ad spots, the Onida Devil jumped out of television screens to perform all sorts of outrageous antics. He drank smoking green cocktails. He beat giant tom-toms. He played the grand piano on top of a mountain amidst erupting jets of fire. He floated through clouds in a lightning storm while caressing a giant television set and dodging a huge celestial ax. Meanwhile, the faceless hordes of envious neighbours tried all sorts of ways to defeat him. They launched him out of cannons; they blew him up with explosives; they stuck his head in a guillotine; they tied him in chains and dropped him into shark-infested waters. But he always survived.

The mascot became an icon nationwide, and was widely seen as being responsible for the company's success in increasing its market share despite heavy competition from more established foreign brands. In a later, more nationalistic iteration, the slogan changed to "World's Envy, India's Pride", with the Onida Devil's stone-sculpted visage appearing next to the American presidents on Mount Rushmore.

David Whitbread, the Bangalorean actor who was first cast in the role, played the devil for fourteen years. After Whitbread hung up the green cape, Ashish Choudhary, Rajesh Khera and Aamir Bashir each took a turn.

The campaign was wrapped up in 2009, only to be rebooted in 2018 with a new, rather more polished-looking black-clad devil and his evil wife.

Ref: 545

ONKOBOYKWE
(AND OTHER BEINGS FROM THE HIGHER PLANES)

The Onge tribe of Little Andaman Island are thought to have remained completely isolated from other human populations for around 50,000 years. The tribe is now highly endangered; in the 2011 census, their population numbered just 101 individuals. Their society, culture, and language have been devastated by colonization and settlement of the islands. As a result, anthropological understanding of their traditional mythology and folklore is limited. What follows is based primarily on a report from interviews conducted in 1963.

According to the Onge, there are thirteen planes of existence, six of which lie above our world and six which lie below. Even lower, beneath them all, is Kwatannange, the primordial ocean, which is full of turtles.

The six planes which lie below Little Andaman Island are dealt with in the entry on **Eaka**. Here, we discuss the beings who live on planes which lie above.

The plane immediately above ours, which lies just beyond the sky, is populated by creatures called Onkoboykwe. These are benevolent spirits who live in large communal huts and subsist on honey and water. They cannot eat anything solid, as they have no teeth. They are generally invisible; but when they choose to be seen, they look—apart from the lack of teeth—just like regular Onge (that is, black-skinned, rather short, with tightly coiled hair.) Onkoboykwe sometimes come to our world in search of honey, but as honey is plentiful in their own world, their visits are rare.

The Onkoboykwe are mortal, as are all other residents of the various planes of Onge cosmology.

Onkoboykwe are said to have created the sun, moon, and stars. They are also responsible for the creation of the human race, though they are not directly our ancestors.

Two Onkoboykwe named Engigegi and Egyabigegi are said to have been the first two inhabitants of Little Andaman Island. They travelled to our world from the land above the sky. One day, after they had been living on Little Andaman for some time, they found some branches of the *tukwege-lego* tree, which have a shape similar to that of human leg bones. They planted these branches in the ground in pairs, and then went away to the jungle. When they returned, they were surprised to find that each pair of branches had turned into an Onge man and woman.

This was the origin of the Onge tribe. But Engigegi and Egyabigegi themselves died childless, at an old age.

Even now, Onkoboykwe are said to play a role in human reproduction. They send down magical energy from above the sky which enters into some kinds of food, such as pork or turtle meat. Only after an Onge woman eats such food can she become pregnant.

Though Onkoboykwe created humankind, there is another myth which says that they themselves are the ghosts of dead human beings—at least some of them. If an Onge is killed by a wild boar or a venomous snake, or if he falls to his death from a tall tree, then his ghost immediately escapes his body and spirals up to the sky. There is a hole in the sky called Ekwachelle through which these ghosts fly, and soon afterwards they arrive in the land of the Onkoboykwe.

The Onkoboykwe catch hold of the flying ghost and make it lie down on a hot stone slab. This alleviates the pain and trauma the ghost felt in death. Soon afterwards the ghost's teeth fall out, and it becomes an Onkoboykwe itself. In its new life, it may marry, take up residence in a hut, and live a comfortable life.

The Planes Above

Above the plane of the Onkoboykwe lie five more planes of existence: the plane of the Goygoge, the plane of the Gabulembes, the plane of the Tetoboy, the plane of the Jugene, and—highest of all—the plane of Tuchenkwaka.

The Goygoge

The Goygoge are malevolent beings who appear like Onge, but with larger bellies. They often travel to the human plane to abduct Onge people to eat. Once a Goygoge arrives on Little Andaman, he sits perched at the top of a gurjan tree, waiting for an Onge person travelling alone to pass by in the jungle below. As soon as he finds one, he jumps down, binds the Onge's hands and feet, and carries him up two planes to his own world. There the Goygoge roast him over a fire and eat him.

The Onkoboykwe are enemies of the Goygoge. They sometimes do battle with them when they visit the human plane, fighting them and killing them with spears.

The Gabulembe

In the plane above the Goygoge plane live the Gabulembe, who are also malevolent towards humans. They too eat Onge flesh whenever they are able to catch a person, but their staple foods are fish and prawns.

The Tetoboy

In the next plane up live the Tetoboy, who seem to be in most respects similar to the Onge; they live in huts, eat fish, and drink honey.

The Jugenes

In the next plane up, the highest but one, live the Jugenes. These beings are tall and light-skinned. They subsist entirely on honey, which they collect from all over. They occasionally come to the human plane to search for honey, but their visits are somewhat rare, as there is plenty available in their own plane of existence.

The Tuchenkwaka

The highest plane of all is populated by the Tuchenkwaka, a pitiable class of beings who have nothing to eat. They are constantly starving.

*

Like the plane of the Onkoboykwe, all five of these higher planes consist only of land, with no surrounding sea. (Presumably, the land stretches out infinitely far). However, there are streams which flow across the land, so river fish and some varieties of prawn are available (except in the plane of the Tuchenkwaka, where there is nothing edible at all).

Ref: 475

OTTE MOLECHI

This ghost hails from Kasaragod, Kerala. She reportedly haunted the national highway in a dark and uninhabited area between Mogral and Kumbla, back in the days when there weren't many electric lights.

When anybody walked that way carrying a kerosene lantern or a torch, the Otte Molechi would appear before them as a beautiful woman, standing topless in the middle of the road, asking in a sensuous voice for some betel-nuts.

As the dazed traveller fumbled for his betel-nut pouch, he would suddenly realize that the woman had only a single breast, and that it was steadily growing larger and larger, drooping down almost to the ground.

Then the ghost would begin to spin, slowly at first and then faster and faster. The elongated monster-boob would extend outwards through centripetal force. If it whacked the traveller, he would be shattered into pieces, completely ceasing to exist. Only by artfully ducking the madly whirling breast could he hope to survive.

Then, abruptly, the Otte Molechi would disappear.

Ref: 268

PADOSOMARU

Among the Kumbri Marathi tribe of the Karnataka coast, a Padosomaru (plural: Padosomarava) is a malevolent ghost that causes illness. They are bad, but not as bad as the **Balishtamarava**.

There are various kinds of Padosomaru.

A **Challi** is the ghost of a child that has died young—after undergoing the naming ceremony and tying of the sacred thread, but before the ceremonies of head tonsure and ear piercing; therefore between a few days and a few years old. A person molested by a Challi spirit may experience burning in the eyes, headache, body pain, and fever. Repeated interventions by a healer over a period of five or six days are required to ward off this spirit.

A **Nirvansh** is the ghost of a child that has completed the head tonsure and/or ear piercing ceremonies, but died before marriage. A **Gandugole** is the ghost of a man who died after marriage, and a **Hennugole** is the ghost of a woman who died after marriage. All three of these spirits can cause fever and other illnesses, but they are generally easier to drive out than a Challi.

A **Kil** is a spirit which causes scabies and other skin ailments.

Ref: 161

⊱ PANDUBBA ⊰

The Pandubba, also called Pandubbi, is an evil water-spirit known from the folklore of Bihar. They are thought to be the ghosts of people who were drowned.

Pandubbas appear as muscular men of short stature, hanging around the rocks at the edge of their lake or river. If you happen by, the Pandubba may approach you and bother you for a bit of tobacco or a drink of alcohol.

If you ignore these requests and walk onwards, you will survive unharmed. On the other hand, if you give the Pandubba something, the Pandubba will suddenly grab hold of your arm, change its shape to that of a slimy, eel-like monster, and drag you into the water. Once it has you at the bottom of the lake, it will pour mud into your mouth and nostrils, until your body becomes so heavy that it will never float to the surface.

Ref: 313

⊱ PAUBI LAI ⊰

Paubi Lai was a giant man-eating python with antler-like horns. According to Meitei legend, it once slept under Loktak Lake in Moirang, Manipur.

After sleeping for ages, the monster was awakened by the noisy fishermen on the lake. Paubi Lai became angry, and started eating all the fishermen. Then it began attacking the Moirang Kingdom itself.

To placate the serpent, the King of Moirang had to provide a daily offering of one bushel of rice and one human being.

Every man, woman, and child in the kingdom lived in terror of being sacrificed to the monster. But one young man, Chauhi Leirong Apanba, decided to do something about the problem. He had heard of a renowned shaman, Kabui Salang Baji, who lived in the hills to the west of the lake. Chauhi Leirong Apanba went to him and found Kabui Salang Baji in his hermitage. He told him about the giant python and the daily sacrifices, and pleaded with him to help. Kabui Salang Baji used his powers to transform a water-weed into a magical nine-pointed spear called a *long*.

Chauhi Leirong Apanba returned to the lake and called Paubi Lai out to fight him. His weapon pierced the serpent's heart, and it perished.

According to some, Paubi Lai is an incarnation of Pakhangba, the supreme god of the Meitei, who appeared on the royal flag of the Kingdom of Manipur.

Ref: 540

⇒⇒ PAVAGADA WOLVES ⇐⇐

This grisly true story dates from 1983. In the village of Pavagada—about 150 kilometres from Bangalore—there was a series of tragic and mysterious deaths of young girls. Each child was carried off in her sleep; only a few body parts or bits of bloodied clothing were ever recovered.

Paw marks were found at the crime scenes, so the first hypothesis was that wild animals had carried the victims off. Strangely, however, there were no signs that any of the bodies had been dragged.

Several wolves and hyenas in the area were hunted down and shot, but the abductions did not immediately stop. Sniffer dogs that were investigating one of the deaths led police to a cave on a nearby hill that had been sealed off with a brick wall.

Each of the victims was an only child, and each was taken in exactly the same way—silently picked up in the night while sleeping next to her parents. These similarities led people to speculate that evil tantrics had stolen the girls for human sacrifice.

The murders—if that is what they were—were never conclusively solved. Even to this day, there are rumours of werewolves, **Werehyenas**, or black magicians lurking in the Kamanadurga hills around Pavagada.

Ref: 66, 378, 390

⇒⇒ PENCHAPECHI ⇐⇐

The Penchapechi is a demon that takes the shape of an owl. It haunts paths through the forests of Bengal, where it waits for people travelling by foot. It flies silently from tree to tree, waiting until the person is completely alone. Then it strikes.

A Penchapechi can eat a person whole. However, like owls, they will later regurgitate a tightly packed pellet of indigestible material, such as the larger bones—the skull and femur—and the hair.

If a Penchapechi comes and alights near a house where a pregnant woman lives, and the woman hears it hoot, she is supposed to cry, "Go away, ghost, or I'll cut off your nose with a fish-knife."

Ref: 418

⤐ PENU ⤏

The word Penu is used among the Kondh tribes of Central and Eastern India for all deities and other supernatural entities. Most Penu are complex figures that can be both protective and malefic, blurring the line between god and demon.

There are several clans among the Kondh (the Maliah Kondh, Dongria Kondh, Kutia Kondh, etc.). Some of the Penu listed below are worshipped only by one of the clans, while others are shared between several.

Tari Penu is the head of the Kondh pantheon. She is also worshipped by non-tribal Hindus of Odisha. Some Kondh tribes used to represent her with an effigy of a bird, other tribes with an effigy of an elephant. Today, however, she is mostly represented by a large stone monolith.

Tari Penu is very fearsome. She is responsible for infant mortality and for failure of crops, and she has the power to destroy the entire world in anger. She can bestow the power of therianthropy (see **Weretigerman**) on those who seek it.

Human sacrifices used to be offered regularly to Tari Penu. This ritual was called the *meriah* sacrifice, and it achieved worldwide notoriety in the early 19ᵗʰ century.

The word *meriah* referred to the person to be sacrificed. Meriahs could be of any tribe or race or creed, but they had to be purchased. (It was not enough to kidnap someone; they had to be paid for.) Alternatively, a family could willingly devote their own son or daughter to the goddess, and raise him or her to become a meriah.

Meriahs were allowed to live normal lives in the community for some time. They were even treated with affection and deference, since the sacrifice for which they were destined was considered very honourable. Many meriahs were children, but some grew to adulthood and were encouraged to start families. (The child of a meriah could also become a meriah.) They grew their hair long, never cutting it.

Finally, in preparation for the sacrifice, the meriah's head would be shaved. For a few days, the whole community would take part in orgiastic revelry. On the morning of the event, the meriah would be given much to drink, until he (or she) became very intoxicated. He would be anointed with oil, ghee, and turmeric, and dressed in a new garment. Then he would be led stumbling from door to door through the village. At each house, people would try to pluck hairs from his head, or collect a drop of his spittle. These relics were thought to be very precious.

Next the meriah would be led to a grove of trees some distance from the village. A huge crowd would gather round. Tari Penu's priests would bind him to the goddess's effigy with a heavy iron chain. A pit would be dug at his feet, to the pounding of drums.

Then the meriah would be pushed into the pit and suffocated to death.

Afterwards, the meat would be cut from the meriah's body. The flesh was divided into two portions. One half of the meat was buried at the base of the goddess's stone, and the other half was distributed amongst the families of the village, for them to plant in their fields to ensure a good harvest.

It was believed that without the blood of the meriahs, the turmeric crop would not have the proper colour.

In the 1830s, some British missionaries were sent to convert the tribals in the area to Christianity. These missionaries were captured by Odias from the princely state of Ghumsur, who sold them to the Kondhs. The Kondhs then sacrificed the white folks as meriahs to Tari Penu.

This act precipitated the Meriah Wars of 1836–1861, during which the East India Company fought against various princely states of Odisha. By the end of these conflicts, the practice of human sacrifice in the area was (mostly) brought to an end.

Today, Tari Penu is usually called Dharani Penu. The meriah rites continue, but now it is a buffalo or a monkey, instead of a human being, that is offered as sacrifice.

Gangi Penu, also known as Bandha Penu, is the queen of the water-spirits. She resides at the headwaters of streams and in large springs, which are thought to be gateways between the worlds of the living and the dead.

She is sometimes worshipped as a benevolent deity, especially during marriages. She is also the patron of crops. But she can cause disease and strife as well. It is said that when Gangi Penu is in an angry mood, she will appear in a dream holding a large cigar in her right hand, and that this is a foreboding of great violence.

Gangi Penu commands a legion of child-spirits whom she has trapped in an embryonic state. These spirits can take the forms of small creatures of the stream, such as insects and salamanders, and Kondh people are generally careful not to harm them.

Some of the most important Penu are the household spirits, or ***Eja Penu***, as they are called amongst the Dongria Kondh. The Kutia Kondh call them ***Elu Penu***. They are symbolized by a small wooden stump called a *munda*, a gourd, and a knife, or else by a copper plate and brass bowl. The Eja Penu articles are kept in a sacred place near the hearth, and protected from disturbance. An outsider's shadow should never fall on them. If a family moves house, the old munda is left behind and a new one is consecrated; but the other articles are transported to the new home.

The Eja Penu are benevolent spirits who look after a family's well-being—unless they are offended, in which case they may bring calamity.

Jugah Penu is the goddess of smallpox; she goes by many other names, such as ***Thakurani***, ***Kamani Penu***, or ***Aja Penu***. She sows the seeds of this disease the way farmers sow the seeds of crops. When a village has been visited by Jugah

Penu, thorny creepers are planted on all the roads leading away from it, so the power of the demoness may not spread. When a goat or chicken is sacrificed to this deity, it must be done by an old woman priestess. This spirit does not have an abode, so sacrifices must be made in lonely places in the forest.

Mardi Penu is also a wanderer, but she sometimes takes up temporary residence in abandoned homes or huts. She is responsible for pushing people off cliffs.

Mahali Penu is a spirit residing in dams. She has the power to pollute the water when she is angry, causing dysentery. She can also cause people to vomit blood and make wounds become infected.

Mahane Penu watches over the funeral ground. She, too, has the power to make people vomit blood.

Bura Penu is the always-furious husband of Tari Penu, associated with the sun. He destroys crops and causes disasters to befall a village.

Lodan Devta is a spirit who causes accidents such as falls, cuts, and broken bones.

Giri Penu or ***Giri Saleni*** is a demon spirit who lives in large trees by the roadside. He attacks passers-by late at night.

Sakhi Penu is the demon of famine. A family who has incurred the wrath of Sakhi Penu will never be able to find enough food.

Salak Penu is the ghost of a foreigner. He is sometimes encountered on busy roads. He causes fever and vomiting.

Sanderi Penu is a spirit who guards a specific area. He attacks outsiders when they enter his territory.

Maolli Penu is another wandering spirit who causes cramps and body pain.

Saora Penu is a thief-spirit who sneaks into a house and causes economic hardship for the family that lives there.

Hani Penu is an angry and tyrannical fire-demon who can wipe out a whole village in just a few moments. He is propitiated with an annual ritual and sacrifices of pigeons and pigs.

There are many more Penu who wander around with evil intentions, causing disease wherever they can. Their names include Chinamali Penu, Rakat Mahali, Gada Dalmi, Lajani Penu, Raki Penu, Dalika Penu, Mutudu Penu, and Kadu Penu.

Penu can be distinguished from one another by their different smells. A trained *kotaku* or healer can perform a detection ritual to sniff out which Penu is causing a haunting or affliction, so as to prescribe the correct remedy.

Ref: 26, 91, 297

✎ PEOPLE WITH NO ANUSES ✎

In the 5th century BCE, the Greek writer Ctesias wrote of a mysterious race of people living in the Eastern Himalayas, past the source of the Brahmaputra, who had no anal orifices. They did have buttocks—but no hole between them.

These people were cattle and goat herders, and they derived all their nourishment from the milk of their livestock. At night, they would chew a sweet root which prevented the milk from solidifying in their gut, so they only ever needed to expel liquid waste. This they did either by urinating or vomiting.

Strange as this legend may seem, there is a corroborating story about an Eastern Himalayan tribe of anusless people in the folklore of Mizoram. It is a tale that involves the folkloric Mizo trickster-idiot character named Chhurbura, called Chhura for short.

It is said that Chhurbura once visited a village called Mawngping, where he discovered that none of the inhabitants had an anus. The villagers, watching Chhura perform his morning rituals, were deeply impressed; they all wanted a hole like that too. They asked him how he came to have it.

Chhurbura told them that when he was a baby, his mother had made the hole for him using a burning hot iron poker.

The villagers asked if Chhurbura could perform this operation for their children, and Chhurbura agreed.

After "operating" on every child in the village, Chhurbura placed all his young patients under a large bamboo basket. He told the villagers to keep them there for a day, and then to lift the basket and take them out.

But when the villagers opened the basket, they found that all the children were dead, except one—and that last unfortunate child was quickly ripped into pieces by all the angry and bereaved parents trying to claim him at once.

Soon they turned their anger upon Chhura, only to find that he had escaped.

There are many stories about Chhurbura running through the jungle with his enemies from Mawngping in hot pursuit. In one story, they nearly have him trapped at the top of a tree; but just as he is about to be caught, he sneezes with such force that all the villagers are blinded by his snot, so he is able to get away.

If such a tribe as described by Ctesias ever really did exist, it seems that Chhurbura may have put an end to them.

Ref: 192, 251

PERI

In Persian mythology, Peris are winged spirits, believed to reside in the Caucasus mountains. Legends of the Peris travelled to India along with the Mughals, who used Persian as the official language of the empire.

The word may originally derive from *Pairika*, a type of beautiful but wicked female demon mentioned in Zoroastrian texts. However, in later Persian literature, Peris are portrayed as benevolent, and as the enemies of the **Devs**. *Peri* usually refers to the female spirit; *Perizad* is used for male Peris, or for anyone born of a Peri mother.

In the *dastangoi* tradition of Urdu storytelling, a Peri is usually a female **Jinn**.

Peris in Indian folk stories act either as celestial nymphs, similar to **Apsaras**, or as trickster spirits of the mountains like the **Anchheri**. They punish those who disrespect nature—especially hunters who shoot for sport rather than for meat.

The similarity with the English word "fairy" is a coincidence; the two words are not etymologically related.

Peris, both male and female, are common in the folklore of Kashmir. They are said to frequently fall in love with humans. Such relationships can be very dangerous, however, and often end with the human partner being consumed by fire.

Kashmiri girls used to say that Peris came in the night to steal the kohl from around their eyelids—either out of love or out of jealousy.

Some Peris have the power to transform into wildcats. In feline form they are extremely fast, much harder to catch than a normal animal would be. They have tough skin, impervious to bullets or bladed weapons, but they can be killed by being strangled or crushed. If a human should kill a Peri-cat, the chances are good that the relatives of the Peri will avenge its death, and the human will die mysteriously in their sleep soon afterwards.

In Bengali folk stories Peris are often more evil, though they still possess supernatural beauty. They sometimes snatch human children and replace them with a lookalike child of their own.

Peris also appear in a folktale of the Baiga tribe of Madhya Pradesh, a community with a history of incorporating a huge variety of supernatural beings from many diverse traditions into their own tribal myths.

The hero of this story is a boy who was magically born from a peacock egg, along with a bull, who acts as his brother and protector.

One day, five Peris descend from the heavens to bathe in a temple tank near where the boy is grazing his bull. The bull manages to capture their clothing; the Peris tell him that if he returns the clothing, the boy may choose one of them to marry. The bull returns their clothes, and the boy marries the youngest Peri.

When the boy grows up to be a man, he and his wife and the bull move to the city. The raja of this city is evil and lecherous, and covets the beautiful Peri. He tries to kill the man so he can possess her.

The bull helps the man to escape and outwit the raja several times, but in the end, both the man and the bull are killed. When the raja attempts to capture the Peri, though, she simply melts from his arms and flies away back into the heavens.

Ref: 127, 163, 541

PESHWA NARAYAN RAO

Peshwa Narayan Rao Bhat was the tenth *peshwa* of the Maratha Empire. He inherited his title in 1772 at the tender age of seventeen. His reign was very short; after just eight months in office, he was assassinated in the Shaniwar Wada in Pune. His ghost is said to haunt the palace to this day.

The peshwas were originally the prime ministers of the Maratha Empire, appointed to the position by the *chhatrapati*, or emperor. In the early 18th century, they became the *de facto* rulers, more powerful than the chhatrapati, and the office became hereditary in the Bhat family.

Narayan Rao Bhat took power after his elder brother Madhavrao died of tuberculosis. But their paternal uncle, or *kaaka*, wanted the office for himself.

His name was Ragunath, and he conspired with his wife Anandibai and the Gardis of the Maratha army to get the young peshwa out of the way.

There is a popular legend that Ragunath merely wanted his nephew kidnapped, and sent a letter to the Gardis that read *Narayan Rao ana dhaara*—"Take hold of Narayan Rao". But his merciless and power-hungry wife Anandibai intercepted the message. She changed one letter of the Marathi, so that it read *Narayan Rao ana maara*—"Kill Narayan Rao"—instead.

As the Gardis came for him, Narayan Rao realized what was about to happen. He ran through the palace screaming for his uncle: *"Kaaka! Mala vachva!"* ("Uncle, save me!")

But no one came to his aid, and Narayan Rao was cut down. Legend has it that he was chopped into so many pieces that he was carried out to the cremation ground in a large pot.

It is said that the young peshwa's voice can still be heard every new moon night, as his ghost runs through the palace screaming: *"Kaaka! Mala vachva!"*

Ref: 543

PEY

In the folklore of Tamil Nadu, a Pey is an evil spirit. Usually, it is the lingering ghost of a human, especially a young adult who has committed suicide due to "love failure" (an intercaste or same-sex relationship blocked by family opposition, or one that ended in a painful breakup.) Sometimes, though, Peys appear to be non-human in origin.

Though the word Pey is thought to be related to the Sanskrit **Preta**, it does not closely resemble the suffering, hungry ghost of Buddhist myth. Instead, the appearance, behaviour, and abilities of the Pey are more akin to the Hindi **Bhoot**. It has the same strength and stamina, the power to stretch its limbs, and the power to transform into a greyish smog and fly away. Unlike Bhoots, though, some varieties of Pey are mortal spirits that can be killed.

Peys typically live in tamarind trees. Late at night or on hot days, they wander around in lonely places. They can even inhabit urban settings such as bus stands or railway tracks. Peys often become infatuated with humans and possess them by sitting on their heads and entering through a lock of hair. The touch of a Pey cannot be felt; it has a tranquilizing or numbing effect.

Complicated exorcisms must be performed to remove these spirits. As Tamil folklorist Ki. Rajanarayanan writes, "There are lots of theories about which sorts of twigs should be used to drive out which sorts of Pey, and which percussion instruments should be played during the session to control them."[291]

Another tool used to bind or control Peys is the iron nail. Exorcists sometimes try to fix a Pey to a tamarind tree by driving a nail into the trunk, preventing it from leaving. A nail driven into the skull of a Pey can have the effect of fixing it in human form; it will be unable to change shape or fly away until the nail is removed.

Sometimes a Pey can be placated with regular offerings of sweets. They are especially fond of *panniyarams*.

When Peys speak—whether in their own body or while possessing an exorcist—they tend to express themselves in rhyme or song.

There is a wide variety of different sorts of Peys, each with its own characteristics and motivations. The Evar Pey is an attendant to a more powerful Pey, or, sometimes, a Pey in the service of a black magician. Echir Pey is a diminutive, gluttonous spirit.

The **Kollivay Pey**, **Kaniam Pey**, **Kanni Pey**, **Kurali Pey**, and **Mohini Pey** are all well-known, and have separate entries in this book.

Ref: 107, 291, 292

PHI

The word Phi means "god", "spirit", or "ghost" in the Thai language, as well as in the several languages spoken in Assam and Arunachal Pradesh that are classified in the same family.

In the Tai-Ahom Faith

The Ahom Kingdom was founded in 1228 by Chaolung Sukaphaa and remained the dominant power in the Brahmaputra Valley for the next 600 years. The traditional religion of the Ahoms was related to the Satsana Phi or "Spirit Faith" practised in Laos; it revolved around worship of the Dam Phi, the ghosts of the ancestors. The old religion is now mostly forgotten, with most Ahom having adopted Hinduism; but ceremonies in remembrance of the Dam Phi are still conducted.

The Dam Phi of a household are categorized according to their generation and their manner of death.

The first three generations of a married couple's ancestors—at least, all those who lived a full life and died a natural death—are called the Griha Dam. These ghosts reside in a pillar in the house called the Dam Khuta, where they are worshipped along with the household god. The next nine older generations are called Chang Dam, who have moved from inside the house to the threshold. The generation above this, and all older generations, are called Chao Phi Dam, who are considered to have merged with the collective ancestors.

Any ancestors who died by accident, violence, or suicide, or who died unmarried or without children, are called Jokorua Dam. These are volatile and dangerous ghosts who are not to be worshipped inside the house, nor with the Chang Dam on the threshold. After fourteen generations, they become Khin, the "Unlucky", and are joined with the evil deities Ra Khin, who causes diseases of the body, and Ba Khin, who causes diseases of the mind.

In Tai Khamti Lore

The Tai Khamti are another community living in Assam whose language is related to Thai. Their stories tell of evil spirits called Phi, and of black magicians called Pee Chew who control them.

In the *Chetuie*, the ancient chronicle of the Khamti, it is said that the homeland of the tribe was a beautiful lake called Mung Khamti. On the banks of this lake grew a miraculous tree whose branches bore fruit of iron, brass, copper, silver, and gold. By harvesting the precious fruits of this tree, the Khamtis grew very wealthy, earning the jealousy of the neighbouring countries.

In one of those neighbouring countries there lived an evil magician named Takasu, who coveted the precious metals of the miraculous tree. He built a gigantic bird out of wood, and used his supernatural powers to bring his creation to life. Then he sent it to attack the Khamti people. The monstrous bird flew to Mung Khamti, perched on the tree, and began to terrorize the Tai Khamti by gobbling up their children.

The Khamti were desperate to get rid of the bird. They burnt down the tree, thus destroying their source of wealth. But it didn't do any good: the bird merely took a new perch on a nearby mountaintop and continued its deadly raids. In desperation, the people began to flee. Some of them ran in the direction of Thailand, others in the direction of India.

It is said that eventually, the people who stayed behind managed to build a gigantic bow and arrow. With it they were ultimately able to kill the bird.

After it was dead, some people took meat from the gigantic carcass and cooked it and ate it. But everyone who did so became a Pee Chew, a black magician who could control the Phi, and who had a ravenous hunger for the flesh of little children.

Some of the Pee Chew followed the Khamti to Assam, and have troubled them ever since.

Ref: 227, 360

PHEICHHAM

In the folklore of the Lushai and other Kuki tribes of Mizoram and Manipur, a Pheichham is a one-legged jungle spirit that grants wishes.

According to some stories, Pheichhams are nimble, able to hop quickly on their single foot. Their footprints, which are the size of a baby's, are found along stream beds in lonely places. A Pheichham has the face of a wild-haired old woman. If a human should come upon one in the forest, the Pheichham will jump away, cackling, challenging the person to chase her. If he should manage to catch her, she will grant him a wish; if he speaks the wish in a single breath, it will be granted. However, if he stops before he has completed the request, the Pheichham will give a short laugh and quickly disappear.

In other tellings, the Pheichham is more decrepit. It may be discovered in the forest having fallen down and unable to get up. It grants wishes to those who take pity on it and help carry it to its destination. In these tales the Pheichham is usually genderless, and appears less human.

While in most stories the Pheichham is a mischievous spirit that brings good luck, other tales say that it is in fact a type of **Ram Huai** or **Thilha**, and warn that it can be dangerous.

Ref: 6

PHUNG

In Mizo folklore, a Phung is a terrifying ogre (the feminine form is Phungpuinu). Phungs are huge, ugly, stinky, and terrifying, with wide-stretched eyes, long talon-like fingers, and wild, unkempt, lice-ridden hair.

Phungpuinu are known for gobbling up beautiful women (they usually swallow them whole), stealing their clothes and jewellery, and then trying to impersonate them. They have the power to put people into hypnotic trances.

So, for example, a Phungpuinu can convince the husband of a woman she's just gobbled up that she is actually his wife, despite her hideous appearance.

Phungs usually stay in the forest, where they live in tree hollows. When they are not eating people they survive on banana flowers. However, there are a few other named varieties of Phung with different habits.

A *Phungkur* is extremely tall and lanky. Its legs are so long that it can step over three houses in a single stride. This kind likes to lurk around the outskirts of villages in a hunched or drooping stance, swaying menacingly.

The *Tualphung* or "local Phung" is stockier and hairier, with longer and sharper teeth. It is said to haunt the village at night, creeping between the houses. This type of Phung loves to eat *piring*, a type of land snail which is part of Mizo cuisine. If two Phungs happen to catch sight of a piring at the same time, they will fight each other bitterly to get hold of it. In the Mizo Tawng language, whenever people are bickering loudly over something, they are said to be "fighting like phungs over a piring".

Most stories tell of Phungs that roam around at night. But according to the folklore of the Hmar clan, they are mostly active in the daytime. These Phung can become invisible. They are held responsible for epilepsy and for sudden attacks of vertigo.

Ref: 6, 192

PISACHA

Pisachas are a major class of goblin-like demons from Hindu and Buddhist mythology. They also appear in folk stories throughout South and Southeast Asia.

Pisachas are described as shorter than humans, with skin the colour of blackened iron. They have bulging eyes and clawed fingers—often more than five per hand. They adorn themselves with grisly jewellery: dead rats for earrings, a string of dead lizards as a crown, a mongoose carcass worn as a pendant. Some have tufts of multicoloured hair sprouting from their heads, or from behind their ears or knees.

They can change their shape, become invisible, or possess people, causing grievous illness. They enter human bodies through the mouth.

Though small, they are extremely vicious, enjoying cruelty for cruelty's sake. They have a taste for hard liquor; their preferred food is raw human flesh; and they indulge in rough, sadistic sex. They haunt abandoned houses and places where violent deaths have occurred.

Pisachas are gregarious. In some myths and epics they appear in huge armies with tens of millions of soldiers. Despite their depravity, they have a complex society and culture. Many are literate and even erudite. They speak a language called Paisachi, sometimes called Bhootbhasha, or "ghost tongue".

It is possible that Paisachi was once an actual historical language. If so, then the supernatural Pisachas of Sanskrit literature derive from a racist portrayal of a real human ethnic group—perhaps a Dardic tribe from the Kashmir foothills, or one of the Adivasi tribes of central India. Some linguists think Paisachi was closely related to the Pali language of Buddhist scriptures; others believe that elements of Paisachi vocabulary survive in the languages of India's west coast, such as Konkani and Tulu.

A different theory holds that the name Pisacha is just an ancient Indo-European word meaning "demon". As the Indo-Aryans migrated into the subcontinent, they applied the term to any and all tribes they encountered who practised cannibalism. If this is true, then Paisachi might have referred to several different real languages, or to a purely mythical one.

The *Brihatkatha*, an ancient Indian epic that is now mostly lost, is supposed to have originally been written in Paisachi. The story goes that Raja Satavahana—a king of Pratisthana in what is now Maharashtra, who lived perhaps around the 2nd century CE—wanted to learn proper literary Sanskrit. One of his ministers, Sarvavarma, boasted that he could teach the raja to master the language in just twelve months. But a rival minister, by the name of Gunadhya, pooh-poohed the idea. Such a feat was impossible, he said; the brightest student on Earth would take at least twelve *years* to master Sanskrit.

The two ministers made a bet. Gunadhya promised that if Sarvavarma could live up to his boast and teach the raja proper Sanskrit in under a year, then Gunadhya would renounce not only Sanskrit, but also Prakrit and any of the other local languages derived from it.

Gunadhya *should* have been right. It is impossible, under normal circumstances, to learn proper Sanskrit in just twelve months. But his rival Sarvavarma prayed to Saraswati, the goddess of knowledge; and through her divine intervention, the raja was able to gain complete fluency in a miraculously short time.

And so Gunadhya lost the bet. He had to stop speaking, writing, and reading. Without the use of language, he could hardly work as a minister any longer, so instead he went into exile in the jungle.

While living in the wild, Gunadhya met a Pisacha named Kanabhuti, who taught him to speak, read, and write Paisachi. (Since this language was unrelated to Sanskrit and Prakrit, it was exempt from his vow.) Kanabhuti told seven long stories to Gunadhya, each of them 100,000 couplets long. Gunadhya, who had access to neither ink nor paper, wrote these stories down in his own blood on tree bark over the course of seven years.

When Kanabhuti finally finished telling his tales, he disappeared. Gunadhya knew he was in the possession of a masterpiece of literature, but he soon realized that none of his own people would pay attention to a work written in blood in the language of demons. Since he had vowed never to use any of the languages they knew, none of them would ever understand what he had written. He fell into despair. Sitting alone at the top of a hill, he read the manuscript aloud to the jungle animals, burning the sheets of bark one by one after he read them.

The animals, who could understand Paisachi, were enraptured by the stories. They became so engrossed in the narrative that they forgot to graze, forgot to hunt. They listened all night until they fell asleep; then they slept all day and woke up again and gathered around Gunadhya's camp, eager to hear the next installment.

Over time they became weak and emaciated. This was soon noticed back in Pratisthana by the raja, who ordered his men to figure out why there was no good hunting in the forest anymore. Soon they found Gunadhya and learned about his strange manuscript. The raja, realizing the value of the amazing tale and its supernatural origin, stopped Gunadhya from burning the last 100,000 couplets. He released Gunadhya from his vow and had the work translated into Sanskrit (though only one-seventh of the original remained). Thus it became known as the *Brihatkatha*.

Though no copy of the original work exists in any language, the *Brihatkatha* is said to be the source material for the *Kathasaritsagara*, "The Ocean of the Streams of Stories", a compilation of legends and folklore dated to the 11th century. This book also contains what is probably India's best-known ghost story: *Baital Pachisi*, or *Vikram and the Vetal*.

Ref: 135

PITR

In Hindu mythology, Pitrs are the spirits of departed ancestors who lived full and righteous lives. After death, they are ferried across the river Vaitarna by the **Yamadutas**, the minions of the god of death. This river, which appears unspeakably foul and horrific to sinners, seems to the Pitrs to be serene and beautiful and filled with nectar. The souls then follow the path of the moon to Pitr Lok, in the southern reaches of the universe.

Living Hindus pay homage to the Pitrs during Mahalaya Amavasya, a new moon day in the month of September. The longer sixteen-day festival of Pitr Paksha begins on this date.

There is also a class of divine Pitrs, who are not the spirits of departed ancestors, but rather ancient gods who dwell along with the human ancestors in Pitr Lok. These deities are reborn every thousand *mahayugas*, that is, every 4.32 billion years.

Belief in the Pitrs as a collective of ancestral spirits is also common to the Sarnaist faith of some tribes, such as the Oraon.

Ref: 544

POGEYAN

The Pogeyan, also called the Pogeyan Puli or Smoke Cat, is a cryptid feline: a big cat thought to live in the Western Ghats rainforest, whose existence has not been confirmed by science. It is said to have a uniform grey coat, a long tail, and rounded ears.

Zoologists speculate that it may be a mutant leopard (*Panthera pardus*); a larger-than-usual jungle cat (*Felis chaus*); or a vagrant Asiatic golden cat (*Catopuma temminckii*) that has wandered far outside its usual range in Southeast Asia.

Others believe it is a supernatural creature which has the power to dissolve into mountain mist and disappear whenever it likes.

The Pogeyan is so rarely glimpsed that not much is known about its behaviour.

Ref: 198, 371

POLYDACTYL WARRIORS OF THE HIMALAYAS

According to the book *Indica* by Ctesias (c. 500 BCE), there once lived a Himalayan tribe of people who had eight fingers on each hand and eight toes on each foot. They also had gigantic ears that hung down to their elbows. They were born with white hair and eyebrows; their hair would remain white for the first thirty years of their life, then slowly turn black, until at age sixty there was no white left in it. They were ferocious fighters, and Ctesias reported that one Indian raja employed five thousand of them as archers and javelin-throwers.

It is said that the women of this tribe only gave birth once in their lives.

Ref: 251

~— PRAMATHA —~

Pramathas are invisible spirits, sometimes said to be a class of minor **Rakshasas**, mentioned in ancient Hindu texts. Along with **Bhoots**, **Pretas**, and **Pisachas**, they are attendants of Shiva, the Lord of Ghosts.

Pramathas are active at night. They possess or torment people for bad behaviour and breaches of etiquette, such as sleeping with their heads in the wrong direction (north and west are considered unlucky). Sleeping at the base of a tree or failing to bathe after sex are also invitations for punishment by a Pramatha.

One can fend off Pramathas by keeping orris root (*Rhizoma iridis*) on one's person, or by keeping the skin of a black cat at home.

Ref: 135

~— PRETA —~

Pretas are hungry ghosts. The feminine version is Preti. They live in Naraka, the abode of the dead, but occasionally they roam the world of the living. Even when they do walk among us, they are invisible; only people in heightened states of awareness, attained through deep meditation, are able to see them.

Pretas are naked, emaciated, and corpse-like, but with huge distended bellies. Their putrid skin is stretched over their bones, making their veins bulge, giving them the appearance of dried-up leaves. They have extremely small mouths and/or long skinny necks.

Some say Pretas are spirits of humans who were greedy, jealous, corrupt, or murderous during their lives, and are therefore condemned in death to suffer from great thirst or hunger. According to others, they are the ghosts of anyone whose funeral rites were not performed correctly, or who died unnaturally as the result of violence or accidents.

Each hungry ghost has a craving for one particular sort of abhorrent food. For some it is blood; for others it is corpseflesh; for others it is the ash from cremation grounds; for still others, it is faeces.

But no matter how much they eat, the food always catches fire in their bellies, and burns up before it can provide them any nourishment.

Pretas suffer other torments too. The heat of the sun scorches them, even in the shade. Any good food that is offered to them turns to dung, urine, pus, or blood as soon as they accept it. If they are given clothes of fine fabric, these transform into scorching-hot sheets of iron the moment they put them on.

Belief in Pretas dates from some of the oldest texts of Hinduism. It was later incorporated into Buddhism and Taoism and adopted over large swaths of Asia. In Bengal they are called *Peta* and *Petni*; in China they are called *E Gui*; in Korea they are called *Agwido*; in Japan they are called *Gaki*. Across most of Southeast Asia and Mongolia, they are called by words derived from the Pali word *Peta*.

The *Petavatthu*

The Buddhist scripture *Petavatthu* was written in the Pali language of ancient Magadha, in what is today the state of Bihar, probably around 300 BCE. It relates how the Buddha and some of his disciples travelled to the realm of the hungry ghosts and conversed with them.

A few of the Pretas and Pretis interviewed in the *Petavatthu* are:

- **Sukarmukh**, the Pig-Headed Ghost. This is the ghost of a man who had verbally abused monks during life. As a Preta, he has the shape of a man with golden skin, but the snout and mouth of a pig.

- **Pootimukh**, the Stinky-Mouth Ghost. This is the ghost of a man who said many vile things during his life, abusing people for no good reason. As a Preta, he too appears golden in colour, and in the shape of a man; but his mouth is being eaten away by worms, and an awful smell hangs about it. This ghost is followed by swarms of mosquitoes and other biting insects.

- **Pancch-Putta-Khadak**, the Devourer of Five Children. This Preti is described as foul-smelling and covered with flies. She explains that in life, she was so envious of another woman's pregnancy that she poisoned her so as to cause a miscarriage. As punishment for this sin, she was condemned in the afterlife to give birth to five children every day at daybreak, and then to devour them all at sunset, and to repeat this for ages.

Not all of the Pretas and Pretis that appear in the *Petavatthu* are suffering as badly as the ones described above. A few of them—despite having sinned in life—even live in beautiful mansions with lotus ponds and mango trees that provide relief from the sun. These lucky ghosts are the ones whose descendants gave donations to charity in their name.

The better condition of these Pretas indicates that the agony of a hungry ghost does not necessarily last for eternity. If a ghost's living friends and relatives give generously to temples and to the poor, they can transfer their merit to the deceased—thus enabling them to live more comfortably in Naraka, or even to be reborn.

The Ghost Festival

In the *Petavatthu*, Sariputra—one of the Buddha's closest disciples—travels to Naraka, where he meets his dead mother. He finds that she has become a pitiful hungry ghost, condemned to eat pus and blood and snot. Sariputra goes back to the world of the living and builds new huts for the monasteries and donates food and drink, thus improving the condition of his mother's spirit, who afterwards gets to live in a beautiful palace and eat rich food.*

This visit is commemorated during the Ghost Festival, a major festival for both Buddhists and Taoists usually held between August and October in countries from Cambodia to Indonesia to Japan.

Possession

Pretas rarely interact with living humans in Buddhist legends. However, in some folkloric traditions, especially of Bengal and Assam, they can possess people in order to speak through them of their woes and torments. It is said that when someone is possessed by a Preta, they will feel that their whole body is on fire.

In Dhivehi and Tamil

The word *Preta* passed into the Dhivehi language, spoken on Minicoy Island of Lakshadweep and in the Maldives, as *Fureta* (see **Faru Fureta**). But there, it is used as a general term for monster or demon. Preta is claimed by some to be the root of the Tamil word Pey, as well, though the Pey has a rather different character.

Ref: 72, 422

....

* In later versions of the legend, it is a different disciple, Maudgalyayana, who saves his mother's ghost from torment.

❧ PRINTER'S DEVIL ❧

In Britain, the term "Printer's Devil" refers to an errand boy or assistant in a print shop. In India, it is more commonly associated with a sort of poltergeist who haunts the printing press, busily introducing misspellings, deleted lines, and other errors into books.

This belief may originate in Europe with the medieval legend of Titivillus, the patron demon of scribes. Titivillus is usually pictured with bird-claw-like feet and horns on his head. He was believed to sit in the rear pews during church services holding a large scroll of parchment. On this parchment, he would write down whatever whispered chit-chat and gossip he heard spoken by the members of the congregation who were supposed to be listening to the sermon. This record would then be used as evidence against them in the afterlife, when they were judged at the gates of heaven.

Other times, Titivillus is shown carrying a huge sack, full of all the grammatical errors people have made while speaking or writing. This he must deliver to his master, Satan, once a day.

Another theory is that the Indian term "printer's devil" arises from Malayalam. In that language, a "printing error" is called an *achadi pisaku*; a change of one Malayalam letter makes this *achadi pisachu*, or "printing devil".

Whatever its origin, the demon is known in other Indian languages too, such as Bengali, where it is called *Chhapakhanar Bhoot*.

Ref: 546

❧ PU PÂWLA ❧

In the mythology of the Lushai of Mizoram, Pu Pâwla (Mr. Pâwla) is a fierce and enormous giant who lives at the gateway known as Zingvanzawl. This is the entrance to Mitthi Khua, the village of the dead, and all human souls must pass through it to reach the afterlife.*

Some claim that Pâwla is the spirit of the first man who ever died.

....

* Many Northeastern tribes have similar myths, though the name of the guardian changes: see **Kolavo**.

Pu Pâwla carries a huge pellet bow, which can fire pellets as big as eggs. When souls (**Thlarau**) approach the entrance, Pâwla interrogates them about their achievements in life. If he is unimpressed—for instance, if they were poor hunters with few kills to their name, or if they died as adult virgins—he shoots them with a giant pellet. It is said that it takes three years to recover from this injury, and during that time the person's spirit must wait in a sort of purgatory outside the gates of Mitthi Khua.

In some stories, this guardian demon forces lazy or weak spirits to submit to a further indignity before they can enter the afterworld: he demands that they pick the lice, fleas, and ticks from his head and body hair and squish them. These parasites are so engorged with blood that they are the size of small brinjals.

A few souls are permitted to bypass Pâwla. One category is the souls of infants who died before the age of three months. These are buried along with an egg, a pinch of rice, and a porcupine quill. The egg would roll the spirit right into Mitthi Khua. The rice was food for the journey, and the porcupine quill a weapon for defence against any **Huai** the infant spirit might meet along the way.

Another category of souls that Pu Pâwla doesn't bother are accomplished hunters who have performed the feast of honour, called *thangchhuah*. These heroes ride into heaven in a great procession, dressed in fine regalia, borne by the spirits of the animals they have killed. For these important souls, Pâwla stands aside.

In the mythology of some Zo tribes, Pâwla is the only guardian of Zingvanzawl. In other stories, he is accompanied by his wife, **Sanu**; in still others, Sanu guards the entrance alone.

Ref: 324

⌁ PUGRI NAAD ⌁

In the folklore of the Kurukh tribe of Central and Eastern India, who are also called the Oraon, *Naad* is a general term for nature spirit, both benevolent and malevolent. A Pugri Naad is a small spirit-familiar in a person's service. They can also be used as ghost-soldiers by battling sorcerers.

These spirits, in their wild state, make their homes at the corners of ancient water-tanks or in peepal trees. It is not too hard to find one: there is an old Kurukh saying that "the world is as full of disembodied spirits as a tree is full of leaves." To enlist the services of a Pugri Naad, a person takes a secret vow near the spirit's place of residence, promising periodical sacrifices in exchange for fulfillment of the person's wish. For example, the person might wish for the romantic attention of someone they admire, or for a coveted object to be magically transferred into their possession, or for some bad luck to befall one of their enemies.

Contracting with a Pugri Naad can be dangerous, especially if the periodical sacrifices are not done according to schedule. Hungry Pugri Naads start performing frantic invisible dances, causing breakouts of disease among people and livestock.

The only way one of these angry, out-of-control Pugri Naads can be contained is if the owner confesses himself. Historically, in such cases, the village council would intervene to oversee proper sacrifices. Afterwards, the Pugri Naad would be contained in a wooden peg and kept in a bamboo basket in the owner's house. In this way, it would be converted to a family spirit.

If a person had more than one Pugri Naad, the wooden peg kept in their house would have as many notches in it as there were spirit-familiars.

Pugri Naads may also be summoned by more powerful magicians. *Dains* (witches; see **Daayan**) and *bishahis* (wizards) may employ them for nefarious purposes, and ojhas or spirit-doctors may use them for supernatural counter-warfare.

Ref: 309, 335

RAHU

In Hindu mythology, Rahu is the demon responsible for the solar eclipse. He is the head of the serpent Svarbhanu, created when Svarbhanu was sliced into two pieces by Lord Vishnu's golden disc. **Ketu** is the other half.

Rahu is associated with greed, cruelty, arrogance, rash judgements, venereal disease, accidents, mass tragedies, the colour black, and the number eight.

In Indian astrology, he represents the northern intersection point of the celestial paths of the sun and moon. A certain span of time each day, usually about ninety minutes in length, is designated as *Rahukaala*. This is considered an inauspicious time to leave the house or to start any project.

Rahu is propitiated as a deity in India, but he is even more popular in Thailand, where he is called Phra Rahu. There his worshippers give him offerings of eight black foods: black grapes, black jelly, black beans, black rice, black cake, black eggs, black liqueur, and black coffee.

Ref: 556

RAKHONDAR

The Rakhondar is a (usually) benevolent guardian spirit, a protector of villages along the Konkan coast. He is associated with the spirit Devchar or with the Holy Ghost of the Catholic Trinity.

Rakhondar walks the village late at night, on the lookout for any enemies. If someone is lost, he may appear to them as an old man with a lathi, and lead them home. When they turn to thank him, they find he has vanished in a puff of smoke.

Ref: 65

RAKSHASA

In Hindu mythology, Rakshasas are a large class of cannibalistic demons. The female term is Rakshasi. These beings were created from the breath of the god Brahma as he lay sleeping at the end of Satya Yuga, the Age of Truth.

Rakshasas are usually described as tall humanoids with blazing red eyes. Each individual has a few features more typical of beasts, such as tails, spotted or striped fur, horns, or clawed feet. Most have two large curved tusks protruding from their upper jaw. Deformities are common: hunched backs, missing ears, fingerless hands... even multiple heads, or tentacles in place of legs. All Rakshasas are fierce warriors. Some are also master illusionists who can appear in different shapes.

Rakshasas are most active at night. They are said to be less powerful in the East, where the rising sun saps their strength. They are mortal.

The Rakshasas of Bengali folklore, called *Rakkhosh*, have a famous catchphrase they use while on the hunt: "*Hau, mau, khau... Manusher gondho pau!*" ("Hau, mau, khau... I smell human meat!")

The female of the species is just as deadly as the male, if not more so. Numerous well-known folktales involve Rakshasis who abduct, fall in love with, and/or eat human males. They typically keep their kidnapped boyfriends imprisoned in deep pits, taking them out every night to use them sexually for a while before finally deciding to have them for dinner. Some Rakshasis are so voracious that, given a few years, they can depopulate whole countries.

According to one source, there are 20,000 Maharakshasas (Great Rakshasas) who rule over lesser Rakshasas as kings. These Maharakshasas reside on islands in the sea, where they attack and swallow ships.

In the *Ramayana* and *Mahabharata*, not all Rakshasas are cannibals. A few even fight on the side of good, such as Ghatotkatcha, who is the son of Hidimbi (see **Hidimba**) by Bhim. Others are considered good or evil depending on whom you ask. Ravana, for example, is considered by most Hindus to be a symbol of evil, but is worshipped as a god by communities in several parts of India and Sri Lanka. His sister Suparnakha, the most famous mythological Rakshasi, was shamed for the impropriety of lusting after Ram and his brother Lakshman by having her nose and ears cut off; in modern retellings she is often presented as a sympathetic character.

The word Rakshasa can be used more loosely as a synonym for **Asura** or any humanoid enemy of the gods. To the consternation of supernatural taxonomists, modern storybooks and cartoons use the word even more generically: *any* sort of fearsome monster is called a Rakshasa, regardless of whether it started out as an **Asura**, **Yaksha**, **Shaitan**, **Pisacha**, or **Peri**. (Though to tell the truth, there is a lot of interbreeding between these clans in the ancient myths as well. Demonic identity politics are complex.)

In Western fantasy art, especially in illustrations associated with role-playing games, Rakshasas are typically portrayed as anthropomorphised tigers. This trend probably owes its origin to an illustration by David A. Trampier in the 1977 book *Monster Manual*, a compendium of monsters for use in the game *Advanced Dungeons & Dragons*, which depicted the Rakshasa as an aristocratic-looking tiger-headed man dressed in a smoking jacket and holding a pipe.

Ref: 135, 257

RAILWAY GHOSTS

The Indian Railways consists of 7,349 stations and carries over eight billion passengers a year. Trains first started running in India in the year 1853, and people have been getting killed on or under them ever since. It is only to be expected that the entire transportation network is teeming with unquiet dead.

Most districts in the country can boast of a haunted station or two. Many stretches of track have a resident **Skondhokata**, a headless suicide or murder victim. Ghost stories set on Indian trains could easily fill a few books on their own.* Here, we limit ourselves to listing a few of the most famous locales.

Cursed railway stations attract legions of young ghost hunters and YouTubers, and all of the sites listed below can be explored further online.

The Kalka-Simla Narrow-Gauge Railway, which winds through picturesque and mountainous country, is said to be haunted by the ghost of an engineer named Colonel Barog. The story goes that when the railway was built in 1898, Barog was tasked with constructing the tunnels. He made some sort of error in calculation in the plans for Tunnel Number 33, which led the two teams of excavators working from opposite sides of the hill to dig right past each other instead of meeting in the middle. The British administrators fined Barog heavily for the mistake, and he was so humiliated and shamed that he committed suicide. His ghost is said to still haunt the tunnel.

There are many variations on this legend. Some say the haunted tunnel is Tunnel 103, not 33; others say the tunnel was never completed and lies abandoned some distance away from the track. Some say Barog killed his horse as well as himself, and that his ghost appears riding the horse beside the train through the tunnel, and that if you try to *walk* through the tunnel the horse will come and trample you to death. There are several other versions of the story involving lady ghosts in white saris who can hypnotize you, screaming children who suddenly vanish, and even some assorted werewolves. Suffice it to say that something on this stretch of track is not quite right.

Rabindro Sarovar Metro Station, Kolkata is a large underground station with oppressive acoustics. The whine of metal as a train pulls in is amplified by the echoing walls into a decidedly menacing roar. Perhaps it is the wicked noise, or something else unseen, that accounts for the disproportionate number of suicides at this station: for it is said that commuters at Rabindro Sarovar are very fond of jumping onto the tracks. (There seem to be no official records corroborating this claim, but then large Indian cities have never been known for reliable crime data.)

The last bogey of the last train that rolls out of the station every night is said to be haunted. There are reports of disembodied screams, mysteriously

---

* In fact, they have: Bengali literature in particular is replete with stories of paranormal encounters on locomotives. Satyajit Ray's *Anath Babur Bhoy* and Syed Mustafa Siraj's *Stationer Naam Ghum Ghumi* are well-known examples.

dimmed lights, and a trio of translucent passengers with gouged out eyes and missing jaws.

Dwarka Sector 9, New Delhi is famous for the ghost, or perhaps ghosts, that live in a peepal tree on the road just outside the metro station. Most sightings are of the ghost of a young girl with blazing red eyes, wearing a torn and tattered school uniform. Legend has it that this girl was killed during construction of the station. Other reports tell of an older woman in a white sari and dishevelled hair who slaps pedestrians, or else chases cars out of the parking lot, bangs hysterically on the windows, and then suddenly disappears.

Begunkodor Station, West Bengal has a long reputation for paranormal activity, and a commensurate tradition of rationalist groups debunking the claims. Some say that late at night a dead woman in a white sari walks the tracks. The story goes that back in 1967 the station master committed suicide after witnessing her apparition. Whether there is any truth to this tale or not, the station was closed that year and remained so until 2009, making it a favourite spot for young thrill-seekers daring each other to spend the night.

After the station re-opened, a "ghost tourism" racket started up at Begunkodor. Out-of-towners were encouraged to visit the empty station at night after the trains stopped. Then a gang of locals dressed up as ghouls and demons would emerge from the shadows, frighten everybody away, and steal their belongings.

Ref: 35

RANTAS

A Rantas, also called a Banbuddhi, is a female **Jinn** that dwells in caves in the mountains of Kashmir. She visits populated areas during the bitter cold nights of winter, striking fear into the hearts of all who catch a glimpse of her. Even wild animals are terrified of her. It is believed that when a pack of howling wolves goes suddenly silent, it is because they have seen a Rantas passing by.

The Rantas appears as an older woman wearing a dirty *pheran*. She has a cascade of messy black hair down to her ankles, and backwards feet with long, yellowed toenails. Some say that her eyes are turned so that their corners point up and down. Her breasts are so saggy that she can throw them back over her shoulders. She can appear and disappear at will, and has the power to imitate the voice of any person or animal.

This is a lusty demon. The Rantas yearns to kidnap men and take them to her lair to bed them. She can disguise her hideousness for a while in order to tempt her victim to come close, and when he does, she grabs him, throws him into a sack, and brings him back to her cave.

The Rantas only ever preys upon lonely travellers—she will never accost people travelling in a group. She prefers to prey on grooms and newlyweds, especially strapping young men with bulging muscles. But she also has a weakness for premature baldness or scald heads: the sight of a hairless scalp makes her all flustered with arousal.

Sometimes, after mating with a man, the Rantas rips his heart from his chest and devours it while it is still beating. Other times, she throws him into a giant pestle, and grinds him up into chutney. If she really likes him, she might keep him captive for a while, using him as a sex slave to breed more Rantas.

The Rantas always consumes her male offspring, but she often has a daughter or two living in her cave with her.

The power of a Rantas lies in her long hair. If you can manage to creep up on a sleeping Rantas and tie her hair to a pillar, she will never wake up.

Ref: 94, 170, 457

RATHA KAATERI

The story of the Ratha Kaateri begins with Kaateri Amman, a goddess whose cult seems to have originated in the Nilgiris district of Tamil Nadu. She is now worshipped in many parts of South India and Sri Lanka. She also travelled with Tamil indentured labourers to Guyana, Trinidad, and other Caribbean nations in the 1800s, and later with the Caribbean diaspora to New York and London. Today there are to be found among her worshippers many who claim no Indian ancestry at all.

In most depictions, the deity has jet-black skin, wears a black sari, and rides a black horse. She is said to have the power to save people suffering from life-threatening diseases and cure infertility in women, but she is also very ferocious. So-called "negative poojas" are sometimes performed for Kaateri Amman, in which the supplicant seeks divine assistance in harming another person. Common offerings include white rum, cigarettes, and—for major requests— the flesh of a black rooster.

Some devotees believe that Kaateri Amman is of purely Dravidian origin, and that she lies outside the Brahmanical Hindu pantheon. Others say she is an avatar of Kali or Durga, and identify her with Kaatyayani, the form of the goddess worshipped on the sixth day of Navaratri.

One myth tells of how Lord Shiva discovered that his wife Parvati had developed the habit of sneaking off in the dead of night. He secretly followed her and found that she was visiting a cremation ground. As soon as she entered the ground, a strange look came over her face. Her mouth widened and her teeth grew into long knife-like blades. With a terrifying monstrous grin, she began to feed hungrily on the corpses.

Instead of confronting his wife immediately, Shiva went out the next morning and dug a huge pit on the path between their house and the cremation ground. That night, when Parvati snuck out of bed and crept away in the dark, she fell into the trap.

Shiva came and found her. He demanded that she stop her disgusting necrophagous habit. Parvati was very apologetic, saying that it was only recently that she had developed a fondness for the taste of corpseflesh. She agreed to give it up, and to shed that part of herself forever. She did so immediately, sloughing off her monstrous form, leaving it there in the pit, and covering it with dirt.

This discarded form of Parvati is said to be Kaateri Amman.

*

In folklore, the undead monster called a Ratha Kaateri is considered either an angry manifestation of the goddess Kaateri Amman, or else an evil witch or black magician who has gained diabolical power by worshipping her. (A few stories give a different origin: when a person born with a *sevvai dosha*—a "Mars defect" in their horoscope—dies a violent death, they come back from the dead as a Kaateri.)

In modern urban understanding, the evil spirit is not often connected with the goddess at all. The term Ratha Kaateri is used in Tamil as a translation for "vampire", on account of the fact that *ratham*, which means blood, forms the bulk of this fiend's diet. But there are major differences between the Ratha Kaateri and the Western vampire. For one, while the vampire has been turned undead by a contagious bite, the Ratha Kaateri has *chosen* to become undead through black magic. Also, while Caucasian vampires are extremely pale, Ratha Kaateris have jet-black skin. They fear neither garlic nor silver, nor wooden stakes, nor even sunlight. The Ratha Kaateri typically bites its victim on the chest, draining blood directly from the heart rather than the neck. Except in more recent stories, where foreign elements have been grafted onto the myth, Ratha Kaateris cannot turn into bats; they can, however, transform into black stag beetles. If a Ratha Kaateri's physical body is killed, it can crawl out of the corpse in beetle form and fly away to regenerate itself.

When a Ratha Kaateri suffers a cut, blood spills from its body in torrents. There is more blood contained in its veins and arteries than should be physically possible.

Ratha Kaateris can change their size so that they stand as tall as hills. They can fly through the air and breathe underwater. They hypnotize bull elephants and keep them to guard their lairs, and if anyone ventures too close, the vicious beasts trample them to death.

Ratha Kaateris derive their magical power through an evil ritual in which the first-born child of a family is abducted and sacrificed to the goddess. The child's skull is then used to prepare a magical black pigment which is applied as a large round *pottu* (bindi) to the centre of the Kaateri's forehead. This pottu is the Kaateri's vulnerable spot. If it is wiped off, the Kaateri will shrink in stature and become so weak and powerless that it can easily be defeated.

At night, Kaateris roam the streets of villages and towns looking for victims. They prefer young adults and children, but a hungry Kaateri will settle for draining the blood of cattle or other livestock if it cannot find a human.

Curiously, despite the great powers and arcane knowledge attributed to the Kaateri, folk wisdom says that it can be warded off by fairly simple tricks: for example, bursting firecrackers, or writing the words *Indru poi, nallai vaa* ("Go away today, come tomorrow") on the door.

Some sources mention various types of Kaateris. An Irusi Kaateri is a demon who invisibly drains the blood of a fœtus *in utero*. A Rana Kaateri appears covered with bleeding wounds. Spells cast on unfortunate women by yet another type of Kaateri are believed by some to be the cause of menorrhagia.

Ref: 158, 169, 291, 292, 547

RAU

Various tribal communities in central India worship a hill-demon or forest god called Rau. While some Raus are considered benevolent, most are feared for their volatile tempers. Possession by an angry Rau is thought to be the cause of all manner of illnesses.

Among the Muria Gond tribe of Chhattisgarh, it is thought that Raus communicate with humans through nighttime visions. If someone dreams of a horse or another large animal, it means that a Rau in the area is in a foul mood.

Raus are particularly fond of eggs, so this is a standard offering when they are believed to be upset. They are also fed rice. When exorcizing a Rau that has taken possession of someone, it may be necessary to distract them with simple toys or figurines made of iron in order to drive them out. A Rau that causes epilepsy should be offered the feathers of a bird.

Some of the well-known Raus of Bastar district mentioned in anthropological literature are Khotela Rau, Markhund Rau, Khamna Rau, Durga Rau, Garba Rau, and the Rau of Markabera. But this list is subject to change and perhaps already outdated, because Raus are reportedly mortal. There are even tales that tell of Rau funerals, where the demons are cremated by other grieving spirits.

In the Gadaba tribe of Odisha, Rau is often compared to the police, because they both "turn up suddenly, bring in principle nothing good, and have to be negotiated with and given what they ask for so that they will leave their victims in peace."[542] As a further extension of the similarity, filing a police complaint about someone is equated with sending a Rau demon against an enemy.

The Gadaba wear a cord around their hips from birth until death as a protection from Rau.

(See also the Kumbri Marathi *Rav*, a type of **Balishtamaru**.)

Ref: 99, 542

⤜ RET KA PRET ⤛

The Ret ka Pret, literally "Sand Ghost", is a demon that lives in the Thar Desert of Rajasthan. It is a shapeshifter, able to mesmerize people with shifting patterns in the dunes. The Ret ka Pret is held responsible for mirages and even full-scale hallucinations. It is also blamed when healthy and sensible people go missing, and their carcasses are later found in the sand.

If you wear brown-, grey-, or beige-coloured clothing while walking in the desert, the Ret ka Pret may take it as an invitation to engulf you and turn you into a Ret ka Pret as well. This is said to be one reason why Rajasthanis prefer to wear brightly coloured turbans and saris, and why they use brightly coloured saddles for their camels.

Ref: 170

⟩⟩⤙ RO LANGS ⤚⟨⟨

Ro Langs means "risen corpse" in Tibetan. There are two types of Ro Langs, distinguished by the type of spirit that inhabits the dead body.

The first type is inhabited by a variety of Tibetan spirit called *Gdon*. In the 8th century, a Buddhist master from India named Padmasambhava travelled to Tibet and converted these invisible spirits to the Buddhist faith. Gdon can be summoned by necromancers to inhabit the body of a dead human, and the resulting animated corpse may be used for magical purposes. This type of being is analogous to the Sanskrit **Vetal**. (A similar type of necromancy exists in the Gurung shamanic tradition of Nepal.)

The second type of Ro Langs, which is the subject of the rest of this article, is more akin to the Western zombie. While they are not as powerful as the first type, they are arguably more dangerous. These corpses are inhabited by a type of obstructing spirit called *Bgegs*, which can manifest in the form of a black cat or a wisp of smoke. A Bgegs steals its way into a dead body lying on a bier before the funeral proceedings are complete. It does this of its own volition, rather than being summoned.

Once the spirit is inside a corpse, the body becomes puffed up and swollen, the whites of the eyes turn a blazing blue, and the undead creature shambles to its feet.

This type of Ro Langs can never be tamed, nor will they ever offer any sort of assistance to humans. They are completely and ruthlessly evil monsters.

By placing the palm of its hand on top of someone's head, a Ro Langs can turn a normal person into another Ro Langs. The victim quickly starts to suffer from slurred speech and ataxia, and his skin becomes deathly pale. Soon, the victim becomes "contagious" as well.

Ro Langs are affected by rigor mortis, which makes their movements stiff and laboured. Tibetan houses are often constructed with low doors in order to keep out Ro Langs, since they cannot stoop to walk in. The monsters are also incapable of speech; they can only communicate by wagging their tongues or gesturing stiffly with their arms.

Ro Langs move especially slowly in bright daylight. They are also susceptible to attack by certain holy objects. Throwing images of the Buddha at them, whacking them with the wooden covers used to bind *The Tibetan Book of the Dead*, or hitting them with the edge of a monk's robe can slow them down or even kill them.

Every Ro Langs has one part of its body which is vulnerable to attack, and the monsters can be classified according to which part of the body it is. A Lpags Langs has vulnerable skin, a Khrag Langs has vulnerable blood, a Sha Langs has vulnerable muscles, and a Rus Langs has vulnerable bones. A Rme Langs is the fifth and most difficult kind to defeat, since its only vulnerable spot is a single small mole or birthmark somewhere on its skin. Even decapitating and dismembering a Rme Langs will not stop the relentless advance of the part of the body that bears the mole.

Ref: 237, 432, 558

ROSE

This urban legend comes from the concrete jungle of Gurgaon, Haryana, that dystopian landscape of call centre complexes and business process outsourcing offices sprawled out for mile after mile under the smog-choked sky. Most of them stay open all night, in order to cater to customers on the other side of the world.

In one of these companies there worked a young woman named Rose. She was the star employee on the late-night shift, consistently exceeding monthly targets and winning employee-of-the-month awards. Her approach to her work was perfectly aligned with the deadline-driven, mission-critical values of the company; she was quick to adapt to new streamlined processes and agile methodologies; she was a team player, who always maintained a cheery and upbeat demeanour around her colleagues. She arrived at office every night at midnight impeccably turned out, and left smiling shortly before dawn every day without a hair out of place.

Some months after she had joined the company, near the end of her shift, she got a strange call which went on much longer than usual. She seemed unusually absorbed. Her supervisor, who had long since learned to trust her judgement, usually didn't bother to monitor her calls. But when she had been on the line over an hour past the end of her shift, he listened in to the call to see what was happening.

He was in for a shock: there was no one on the other end.

When he got up to ask her what was going on, she ended the call, but she still seemed to be in a trance. She gathered her things and left the office slowly and quietly, like a sleepwalker. In the early morning light, she looked haggard for the first time, her skin pale and stretched over bluish veins. The supervisor and other colleagues, not sure what to make of it all, let her go.

She never returned to work. When her employers tried to investigate, they found that no one by the name of Rose had ever lived at the address they had on file.

Eventually it was discovered that the woman named Rose had died eight years earlier. Her body had been buried in a graveyard which had been relocated when the office building was built.

Ref: 548

⤚ RUKH BALU ⤜

Rukh Balu means "tree bear" in Nepali. There have been several reports from Himalayan villages of a reclusive, tree-dwelling animal with an estimated weight of about seventy kilograms. The only bear in the region is the larger Asiatic Black Bear, which does not climb trees, and the descriptions do not match any other animal known to science. Some cryptozoologists claim to have found prints showing that the animal has an opposable thumb, and have speculated that the Rukh Balu may be a type of **Yeti**.

Ref: 365

⤚ RULEIPA ⤜

The story of Ruleipa comes from the Mara people of Mizoram.

Ruleipa was originally a man who fell madly in love with a woman. He proposed to her, and she agreed; but before they could consummate the marriage, she was suddenly stricken ill with a raging fever, and died a few days later.

Ruleipa, out of his mind with grief, longed for just one chance to make love to his wife.

His in-laws were aghast. They told him that such a depraved act was against nature. But Ruleipa promised that he would pay a death due, called *ru*, a large sum of money—and he was so distraught that the family finally agreed to allow it.

After the act was finished, though, Ruleipa did not keep his word, and refused to pay.

His wife's brothers were furious. To punish him for his revolting and contemptible behaviour, they removed all the bones from his body, transforming him into a slow loris, a small and very flexible nocturnal primate that creeps through the trees.

It is the result of Ruleipa's sin that a death due must be paid whenever a married Mara person dies. When a man dies, his eldest son or heir pays it to his maternal uncle; and when a woman dies, her husband or son pays it to her brother.

The slow loris is considered very unlucky among the Mara. Anyone who catches sight of one, especially during the day, is cursed to die prematurely. The curse can also fall upon the person's spouse. To see a a slow loris in one's dreams, on the other hand, is very lucky.

Among some Kuki people, Ruleipa the Slow Loris is thought to be a priest to the gibbons, and to possess very dangerous magic.

Ref: 259

⤞⤝ RULPUI ⤞⤝

Rulpui is a fearsome, giant, feathered serpent-demon in the folklore of the Lushai and other tribes of Northeast India.

Once upon a time there was a girl called Chawngchilhi. Her mother had passed away when she was very young. She lived in a small house with her younger sister and their father near their jhum field. At the bottom of their jhum field was an even smaller hut where they would rest and cook whenever they needed a break from farming.

Nearby the small hut was a hollow tree in which a large snake had its nest. This snake and Chawngchilhi were secret lovers. Whenever Chawngchilhi and her sister went to the jhum, Chawngchilhi would ask her sister to call the snake. The snake would come out and coil itself up in Chawngchilhi's lap. The little sister was very much afraid of the snake, and did not dare tell her father what was going on.

Whenever the girls were going out to work, their father would cook some rice and vegetables and wrap it up for them to take with them. But on account of her fear of the snake, the little sister could not eat anything. So Chawngchilhi and the snake ate up all the food, and the little sister stayed in the jhum hut all day and got very thin.

Her father used to ask her, "Oh, little one, why are you getting so thin?" but she always said, "Oh, father, I can't tell you." He pressed her and pressed her to tell him, and at last she said, "My sister and the snake are constantly making love; as soon as we get to the jhum she says to me, 'Call him to me', and I call him, and he comes up and coils himself up in her lap, and I am so frightened that I cannot eat anything, and that is why I am so thin."

The next day the father asked Chawngchilhi to stay home and rest. Meanwhile, he and the younger sister went to the jhum. Her father dressed himself in Chawngchilhi's clothing; but he also carried his dao, a machete-like weapon which he always kept sharp.

When they got to the tree, the little sister called to the snake, who came out and tried to curl itself up in her father's lap, thinking he was Chawngchilhi.

But the father quickly chopped off the snake's head. Then he hacked up the rest of the snake's body, scattered it around the field, and threw the head into the fireplace of the jhum hut.

With that, they returned to the village.

On the next day Chawngchilhi took her sister and went to the jhum. Her little sister called out to the snake as usual. When it didn't emerge, Chawngchilhi searched the area, and soon found the pieces of her lover's body. She also found the snake's head in the fireplace. Sobbing, she took the head and stuffed it up between her legs.

They came back to their house and found their father reclining on his back right in front of the front door. Chawngchilhi said, "Get up, father, I want to go in", but the father said, "Just step over me." When she did, the snake head fell out of her vagina onto her father's face. Her father jumped up in a rage, picked up his dao, and sliced open his daughter's belly.

But Chawngchilhi was pregnant by her dead lover. As soon as her father cut her open, hundreds of baby snakes spilled out of her, slithering everywhere, both inside and outside the house.

The man and his younger daughter tried to kill the snakelets as fast as they could. They got almost all of them. But one of the snakelets quickly slid under a dried pat of cattle dung, and managed to escape detection. It waited until nighttime, and then, under cover of darkness, it snuck off into the hills.

Over the years, this snake grew and grew. It preyed upon small animals at first. Then it graduated to goats and pigs. It no longer looked like a snake, now, but a gigantic black dragon with feathers around its neck and a comb on its head like a monstrous rooster. This was the demon Rulpui, and it made its residence in the cave known as Rulchawm Kua.*

Rulpui began demanding offerings of livestock from the people who lived in the surrounding villages. Soon it began demanding human meat as well. Some of the clans obeyed, performing an annual human sacrifice at Rulchawm Kua.

One day, a traveller who was staying in a village in that area overheard a young couple weeping despondently. He learned that it was their turn to sacrifice their child to Rulpui.

"I will slay this demon," the traveller proclaimed; and he purchased a goat and slaughtered it. Then, gripping his dao in his right hand, he wrapped the flesh of the goat around his blade and forearm, went to Rulpui's cave, and held out his arm.

....

* This a real place that can be visited today. It is a protected monument in Mizoram.

The giant serpent tried to gulp down the goat carcass, but now the dao was inside it. The traveller wrenched his arm this way and that, slashing the monster to pieces and ripping out its guts.

Soon, Rulpui was dead.

*

In some versions of the story, there is an epilogue in which the local people all divide up the meat of the dead serpent to eat. An old widow takes home the head and begins to cook it. But as she stirs the pot with her ladle, Rulpui's head snaps at her in a loud voice: "Don't spoil my eyes!" This scares her so badly that she throws the head out of her house into the neighbouring field of bottle-gourd creepers.*

After a few days, one of the bottle gourds grows as big as a house. All the crows in the area start cawing madly. As people gather around to marvel at the huge vegetable, there is a massive landslide, and everyone who ate the meat of the serpent is buried alive. Only the old widow is spared.

*

The Mizo story of Chawngchilhi bears strong similarities to a story told in the Kokborok language of Tripura about two sisters named Raima and Saima—Raima is the older sister, and Saima is the younger. Just as in the Mizo version, Raima has a python lover who is cut to pieces by their father. In the Tripuri story, though, the python is not an evil monster, but an avatar of Lord Shiva. When Raima discovers that her snake-lover is dead, she cradles his severed head in her lap and weeps. Her torrent of tears is said to be the source of the Gumti River.

In yet another version, instead of throwing the snake's head in the field, the father throws it into a spring. Raima later discovers the spring because there are magical *khumpui* flowers growing thickly along the banks. When Saima puts these flowers in her hair, they wither, but when Raima wears them they stay fresh. She realizes that her snake-spirit-husband is still alive within the water and, with a loving farewell to her sister, decides to join him. She walks slowly into the spring, drowning her human body, but living on as a queen in a magical underwater palace with the python.

Ref: 95, 192, 382

----

* Compare with the Khasi story of **U Thlen**.

⤙ RUNIYA ⤚

The legend of Runiya comes from Kumaon and other parts of the Himalayan foothills. This handsome young demon is the spirit of avalanches and landslides. He rides a giant boulder, which can sometimes be heard rumbling along roads late in the night.

Runiya has a tendency to become infatuated with young maidens. He starts appearing in their dreams to seduce and make love to them. These dreams feel blissful to the girl, but the effect on her body is devastating; she begins to waste away, sleeping through the day and becoming thin and gaunt. In the end she dies; and Runiya, who has no time for mortal emotions like grief or remorse, rolls away on his boulder to find a new love interest.

Runiya also likes to impersonate newlywed grooms. There is a legend that during a Kumaoni wedding, Runiya hides in the soles of the groom's shoes, trying to steal his way into the marriage bed to have his way with the bride. This is the reason given in Kumaon for the custom of *joota chupai*, which involves the bride's sisters stealing the groom's shoes and shaking them out before the groom puts them on to leave at the end of the ceremony. As a further precaution, the room with the bridal bed always has its windows closed, so that Runiya cannot sneak in.

Runiya can also attack women during labour. Women are cautioned not to shout too loud while giving birth, or else Runiya may steal in through the mouth.

Runiya is propitiated with prayer and offerings to avoid landslides. His shrines take the form of small stacks of stones a few feet high, sometimes with a flag stuck in the top.

Ref: 74, 447

⤙ RURU ⤚

According to the Hindu scripture called the *Bhagavata Purana*, Rurus are giant monsters that reside in two of the twenty-eight hells of Naraka.

A selfish man who works only for the benefit of himself and his family, unmindful of the harm he does to other living beings, must suffer after his death in the hell called Raurava. In this place, all the living things that the man harmed in life are reborn as Rurus. They are vicious creatures with long fangs, equipped with a venom that causes immeasurable agony.

The Rurus torture the man for billions of years. Only then can he progress to the next level of hell.

An *extremely* selfish man, who was so heartless in life that he did not even care for his family, but only for himself, and hurt many others in the process of satisfying his desires, meets an even worse fate. His soul travels to a different hell called Maharaurava. In this hell there lives an fiercer class of Rurus called Kravyadas, who kill the man, eat him, and excrete him, over and over and over and over.

This, too, lasts for billions of years before the man can progress to the next hell.

Ref: 278

⟫⟶ SAAMRI ⟶⟪

Saamri is a fictional undead monster-demon featured in the popular 1980s B-grade Bollywood horror films *Purana Mandir* and *Saamri 3-D*, directed by the Ramsay brothers: Shyam and Tulsi Ramsay. Anirudh "Ajay" Agarwal played the monster in both films, and reprised the role in the 2010 film *Mallika*, directed by Wilson Louis.

At the beginning of the first film, Saamri is an evil magician who lives in the ruins of an old fortress. He is notorious in the surrounding towns and villages as a rapist, murderer, cannibal, and necrophage. He has the power to steal the life force of a person by fixing them with his stare: Saamri's eyes go blazing red, and his victims' eyes gradually turn blank white.

When Saamri tries this trick with the local raja's daughter, he is caught by the raja's soldiers. Before he is executed, he pronounces an awful curse: he proclaims that every one of the raja's female descendants will die in childbirth.

The raja's soldiers proceed to cut off Saamri's head and lock it in a box with a sacred *trishul* (trident). Then they bury his body in a nearby ancient temple.

The rest of the film—and its sequels—take place in modern times, when Saamri's head is reattached to his body and he begins his reign of terror anew.

The popularity of the films led to the name "Saamri" being used by other Hindi horror writers as the name of an undead vampire.

Ref: 549

⊱ SAKAINJEEK ⊰

In the beginning—so say the Dimasa Kachari people of the Brahmaputra Valley—there was Bangla Raja, god of earthquakes, and his consort Arikhidima, a divine, gigantic bird. These deities settled near the confluence of two rivers, where Arikhidima laid seven eggs.

From the first six eggs hatched the gods Shibrai, Alu Raja, Naikhu Raja, Waa Raja, Gunyung-Braiyung, and Hamiadao, who are said to be the ancestors of the Dimasa people.* These were all benevolent gods; but the sixth, Hamiadao, was naughty and prone to mischief. When he saw that the seventh egg was taking too long to hatch, Hamiadao cracked it open.

This act unleashed a myriad of bothersome demons and evil spirits, who immediately flew out into the hills and springs and forests to make mischief.

These spirts—called Deo or Madai—are capable of causing all manner of disease and affliction. In order to keep their depredations to a minimum, they must be propitiated with animal sacrifices, performed carefully at certain times and places. The spirits go by many names: Daujidaimba, Daujar, Dakhinsa, Dikhongnarni, Diphuraja, Dipangiraja, Disinraja, Jompara, Hagrani, Haklini, Halebdi, Hapai, Haremdi, Khorongaji, Khorongner, Londisa, Madaima, Padumaniban, Sainni, Singkharao, Simangkhuba, and so on.

But the most fearsome of all is Sakainjeek.

Sakainjeek is the Dimasa analogue of the Tripuri witch-spirit **Swkal** or Swkaljwk. She is sometimes thought of as a single entity, but others say the term refers to seven sisters. Some of the sisters are scarier than others, and it is not always easy to know which sister one is dealing with.

To work her power, a Sakainjeek must first possess a mortal woman. Her evil spells are cast through her eyes. By fixing a victim with her gaze, Sakainjeek can cause sudden unexplained illness, or even turn a person into a pig or a chicken.

A shaman called a *samanaiyaba* is tasked with deciding which Sakainjeek spirit has caused the problem and how to propitiate her.

When sacrifices are performed to drive Sakainjeek away, it is important to keep them secret. If the person whom Sakainjeek has possessed comes to know about the ritual in advance, she can launch counter-measures to spoil its efficacy. So the ritual must be conducted in the dead of night in an unknown place.

Ref: 308

* Alternatively, according to a later Hindu myth, the rulers of the Dimasa Kingdom were descended from Hidimbi and Bhima; see **Hidimba**.

SALYASURA

Salyasura is a porcupine demon character in the 16ᵗʰ-century Telugu novel *Kalapurnodayamu* by Pingala Suranna.

His otherwise humanoid body is covered with quills as thick as crowbars with needle-sharp points—thus his nickname, "Crowbar". When he shakes his body, he shoots these deadly quills with enough force to shatter boulders, splatter elephants, or pierce through a row of thick tree trunks and pin them together.

Salyasura is a cousin of the buffalo-demon Mahishasura, who was killed by Durga. He nurses vengeance against the goddess in his heart.

At one point in the story, he madly falls in love with an **Apsara** named Abhinavakaumudi, and this is his undoing. The Apsara spurns Salyasura, vowing that she will only marry the man who kills him.

This gets Salyasura looking for some sort of magical protection. He comes upon a Durga temple where the idol carries a large blade; and on a stone pillar he sees an inscription which says that anyone brave enough to chop off their own head with the blade will be able to reattach it and survive; and that anyone else who tries to kill them will be killed *by* them.

Seeing his chance, Salyasura cuts off his head and then fixes it back on. Convinced that he is now invincible, he starts demolishing the goddess's temple. But Abhinavakaumudi and the goddess find a loophole in the protective spell. They enlist the help of a **Gandharva** named Manikandhara, presenting him with a magic sword which is his rightful inheritance. He attacks Salyasura, and gets impaled by a volley of quills; but he manages to hack his way through and cut off Salyasura's head before expiring, thus obeying the letter of the prophecy. Manikandhara is then reborn as a man named Kalapurna, and Abhinavakaumudi marries him, fulfilling her vow as well.

Ref: 474

SAMBANDH

In the folklore of Maharashtra, a Sambandh is the ghost of a greedy person who dies without an heir, or without someone to perform the proper funeral rites.

Sambandhs reside in old and abandoned houses, guarding hidden gold. If anyone tries to search for the treasure or dig it up, the Sambandh will possess a member of their family, usually a daughter-in-law, causing her to dance wildly and scream at the top of her lungs.

Even if someone does manage to get hold of the wealth of a Sambandh, the ghost will not allow them to enjoy it. Valuables will break or get lost; businesses will fail; vacations will go horribly awry.

When a person has trouble finding a spouse, or is unable to advance in their career, these problems are blamed on the Sambandh of an unhappy relative. Priests and astrologers are consulted to find out how to propitiate the spirit.

When two people have a long-standing feud over property or money, the one who dies first may become a Sambandh and haunt the living person, causing him all sorts of problems—even possessing him and causing his death.

A similar heir-less ghost from Punjab is called Gayaal. He is especially troublesome to young boys.

Ref: 463

⊱— SAMON —⊰

This Assamese spirit, named for the *sam* or *cham* tree in which it lives, is a ghost of very few words. Not only does it dislike talking, it also hates to have to listen to anyone else.

Anyone who disturbs the spirit's tree by hacking off a branch, or urinating at the base of it, or simply yammering on too loudly in the vicinity, will find himself suddenly and completely unable to speak.

A complex exorcism must be performed to remove the possessing Samon.

Ref: 294

⊱— SANAMAHI APOIBA —⊰

Sanamahi is an important god worshipped in Manipur. His name has been translated as "liquid gold". His main aspect is a benevolent household god, associated with the hearth.

However, there is also another aspect to Sanamahi, a demonic one, called Sanamahi Apoiba. This is the god of damage and destruction; he is wild and untamed, the lord of all evil spirits. He hovers over mankind with diabolical intent.

A sorcerer (*maiba*, male, or *maibi*, female) who wishes to bring harm upon someone can introduce Sanamahi Apoiba into that person's household. To do this, the house should be empty; the maiba must use some trickery to convince everyone living there to leave for a while. Then the maiba sneaks in and plants a coin, which represents the god, somewhere under the house or in the garden. This coin then brings ill luck and misfortune upon the house and its residents. It is especially dangerous for someone to sleep on top of the place the coin is buried, or to undress in front of it; this can cause serious illness or death.

Sanamahi Apoiba can also attack people outside the house. He has different names and aspects in different places. One of these names is Thangkhul Sanamahi; this is the most terrifying aspect of the god, the one in which he attempts to destroy the world.

Ref: 68, 87, 375

SANU

In the mythology of the Mizo and Kuki people of Mizoram and Manipur, Sanu is a fierce giantess who guards the gateway known as Zingvanzawl, the entrance to Mitthi Khua, the village of the dead. All souls (**Thlarau**) must pass by her on their final journey.

Sanu is said to know the life history of all souls who try to enter Mitthi Khua, and she is a harsh judge of character. If a man was such a poor hunter in life that he never killed even a single deer, then when he approaches her, Sanu catches him and breaks his ribs before letting him proceed. If he was indolent and failed to provide for his family, she flays his skin. Women, too, are punished if they didn't contribute enough to the household; for instance, if a woman never learned to weave properly during her life, Sanu gives her a sound beating with the beam of a loom.

Sanu may also try to delay the entry of spirits to the village of the dead by giving them difficult chores, such as weaving cloth on her special loom of spider-silk, or picking giant fat lice out of her hair. Even the spirits of infants are not exempt from these duties.

According to some stories, Sanu is the wife of the giant **Pu Pâwla**. She runs around trying to catch the spirits who are on their way to Mitthi Khua and get them to stand in one place so that Pâwla can shoot them with his pellet bow.

Some traditional Kuki funerals involve a ritual sacrifice. The liver of the sacrificed animal is split into two and placed in the palms of the deceased. These pieces of liver are meant to be presented to Sanu and Pu Pâwla as gifts, so that the spirit is not detained on its journey.

Sanu goes by different names in the folklore of different sub-tribes, such as Kulsamnu, Suahnu, and Tawminu.

Ref: 154, 324, 570

SANVARI

Among the Warlis of Maharashtra, a Sanvari is a female spirit believed to reside in large boulders in the forest. People used to mark these boulders with designs in red lead paint to indicate the spirit's presence.

Sanvaris spend most of their time staying invisible, but when they do show themselves, they appear as attractive young women. They often visit human villages during the harvest season. They are fond of eating grain from the threshing floor, and their footsteps sometimes appear mysteriously among the husks.

On these visits, it may happen that a Sanvari's eye falls on a handsome young man and she becomes infatuated with him. In such an event, she will use her magic to lure him back to her boulder to have her way with him. If the young man goes along with this, he can usually emerge from the encounter unscathed, and the Sanvari won't bother him again. However, if he tries to refuse the Sanvari's advances, the spirit will become enraged and kill him.

Sanvaris do not appreciate being spurned.

Ref: 450

SAROI

The Saroi are a class of evil spirits in Sanamahism, the pre-Hindu religion of the Meitei people and other tribes of Manipur.

There are sixty-one Saroi. According to an ancient belief among the Meitei, these spirits become especially active on Saturday nights, particularly during the lunar month of Lamta (February–March), which is the first month of the Meitei calendar. The first Saturday of this month, which is called Lamta-gi Thangja, is considered the most dangerous date of all. On this day, children are advised not to go outside. The spirits of the forest gather together and make a list of all those who will die in the coming year, counting out each name with a small broken twig. Then, as night falls, the Saroi wander the streets looking for human victims.

The ritual known as Saroi Khangba (propitiation of the Saroi) is performed on the day of Lamta-gi Thangja. In the morning, elderly women prepare a huge feast for the Saroi and the other gods to appease them. They also plead for the lives of those whose names will be counted out. The women go to a crossroads and lay leaf plates on the ground, one for each of the deities and spirits, and pile the plates high with fruit, fermented fish, salads, rice, salt, chilli, tobacco, and a number of other articles. Then they sing a prayer to the nine gods, the seven goddesses, the forest spirits, and the sixty-one Saroi, asking for deliverance from evil.

The processions of old women preparing and returning from these feasts are treated with fearful respect. If people should pass by, they will be sure to drop something to the ground as an offering—even a pebble or a blade of grass will do, if one has nothing else.

There is a famous Manipuri legend about two lovers, Henjunaha and Leirourembi. Henjunaha was the poor son of a single mother, while Leirourembi was the daughter of an officer. The two fell in love at first sight, and Leirourembi arranged for him to come visit her a few days hence.

However, it so happened that the appointed night coincided with Lamta-gi Thangja. As evening fell, the spirits were out in force. Henjunaha's mother warned him not to go, but he was adamant; he simply had to visit his love.

Shortly after Henjunaha left his house, the Saroi began chasing him. He ran and ran through the night. Whenever he glanced behind him, he could see the glowing green eyes of the spirits gaining on him.

Finally, just as he reached the threshold of Leirourembi's house, the spirits caught up with him and killed him on the spot.

Leirourembi was so distraught that she committed suicide.

The story of Henjunaha has been adapted for many different media, including a radio play, which is always aired on the day of Lamta-gi Thangja.

Ref: 73

⊱— SEVEN SISTER SPIRITS —⊰

There is something mystical about the number seven.

Most people can subitize up to five objects—that is, count them without actually counting. You can look at a picture of five dots and know that there are five of them without actually enumerating each one. Six is a little trickier, but can still be quickly recognized—especially if the dots are arranged in a two-by-three array, as they are displayed on dice.

But seven is different.

As a prime number it can't be divided evenly into smaller groups. A group of seven things requires us to count each one individually to be sure how many there are. It is the smallest whole number that can't be instantly grokked by the human brain.

Perhaps this is why supernatural beings so often come in groups of seven. Or perhaps there are astronomical reasons; the ancients recognized seven "planets", or wandering celestial bodies, which were visible to the naked eye but did not move according to the same pattern as the rest of the stars—the Sun, the Moon, Mars, Mercury, Jupiter, Venus, and Saturn. These entities were deified, and their names were used, in the order listed above, for the days of the week. There are also legends pertaining to the seven stars of the Big Dipper constellation, or the seven stars of the Pleiades star cluster.

Whatever the case, myths about seven mothers, seven brothers, or seven sisters are found in mythological traditions from around the world, from Aboriginal Australia to ancient Sumer, and in modern urban legends from Hong Kong to the American state of Nebraska.

It seems that in a majority of these legends, the spirits are female.

Hindu mythology has several groups of seven goddesses. The best known are probably the Saptamatrikas, the mother goddesses. In early Hinduism, they were portrayed as fearsome deities who caused illness, famine, and infant mortality. Later, they came to be viewed as protectors, but they still have ferocious aspects. Their names are Brahmani, Vaishnavi, Maheshvari, Indrani, Kaumari, Varahi, and Chamunda.

Then there are the Kritikas, the wives of the Saptarishis, or seven great sages. These are associated with the Pleiades star cluster.

Shitala the Smallpox Goddess is the eldest of another set of seven sisters, each of whom represents (and offers protection from) a different sort of fever. The names of the others are Masaani (see **Masaan**), Basanti, Maha Mati, Polamde, Lamkaria, and Agwani.

319

South India has yet another set of Dravidian sister goddesses: Poleramma, Ankamma, Muthyalamma, Dilli Polasi, Bangaramma, Mathamma and Renuka.

In Meitei folklore, the **Helloi** are seven sister-nymphs who hypnotize men with their powers of illusion. This legend is possibly related to the seven music-loving **Nelhaoloi** brothers of the Thadou Kukis.

In Tripura, Swkalmwtai, the goddess of witches (**Swkal**), is sometimes thought to be seven-sisters-in-one. The same is true of the **Sakainjeek** spirit of the Dimasa people of Assam.

In Kumaon, there is a legend about seven maidens who were captured by **Runiya** and taken to a hilltop, where their ghosts become **Anchheri**.

The Ghosts of Lalitpur

Several famous Indian ghost stories involve seven sisters who were pursued or molested by an evil man. One such tale comes from Lalitpur in Uttar Pradesh, where, in the early 1800s, the lecherous Raja Prahlad Singh is supposed to have abducted seven sisters and held them captive in Talbehat Fort. The women escaped his torture by jumping to their deaths from the fort walls. Their ghosts are said to still haunt the place, and can be heard screaming and wailing late at night.

The Asras

Another legend comes from the Konkan coast, where the spirits are called Asras, a type of Jal Devta or water-spirit. The Asras are the ghosts of seven young mothers who committed suicide together by jumping into a well. They became wicked water-nymphs who lurk around old wells, ponds, or streams in lonely places. When a person walks into their territory alone—especially a young, good-looking man or woman—the Asras will show themselves in the form of alluring, scantily-clad bathers. If the traveller approaches too closely, the spirits will pull them into the water to be drowned.

Asras are especially dangerous at noontime and around sunset. They are propitiated with coconuts, flowers, and bhel.

Ref: 56, 372

❧— SHAITAN —❧

In Arabia, a Shaitan is a **Jinn** who has not accepted Islam. Iblis, the devil, was the first Shaitan; the others are his offspring, and he rules over them as their king.

(In Hindi and Urdu, the word Shaitan can be used more generally to refer to any sort of wicked demon. In most contexts, though, it is the evil Jinn that is meant.)

Iblis has five sons, hatched from eggs, to which he is both father and mother. Their names are Teer, who causes accidents and injuries; Aawar, who encourages lust and debauchery; Sot, who makes people lie; Dasim, who causes family strife and domestic violence; and Zalamboor, who advocates cheating, embezzlement, bribery, false advertising, Ponzi schemes, and every other possible variety of corrupt business practice.

According to some, these five arch-Shaitans are only the most powerful of Iblis's children; he has countless others. He lays ten eggs every day, and from each egg, seventy male and seventy female Shaitans are born. These spirits roam about invisibly, whispering temptation in the ears of humans. They are believed to be the first teachers of witchcraft.

Shaitans look unspeakably hideous in their natural shape. They more commonly appear to humans in human guise. They always retain the hooves of a goat, however, rather than human feet.

There are limitations to the powers of a Shaitan. For example, they are incapable of directly causing physical harm to faithful Muslims. Still, they are very crafty, and often find a way to trick and deceive people into hurting themselves—or one another.

In the folklore of the Dom community of Kumaon, the name Shaitan refers not to a whole class of demons but to one particularly loathsome ghostly individual. This evil spirit appears as a bald, skinny old man with a string of drool hanging from the corner of his mouth. He is constantly on the prowl for liquor and women.

This Shaitan is said to be a devotee of Yama, the Hindu god of death.

The story goes that in life, this dirty old man molested his own daughter. Furthermore, after his sons got married, he used to pimp his daughters-in-law out to his drinking buddies. Finally his wife had had enough of him; she got a large and very fierce dog, fed it a magical potion that sent it into a frenzy, and sicced the dog on her drunken husband. The dog tore Shaitan to pieces.

Ever since then, the ghost of Shaitan wanders on roadsides and forest paths late at night. He possesses anyone guilty of incest or excessive boozing.

Intriguingly, there is an echo of this folkloric figure far to the south of Kumaon. In Tamil Nadu, stories of a similarly lecherous, drunken, ghostly Shaitan are part of the folklore the Vagriboli-speaking Narikurava community.

Ref: 165, 490, 495, 496

⤐ SHAKINI ⤏

A Shakini is the ghost of a bride. It may be that she was harassed by her in-laws for being from the wrong community, and driven to suicide before the ceremony. Or it may be they murdered her after the wedding for failing to bring a dowry. Whatever the specifics, this is the ghost of a woman who was terribly wronged, and seeks vengeance.

While the similar spirit **Shankhchunni** is specifically Bengali, belief in Shakinis is widespread across North India among various communities. They are thought to be one of the most dangerous and powerful types of ghosts. They can show themselves or become invisible at will; they are able to fly; and they are immensely strong.

When a Shakini haunts a house, guilty family members may fall victim to illness or accidents. Even their descendants may not be spared. The Shakini may haunt them for generations unless certain rituals are performed to drive her away.

Shakinis have shrill, high-pitched voices which they use to hurl vile insults and abuse at those who wronged them in life. They can use technology to deliver this discordant screeching, invisibly switching on and commandeering speakers, televisions, or public address systems. They can also use metal panels and Thermocol blocks as amplifiers.

When a Shakini possesses a person, she causes the entire body to be wracked with pain. The eyes of the victim, in particular, grow bloodshot and bulge out, pounding with pressure. If the ghost is not exorcized, the eyeballs will eventually explode.

The word Shakini is sometimes used as a synonym for **Dakini**, or in combination with the names Dakini, Kakini, and Kamini as forms of the goddess Shakti.

Ref: 550

⊱ SHANKHCHUNNI ⊰

The Shankhchunni name derives from *shankha*, or shell, used in the bangles traditionally worn by married Bengali women. This ghost, common in Bengali folk tales, is thought to be the spirit of a woman who was wronged by her husband.

Shankhchunnis have very pale white complexions. They wear white saris with the red-and-white conch-shell bangles of married Bengali women. They appear in the middle of the night, standing near the tamarind, mango, or banyan trees which are their homes, swaying slightly, looking at first glance like a white sheet of cloth.

Shankhchunnis don't like to be approached too closely. If a woman touches a Shankhchunni or otherwise disturbs her at night, the Shankhchunni will grab hold of her, strip her of her clothes, and hide her in a hollow of her tree in a senseless state of unconsciousness. The ghost then puts on the woman's clothes, changes her face to look like hers, walks back to her house, and attempts to take her place in the family.

Shankhchunnis share several attributes of normal **Bhoots**. They are extremely strong, and they can stretch their arms or legs very far, for example to fetch an article from another room. Like **Mohini Peys**, they can set their limbs ablaze and use their legs as logs for cooking without suffering any pain or ill effects. These abilities make them especially good at housework.

Shankhchunnis cannot bear the smell of burning turmeric, so exorcists use turmeric to detect whether a person is actually a Shankhchunni in disguise.

Ref: 40, 418, 456

⊱ SHEEP-KILLER OF NIALI ⊰

In the summer of 2017, livestock keepers in Odisha's Niali district began reporting strange killings of their goats and sheep. The dead animals were found in the morning with their bellies slit open. It seemed as though whatever was killing them was not interested in eating their meat—only in devouring their intestines and drinking their blood.

Government officials took notice and called in wildlife experts. They quickly tracked and got pictures of some nocturnal predators in the area, but the images were inconclusive. Maybe they were wolves; maybe they were jackals or hyenas. The necks seemed too elongated to be safely identified as any of those species.

Even after a couple of the animals were caught and provisionally identified as wolves, some farmers were sure that the real culprits weren't ordinary canines. A few of them pointed out that there were no pugmarks to be found leading in our out of the sheep pens where the attacks had taken place. They told stories of shadowy forms that evaporated into smoke.

Photographs and videos of weird alien monsters soon began to circulate on WhatsApp and YouTube and were quickly picked up by local television news channels. Some showed tall monsters with curved horns, fangs, and goat legs. Others featured hunched, grey, wrinkled, monkey-like figures with protruding ribs and misshapen hands.

The sheep-killing incidents recurred in several other districts later that year, and in 2018 as well. In all, many hundreds of animals were killed. They were always found disembowelled and drained of blood.

Ref: 551

⋟⋞ SILESALOMA ⋟⋞

Silesaloma was a fearsome **Yaksha**. He appears in the story "Prince Five-Weapons and the Sticky-Haired Demon", one of the Jataka tales of the Pali Buddhist canon.

The tale of the Sticky-Haired Demon is interesting to cultural anthropologists because of its similarity to other folktales told in places as far-flung as Iran, South Africa, the Philippines, and Jamaica. The question of where the story is *originally* from is still a matter of debate. Some believe it originated in Africa. Others suggest that Buddhist missionaries carried it from India to Africa about 1,500 years ago, from where, over a millennium later, it travelled in chains on slave ships bound for the Caribbean, took root on cotton plantations in the American South as the story "Br'er Rabbit and the Tar Baby", spawned a racial epithet, got adapted by Disney Studios for the controversial animated film *Song of the South*, and was eventually reclaimed as a symbol of the resilience of African-American women in the novel *Tar Baby* by Nobel laureate Toni Morrison.

If India is indeed the ancestral home of the tale, then surely we must award Silesaloma with a prize for being the best travelled of all Indian demons.

The Jataka version of the story begins in the city of Varanasi with the birth of a prince. This prince was a bodhisattva—a being destined for enlightenment. His birth was attended by 800 fortune-tellers, who prophesied that the child would become a great king and win glory through the mastery of five weapons. So it was that his parents named him Panchayudha, "Prince Five-Weapons".

When the boy turned sixteen, his parents gave him a thousand gold coins and sent him off to study with a world-famous guru in Taxila, in the kingdom of Kandahar (now in the Pakistani part of Punjab).

The prince applied himself diligently and became the guru's star pupil. Upon completion of the course, his guru awarded him with five deadly and expertly made weapons: a bow, a quiver of fifty poison-tipped arrows, a long sword, a spear, and a mace. Then he sent him on his way back to Varanasi.

On his return trip, Panchayudha had to pass through the forest where the fierce ogre Silesaloma lived.

The local people warned him not to go in, saying that Silesaloma was sure to find him and kill him. But the young prince was fearless and bursting with confidence, and he paid them no mind.

It didn't take long after Panchayudha entered the forest for Silesaloma to sniff him out and appear in front of him. He rose up to the height of a palm tree, his head as big as a temple-roof, his bulging eyes as wide around as dinner plates. His mouth was full of teeth that were stained and crooked but razor sharp; two huge yellow tusks stuck out from his upper lip and curved downwards. His whole body was covered with thick matted hair. Most of it was brownish-black, but his belly was covered with white spots, and the fur on his hands and feet was blue.

"Where do you think you're going, little man?" growled the demon. "You look tasty. I think I'm going to gobble you up!"

Panchayudha stood before him, lion-hearted. "Silesaloma," he said, "I am Prince Five-Weapons, and I have come to kill you."

With that, he nocked one of his poisoned-tipped arrows and shot it straight for the heart. But the arrow merely got stuck in the demon's fur, without piercing his skin.

Panchayudha let arrow after arrow fly until there were none left in his quiver. But all the arrows merely stuck in the demon's hair. Then Silesaloma gave his gigantic body a tremendous shake, and all the arrows fell harmlessly to the ground.

Undaunted, the prince took up his third weapon, the long sword. He advanced on the demon and dealt him a mighty blow. But the sword stuck fast in the hair, and when the prince tried to draw it out again, he couldn't budge it.

Next he tried with the spear. This, too, got stuck in the gooey morass of the demon's hair.

Finally, he tried with his fifth weapon, the mace. But the result was the same.

Panchayudha didn't give up. "My name may be Five-Weapons, but watch out! I'm so strong that even bare-handed I can pound you into dust!"

With that he gave the demon a mighty punch. But his right fist stuck fast in Silesaloma's hair. He wound up with his left fist, and hit him again, but that stuck too. Then he gave a strong kick with his right foot, which stuck fast, and another kick with his left foot, which got stuck as well.

Even with all four limbs immobilized, Panchayudha kept fighting. He leaned his head back and head-butted the monster furiously. But now the top of his head was stuck too!

Silesaloma was astonished by the prince's fearlessness. Even now, with his arms and head stuck to the demon's hair and wholly unable to move, he was shouting threats!

"How is it, young man," asked Silesaloma, "that you do not fear death?"

"Why should I?" replied the prince. "We all have to die someday."

As he said this, the bodhisattva thought to himself, *The five weapons my guru gave me turned out to be useless in fighting this monster. Even my youthful strength is not enough. I must go beyond the teachings, and beyond my body, and use the most powerful weapon of all... the weapon of my mind.*

"Besides," he told the Yaksha, "should you eat me, you won't just cause my death, but yours as well. For inside me there is a *vajra*, a thunderbolt-weapon, which you cannot digest; it will rip your guts to shreds, and both of us shall perish. That's why I'm not afraid."

The demon thought, *What this young man says seems to be true. He is so ferociously brave that I wouldn't even be able to digest a tiny scrap of his flesh. I'd better let him go.*

And so, to the prince, he said, "You are lion-hearted indeed! I will not eat you after all. Instead I will release you, just as Rahu disgorges the moon after an eclipse. Go back to your home and loved ones."

Freed at last from the gluey tangle of hair, Prince Five-Weapons said, "Silesaloma, you were born as a murderous bloodthirsty demon because of the wicked deeds you performed in your past lives. If you were to go on killing like this, there would be no end to it—you will suffer in countless lives, in hell, as a hungry ghost, or as an animal. But now that you have encountered me, you shall do no more wickedness."

Prince Five-Weapons taught Silesaloma the five precepts, and from then on the Yaksha renounced violence and became a friendly forest spirit. Afterwards, the Bodhisattva travelled safely back to Varanasi, where he soon became king, and ruled long and justly.

Ref: 146, 399

⤐ SIMEKAR ⤐

In the folklore of the Konkan coast, a Simekar or Girha is a water-dwelling spirit, the ghost of a person who died by drowning. Simekars are typically encountered by fishermen who go out to catch crabs at night. They are slow-moving and not very powerful, but they can still be dangerous, especially if they hold any grudges against people they knew in life. If this is the case, the Simekar will track down his enemies, calling their names at night, luring them to the backwaters, and abandoning them in dark and lonely places where the water is deep and the current is strong.

By drowning others, it seeks to increase the numbers of its undead tribe.

A Girha can also haunt the houses of people who live near the water, causing minor annoyances like stealing trinkets or mixing dirt in the food.

These ghosts wear their hair tied in a topknot. It is said that if one can get hold of this topknot, it will bring great fortune. However, if a Girha's hair is stolen, the ghost may visit the thief once in a while, knocking on the door in the dead of night to ask for its return. It is vitally important not to give back the stolen hair, or the person's luck will turn dire.

Simekars fear scissors and razors.

Ref: 115

⊱— SIVATHERIUM —⊰

Those of a rationalist bent will deny the reality of most of the monsters in this book; but the existence of *Sivatherium giganteum* is well supported by scientific evidence. An outsized member of the giraffe family that once roamed Western and Southern Asia, *Sivatherium* had two sets of giant ossicles, or antler-like structures, on its head and snout. The beast likely grew to over three metres tall and weighed more than 1,200 kilograms.

There are, of course, dozens of other extinct prehistoric "monsters" that lived in what is now India: from the large carnivorous dinosaur *Rajasaurus* to truly massive herbivores like *Titanosaurus*, these beasts could fill a whole book on their own.

But while their long-dead fossils have had negligible influence on myth or legend, *Sivatherium* may have actually been encountered by humans.

The first Sivatheriums evolved around seven million years ago, and the youngest fossils are around 780,000 years old. But some believe it survived much longer—becoming extinct only about 8,000 years ago, due to pressure from human hunters. Evidence for this theory comes from an ancient cave painting found in Amravathi, Maharashtra, which appears to depict a *Sivatherium*.

It is perhaps remotely possible that a population of *Sivatherium* survived in the Indus River region long enough for Alexander the Great to have encountered one (see **Odontotyrannos**), or for cultural memory of the animal to have contributed to the legend of the **Unicorn**.

Helena Blavatsky, the Russian occultist who co-founded the Theosophical Society, claimed to have encountered a restored skeleton of a *Sivatherium* in a ruined temple of "devil-worshippers" in Mandu, Madhya Pradesh. The fossil, which was wrapped with rhinoceros skin and adorned with an elephant-like trunk, was reportedly worshipped and decorated with flowers and kumkum. The incident is related in her book *From the Caves and Jungles of Hindostan*.

Ref: 552

 SKONDHOKATA

The Skondhokata is the ghost of a person who had his head cut off, often in a train accident. They are doomed to haunt the place they died forever, searching for their lost heads.

Skondhokatas are usually invisible, but they can be glimpsed at night on empty platforms or from the windows of moving trains. A recently deceased Skondhokata may still have torrents of spectral blood spilling from its neck.

Once in a while a Skondhokata will board a train and ride it for a while. One tale tells of a passenger who looked up from his newspaper to see a headless body sitting next to him. That very second the train entered a tunnel. The man felt an eerie cold touch in the darkness—but when the train emerged into the light, the ghost had disappeared.

Skondhokatas occasionally approach the living and angrily demand help in searching for their heads. Luckily, these ghosts are not terribly clever—perhaps because they don't have brains—so it is pretty easy to outwit them and escape.

Ref: 40, 418

SONGDUNI ANGKORONG SAGALNI DAMOHONG

In Songsarek mythology from the Garos of Northeast India, Songduni Angkorong Sagalni Damohong is a humungous crab-monster that travels between the sea and the Brahmaputra River. Like most normal-sized crabs, it is primarily a scavenger, feeding on whatever carrion it finds; but it can also hunt and kill humans if it gets hungry enough.

Dewan Singh Rongmuthu, in his book *Folktales of the Garos*, describes it as "a hideous, loathsome-looking being. It had projecting eyes that seemed to be

constantly glaring, flexible feelers, and gigantic claws with which it used to nip its victims to shreds."

Goera, the god of strength, used the crab to threaten his grandmother into giving him information about the boar-demon Wakmangganchi Aragondi, who he planned to kill to avenge the deaths of his relatives.

Ref: 306

⊱— SONUM —⊰

The word Sonum comes from the traditional shamanistic tradition of the Sora tribe of Eastern India. A person becomes Sonum, or part of a Sonum, when they die; but Sonum cannot be accurately translated as ghost or soul. The British anthropologist Verrier Elwin, who wrote a book on Sora religion in 1955, described them as gods. Piers Vitebsky, another British academic who studied the tribe in the 1970s and 1980s, translated Sonum as "Memory", with a capital M: "A Sora Memory of a dead person remains outside the mind of the rememberer."[396]

A Sonum is a sort of collectivity, containing all the people who have died from a similar cause. That Sonum then returns to trouble the living, and tries to effect their deaths in the same way. For example, someone who was killed by a leopard becomes a member of Kina-Sum, the Leopard Sonum, an entity which is responsible for sending leopards to attack his or her descendents.

As time passes, the mode of death becomes less important. Instead of trying to kill their descendents, the deceased now takes up a role as an ancestor-spirit. Soon the person's name is reused for a newborn child among their descendents. Eventually, when the deceased has passed out of living memory, they die a second death in the underworld. At this point they become a butterfly, and can no longer communicate with the living.

Some of the main Sonums are as follows.

Labo-Sum is the Earth-Sonum, which causes death by swollen organs or blocked orifices. This includes most people who die gentle deaths in old age, but also some mothers who die in childbirth. Labo-Sum is associated with springwater, coolness, and the soil. In iconography, it is often shown riding an elephant.

The dead who reside in this Sonum are thought to have some positive influences; for one, they help the crops grow. But they can also sexually assault the living. If an unmarried woman becomes pregnant, she may claim that Labo-Sum is responsible. Dead women who reside in the Earth-Sonum are said to molest good-looking double-reed musicians—they are attracted to the way they puff out their cheeks when they play.

Uyung-Sum is the Sun-Sonum. It is responsible for accidental or violent deaths: murders, suicides, deaths from falling. Sun-deaths are highly contagious, with the dwellers of Uyung-Sum often coming back to attack their descendents and kill them in a similar way. When an accidental death occurs, a pig is sacrificed; everyone in the village should drink some pig's blood and bathe in it, as this helps wash away the contagion.

When a person is killed and loses blood, it is thought that the soul cannot find the way to the underworld, so instead it rises to the sun like smoke.

The Sora goddess of the sun, Uyung-Boj, is a Telugu-speaking blacksmith. She commands several other imbecilic blacksmiths, as well as a giant python who is responsible for swallowing foetuses in the womb, or for placing its tail in the mouth of a nursing child instead of the mother's nipple. Thus Uyung-Sum includes miscarriages, stillbirths, and deaths in infancy. The god of leprosy, Madu-Sum, also works for the sun goddess. Uyung-Sum is associated with scorching heat, fire, menstrual blood, and molten metal.

Ural-Sum or **Uralba-Sum** is the Sonum of babies swallowed by the Sun's python, a sub-Sonum within Uyung-Sum. She is a baleful spirit with a terribly sad origin: the ghost of a woman who lost one child after another—through stillbirth or crib death—until she became so despondent that she killed herself.

She returns to attack healthy babies out of jealousy. She causes fevers and makes them refuse their mothers' milk. She is also held responsible for miscarriage.

Uralba-Sum can be placated with the sacrifice of a fowl at the base of the Uralba tree.

Ra'tud-Sum is a Sonum of vicious anthropophagous spirits who wander lonely paths in the forest. They exult in torture and killing, and they feast on children. They cause acute diseases that come on quickly and—without the prompt intervention of a healer—end in death. The Ra'tud-people are also held responsible for night-blindness. When they catch a person, they skewer them through the anus and roast them over a fire like squirrels.

When a soul is taken by these spirits, the Ra'tud-people torment it in the afterlife, forcing it to carry heavy loads without rest and whipping it until it bleeds. Luckily, a shaman can sometimes bribe them to release it.

People who are overly aggressive and do bad deeds in their lifetime may have to spend time troubling people as a Ra'tud after death.

Rituals to propitiate Ra'tud-Sum must be performed at midnight, and only black animals should be sacrificed. Offerings of liquor made to this Sonum must be given in cups made of a peepal tree leaf. There is a Ra'tud-house at a junction of paths outside the village where these spirits are thought to reside.

Kina-Sum is the Big Cat Sonum, which causes deaths by tiger or leopard attacks. This, too, is a highly contagious form of death; those who die by leopard come back as ghosts to incite leopards to kill their descendants. They can also cause virulent fevers. The contagion enters the body by the way of a hairy black caterpillar or other insect grub, which must be removed by a healer. Kina-Sum resides in a rock or termite mound outside the village.

Kani-Sum is the Epilepsy Sonum. This Sonum is thought to reside in a big tree or clump of bushes outside the village. Kani-Sum is associated with drunkenness, and should never be propitiated with liquor.

Rugo-Goj is the Smallpox-Woman, the elder sister of the sun. Her Sonum resides in the plains, at lower evelations than most Sora live. Included in this Sonum are deaths from cholera, called Mordi-Sum, and other epidemic diseases.

Ranggi-Sum is the god of wind and airplanes. He lives on the moon. Ranggi-Sum is generally a bad-tempered spirit. He can flatten crops, or blow hot so as to aid the spread of cholera. He causes hernias and constipation. When a person dies far from home, his spirit sometimes meets Ranggi-Sum on its way back, and they combine with a tumultuous noise to form a whirlwind.

Ilda-Sum are a special kind of Sonum who reside in the underworld; they become the supernatural spouses of Sora shamans. Sora shamans are usually women (but not always); and the women shamans typically choose their professions earlier than the men do. Thus, even before they reach puberty, these women will have got married in their dream-lives to Ilda-Sum in the underworld, where they lead a full family life complete with underworld children. These Ilda-Sum families are independent of the shaman's above-ground, living family.

Shamans also have helpers called Rauda, who are the ghosts of dead shamans who preceded them.

Ref: 395, 396, 531

SRIN MO

The Srin Mo are female demons of Tibet; Srin Po are the male versions, less commonly encountered. They are bloodthirsty and lascivious spirits. Srin are associated with the Bön religion that preceded the arrival of Buddhism, and even more so with the nameless animist tradition that preceded Bön. After the coming of Buddhism, they were identified with the **Rakshasas** of Sanskrit lore.

The founding myth of the Tibetan kingdom says that the entire landscape of Tibet is a giant Srin Mo demoness lying on her back, pinned down and held in place by thirteen Buddhist monasteries.

This myth is echoed in Zanskar, in the Kargil district of Ladakh. Here, too, the valley is said to be a gigantic Srin Mo, pinned to the ground by three Buddhist monasteries.

Ref: 553

❧— SUNGUR BHOOT —❧

Sungura means "pig" in Nepali; a Sungur Bhoot is the ghost of a pig or wild boar. These ghosts have been reported from Darjeeling and Kalimpong districts in West Bengal. They are only ever encountered exactly at midnight.

Sungar Bhoots are invisible, but can be heard grunting and foraging in the dark. Sometimes two ghost animals can be heard rutting.

They can attack living humans if they feel disturbed or threatened. Anyone who hears the sound of a heavy animal charging through the foliage should try their best to get out of the way, or they risk being badly gored by unseen tusks. Wounds inflicted by a Sungur Bhoot can quickly become septic or develop necrotizing fasciitis.

Ref: 554, 555

❧— SVARBHANU —❧

The Hindu mythological episode known as *Samudra Manthan* ("The Churning of the Ocean") tells of the aftermath of a fierce battle between the Devas and **Asuras**, in which the Asuras emerged victorious.

On the advice of Lord Vishnu, the Devas accepted their defeat graciously. They even offered to assist with the project of churning the Great Ocean of Milk.

The Devas and Asuras worked at this task for a thousand years. Eventually, the churning produced the nectar of immortality, called *amrita*, along with many other wondrous things.

Once the amrita emerged, all the Asuras planned to drink it. They meant to become undying gods, the permanent lords of the universe. But at this point Vishnu appeared to them in the form of **Mohini**, a seductively beautiful woman, and distracted them. Performing a quick sleight-of-hand trick, he switched the amrita for alcohol, and gave that to the Asuras. Then he began distributing the real amrita to the Devas, who drank it.

However, one Asura, a dragon named **Svarbhanu**, disguised himself as a Deva and switched sides. He too got a taste of the amrita, and thus became immortal.

Surya the Sun Deva and Chandra the Moon Deva both noticed the deception, and quickly alerted Mohini. She swung around and threw her bladed flying disk—the *sudarshan chakra*—at Svarbhanu, decapitating him. Since he had already drunk the amrita, this didn't result in his death; instead, it merely split him into two beings, a severed head and a headless body.

Svarbhanu's head is called **Rahu**, and is responsible for solar eclipses. His body, which ends in a serpent-like tail, is called **Ketu**, and is responsible for lunar eclipses.

Ref: 556

⊱⊱— SWKAL —⊰⊰

In the Kokborok language of Tripura, Swkal is an evil spirit that possesses women. Once possessed, the woman becomes a witch called a Swkaljwk.

A Swkaljwk usually appears completely normal, with nothing to give a clue as to her true nature.

At any time, though, it may happen that the Swkaljwk enters a state called *twimaromjago*. In this state her eyes bug out and her hair becomes dishevelled; she withdraws from friends and family and starts acting bizarre, hiding under the bed or in a dark closets. A Swkaljwk in this state often appears afflicted with what medical doctors call opisthotonos—a backwards arching of the head and neck. In extreme cases, her limbs and necks become completely disjointed and bend at bizarre angles, and she begins crawling about like an evil giant spider hunting for prey.

Swkaljwks can leave their physical body at night and take the form of a bird, named *owang* for its call: "Owang! Owang!" They can also turn into small fireballs called *swkal chwngw*, which are sometimes seen floating in lonely places, or near the corner of the house of a person the Swkaljwk seeks to harm.

These witches are also associated with the chameleon, which is called *swkalthuinungnai*, "witch blood drinker".

It is thought to be very dangerous to refuse any request of the Swkaljwk, as she will always be able to get what she wants one way or another. If someone is suspected of being a Swkaljwk, everyone will be very careful in their dealings with her.

A Swkaljwk doesn't usually admit to anyone what she is; but on her deathbed, she can pass the art of witchcraft on to her daughter.

Some say that the word Swkal is derived from the name of the goddess Kali: the word in the related Reang dialect is *Skali*. There is a male counterpart to Swkal called Bedua, who possesses men.

Swkalmwtai is the deity of witches. Some say she is a collective of seven sisters. Whenever one is troubled by a Swkal, this goddess should be propitiated by offering pork or tortoise meat at her forest shrine in the middle of the night. She is one of the Chaturdasha or 14 gods of Tripura, and is associated with Himadri, the goddess of the Himalayas.

The Garo people of Meghalaya—who speak a language closely related to Kokborok—believe in a similar witch called Skal, which can be male or female. The Garo deity that rules over the Skal spirit is simply called Daini (see **Daayan**). Once a person becomes Skal, they begin attacking others by magically eating their livers from within. This is done by fixing them with an intense gaze. A Skal can also send its spirit in the shape of a sort of giant firefly, a ravenous insect which flits about at night eating up other insects with its long tongue.

The saliva of a Skal is contagious, and can turn others into Skals.

If it is thought that a person is being attacked by a Skal, a ritual is performed at dusk just outside the victim's neighbourhood. A chicken is sacrificed, and the blood is poured into a bamboo tube. This is supposed to attract the Skal insect. The tube is then placed over a fire, roasting the insect inside, and killing the human body of the attacking Skal as well.

Though today most Garos profess Christianity, belief in Skal is still widespread. It is thought that Skal have no fear of the Christian cross or bible; indeed, it is entirely possible for a preacher to become a Skal.

Ref: 39, 77, 207, 372, 459

TAKTE RAGRE

In the folklore of the Adi people of Arunachal Pradesh, Takte Ragre is an evil creeper vine which grows out of the earth, coiling itself around farmers while they are busy working in the fields. The vine has an intoxicating effect on those it ensnares; they become weak and delirious, as if they have taken opium.

The Takte Ragre vine is incredibly tough and difficult to cut or saw through, even with the sharpest tools.

Ref: 262

⊱⊱ TANDEI ⊰⊰

Tandei is a fearsome witch known from the folklore of Odisha, especially the Sambalpur region. She is especially active on the night of Chitalagi Amavasya, the new moon night of the month of Shravan (July–August); at other times, she appears and acts like a normal woman.

Late at night on Chitalagi Amavasya, the Tandei goes out walking upside down on her hands through the darkness, holding a kerosene lamp in her mouth. She is on the prowl for young children, to quench her thirst for blood.

To ward off the Tandei, mothers draw magical designs beneath their children's navels. They also leave out a dish called *chitau pitha*—a rice and coconut pancake—to propitiate her.

(On the same day, bits of *chitau pitha* are also scattered in the paddy fields to appease Gendeisuni, the goddess of snails, and to ask her to spare the feet of the farmers from the sharp edges of the snail shells.)

Ref: 581

⊱⊱ TASMA-PA ⊰⊰

The Tasma-pa live on a small uncharted island somewhere in the Indian Ocean. When ships with human crews drop anchor and visit the island, the sailors find a number of old, disabled men sitting near the beach, unable to walk. The old men beg the strong sailors to lift them on their shoulders and carry them home. But as soon as they are mounted, the legs of the Tasma-pa extend and become leathery tentacles, which they wrap tightly around the men's bodies. Then they start riding the humans as though they were jockeys riding horses.

The Tasma-pa are very susceptible to the effects of alcohol, and the best way to free oneself from the grip of one of these demons is to trick it into getting drunk.

Tasma-pa appear in the Urdu version of the *Hamzanama*, the epic story of Amir Hamza, and in other Urdu fantasy literature. The same creature is called Daval-pa in Kurdish folklore, and appears in the story of Sinbad the Sailor as "The Old Man of the Sea".

Ref: 191, 277

⤳⟶ TASRUFDAR ⟵⤳

The Tasrufdar are a race of small elf-like beings that live in the springs and ponds of Kashmir. They usually avoid humans and dislike being disturbed. If their springs get polluted, they can punish those responsible by causing bad luck and trouble.

Tasrufdar often inhabit the same springs used by the serpent-like **Nagas** as portals to Paataal Lok.

Some springs go dry part of the year, but start to run with good clear water during the growing season. Such springs were worshipped, and offerings made to the beings thought to live within them.

The pools of the Tasfurdar were also used as oracles. One method was as follows: a farmer would fill a clay pot with rice, seal it closed, and write his name on it. Then he would throw it into the spring. After a while, the pot would float back up to the top. If, when he opened it, the rice was warm and good-smelling, it meant the coming year would be prosperous, with a good harvest; but if it were filled with mud, the crops were likely to fail.

Another method was to cut a nut into four pieces and throw the pieces into the spring. If an even number of pieces floated, this was a good omen; if an odd number of pieces floated, it was bad.

Ref: 94, 457

⤳⟶ TEGHAMI ⟵⤳

In Sumi Naga folklore, the Teghami are a class of capricious, amoral nature spirits. They are rarely glimpsed; those who claim to have seen them say they look like small, diminutive humans. More often, people walking quietly in the forest may hear them talking to each other.

In contrast to the **Kungumi**, the sky-spirits of Sumi Naga lore, the Teghami are earth-bound. They usually reside in the jungle or other wilderness areas.

According to legend, the first man, the first tiger, and the first Teghami were brothers. Man learned many arts and crafts from the Teghami, including the manufacture of weapons. Eventually though, they parted ways; the man settled in villages, while the tiger and the Teghami went off to live in the wild.

There are some malevolent Teghami who hate newborn human boys, and try to kill them. They learn about male births from sand lizards, who act as their spies. Naga men used to try to kill these lizards whenever they saw them around a male baby, to prevent news of the child from reaching the spirits.

For some reason, the Teghami do not trouble newborn girls, nor does the lizard bother to bring them the news of a birth.

Most Teghami are rather stupid. It is easy to fool them—for instance, by calling someone by the wrong name, or announcing loudly that an event will happen on a certain date when you actually plan for it to take place earlier. They also hate the smell of ginger, garlic, and lemongrass, and these plants can be used to ward them away.

One of the most feared Teghami is Muzamuza, who causes people to hallucinate and get lost in the jungle. He fools people who are walking on the edges of cliffs into thinking they are on even ground, so that they trip and fall and crash; or else he makes people who are walking on even ground believe they are walking on craggy cliffs, so that they tiptoe slowly along, carefully choosing where to place their steps, looking completely ridiculous to anyone who might be watching. Those who are wrapped up in Muzamuza's illusions often decide to eat worms (thinking they are some rare delicacy), or make necklaces for themselves out of worms, or stuff worms into their ears.

Muzamuza is also the spirit of the echo.

If you get lost in the jungle, you should cut off a bit of the fringe from your clothes and stick it in the fork of a tree. This is usually enough to satisfy Muzamuza, and he'll stop bothering you. But if you fail to do this and come under Muzamuza's spell, then it is up to your friends to save you. Someone should let a chicken loose in the forest and sing, "Muzamuza! Tell me where my friend is!" The chicken will then lead your friend straight to you.

Once a person has been led astray by Muzamuza, though, even if he is found and brought home and regains his sanity, he will never really be the same again.

Other Teghami with individual names are Tegha-aghuzuwu, the spirit of fever and delirium; Tegha-kesa, a demon who ruins crops and breaks things; and Shikyepu, who rules over wild animals, and bestows favour on certain hunters, allowing them success.

Kukwobolitomi are a class of Teghami who harass pregnant women. They are held responsible for miscarriages.

Loselonitomi, another group of Teghami, cause marital disputes, family squabbles, and disagreements among friends.

While most Teghami are jealous, greedy, and troublesome, a few of them help farmers produce bountiful crops, and are propitiated with offerings. The best known of these benevolent Teghami is Litsaba, also known as Kichimiya.

Another is Aphowo, who is worshipped on alternate years, as the spirit governing shifting cultivation.

Ref: 140

⟿ TENGTE ⟾

In Garo lore of Meghalaya and Assam, the Tengte are a race of diminutive humanoid creatures. (The word is sometimes translated into English as "elves".) They are very short—at most around two feet tall—with very large slanted eyes. They live in caves, where they hoard gold and precious gems.

It is said that in ancient times, the Tengte used to be on friendly terms with humans. They would meet at certain markets to trade, along with the Matchadus (Weretigers) and other spirits. One Tengte chieftain even helped the great hero Goera defeat the abominable boar-monster **Wakmangganchi Aragondi**. In modern times, though, Tengte are rarely seen by humans.

Tengte have supernatural powers and can be formidable enemies. However, some human beings know secret mantras and herbs by which they can control them.

When Tengte visit the surface world, they must also be very careful to avoid tigers, for whom they are a favoured prey.

Tengte are extremely strong, capable of lifting and hurling huge boulders many times their size. Curiously, however, they find it absolutely impossible to lift a leaf of the colocasia plant. If you put a colocasia leaf on top of a Tengte, it will be pinned to the spot, unable to roll out from underneath. There are tales of humans who managed to catch Tengte using this method and ransom them to their underground-dwelling families for great riches.

The patriarch of the Tengte is called Tengte Bandok Mikpil Jahphil. He is incredibly wealthy, but also very miserly.

Ref: 306

⟿ TERHOMA ⟾

In the language of the Angami Naga people of Nagaland, the term Terhoma was originally a catch-all term for deities, ghosts, and other supernatural entities—whether benevolent, malevolent, or a mix of both. However, the Christian missionaries translated the term as "Satan" or "devil", so that in modern times it is used to mean "evil spirit".

In traditional lore, there are many different Terhomas. Some are nameless, such as the spirit that is responsible for smallpox. (When the Angami Nagas practised headhunting, this Terhoma could be propitiated by offering it the head of an enemy.)

Other Terhomas have names. Aside from the creator deities, a few of the best-known Terhoma are as follows.

Rutzeh is a demon who kills people in their sleep, causing blood to run from their mouth and nostrils. Rutzeh attacks with no warning; his victims are people who have enjoyed good health and have no other symptoms of illness.

Telepfü is a mischievous female Terhoma known for rendering her victims unconscious and carrying them away. Rather than kill them, she just leaves them lying in a secluded place. When search parties of friends and relatives finally discover them, they have no recollection of how they came to be sleeping there.

Tekhu-Rho is a feline god. He is held responsible whenever someone goes missing in the jungle. If a human hunter kills a tiger or any other big cat, Tekho-Rho will try to avenge its death—but first, he must go to the dead animal and find out the name of the hunter who killed it. Tiger-killers, fearing reprisals from Tekhu-Rho, used to cut off the head of the tiger they had killed and lay it down in a running stream, propping its mouth open with a stick. Then, when Tekhu-Rho came to ask it to identify its killer, he would hear no sound but the babbling of the water.

Ayepi is a tiny fairy-spirit that sometimes takes up residence in people's houses. They bring luck and prosperity. Like most Terhomas, they are invisible, but their small footprints are occasionally seen in a path across a dusty floor.

Temi is the ghost of a person who died as a result of murder, suicide, drowning, or attack by another Terhoma. These ghosts can be terrifying, but they are actually powerless to cause any harm. The worst they can do is to give a coward a good scare.

Ref: 141

⤳ THAN-THIN DAINI ⤝

In the folklore of the Bodo and Rabha people of northwest Assam, the Than-Thin Daini is a type of evil witch.

When the Than-Thin Daini goes to bed, she lies on her back, places a blade of grass across her neck, and begins to chant a secret mantra. Then, in the dead of night, her head detaches from her body and roams about on its own, floating through the air. The witch's head is ravenously hungry, and will eat almost anything it comes across, including animals and children. While it cannot quite manage to devour a whole adult human, it has the power to slowly eat away at a sleeping person's internal organs, shrivelling them and turning them black.

The Than-Thin Daini cannot attack a person through a net. So sleeping with a mosquito net is said to be a good defence against it. If people fear there is a Than-Thin Daini about, they may set aside a portion of their dinner for it before eating.

Nearly every country in Southeast Asia has a detachable-headed monster analogous to the Than-Thin Daini. In Malaysia, it is called the Penanggalan; in Thailand, the Krasue; in Cambodia, the Ap; and in the Philippines, the Manananggal. In many of these legends, the witch must store her body in a giant vat of vinegar to prevent it from decomposing while her head is out flying around. This makes her reek of vinegar during the day. While this vinegar smell is not reported for the Than-Thin Daini, some say that she must cover her headless sleeping body with thatch.

If the Than-Thin Daini ever teaches her unholy mantra to another person, she will shrivel and die. In most stories, the secret is passed on from mother to daughter.

Ref: 159, 279

⤳ THENDAN ⤝

Tripunithura today is a district in the city of Kochi, Kerala. But it was once the capital of the Kingdom of Kochi, a state that exsted from the 6th century up until it joined India in 1947. In this place there is an ancient temple dedicated to Sri Poornathrayeesa, the family deity of the Kochi royals. The temple is very ancient—so ancient that no one is really sure how old it is. Legend says it has been there since the Dwapara Yuga, which would put it anywhere between 5,000 and 869,000 years old.

A nocturnal spirit known as Thendan makes its home in the trees near this temple. He strongly dislikes human attention. People are warned *not* to make offerings to Thendan under any circumstances.

Late at night, Thendan awakens and stretches himself to his true height. He can grow several hundred metres tall. He stands with one leg on each side of the temple complex, bends down, and laps up water from the temple tank.

It is very dangerous to witness the giant Thendan while he is drinking. If any mortal should glimpse him, Thendan will fix him with the glare of a burning eye. The person is then doomed to die within three days.

Sometimes Thendan gets restless. He leaves the temple area and goes out of the city, looking for people walking alone through forests or paddy fields. He stalks these travellers on dark paths late at night.

You might hear the crunch of leaves or twigs behind you. If you turn around to look at Thendan, you will catch a split-second glimpse of a tall, shadowy, faceless figure—just before he gives you a brutal slap to the face that knocks you unconscious.

If you're lucky, you might come to your senses in some strange location, with no idea how you got there.

If you're not so lucky, Thendan might eat you.

On the other hand, if Thendan is following you and you *don't* turn around to look at him, you are still in danger of getting lost, for Thendan has a way of making the paths ahead shift and turn and cross each other. The best course of action is not to look around, but to chew a betel-leaf and spit over your shoulder. This will make Thendan decide to leave you alone, and the paths ahead of you will straighten themselves out.

Ref: 243, 341

THILHA

In the languages of the Kuki tribes of Northeast India, Thilha literally translates as "spirit of the dead". Somewhat confusingly, though, it does *not* refer to the souls of dead humans, which are Lha, but to evil non-human demons or entities, usually immortal. Thilha are analogous to the **Huai** of Mizoram; the word is also used today by Christian Kukis to mean Satan.

In pre-Christian lore, it was said that Thilha used to live together with mortals in the same village, and the human children and Thilha children used to play together.

Once, the human and Thilha children were having a high-jump contest. The two teams were taking turns; a human would jump, and then a Thilha. When it was a human child's turn to jump, one of the Thilha children tried to cheat by surreptitiously dislodging the bamboo bar, even though the jumper had not touched it. He was caught in the act, and this sparked off a fierce argument, which soon devolved into a bloody fight. The human children took up spears with poisoned tips and killed all the Thilha children—except for one Thilha girl who was able to escape. She ran off to tell her parents what had happened.

The Thilha wanted revenge, but they were afraid of the poisoned spears. So they asked the creator god, Pathen, for help. Pathen gave them a magical charm in the form of yeast cakes with black centres called *chollaivom*, and instructed the Thilha to drop these cakes into the well from which the humans drew their drinking water. As soon as the humans drank the water, the chollaivom became the black pupil at the centre of the eye, and this is what prevents us from being able to see the Thilha to this day.

There are numerous different types of Thilha, including:

- *Nelhao*, who lives high in the hills.

- *Khemkhum*, who resides in trees.

- *Tuivamit*, a spirit of saline springs.

- *Tuivalha*, a spirit of cave mouths where water drips slowly and rhythmically.

- *Tuikhumngah*, the spirits of the streams and lakes, who are ruled by a king named Tuikhumlen.

- *Thingjungkai*, who dwells in trees that have roots growing on both sides of a stream.

- *Thinglubul*, a spirit of trees whose trunks grew in unusual shapes.

- *Thinggunei*, a spirit of the poison-tree, which causes a painful rash when touched.

- *Thinglusum*, who lives in a tree that is leafless and branchless, but not yet dead.

- *Thinggophel*, who lives in a tree where the wood of the trunk separates and joins again to form a hole.

- *Thingbulacheng*, the spirit of the largest trees.

- *Songbulngah*, the spirit of the rocks and stones.

- *Noijinmang*, who dwells underground.

- *Saote*, who is found near veins of gold or silver or other precious metals.

- *Vetvut*, who is a jungle dweller.

- *Gamlalhen*, a male spirit which causes sickness or disease, also found in the jungle.

- *Gamnupi*, a female jungle spirit with red teeth and breasts that hang down to her hips.

- *Nomnoh*, who lives in fetid swamps in the foothills.

- *Khukseko*, also found near swamps.

- *Sontepel*, who haunts jungle trails.

- *Melmul*, who lives beneath wild fruit trees.

- **Zasam**, who builds dwellings in the forest.

- *Chomnu*, a harmless female dwarf spirit, who disappears when about to be caught.

The Thilha also have a king and a queen, whose names are Gamhoise and Inmunse. Gamhoise lives in the densest forest on the highest hills, while his wife Inmunse haunts the villages and even the insides of people's houses. When travelling through forested hills, one must never speak Gamhoise's name; to do so would ensure a swift and grisly demise. Likewise, Inmunse's name should never be spoken at home.

In Kuki belief, the Thilha associated with springs and water are by far the most powerful and evil, and they demand the biggest sacrifices.

All sicknesses, ailments, and deaths are thought to be caused by one Thilha or another.

Ref: 59, 178, 215, 570

⊱ THLA AI ⊰

In Mizo folklore, when someone is critically ill, it is said that part of their spirit manifests in the forest nearby at night as a Thla Ai.

It then becomes the job of someone in the family to go and call this spirit out from the trees. Once the caller hears the spirit approaching, he should turn back and face the house. Behind him, he will hear horrible noises: shrieking, crying, the howling of an unearthly voice. The relative must lead the Thlai Ai all the way back to the house of the sick person without once turning around to look at it. If he does, the spirit instantly vanishes, and the sick person is doomed.

However, if the relative is able to lead the spirit all the way back into the house, then the sick person's recovery is assured.

Ref: 6

⊱ THLARAU ⊰

Thlarau (or simply Thla) is a word in the Mizo language that can be translated as spirit, ghost, or soul. In Christian understanding, this is the spirit which enters heaven or hell after death. The Holy Spirit of the Christian trinity is known in Mizo as Thlarau Thianghlim.

In pre-Christian Mizo belief, the Thlarau escapes the body through the top of the skull after death and makes its way to a lake called Rih Dil, just over the border of Mizoram with Myanmar. Once it crosses this lake, it travels onwards to the peak of Hringlang Mountain; it stops there and looks back over the land where it lived, and a great sadness and nostalgia for life washes over it.

The Thlarau's next stop is at a spring called Lungloh Tui. After drinking from this stream, its sadness falls away. It then plucks a flower called *hwilo pâr*, the "no-looking-back flower".

Next the Thlarau makes its way onwards to Zingvanzawl, which is the gateway to Mitthi Khua, the village of the dead. This gateway is guarded by a giant named **Pu Pâwla** and his wife **Sanu.**

Once the Thlarau gets past Pâwla and Sanu, it enters Mitthi Khua. Life in the village of the dead is thought to be similar to regular life, complete will all the usual joys and hardships.

However, if the person was much honoured in life (for instance, as a renowned hunter), their Thlarau could proceed further, past another river, to the land of Pialral, a sort of heroes' Valhalla. In Pialral, spirits are waited on hand and foot for eternity; they are fed milled rice every day, and they never have to work.

Tlingi and Ngama

The legend of Tlingi and Ngama tells of a boy and a girl who fell in love in childhood. Their love increased year after year until finally, when they were grown to adulthood, they were married. But tragically, soon afterwards, Ngama fell ill and died.

Her husband Tlingi wept with grief so hard and for so long that he was granted access to Mitthi Khua even though he was still alive. There he saw Ngama's ghost looking very thin and frail. When he asked her what happened, she told him that there wasn't enough to eat in Mitthi Khua.

Tlingi returned to the world of the living. The next day, he left some food out for his wife.

That night, Tlingi cried himself into the village of the dead again. This time, however, he found her ghost looking much plumper, healthier, and happier.

From that time began the custom of leaving some portion of the harvest aside for the Thlarau of the departed. This is celebrated annually in Mizoram as the festival of Mim Kut.

Mara Belief: The Journey of the Thlapha

The Mara tribe of Mizoram has a similar conception of the journey of the soul after death. They call the soul Thlapha, and the village of the dead Athikhi. The guardians of this realm are the **Chhongchhongpipa**, the ghosts of men who died as virgins.

Interestingly, the Mara believe that the Thlapha, after living a second life in Athikhi, dies a second death. After this final death, the souls of people who were chieftains in life evaporate into the air as mist, while the souls of poor men turn into worms, fall to the ground, and are eaten by birds.

Ref: 215, 324

TIMITIMINGALA

In Hindu and Buddhist mythology, a Timitimingala is a gigantic sea monster which can eat whole ships, as well as prey upon the largest whales.

The words "Timi, Timingala, Timitimingala" are often used together in Sanskrit to refer to a variety of enormous sea creatures. The Timi is a huge fish, perhaps a great white shark; the Timingala is a giant whale; and the Timitimingala is a fantastic creature much larger than both.

There is a Buddhist legend about a Timitimingala which terrorized sailors in the Bay of Bengal. It preyed upon ships, swallowing many trade vessels whole. When the crew of one ship found itself under attack, the crew members gathered together to pray, invoking the name of the Buddha. The Timitimingala heard their prayer and was instantly converted. It took a vow of *ahimsa* (non-violence), and from that point onward the leviathan ate nothing but seaweed. After it died, it was reborn as a monk and achieved nirvana.

Ref: 557

⟶ TISSO JONDING ⟵

In the folklore of the Karbi people of Assam, Tisso Jonding ("Tall Tisso") is a mysterious and menacing being who makes his lair in a gnarled banyan tree deep in the jungle.

Tisso Jonding is tall, bipedal, and covered with reddish-brown fur. It looks something like a giant Hoolock gibbon, with recessed eyes outlined in black. But it rarely allows itself to be seen by human eyes and may even have the power to turn invisible. Despite its animalish appearance it is highly intelligent. It can imitate the human voice and is completely fluent in Karbi. Some say it can speak in other languages as well.

This creature has the habit of raiding human villages at night for chickens or other livestock. But it also hungers for human flesh. It lures its victims into the forest with its beautiful singing voice, or by crying like a human baby. Then it steals their senses and gobbles them up. It often preys on opium addicts, who are easy to hypnotize.

There are a few tricks you can use to defeat a Tisso Jonding, if you can manage to keep your wits about you when you meet one. They are mortally afraid of cassumunar ginger, and can be threatened with it; for if they touch this plant, they will lose their powers and be excommunicated by the others of their kind. Also, if you look the Tisso Jonding in the eyes when it is standing in front of you, it will seem to grow taller and taller, to giant proportions, until it eats you; but if you look at its feet, then it shrinks and shrinks until it becomes a tiny, powerless creature, and finally disappears altogether.

Tisso Jonding is classed as one of the **Hi-i**, the evil demons of the Karbi pantheon. But paradoxically it is also revered, for this creature is said to have given the Karbis the gift of music. Traditional Karbi drummers consider it as their guru, and they always offer it rice beer and seek its blessings before a performance. With its voice, the creature can produce the sounds of a variety of instruments, such as flutes and veenas, which are sometimes heard emanating from the jungle. Tisso Jonding has certain favourite melodic patterns, and these can be used by Karbi musicians to call the creature out from the trees.

During festivals, the Tisso Jonding assumes the guise of a human being, and visits the village at night to take part in the celebration. However, it must return to the forest by dawn—the hour known as *Tisso rongdam*—or else it will return to its monstrous form. If the young bachelors at the festival suspect that someone is really a Tisso, they sing and dance and drink with him to get him to forget the time. If he gets carried away or passes out drunk and stays in the village past Tisso rongdam, then everyone will get a chance to glimpse his hairy body and strange-looking eyes before he wakes up and runs back to the forest.

"Tisso" is also the name of a subclan among the Karbis. This clan is said to actually be descended from a group of Tisso Jondings who, in the distant past, decided to give up their supernatural powers and come out of the jungle to become human.

Ref: 93, 276, 368, 369, 370

TSINE NAT

In Garo folklore, a Tsine Nat is a type of shapeshifting, jungle-dwelling **Memang Gitting**, or ghoul. It feeds on human flesh. While Tsine Nats sometimes attack the living, they are even fonder of corpseflesh.

Tsine Nats are repelled by heavy metals like iron, steel, or copper. Anyone carrying such metal articles on his person is completely safe from the depredations of a Tsine Nat, and the demon cannot enter a house that contains metal tools or metal furniture.

A Tsine Nat can change its shape and appear as a human, even imitating the appropriate clothing and affecting a pleasant voice. In this disguise, it may cleverly try to convince a person to put their metal articles aside, or to clear all the metal articles out of their house. This trick is employed to gain access to a house where someone has recently died so that the Tsine Nat can feast upon the dead body.

In its true form, the monster appears as a hideous cyclops, with a single bright phosphorescent eye set strangely in the middle of his forehead. It speaks in guttural monosyllables.

Ref: 306

ᠵ᠊ TSUNGREM ᠊ᠵ

Tsungrem is an Ao Naga word meaning "god" or "supernatural creature". The Lotha Naga version is Tsungrham. Like the Angami word Terhoma, this includes both the benevolent gods and the evil spirits of the springs and wet places, the bamboo groves, and the boulders.

According to Lotha Naga folklore, the first Tsungrham was Khyuham, who used to abduct human children and eat the meat from their bones. Once he finished this grisly snack, he would collect his victims' skulls in a basket which he always carried around on his back.

It was believed that Khyuham lurked inside every house, and was always waiting to snatch another child—so it was very important never to leave a child unattended at home. Finally, Rankhanda, one of the the Lhota Naga ancestor heroes, fought and defeated him, and entombed him in the earth. And yet he did not die. A yearly ritual was performed to ward off Khyuham's evil, in which the demon would be offered the paws and nose of a dog, cooked with ginger.

Malicious Tsungrham can attack humans by magically placing pebbles, bits of wood, or clumps of hair into their bodies. These insertions cause illness, and they must be detected and extracted by a priest (*ratsen*).

Tsungrham Eyimo is a mad, merciless spirit who cannot be propitiated in any way. When a person falls sick due to affliction by Tsungrham Eyimo, no sacrifices can help them.

Ahlachetla, a water-spirit (Atsu Tsungrem), is the most feared of all the Tsungrem of the Ao Naga. Any person who encounters Ahlachetla is doomed to die.

Alonglamla is sometimes also classified as one of the Atsu Tsungrem.

Ref: 58, 80, 103

TUALSUMSU

In the folklore of Mizoram, a Tualsumsu is a person—usually a woman—who has been possessed by a peculiar sort of evil spirit. This spirit makes her do something very curious.

Late at night, without being aware of her actions, the possessed woman goes outside and starts hopping upside down on her head, all around the streets of the village.

In the morning, she wakes up with a splitting headache she can't explain.

When people hear strange rhythmic thumping noises at night, they lock their doors and stay at home in case there is a Tualsumsu about.

Ref: 6, 150

U DIENGIEI

In Khasi mythology, U Diengiei was a tree of gloom that once spread its branches over the Earth, cutting mankind off from the heavens. It is a symbol of evil, ignorance, and human greed.

It was at the end of the Golden Age, as a punishment for the sins of humanity, that the god U Blei planted the U Diengiei. He placed the seed in the soil at the top of a mountain, some distance west of Shillong. It grew into an oak sapling, and then a tree; it went on growing and growing until it blotted out the sky. Its branches became so thick with leaves that no sunlight could get through at all. In the land beneath the tree, all the crops began to fail, animals began to sicken and die, and people's minds became dim and confused.

People tried to cut down the tree. It was a big job. The trunk was far too thick to chop through in a single day. After a large team worked for hours and managed to make some progress, they called it a night.

But in the morning, when they came back to the tree, they found it had magically regenerated; the trunk was whole again.

This happened over and over, day after day, and the people were on the verge of giving up with despair. Finally a tiny wren—the bird known in Khasi as Ka Phreit—came up to them. She told them that she had some information which would help them cut down the monstrous tree. In exchange for the information, Ka Phreit made the people promise that she could eat freely of the crops in the fields once the sun shone again.

The people readily agreed to this deal, so Ka Phreit told her secret. Every night, U Khla, the tiger, was coming to the injured tree trunk and licking it. The tiger's tongue was magically healing the wood of U Diengiei, preventing them from cutting it down. U Khla wanted the tree to stay, because its dark shadow made it easy for him to stalk and hunt his prey.

To guard against the tiger, Ka Phreit told the people to leave their axes leaning against the trunk at night as they slept.

They did so. That night, when U Khla arrived in the darkness and tried to lick the tree, his tongue was slashed to shreds and he ran away in pain.

This allowed the Khasis to complete the job of cutting down the evil tree, restoring light to the world.

Ref: 254, 287

⤙⤙— U KSUID TYNJANG —⤚⤚

The story of U Ksuid Tynjang comes from a Khasi folktale told around Sohra (Cherrapunji), Meghalaya. During the day, this monster sleeps in a den in the forest. But at night, he turns into a hideous ape-like demon with long clawed hands. U Ksuid Tynjang walks with a limp. He suffers from a frightful itching disease. His fur is mangy and scabby; his skin is chafed and covered with sores. The pus that drips from these sores is incredibly foul-smelling.

U Ksuid Tynjang has an obsessive need to be scratched by human hands. To this end, he wanders the forest at night calling out "*Kaw-hoit! Kaw-hoit!*", which is the sound Khasi people make to find each other in dense vegetation. He also carries a torch, which appears to blink on and off. Anyone who hears the calls and unwittingly goes to U Ksuid Tynjang is caught and ordered to scratch ("*Kboh!*") his skin. This is a difficult job, because his skin is so disgusting and the smell is stomach-turning; if his captives do not satisfy his itch, he can become angry, and tickle them to death.

Other times he hypnotizes his victims, so that they follow him in a trance. He may lead them to the edge of a high cliff and abandon them there, so they are frightened to death when they awaken.

Once, U Ksuid Tynjang captured two girls named Ka Thei and Ka Duh. "*Kboh!*" he ordered them, and they scratched his nasty skin for so long that he went to sleep. As he slumbered, Thei kept rubbing him while Duh built a fire. Duh searched the area and found a dao (a type of machete) nearby. She heated the dao in the fire and then drove the hot iron deep into the demon's heart.

The attack did not kill him—Ksuid are immortal—but it caused him to shrink until he took the shape of a creeper vine, so the girls were able to run to safety.

Some say that the spirit of U Ksuid Tynjang remained forever in the form of a creeper vine, and this is why the creeper vine strangles trees, ruins crops, and trips up hunters.

But according to others, he did not remain in that shape for long. The very next night, the vine straightened out, grew thicker, and took the shape of U Ksuid Tynjang once more. Again the demon roamed through the forest, calling out "*Kaw-hoit! Kaw-hoit!*"

*

The Atong people of the Garo Hills have a similar female ghost called Ambi Chakkhen. She, too, turns into a liana vine during the day, but at night she appears as an old woman with very long arms and fingernails. She demands that you scratch her, and if you refuse, she will claw you to death.

Ref: 9, 51, 254, 287

⤜⤛ U THLEN ⤜⤛

U Thlen is an evil dragon, a devourer of men, and probably the most powerful and diabolical of all demons or **Ksuid** in the pantheon of the Khasis of Meghalaya. He is, allegedly, kept by some people as a household deity; but since anyone who worships Thlen at home must feed him human blood, these worshippers are considered very dangerous people.

U Thlen's grandfather was U Mawlong Siem, the god of a mountain who still bears his name. U Mawlong Siem had a daughter named Ka Kma Kharai, the goddess of caves and ravines. She was a shapeshifter who loved to wander about incognito among both mortals and spirits. Her father was fiercely overprotective, and forbade her from taking lovers; but Ka Kma Kharai rebelled, and soon became known as a debauched goddess. She was so fond of getting drunk, partying, and having promiscuous sex that her own divine family excommunicated her.

Ka Kma Kharai conceived U Thlen out of wedlock. He was born small and deformed, with a snake-like shape. His mother couldn't be bothered taking care of him, so she soon abandoned him.

She was, at least, considerate enough to leave him in a spot where he would be able to get enough food. She dropped him at the base of Pomdoloi Falls, a place which saw a lot of foot traffic, as it was on the route between the towns of Rangjyrteh and Sohra (Cherrapunji). U Thlen began gobbling up unsuspecting travellers along the path. Whenever an odd-numbered group of people passed by, Thlen would lie in wait and eat the last one.

Soon he was no longer small. He grew into a giant, sluggish, dragon-like monster.

Thlen's appetite grew and grew, and more and more travellers started disappearing. Now whenever a group passed by, he would eat half of the travellers. Desperate, the people of the area prayed for help to every god they knew.

One of the beings they beseeched was U Suidnoh. Some say Suidnoh was simply a brave man. Others say he was an avatar of U Syiem Kyrsan, the chief of all guardian spirits. Still others say Suidnoh was a fleeting ghost who haunted the forest Lait-rngew to the north, and had not been thought much of before now; but people were desperate.

In any case, Suidnoh agreed to help, and slowly he tried to gain Thlen's trust. First, he bored a hole through the top of the dragon's cave. He asked the people of Sohra to bring him lots of fat pigs and goats. "O Uncle, open your mouth so I can feed you," he would say, and then drop the meat down to him. Thlen had grown so lazy and gluttonous that he no longer bothered to come out, and he didn't notice that human meat had been removed from his diet.

Next Suidnoh conspired with a giant named U Ramhah to construct an iron smelter not far from Thlen's cave. He had the giant fashion a huge pair of iron tongs and a gigantic iron ball. Once these were made, he left them with U Ramhah and headed over to Thlen's lair.

There he struck up a conversation with the demon. He said he was going to Sohra, and asked if Thlen wanted anything. U Thlen asked for some of the famous Sohra pork, and Suidnoh promised to bring him some.

But instead of going to Sohra, Suidnoh went back to U Ramhah. Together they heated the iron ball over a fire until it was red hot.

Suidnoh picked up the ball with the tongs and walked back to Pomdoloi Falls. He stood over the hole he had bored, and again he asked, "O Uncle, open your mouth so I can feed you." But this time, instead of giving him meat, he shoved the red-hot ball of iron deep down into the dragon's throat.

Thlen began to writhe in agony, shaking the earth. So much dirt flew into the sky that the sun was blotted out. His thrashings caused a tremendous earthquake, which created the gorges of Cherrapunji that can still be seen to this day.

At last the strength went out of him, and U Thlen was still.

Suidnoh called people from all around for a gigantic feast, and insisted that every last scrap of the dragon's flesh be eaten. It almost was; but one foolish old woman kept a bit of meat in a basket, without telling anyone, and took it back to her house for her son, who was out of town. Then she forgot about it.

After a few days, when the old woman was alone, a voice from the basket started to speak to her. She opened the basket and was shocked to see a tiny snake-like creature there. It told her that if she kept it and fed it, it would make her rich.

Too scared to admit that she had made a mistake by not following Suidnoh's instructions, and greedy for the gold that was promised, the old woman did as Thlen asked. But soon it started to demand blood. And only Khasi blood, the blood of her own people, would satiate it.

The old lady was too frail to go out murdering people by herself. She had to find a way of getting others to do her bidding. She accomplished this by feeding them a special brew of triple-distilled rice beer, *kyiad tangsnem*, which had been kept for a year and consecrated to the demon. Under the influence of this brew, people turned into a sort of drugged zombie, or **Nongshohnoh**. They were more than happy to kill in service of U Thlen.

Thus began the tradition, which some claim continues up to this day, of nong-ri-Thlen, "keepers of Thlen"—that is, families who keep and worship the evil spirit in their homes.*

If a nong-ri-Thlen cannot offer Thlen blood, they may secretly cut a bit of hair from a victim, or a bit of the person's clothes, and offer this to the demon.

....

* In one version of the story, the first worshippers of Thlen were given magic rings by his mother Ka Kma Kharai, called the Yngkuid rings. These ensure that they will be able to possess anything they desire, as long as they keep feeding human blood to Thlen. Nong-ri-Thlen refer to Thlen as their maternal uncle.

By this method, Thlen may capture the victim's *rngiew*, or essence.* Then, at midnight, to the beat of a small drum, Thlen forces the victim's captured rngiew to dance on a silver plate; and, starting from the feet, slowly swallows him completely, until the owner of the rngiew falls dead at home.

It is said that this spell can be broken only by the *syiem sad* or matriarch of the victim's clan. To release the victim's soul from captivity, she has to heat an iron rod in the hearth and touch it to the hair on the victim's forelock while chanting prayers to the god U Blei.

U Thlen rewards his keepers with great riches. But if they cannot keep him fed, he may punish them by killing one of their children; or by taking the form of a fish which appears on top of their roof, or of a cat which perches there, exposing them for what they are before their neighbours.

In some interpretations of the myth, the nong-ri-Thlen represent people who are so greedy that they no longer value human life over money; and the Nongshohnoh are those who, in order to please their masters or employers, are willing to follow any orders, no matter how immoral—up to and including taking another person's life.

Ref: 254, 287

UCHU

The Uchu are mythical man-eating monsters known from the folklore of the Pucikwar people of the Andaman Islands. The Pucikwar and their language went extinct in the 1930s, and no detailed description of the Uchu survived. There is, however, a story about them.

The monitor lizard, Ta Petie, was the first ancestor of the human race. The story goes that he once went into the jungle and climbed a fruit tree, and a group of the early people followed him. He began tossing fruit down to them, to their great delight.

---

* In Khasi metaphysics, there are three components to the self: *Ka Met*, the body; *Ka Mynsiem*, the soul; and *Ka Rngiew*, the essence. The folklorist Desmond L. Kharmawphlang describes this last component as "the power that shapes and determines man's action, thought and motivation. It gives shape to his dreams and visions, and charts the course of his life, is imperishable and immutable."[572]

Soon the crowd grew, and they began clamouring for more and more fruit. Ta Petie got annoyed, and told them, "Stop shouting or I'll call the Uchu out from the forest, and they'll come and kill you all." But the people only laughed.

So Ta Petie called the Uchu. Two of the monsters came running out from the jungle, one male and one female. The people scattered, but the Uchu were too fast for them; they chased them down and gobbled them up. In almost no time at all, they had devoured everyone—all except Ta Petie, who was safe up in the tree, busy eating fruit, not paying much attention to what was happening below.

The two Uchu then went to the edge of the mangrove swamp and tried to cross the strait to the next island. But they were so weighed down by all the people they had eaten that they got stuck in the mud.

Later, when Ta Petie finally came down from the tree, he couldn't find any people. Understanding that they must have been eaten, he went looking for the Uchus, and found them still stuck at the edge of the swamp. Ta Petie slashed open their bellies, and all the people came swarming out (alive and safe, for the Uchus had swallowed them whole). The two dead Uchus turned into huge limestone rocks, which can still be seen rising from the water a few miles south of the place called Wota-emi.

When elephants were brought to the Andaman Islands, the Pucikwar, who had never seen such large land animals before, called them "Uchu".

The folklore of other Andaman tribes includes tales of similar monsters. In Akar-Bale (another extinct language), there was a monster called Kochurag-boa, and in North Andaman there was a monster called Jirmu. The Nicobar Islands have a comparable legend about a creature called Tamakung.

Ref: 54

UKA

The Uka, also known as Guloi or Dhonguloi, is a spirit known from the folklore of Assam. It dwells in fields, near buried treasure.

During the day it is shadowy and incorporeal. But at night it takes the form of a greater adjutant stork—a huge bird which feeds on carrion, known for being able to swallow large bones. The Uka then spreads its wings and flies off in search of food.

The mouth of the Uka can emit glowing flames.

Ukas generally do not harm humans. However, if you are walking alone and you see several Ukas flying in the sky, it is best *not* to try to run away. The Ukas, sensing fear, may flock down and chase you and peck out your eyes.

Adjutant storks were once widespread across South and Southeast Asia, but are now an endangered species. The same may be true of the Ukas as well.

Ref: 294, 448

⤛⤛ UNICORN ⤜⤜

The Indus Valley civilization, which flourished between 3300 and 1300 BCE, is known for its advanced architecture, bronze carvings, and soapstone seals, written in an as-yet-undeciphered script. One of the most common images on these seals is a bull-like creature, shown in profile, with a single horn. Some historians argue that this image represents a two-horned animal, with the second horn merely hidden behind the first; but others believe that the seals depict the mythical animal known today as the Unicorn.

The first known historical mention of a Unicorn—that is, in a language we can read—comes from the book *Indica*, by the Greek physician Ctesias, written in the 5th century BCE.* Ctesias himself never visited India, but he did work as the court doctor to Artaxerxes II in Persepolis, the capital of ancient Persia, where he met many Indians and recorded their descriptions of their homelands. His book lists several fantastic-sounding monsters from Sindh and the lands beyond. But it also gives accurate descriptions of some *real* creatures that were hitherto unknown to the Greeks, such as the Indian elephant and the parrot; so some people have wondered whether his stories of creatures like the Unicorn and Manticore were based on fact.

Ctesias described the Unicorn of India as a wild ass, the size of a horse or larger, which could run faster than any other animal (though it took a while to reach top speed). It was very ferocious, able to kill men and horses easily by kicking, biting, or piercing them with its horn. For this reason Unicorns were never captured alive. The only way to hunt them was to surround them while

....

* There are unicorns in some versions of the Christian Old Testament, but it is generally agreed that this is a mistranslation of the Hebrew word *re'em*, which meant "auroch"— an ancient type of wild cattle.

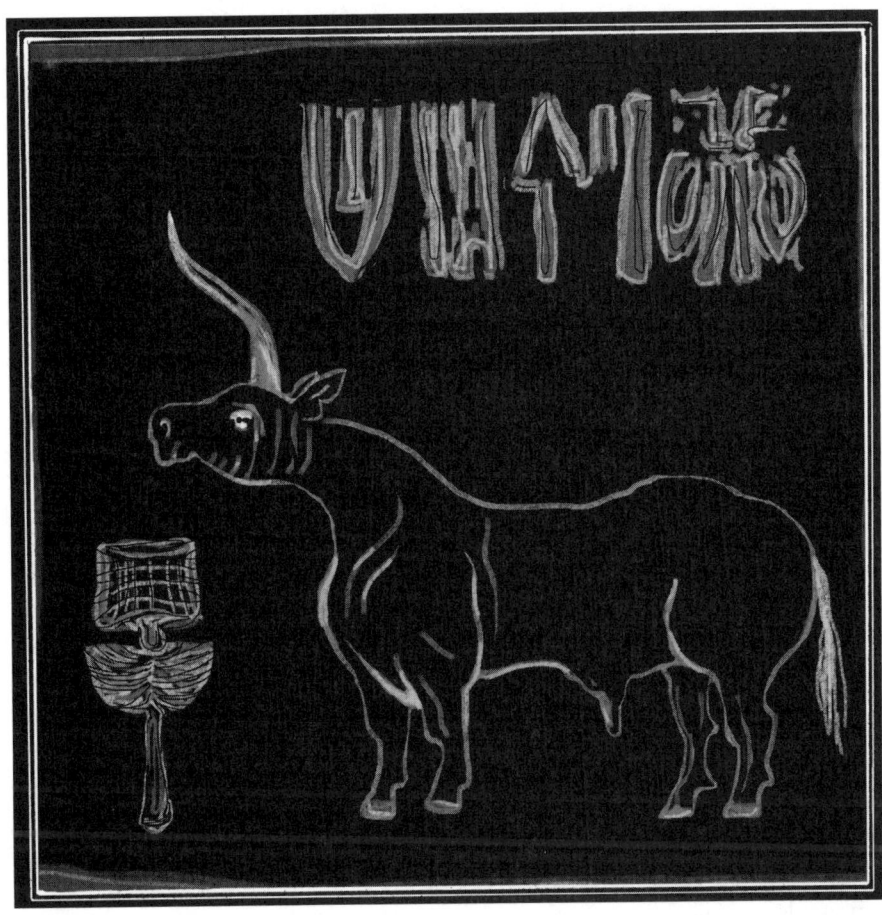

they were grazing with their colts, and attack them with ranged weapons like javelins and arrows.

The Unicorn had a white body, crimson head, and deep blue eyes. The single horn in the middle of its brow was 1.5 cubits long (about 70 cm). The horn was white at the base, black in the middle, and crimson at the tip. It was very sharp. Ctesias wrote that the richest and most powerful Indians drank from Unicorn-horn cups that had been decorated with gold rings. The belief was that anyone who drank from a Unicorn horn would never fall ill, and would be immune to poison.

The Unicorn's astragalus, or ankle bone, was also highly prized. It was said to be as heavy as lead and the colour of vermillion. These bones were often used to make dice.

Unicorn meat was said to be too bitter to eat.

Ælian, who lived around six hundred years after Ctesias, described a one-horned beast living in the heart of India called the Cartozonas, which was similar in many respects to Ctesias's Unicorn. This animal was also about the size of a horse, a fast runner, and very ferocious. However, according to Ælian's sources, it had reddish fur all over (not just the head), and the horn was completely black, with rings or spirals on it. The Cartozonas could make a very loud and obnoxious noise.

Ref: 195, 250

⊱⊱ VANCHUNGNULA ⊰⊰

In Mizo folklore, a Vanchungnula or Vantrikoh is a winged spirit of the clouds and rain. They appear as beautiful women with large, white wings. They are the daughters of Pu Vana, the god of thunder and lightning.

Vanchungnulas sometimes descend to Earth to bathe. Men used to try to catch them, but as soon as they looked directly at them they would be paralyzed by the creatures' dazzling beauty.

One story tells of a man who did manage to catch a Vanchungnula by the name of Sichangneii. He did this by sneaking up on her from behind. He took her home, ripped off her wings, and hid them in a bamboo basket on the highest shelf. Then he forcibly married her.

Sichangneii bore seven sons. Though she loved them all, she was still miserable.

She and the man used to take turns looking after their children. One day, she stayed home and he would go to work in the jhum field, and the next day, they would switch roles.

Sometimes, when the father stayed home with the children, he would take the wings down from the shelf and let the children wear them and dance around. He warned the children strictly never to mention this to their mother, or to tell her where the wings were kept.

But when Sichangneii stayed home with the children, she was so glum and mournful that the children got bored. One day, the youngest one, whose name was Tlumtea, asked if she could get down the wings, like father sometimes did.

Sichangneii's eyes lit up. "Where does he keep the wings?" she asked.

Tlumtea showed her. Sichangneii got the wings down and put them on. Then she went to the verandah and spread them out wide.

"How do I look?" she asked.

Her children were dumbstruck by her radiance. Tlumtea was the only one who could manage to speak. "You look very beautiful," she said in a hushed voice.

Sichangneii smiled, and then she flew away into the sky.

When the father returned home, he was so despondent that he took a hammer and smashed his own testicles with it. Shortly afterwards, he died.

In some versions of the story, Sichangneii's children later travel to meet her in the clouds. There they encounter her brother, who is a murderous cannibal, and narrowly escape with their lives back to Earth.

Ref: 6, 229

VANTRI

This ghost hails from Gujarat and Rajasthan.

In many respects the Vantri is similar to the **Chudail**. She is a wrathful, wicked spirit who wears a white sari. A Vantri is the ghost of a woman who died while giving birth to a child, or a few days afterwards; or a woman who died childless; or a widow who was murdered.

The Vantri's hair appears as if dyed with red henna. She is usually encountered bathing in a river below a bridge, or floating in a well.

While a Chudail's victims are most often grown men, the Vantri preys primarily on children.

Ref: 260, 284

VETAL

A Vetal is a spirit which haunts cremation grounds. Vetals like to eat flesh and drink blood.

Folk stories about the Vetal are told in many different languages, across India and even beyond, so the description of the creature can vary quite a lot. (As can the spelling: Betaal, Baital, and Vaital being a few of the variants.) The most familiar Vetal, and possibly the original on which other tales are based, is found in the ancient story *Vetala Panchavimshati* ("The Twenty-Five Tales of the Vetal"), or its many modern adaptations, *Vikram and the Vetal*.

"Vetal" is often translated to English as "vampire", but the two myths are quite different. A Vetal does not actually have a body of its own, though it can inhabit human corpses at will. (In one ancient story, a Vetal inhabits a "body" made out of parts of several different animals sewn together.) By most accounts, it is not the ghost of a human, but a different sort of spirit entirely, perhaps a type of **Pisacha**. In fact, Vetal and Pisacha are sometimes presented as synonyms. (The original version of *Vetala Panchavimshati* is supposed to have been written in Paisachi, the language of the demons. But that version has been lost. The oldest surviving version was written in Sanskrit by Somadeva in the 11th century CE.)

When inhabiting dead bodies, Vetals are fond of hanging upside-down from tree branches by their toes. In most legends, the Vetal's home is a moringa tree (though sometimes a banyan, rosewood, or mimosa tree is preferred). A corpse which is host to a Vetal appears motionless, limp, and cold, but it can magically transport itself across distances nearly instantaneously, usually using this power to return to its home tree.

Despite their diet, Vetals are not always completely evil. The Vetal in *Vetala Panchavimshati* eventually helps the good King Vikramadityan defeat a power-hungry tantric magician, and later assists him in overthrowing the King of Kalinga.

The Sanskrit word Vetala is masculine in gender, but females (Vetali) are also found in stories and religious art. It is debatable whether the Vetal spirit itself has a gender, or whether the gender only depends on the body it is occupying.

Tamil Nadu: The Vethaalam

The Tamil word Vethaalam is used for the creatures in translations of the same Sanskrit stories mentioned above. However, Tamil folktales describe a different sort of Vethaalam, one that has the outward appearance of a normal human during the day, but turns into a voracious monster at night. This type of Vethaalam can have a staggering appetite; they are capable of gobbling up a hundred elephants at one go. They also eat humans.

If a childless couple seeks instructions from a holy man on how they may conceive, but then fail to follow the instructions exactly—*knowingly* making some small but significant change—the resulting child may grow up to be a Vethaalam, and will usually end up devouring the parents.

This type of Vethaalam can only be killed by sneaking up behind it and stabbing it with an enchanted sword.

Goa: The Betal Deity

In Goa and parts of Maharashtra and Karnataka, the god Betal is worshipped. He is said to be the King of Ghosts. He is a powerful protector, since all evil spirits obey his command. His idol appears as an emaciated man with large fangs, holding a sword and wearing a garland of human heads. Traditionally, he was always naked, though today the idol is sometimes dressed in a dhoti.

Offerings to Shri Betal are made in the form of liquor, meat, cigars, and Kolhapuri chappals (leather sandals), which the god is said to wear when he roams the town in the dead of night. Betal shrines are usually constructed without a permanent roof over the deity, as it is believed this will bring bad luck.

One legend says that Betal arrived in Goa after conquering twelve kingdoms. He was about to conquer Poinguinim as the thirteenth, and put all the inhabitants to the sword, but a local chieftain named Nagizan intervened. He asked Betal to stay and reside in the village as its guardian. Betal agreed, on the condition that a sacrificial offering be made: he should be given a two-legged animal, a four-legged animal, a ten-legged animal, and a fœtus.

Nagizan agreed, and offered Betal a chicken, a buffalo, a crab, and an areca nut palm sprout (which has an uncanny resemblance to a human fœtus). Thus Betal was tricked into staying on as protector.

While Betal is generally thought to be merely an alternative pronunciation of Vetal, there is at least one shrine in Dharbandora Taluk of Goa where Betal and Vetal are worshipped as two separate gods, with their idols joined at the feet. Here Shri Betal is considered an incarnation of Shiva, while Shri Vetal is the ghost god.

The Betal temples of Goa celebrate a festival every three years known as Gadyachi Zatra. During one such festival four male devotees (called *gade*) are pierced through the back with hooks, suspended from a wheel high above the ground, and rotated. It is said that in ancient times, the wheel was rotated until one of these men fell to their death, and his body was given as a sacrifice to Betal; but that practice has been banned.

During the Gadyachi Zatra, the gade play a game of hide and seek with the devil called **Devchar**. Fifty-two devotees run in all directions while the Devchar appears and does tricks with fire.

Worship of Betal may be very ancient, originating with the Adivasi tribes of the Konkan coast or possibly from far beyond. The Raji tribe of Uttarkhand worship a god named Betal too, and there is a Betal temple in Srinagar, Kashmir as well.

Vetalasiddhi

Vetalasiddhi is a supernatural power over vampires. It is said that this power can be attained by drinking alcohol, chanting a mantra one lakh times, and giving an offering of goat's blood. If performed correctly, a Vetal will appear and do the yogi's bidding.

Agiya Vetal

This is a special breed of Vetal, the "Fiery Vetal". Tantriks are supposed to be able to harness the power of this Vetal by giving it a home in the palm of their hand.

In the folklore of Chhota Nagpur, Agiya Vetal is the servant of Van Devi, the goddess of the forest. When she is angry, she gives him the order to start a blaze. Agiya Vetal is associated with a medicinal herb, *Pygmaeopremna herbacea*, which is believed to spontaneously combust when very dry.

Catching Vetals by the Tongue

There is a Buddhist tale from the time of the Pala Empire (around 750 CE in Bengal) about a yogi named Narada who was powerful with magic. He conscripted an assistant to help him catch a Vetal.

Narada planned to summon the being to them, and he instructed the assistant to try to catch it by the tongue. Narada told him that if he caught the Vetal on the first try, they would attain a *mahasiddhi*, or great power, which would result in every person in the world being able to live for a thousand years. If he missed the Vetal on the first try, but caught it on the second, they would attain a slightly weaker power. If he caught the Vetal only on the third try, he would get a low-level siddhi. But if he missed the Vetal three times in a row, the Vetal would devour them both, and then go on to ravage the entire country.

When the Vetal appeared, the assistant missed on the first try. He missed again on the second. But on the third try, he managed to clamp down on the Vetal's tongue with his own teeth. Instantly, the Vetal's tongue turned into a magic sword, which gave its wielder the power of flight. As for the body of the Vetal, it turned to solid gold.

Narada instructed his assistant to remove the parts of the Vetal's body that had been flesh and muscle, but to leave the parts that had been bone. He further told him that if he spent the gold only for virtuous purposes, then whatever he spent during the day would be magically replenished at night. This prediction came true, and the assistant used the wealth from the Vetal's body to build a great monastery and do many charitable deeds.

Vajra Vetali, Queen of the Vampires

In Vajrayana Buddhist mythology, the undead have a Buddha-nature, just as the living do, and can progress towards enlightenment. There is a tale of one Vetali who actually attained nirvana through her practice of *karmamudra* (sexual yoga) and meditation. She is known as Vajra Vetali, sometimes rendered in English as "Queen of the Vampires".

Vajra Vetali has dark-blue skin, flaming red hair, and four arms, in which she holds a skull cup, sword, mirror, and *phurba* (triple-bladed dagger). From the skull cup she drinks blood, representing the ego of her enemies. She wears a crown made of five skulls and has chains around her ankles. She rides a donkey, sitting on a saddle made of human bone with a saddle cloth of human skin.

Vajra Vetali is the consort of Vajrabhairava. She is also known as Dakini Vetali, one of the **Dakinis** of Wisdom. Her mantra is *Om Vetali Hum Svaha*. She is associated with the sense of smell, the direction west, and the tortoise.

When Vajra Vetali lived in the realm of gods, she was extremely naughty, always pulling pranks and breaking things. Yama, the Lord of Death, got fed up with her and tied her up in chains. But she managed to free herself and fled on the back of her donkey. The gods shot arrows at her as she made her escape; one of them found its target, wounding the donkey's hindquarters. This wound transformed itself into an eye, so that now when Vajra Vetali rides, she can see any enemies behind her as well.

Odisha: Vaitala Deul Temple

The Vaitala Deul temple in Bhubaneshwar, Odisha was built in the 8ᵗʰ century, during a time when Buddhism and Hinduism were equally popular in the Kalinga region. The presiding deity in this temple is the goddess Chamunda, known locally as Kapalini, and associated with Vajra Vetali. According to some legends, Chamunda is herself a Vetal.

The Seven Mahavetala

A Tibetan Buddhist text called the *Saptavetalakanamadharani* includes a story in which Buddha's disciple Ananda is attacked by seven powerful Vetals. He is unable to see them, and doesn't know what is causing his intense pain. He goes to the Buddha, who tells him about the seven Mahavetala (powerful Vetals), whose names translate to "Garland-Carrier", "Jewel-Carrier", "Ferocity", "Terror", "Heart of the Peacock", "Consumer of Life", and "Soldier".

The Buddha tells Ananda: "These seven Mahavetala are great in strength, difficult to tame, difficult to propitiate; and, their powers of deception and magic are great. Ananda, each of these Vetala could, if he wished, cast down even Mount Meru, King of Mountains, with the toe of his left foot; it would be completely reduced, until it was about the size of a mustard seed. If each looked upwards, he could make the earth split open; if each looked in the cardinal directions, there would be death in them; if each looked in the intermediate directions, they would be burnt by fire. It is they that have touched you!" (Translation: Michael Walter.[558])

Ref: 109, 157, 241, 366, 558

VIR

Vir means "hero" in many Indian languages; when referring to a supernatural being, a Vir is a hero ghost, often the ghost of a warrior who has died in battle. They are generally benevolent spirits. Offerings are made to Virs in many parts of India, including Mysore, the Konkan coast, Rajasthan, and Varanasi. In Gujarat, there are said to be forty-nine of them.

A Vir may spend his afterlife as a soldier in the personal army of a deity. Sometimes powerful tantrics manage to press them into service as well.

Ref: 115

VIRIKA

Virikas are small ghosts with long sharp teeth. They are either red in colour, or surrounded in a weird red mist. They wander around in dense forests at night making bizarre gibbering and slobbering noises.

They like to sneak up on humans and drink their blood. The victim will be unaware of being bitten until he or she notices the bite mark, which later begins to throb with pain.

Virikas are rarely deadly. They can be easily driven away using fire extinguishers, of which they are mortally afraid.

The term "Virika" was originally used in the area around Mysore for the spirits of heroic ancestors, who would appear in dreams to trouble descendents if they forgot to worship at their shrines. The small, red, noise-making Virika, on the other hand, seems to be more common in foreign lists of ghosts than in Indian folklore itself. It's possible that these ghosts prefer to trouble tourists.

Ref: 559, 560

VRITRA

In Hindu mythology, Vritra was a gargantuan demon, the personification of drought. His name means "the enveloper".

He appears in the *Rig Veda* as the first and most powerful foe of the god Indra. In these ancient hymns, "Vritra" is actually the first-born and most powerful of a whole clan of Vritras. The Vritras in turn belong to a class of demons called Ahi—evil, dragon-like beings, connected by ancient Indo-Aryan mythology to the Zoroastrian Dev of greed called Az, and to the Azhadars of later Persian myth. The Ahis were skilled in the use of magic, and were so huge that they could wrap themselves around mountains.

The eldest Vritra captured the rainclouds and blocked the rivers so that nothing could grow, hoarding all the water that there was in the world. He had ninety-nine towering fortresses to defend it.

In later tellings, Vritra is an **Asura**, appearing less like a dragon and more like a humanoid giant. The version in the *Bhagavata Purana* says that he was created by Tvashta, the artisan and inventor of the gods, in order to avenge the killing of Tvashta's son by Indra. In this version, Vritra grew rapidly—as fast as an arrow flies, in all directions, day after day after day—and his mouth yawned so wide that he threatened to devour the entire universe.

The *Rig Veda* says that Indra killed Vritra—along with all the others of his evil clan—using his divine thunderbolt, the *vajra*, which was expressly created for this battle. The *Bhagavata Purana* says that this weapon was made from the bones of the great sage Dadhichi, who sacrificed himself for this purpose.

In the *Mahabharata*, on the other hand, Indra is said to have killed Vritra with foam from the waves of the sea.

Ref: 56

☙━ VRIYABHOOT ━❧

Among the Muria tribe of Chhattisgarh, a Vriyabhoot is the ghost of a boy or girl who has died at a young age. These ghosts are thought to be playful rather than harmful; the worst they do is to blow dust in the eyes or scatter leaves in the house.

Not all spirits of dead children are so harmless: see also **Mirchuk** and **Matiya**.

Ref: 381

WAKMANGGANCHI ARAGONDI

In the Songsarek mythology of the Garo people, Wakmangganchi Aragondi was a colossal demonic boar who ruled in terror over the land for many years, before he was slain by the hero-god Goera.

This beast was said to be as big as a mountain. Its neck branched into seven heads, each of which had two gigantic tusks as sharp as double-edged scimitars, and a single eye in the centre of the brow that shone like a full moon. On its back were seven stands of bamboo, seven meadows of thatch grass, and seven marshes of bulrushes. Seven streams flowed through this forest, and these streams never went dry. A family of langur monkeys lived there too, and seven families of moles. When Wakmangganchi Aragondi stretched itself out, it was so long that one of its snouts could touch Tura Peak while its tail lay in the Brahmaputra River.

The monster-boar was born in Aning Chining, the Garo underworld or realm of the gods. There is a story about how it was brought to the surface world.

A man named Gonga Tritpa Rakshanpa was fishing in a stream when he accidentally caught a serpent-spirit. This was the patriarch and progenitor of kraits, by the name of Chongmitchang Pantdrang Chipuch Rodachi. Gonga took the snake home and was about to offer it in sacrifice to the gods, but Susime, goddess of fortune and of the moon, came to him and advised him not to kill it. Instead, she said, he could ransom it back to the dwellers of the underworld in exchange for some of their fowls that they kept in one of their deep caves.

Eventually, a search party from Aning Chining did arrive, looking for their compatriot Chongmitchang Pantdrang Chipuch Rodachi. Gonga agreed to give the krait-spirit back, on the condition that he and his friends could visit their subterranean realm and take some of the fowls they kept there.

And so Gonga travelled to the seventh level of the underworld, along with his dog and three of the hero Goera's maternal uncles. (This all happened before Goera himself was born.) Gonga returned from the underworld carrying with him the spirit named Doha Ahning Ruram Sureng, the progenitor of chickens and ducks and all other birds, along with all of this spirit's descendants, in seven huge cages. This is how birds came to the surface world.

Goera's uncles also brought up a small piglet, which was then called Wakmabitchi Warak Wakkimbi. (Remember that Susime, the goddess of fortune, had advised them to bring back the fowls; but she never mentioned this piglet.)

They kept the piglet as a pet, in a pen they built with heavy stones.

Soon, the piglet began to grow. It grew and grew and grew until it was a formidable boar. When the stone pen could hold it no longer, it was allowed to roam free. Though it was fearsome, people would sometimes feed it with leftovers.

One day, three of Goera's uncles tried to feed it some rice husks. But the boar charged the feeding trough and gobbled all three of the men right up!

After that the boar grew larger and larger still. Soon no one could farm rice, yams, gourds, or melons anymore, because the monster-boar would tear through the fields and eat the entire crop. It began eating everything and anyone it found in its path, leaving a trail of destruction and trampled earth. It seemed unstoppable and all-powerful. It was then that it sprouted its other six heads, and became known as Wakmangganchi Aragondi, the most fearsome beast in the world.

When the hero Goera was about to be born, two more of his uncles were on their way to the market to buy a goat for the celebration. But they never made it to the market, because Wakmangganchi Aragondi came upon them, and quickly devoured them both.

Years later, when Goera came of age and learned this history, he wanted to avenge the killing of his uncles. He also wanted to free his people from the shadow of the terrible monster-boar.

In preparation for the fight, Goera obtained a magic sword from Dykgyl Khongshyl, the god of smiths and metalworkers. Dykgyl Khongshyl also made him a magic bow that could shoot twelve fiery arrows at once.

Goera then made alliances with the Tengte, a race of subterranean elves, as well as with a dwarf god named Maal.

Together, they made war on Wakmangganchi Aragondi.

It was a tremendous battle. For seven summers and seven winters, the Earth trembled as they fought. But eventually, Goera and his allies were victorious. The beast was felled, and its meat was shared at a huge feast attended by humans and supernatural creatures alike.

There are stones and rock formations all over Meghalaya that are explained as evidence of this epic battle. Some are said to be droppings of the monster-boar, while others are said to be piles of leftover boar meat from the feast that followed.*

Ref: 306

---

* Some of these landmarks overlap with those identified in the Khasi story of **U Thlen**, which also tells of an epic battle with a giant monster whose meat is eaten in the end.

➤— WAI WHOP —➤

The Wai Whop is a supernatural creature from the folklore of Kashmir. It is named for the eerie sound it makes. It appears like a civet cat or hyena, but wears a skull cap on its head.

Wai Whops skulk about in deserted houses and lonely roads. They sometimes snatch newborn human children and carry them away to eat.

The skull cap of the Wai Whop has magical powers, and anyone who is able to capture it gains control of the creature. The Wai Whop can then be made to run errands or even grant wishes. However, one must be vigilant. If the Wai Whop ever gets the opportunity to steal the cap back, the owner will surely be killed, along with his or her entire family.

The legend of the Wai Whop's cap bears some similarities to the story of the **Yach**, and in fact, these two spirits may be different manifestations of the same being.

Ref: 7, 94, 457

➤— WAN MOHNIYU —➤

The Wan Mohniyu is a restless forest-dwelling man-beast from Kashmiri folklore. He is tall and strong and long-limbed, a humanoid giant covered with fur. He can run on all fours like a dog, or climb trees like a monkey, or walk on two legs like a man. He cannot speak, but babbles in a childlike voice.

The Wan Mohniyu lives in a cave deep in the woods; some say it is a log cabin with a boulder for a door. He is usually nocturnal. The Wan Mohniyu sometimes begins to hang around human settlements at night, and this is because he has become infatuated with a beautiful woman who lives there.

Wherever a Wan Mohniyu was sighted near a village, women would dread going outside after dark, for fear of the creature abducting them and spiriting them away to his cave. But some people say that the Wan Mohniyu's evil reputation is undeserved. When there is a disappearance, they say, it is because a human woman has fallen deeply in love with the Wan Mohniyu, and eloped with him by choice.

Ref: 94, 457

⤳ WEREHYENA ⤳

The Werehyena is a therianthrope found in stories from Punjab and Sindh. In human form, these beings appear tall and muscular, with strange yellow-tinged eyes. As animals, they take the form of giant striped hyenas (a species whose range formerly included most of Western India, though it is much rarer today). In hyena form they can hunt and eat humans, just as real hyenas occasionally do.

Werehyenas can assume animal form at will, though they usually only do so at night. Unlike werewolves, they seem to be oblivious to the phases of the moon.

A 1922 story by the British officer C.A. Kincaid tells of a Werehyena that was believed to be the reincarnation of a real-life serial killer named Anud Kasai, who lived in the city of Sehwan, in Sindh, in the 12th century.

This Anud Kasai was a butcher. When times were tough and there was very little meat available, he used to kill people, chop them up, and sell their flesh, pretending it was mutton—thus turning half the population of Sehwan into unwitting cannibals.

He got away with this for months. But one day he killed a man named Bodla Bahar, who was a disciple of the great Sufi saint Lal Shahbaz Qalandar, also known as Jhulelal.

Bodla Bahar was soon missed, and Qalandar walked through the city looking for him, calling out his name. As he passed Anud Kasai's shop, he noticed that every time he called out the name "Bodla Bahar!", the pieces of meat on the butcher's table jumped and danced. Qalandar realized what this meant, and he was able to reassemble Bodla Bahar's body and restore him to life through his spiritual power.

Anud Kasai was arrested. The authorities searched his shop and found many human bones.

The butcher was bricked up alive in the walls of Sehwan Fort. Visitors can still go to look at the place in the battlements where his body is entombed.

Ref: 562, 563

⸙⸎ WERELEOPARD ⸎⸙

There is an ongoing dispute as to whether Wereleopards are humans who gained the power to turn into leopards, or leopards who gained the power to transform into humans. According to most stories, if a Wereleopard is shot and killed while in leopard form, its corpse changes into a person, and some argue that this evidence supports the former hypothesis.

However, others say that when a Wereleopard is killed, the shapeshifting spirit which inhabits it can jump out and possess the killer, turning him or her into a Wereleopard in turn. This is true regardless of whether the killer is human or feline. (Normal leopards hate and fear Wereleopards just as much as humans do, and the monster must hide its true nature in order to live among either species.)

While they are in human form, Wereleopards appear strangely proportioned. The torso is large and muscular, the arms and legs a bit too short. The effect is too slight to make the person appear truly deformed or monstrous, or even unattractive; indeed, Wereleopards of both sexes have a certain magnetism and great powers of seduction. Nevertheless, their unusual build is noticeable. It is unknown whether regular leopards can see a symmetric effect when the creature is in animal form.

Wereleopards are reported from Dharwad district in Karnataka and Mudumalai National Park in Tamil Nadu.

Among some Naga people and other tribes of the northeast, there is a different type of "psychic wereleopard" or "wereleopardman". Here the person doesn't actually undergo any physical transformation; instead the soul is able to leave the body and possess the body of a leopard, or take the form of one. These beings may be juvenile **Weretigermen**.

Ref: 563

⸙⸎ WERETIGERMAN ⸎⸙

The word *Weretiger* is usually understood to mean a creature that can actually transform from a human into a tiger and back again. Such creatures do occur in South Asian folklore, for example in Mizo mythology, where they are called **Keimi**, and in the Koya legend of the **Chedipe**.

But there is a different—and, in India, more widespread—supernatural phenomenon in which the human body never actually changes its shape. Instead, the person has an ability to project his or her soul outside the body, where it takes the shape of a tiger and roams about.

The Naga writer Easterine Kire has coined the word "Weretigerman" for this type of being, to distinguish it from the other sort of weretiger. The Nagamese word is *Tekhumiavi*. In Kondh languages of central India, they are called *Kradi Mleepa*; in Oriya, *Palta Bagha*; and in the Khasi language of Meghalaya, *Khla Phuli*. The Khasis use pugmarks to distinguish the *Saw Saram* or "four claw"— the natural tiger—from the *San Saram* or "five claw", which is a human spirit in tiger form.

Outside these communities, there is a common belief that tribal Weretigermen acquire the ability to project their souls through sorcery and dark magic. On the contrary, at least according to Kondh folklore, the ability cannot be learned; it is bestowed by the goddess Tari **Penu** upon certain individuals at a young age, perhaps even at birth. According to the Khasis, the ability is inherited, passed down by a mother to a daughter or from a maternal uncle to a nephew. The Nagas, too, believe that the tiger-spirit is inherited, though usually from parent to child. Some say that the ability can also "rub off" on a person who spends a lot of time around a Tekhumiavi, or who shares certain food items with one— fresh ginger root, for example, or chicken liver.

The projected spirits of children who develop the ability do not immediately take the shape of a tiger. Instead, they start by becoming small insects, then butterflies, progressing as they grow up to squirrels and dog-like animals before finally taking the shape of big cats.

The soul of a Weretigerman usually migrates into the body of a tiger only during sleep, and returns to the human body when it wakes. Sometimes, though, the soul remains in the tiger for days on end. If possible, the person stays asleep in a darkened room all the while. If forced to get up, he will go through the motions of a daily routine while acting listless and distracted.

While in tiger form, Tekhumiavis have a complex social structure. They are organized into ranks and battalions, and follow many rules and laws. Monthly meetings are held during full moon nights at secret locations in the jungle. An annual conference of Weretigerpeople is said to be held on the 5th of August. On this day, they discuss which animals they may prey upon, and how to divide up the hunting grounds.

If a Weretigerperson is shot dead while in tiger form, the person's human body will die in its sleep at exactly the same instant.

Ref: 26, 129, 206, 572

⭒⟶ WIYU ⟵⭒

The Wiyu are a broad class of spirits in the traditional religions of Arunachal Pradesh. The pronunciation and spelling varies in different tribal languages. *Wiyu* is the Nishi word, while the same or very similar spirits are called *Ui* by the Apatani, *Uie* by the Mising, and *Uyu* by the Adi people.

Most Wiyu are not evil for evil's sake. Rather, they hunt humans the same way humans hunt wild animals. They compete with humans for natural resources, and they sometimes enter alliances with us.

According to the Arunachali creation myth, there were originally three brothers: the ancestor of the Wiyu, the ancestor of the humans, and the ancestor of the wild beasts. At some point, the human brother lost the ability to see the Wiyu brother, and the Wiyu went to live on their own in the jungle.

Though they are normally invisible, the Wiyu are thought to have physical presence. They can be fought with blades and other physical weapons. For example, when a person dies, men stand guard over the corpse with machetes so that the Wiyu will not occupy it. When a pregnant woman is having a difficult labour, her relatives take up positions around the house, brandishing their weapons, shouting, and striking the walls.

A few Wiyu from the pantheon are listed below.

The **Epom** are a large class of Wiyu who reside in the forest, especially around large trees. They are the descendents of Robo, who was the brother of Nibo, the father of man. Epom sometimes make themselves visible to humans; when they do, they are armed with swords and spears, and they wear helmets.

They occasionally abduct people. One favourite trick is to hide at the top of a banyan tree and make a sound like a crying baby. When a person arrives to investigate, they will find at the base of the tree the carcass of a wildcat missing its head. As they stand over it looking stunned, the Epom swoops down from the branches of the tree and catches hold of the person. Then the spirit carries them off deep into the jungle.

Epom can marry and have children, just as humans do. The long-legged arachnids known as harvestmen are thought to be manifestations of Epom bridegrooms.

Nipong is a Wiyu (or class of Wiyu) who reside in springs and streams and attack pregnant women.

Jimu-Tayang is the Wiyu who rules over the highest peaks.

Sikkom-Tanom are jungle spirits who can take the form of stick insects. They cause boils and spread diseases.

Babang is a healer spirit. He possesses shamans and helps them set broken bones. Babang is mute, and communicates only through gestures.

Urom are spirits of dead humans—especially those who have died unnatural deaths—who have gone to live among the Wiyus. Sometimes included in this class are the **Niji-Nipong**, spirits of women who died in childbirth. The Urom use grasshoppers, *urom takom*, as their messengers.

Mite and *Miname* are twin spirits who bear a grudge against humanity dating back to the earliest days of creation. At the very first village council, at which all the wealth of the world was apportioned, they arrived late, and the humans got what should have been their share.

    Their pestilential breath causes breakouts of contagious disease.

Pet-pum causes epidemics among swine.

Taleng Wiyu causes accidents, from small cuts and scrapes to fatal falls and impalements.

Ref: 46, 121, 188, 202, 222, 262, 267, 295, 318, 384

 YACH

The Yach is a Kashmiri spirit who is known for his vanity and stylishness. He likes to dress up as a film star in fancy clothes, and always wears a cap. (Muslims say it is a white *karakul* cap; Kashmiri Hindus say it is red and encrusted with jewels.)

    Yaches are usually portrayed as mischievous and fun-loving, but they can be fearsome and even murderous if they feel insulted.

    The Yach is slowly balding, and he's terribly worried that people will notice. This is the reason he never removes his cap. He is also, for some reason, dreadfully scared of sieves; he thinks this kitchen utensil will somehow be used to make him lose more hair.

Therefore, the secret to controlling a Yach is to steal his cap and hide it under a sieve. (Some say it can also be hidden under a mortar, or a pitcher of water.) If one does this, the Yach will be totally under one's power. And as a Yach has the power to grant nearly any wish, it can be very profitable to subdue one in this manner.

Though most Yach stories feature only a single male creature, a few tell of a larger Yach community with families and clans.

There is a season of the year during which articles of fine clothing have a tendency to go missing from people's closets. This is because it is the Yach wedding season, and the spirits borrow them for their functions. Yach weddings are held in well-lit, elaborately decorated underground chambers, and everyone tries to dress up as extravagantly as possible.

The Yach never fail to return the clothes in perfect condition.

Once in a very rare while, a human will get an invitation to attend one of these underworld weddings. This lucky individual is sure to come away from the function with some valuable magical gift.

Many say the Yach are the Kashmiri version of **Yakshas**. A minority opinion is that they are a variety of **Yeti**, descended from bears, and that they only have one eye in the centre of their foreheads.

According to some legends, the Yach may take the shape of a civet cat. In this form it may be synonymous with the **Wai Whop**.

Ref: 7, 94, 105, 564,

⟫— YAKSHI —⟪

A Yakshi or Yakshini (or Yaksha, masculine) is a member of a class of supernatural beings who appear in folklore across the length and breadth of India. They are also known from Nepal, Bhutan, Tibet, and Sri Lanka, and eastwards as far as Indonesia and Japan. They are found in Jain, Buddhist, and Hindu mythology, in the traditional religions of northeastern tribes, in ancient Christian legends of Kerala, and in the folktales of Kashmiri Muslims. Even Sikhism—of all Indian faiths, probably the least encouraging of belief in ghosts and spirits—includes mentions of Yakshas in its sacred texts.

The legends stretch far back in time, as well. At Pataliputra in Bihar and at Sanchi in Madhya Pradesh, stone statues of Yakshas have been found that are over 2,200 years old. They represent some of the oldest monumental sculptures ever discovered in India, only slightly younger than the great pillars of Ashoka.

Given this staggering scope of history and geography, it is difficult to focus on exactly what a Yakshi is.

Many believe they were deities of a very ancient animist faith that later was incorporated into the Dharmic religions. In the oldest scriptures of Hindu and Buddhist tradition, they appear as tree-spirits—angelic, mostly benevolent figures. Females are portrayed as beautiful women with large breasts; in ancient art, they always wear their hair tied in a knot. Males can either be tall and imposing, or rotund and dwarf-like; in either case, they are depicted as strong and virile warriors.

Yakshas are mortal beings, but they have the power of transmigration through time and space. They are attendants of Kubera, the Hindu god of wealth* (or his analogue in Buddhism, Vaisravana, the Treasure Lord.) Many of them live with him in the mythical city of Alaka, over which he rules. An elite group of invisible flying Yakshas called Guhyakas are said to hold up the corners of Kubera's floating palace. These Guhyakas also serve as messengers, and can take the form of ferocious demons during wartime; in times of peace, they dwell in the ground as earth gnomes.

The Yaksha Manibhadra is sometimes named as the general of Kubera's army. In other legends, he is the Yaksha king himself. He is a fierce fighter who can take the form of a hawk with a crest of flame. Manibhadra is worshipped as a demigod by many Jains. In fact each of the twenty-four Jain *tirthankaras*, or spiritual teachers, are associated with a particular Yaksha and a particular tree.

Yakshas in the *Mahabharata* are generally helpful to the lead characters. In one episode, a Yaksha standing in a poisoned lake in the form of a crane challenges Yudhishthira to answer a series of philosophical riddles. When the Pandava acquits himself admirably, the Yaksha resurrects his dead brothers and gives him a blessing. In another episode, a Yaksha named Sthuna finds a trans man named Shikandi in his forest, weeping and despondent because he was outed as a biological female in the marriage bed. Sthuna agrees to swap genitals with Shikandi so that Shikandi's wife's family will accept him. (Sthuna, however, is cursed for this action by Kubera.)

In the *Mahavamsa*, the 5th-century epic chronicle of Sri Lanka, Yakshas are among the indigenous inhabitants of the island. They were conquered by the Indian Prince Vijaya, who married their queen. The Yakshas then retreated to the mountains, where they harnessed the winds of fierce monsoon storms to work iron.

In Buddhism, Yakshas are counted as one of the eight classes of non-human supernatural beings, alongside **Kinnaras**, **Asuras**, **Garudas**, **Nagas**, Devas, **Gandharvas**, and **Mahoragas**. The Yakshas of many Buddhist stories are ugly, deformed ogres, reborn in that form because of sinful deeds in their past lives as humans.

One such tale is the story of **Silesaloma**, who has his own entry in this book. Another tells of Kharaloma, whose body was covered with rough scales, and his friend Suciloma, covered in hairy spikes. These two Yakshas planned to torment

---

*   In very ancient Hindu texts, Kubera is said to be the king of all evil spirits. He appears as a dangerous nature spirit in some tribal folklore as well—for example, among the Boros of Assam.

the Buddha; but instead, after conversing with him on the source of lust and hate, their hideousness fell away and they achieved *sotappana*, the first stage of liberation on their way to Nirvana.

In folklore and in pop culture too, Yakshas often appear less angelic and benevolent than they do in texts of Hindu tradition. They can resemble ogres, evil spirits, vampires, succubi, or cave-dwellers who waylay travellers on lonely mountain passes. Their Tibetan name, *gNod-sbyin*, means "doer of harm".

In Assam, where they are known as **Jokh** and **Jokhini**, Yakshas have distinct local characteristics. Accordingly, we have dealt with these versions in a separate entry. So too with the Kashmiri **Yach**.

Yakshis are an especially popular fixture of horror stories in the state of Kerala, whether in movies, on television, or in literature. One variety, called Vada Yakshis, live in palm trees, and descend at night to seduce men. They appear as ravishingly beautiful women in white saris. They wear fragrant flowers in their hair, preferring either jasmine (like the **Mohini Pey** of Tamil Nadu) or blossoms from the *yakshi pala*, the Indian devil tree, whose wood is used for coffins.

In this bewitching garb, the Vada Yakshi may approach a man to ask for a bit of lime to add to her betel-leaf. The man readily agrees. They walk along together for some time, chewing their betel-leaf and chatting; then the Vada Yakshi invites him into an abandoned house, which she claims is her own. Once they are inside and the door is closed, her form changes to that of a hideous demon with bloodshot eyes and long fangs…

In the morning, all that is left of the man are his hair and fingernails, strewn about at the base of the Vada Yakshi's palm tree.

Some tantric practioners of the *vamachara*, or left-hand path, are said to be able to gain the magical power of *yakshini siddhi*—basically, enlisting the services of Yakshi to attain their desires. The more powerful and dangerous *vada yakshini siddhi* can be used to kill one's enemies; by using this power, the magician conjures a Vada Yakshi and "keeps" it in a yakshi pala on his or her property. Sometimes the Vada Yakshi stays in the family for generations. It is not at all uncommon, though, for a Vada Yakshi to turn on her conjuror and consume him.

Yakshis are said to live in Paataal Lok, a subterranean realm full of treasure. The 1967 Malayalam novel *Yakshi* by Malayatoor Ramakrishnan describes their world as having a blue sun which shines down on rolling carpets of crimson grass. The flowers that grow there are made of sapphires, emeralds, garnets, and topaz. Young Yakshis fly around on the backs of giant dragonflies over streams of molten silver.

Adult Yakshis, according to Ramakrishnan's book, are required to ascend from this world to the land of the living once per year to feed on the blood of mortal men.

The Kanjirottu Yakshi

Many Malayalam folk stories revolve around a murdered woman reborn as a vengeful Yakshi. One such legend is the story of Chiruthevi, a famous courtesan. She was renowned for her beauty, and men from all around used to desire her. She had her pick of clients from the richest and most famous men of her day.

All this constant adoration soon went to Chiruthevi's head. She began to get a sadistic thrill out of stealing men's hearts, driving them to financial ruin, and destroying their lives.

There was only one man for whom Chiruthevi had any real feelings. This was Kunjuraman, her palanquin-bearer, who used to carry both her and her brother Govindan around on his back. But Kunjuraman was married, and had no interest in getting involved with Chiruthevi.

Govindan and Kunjuraman, on the other hand, were very close. In fact, according to some versions of the story, they were lovers themselves.

Eventually, frustrated that she couldn't get Kunjuraman's attention, Chiruthevi contrived to have the palanquin-bearer's wife killed. After the deed was done, Govindan came to know that his sister was responsible, and he told Kunjuraman about it.

Kunjuraman finally consented to sleep with Chiruthevi. But then, to avenge his wife, he strangled her to death in bed.

Govindan lied to protect his friend from the authorities, so that Kunjuraman escaped punishment.

Immediately after her death, Chiruthevi was reborn as a Yakshi in the village of Kanjirottu. Within minutes of her birth, she magically grew up into a full-figured woman of otherworldly beauty. She went right out and began seducing men and drinking their blood.

The Yakshi also kept harassing the still-living Kunjaraman, whom she desired now more than ever. She finally made a deal where she was able to cohabit with Kunjaraman for a period of one year—promising that afterwards she would become a devotee of Lord Vishnu, in his lion-headed avatar Narasimha.

Today, Kanjirottu Yakshi is supposed to reside in the mysterious "Vault B" of the Sri Padmanabhaswamy Temple in Thiruvananthapuram, Kerala, deep in prayer.

This temple is so ancient that no one is quite sure how old it is. References to the shrine appear in literature that dates back to the Sangam Era, before the time of Christ. For the past several centuries, it has been managed by the royal family of Travancore.

There are at least six vaults in this temple, designated by the letters A through F.* Five of these vaults were opened in 2011 following a Supreme Court order, revealing one of the largest hordes of gold and jewels anywhere in the world, estimated to be worth more than US $20 billion.

As of this writing, the huge iron door of Vault B remains unopened due to ongoing legal challenges. There are rumours of an even bigger treasure lying within; but there is also a legend which says that any attempt to open the vault will result in catastrophe. To start with, it will summon up a swarm of vicious demonic king cobras, but that's not the worst part: it will also set free the fearsome Kanjirottu Yakshi, who has been inside the vault praying to Lord Narasimha for centuries. If her long meditation is disturbed, she will likely become more evil, powerful, and destructive than she ever was before.

Other people believe that this is all superstitious nonsense. They say that the stories about Vault B only serve as a cover for corrupt temple officials and government authorities who are slowly looting the temple's treasures, selling them to black market antiquities traders for huge sums of money.

Chempakavally Ammal and Neelapilla Ammal

Another Yakshi legend comes from Thakkalai, near Nagercoil in Tamil Nadu.

There were once two beautiful girls named Chempakavally and Neelapilla. Their mother died when they were very young, and they were raised by their father.

The wicked and lecherous raja who ruled that part of the country happened to lay eyes on the two girls, and he desired them. He sent a message to the father that his daughters were wanted at the palace, and that he should deliver them the next day.

The father had heard the rumours about what went on at the palace when the raja called young women there to meet him. He also knew that if he refused, the king was sure to have him killed. With a heavy heart, he told his daughters to get ready for the journey.

The family set off the next morning. When they were halfway there, though, the father stopped. He explained to his daughters why they had been called to

---

* A 2014 report tells of two more underground vaults, G and H, bringing the total to eight. Vaults G and H remain unopened.

see the raja, and what he wanted from them. Then, out of a sick and twisted sense of honour, he picked up a rock and smashed both of his daughters' skulls.

After death, the two girls turned into revengeful Yakshis. They travelled to the palace and killed everyone in it, including all of the raja's family members and every one of his heirs. They saved the raja for last. He underwent unbelievable torture as they broke every bone in his body, and then began ripping off strips of his flesh, slowly devouring him alive.

After this grisly meal they went back and took revenge on their father, murdering him as well.

For years afterwards, the two Yakshis haunted the place where they had been killed. The area grew wild with cactus and thorny vines. Nobody could set foot there without the Yakshis harassing them, even in the daytime.

Finally, through many rites and poojas, the Yakshis were placated somewhat. A temple to them was built on the site. The older sister, Chempakavally, travelled to Mount Kailash to worship Lord Shiva, and was eventually transformed into a benevolent deity. Her idol in the temple is smiling.

The younger sister, Neelapilla, has not been reformed. Her idol stands behind Chempakavally's, full of rage and as ferocious as ever. It is said that some of those who pray to Neelapilla Ammal offer her fingernail clippings or cuttings of hair of their enemies, beseeching the Yakshi to seek them out and cut them down.

Ref: 4 101, 228, 252, 342, 425

YALI

A Yali is a chimeric animal most frequently encountered on the stone pillars of South Indian temples. It usually has the body of a lion and the tusks—and sometimes the trunk—of an elephant. Yalis started out as fearless beasts wandering in the jungle, and later became guardians of the temples and the entryways. They are often depicted standing on **Makaras**, or on elephants. Sometimes, there is one elephant under each foot.

A carved Yali-head can also be seen as a decorative ornament at the end of the neck of a veena, in the same place that a violin has a scroll. In olden days each instrument-maker would carve the head in a distinctive way, and an expert could identify the artisan by the style of the Yali.

Today, many of these distinctions have vanished. Most modern veenas feature a standard, Thanjavur-style Yali.

Ref: 376, 414

➤— YAM BHAYA AKHOOT —➤

The Yam Bhaya Akhoot is a protoplasmic entity believed to haunt Chittorgarh in Rajasthan, the erstwhile capital of the Mewar Kingdom.

Chittorgarh Fort is very ancient, and the details of its original construction are lost to the mists of time. Folk legend has it that Bhim, strongest of the Pandava brothers, travelled here; feeling thirsty, he stomped his mighty foot into the ground, and a gushing spring burst up through the hole. Around the reservoir thus formed, over hundreds of years, the fort was built up. It was controlled by a succession of dynasties—the Mauryas, the Guhila Rajputs, the Umayyad Arabs, the Delhi Sultanate, the Sisodia Rajputs, and the Mughals.

Somewhere along the course of this history, it became a sacred place for the Gadulia Lohars, a community of nomadic blacksmiths whose ancestors forged the fort's cannons. The Gadulia Lohars believe that their souls travel back to Chittorgarh after death.

The tallest tower in the fort complex, called the Vijay Stambha, was erected in 1448 by the Raja of Mewar to commemorate his victory in war. It is at the bottom of the stairwell of this tower, in the shelter of its cold and ancient stone, that the amorphous Yam Bhaya Akhoot is thought to reside. At least, it stays here in the daytime: at night, it rests in the Bhimlat Kund, the water tank attributed to Bhim.

The being is believed to be attracted to spiritually advanced individuals. On quiet days, when there are not many visitors, it follows lonely tourists up the stairs of the tower. At first it is invisible, but as it rises, it begins to glow with a blue light, and tentacular appendages start to take shape. An old legend says that it follows only as far as the person is self-realized; most of the time, it gives a tiny sigh and tumbles back down the stairs. But if it accompanies the climber all the way up to the top of the tower, it becomes his aura, and guides him to Nirvana.

Unfortunately, at some point, the top of the tower was damaged in a lightning strike and replaced with a dome. So today, even if a fully enlightened visitor should happen to climb the staircase, it is no longer possible for the creature to complete its journey.

The Yam Bhaya Akhoot has never been one of India's best-known mythological beings. And yet, there is a fertile underground river of stories regarding this strange entity and how it came to live in the fort. Tales of the mysterious, barely visible bluish blob have travelled widely around the world, becoming entangled with a chaotic mix of other legends, philosophies, and fictions—including the Jain *Kalpasutra*; legends of the Chisti order of Sufi saints; Kannada and Konkani folk traditions about invading sea monsters; Dogon mythology from Mali; the folklore of the Orang Asli (the indigenous tribes of Malaysia); even a bizarre European Neo-Nazi superstition about chthonic angels called Vril-ya, with roots in a 19th-century British science fiction novel. Further connections and comparisons have been drawn to the Greek myths of Sisyphus and Prometheus, the Exu spirits of the Afro-Brazilian Umbanda faith, Luristani versions of *The Thousand and One Nights*, the esoteric cosmology of the Lotus People of Early Hind, the Armenian mystic George Gurdjieff's "organ kundabuffer", the New Chronology of Russian mathematician Anatoly Fomenko, MK-Ultra, the Montauk Project, and an obscure 1942 Argentinian film called *Ponchos Azules*.

The cult continues to surface in unexpected places. In 1998, a temporary kinetic shrine to the Yam Bhaya Akhoot was erected in Black Rock City, USA as part of the anarchic Burning Man arts festival, whose theme that year was "The Nebulous Entity". The anonymous artist responsible for the sculpture, who hailed from the South American micronation of Parva Domus, claimed to have spent several days the previous year communicating with the Yam Bhaya Akhoot in Chittor while under the influence of a potent cocktail of psychedelics. In recent years in Japan, a subgenre of devotional art in praise of the creature has emerged, especially within the experimental heavy metal scene.

In Rajasthan itself, the entity is said to be either one of Shiva's ganas or a cousin of Yama, the god of death (see **Yamaduta**; Yama Bhaya means "Yama's brother" in Mewari, or possibly, "fear of Yama"). Others believe that it is an accretion of souls of generations of Gadulia Lohar patriarchs, or else a fragmented piece of the divine aura that surrounds the gods. Competing theories as to its nature have been the subject of clashes between rival camps of Rajasthani ojhas; there are indications that a sort of protracted magical war is being waged for control or possession of the Yam Bhaya Akhoot. Meanwhile, another sizeable contingent of tantrics believes the being to be firmly beyond the influence of human sorcery.

In several versions of the legend, the creature is said to be of extraterrestrial origin: a visitor from another solar system, or perhaps even another universe, trapped in our world due to a quark-nova disaster that caused an interdimensional portal to slam shut.

The Dogon people of West Africa—at least those who still follow their traditional religion—worship at shrines that are said to contain the fragments of a being called a Nommo, who was chopped into pieces by the sky god Amma to restore order to the universe, and then scattered across the Earth. Nommo were supposed to be amphibous, fish-like things with long arms or tentacles. They had greenish-blue skin, but could change colour like chameleons.

In the 1940s, two French anthropologists claimed to have uncovered secret knowledge about the Nommo through hard-won interviews with venerable Dogon spiritual leaders. The Nommo, they said, were in fact aliens from a planet orbiting the binary star Sirius, eight light years away, who had landed on Earth in the distant past. The Nommo were believed to have punctured the Earth to create reservoirs of water in which to live. At some point, presumably via Malian or French visitors to Rajasthan, this legend became conflated with the origin of the Bhimlat Kund; and so it is believed by some that the Yam Bhaya Akhoot is is a Nommo, or a piece of a Nommo—an extraterrestrial from Sirius.

In another tradition among the *bomohs* or occult practitioners of Malaysia, the being is called Abang Aku. Apparently a corruption or mishearing of the Mewari name, this phrase means "elder brother" in Bahasa Melayu; and so the Abang Aku is conceptualized as a sort of cosmic sibling of mankind, an incarnate extragalactic god that has become tethered to Earth and to human destiny. "Abang Aku" was further corrupted to "A Bao A Qu" by researchers on Malaysian witchcraft, and this became the most commonly seen Romanized form of the name, due to its popularization by the Argentinian writer Jorge Luis Borges.

Yet another story assigns an underground or deep-sea origin to the Yam Bhaya Akhoot. This legend holds that it is the ghost of the leader of the giant brittle stars (see **Nakshatra Meenu**) that attacked the Konkan coast in the 16th century. The spectral invertebrate was trapped and held captive by ojhas in the employ of Krishna Deva Raya, emperor of Vijayanagara, until it was presented several generations later to the Sisodia ruler of Mewar as a gift.

Ref: 12, 47, 143, 168, 245, 310, 436

❧— YAMADUTA —❧

In Hindu belief, Yamadutas are responsible for conducting the spirits of the dead to the afterlife. In some cases, they transport them to Swarga (heaven), or back to Earth to be reborn. But those who led ignorant and impious lives are destined for more gruesome fates.

First, the souls of sinners must cross the river Vaitarna, a turbulent channel one hundred yojanas wide.* The banks of the Vaitarna are gigantic piles of bones, with dark clouds of insects swarming above them. The river itself is not a river of

---

* About 1,500 kilometres—the distance from Delhi to Kolkata.

water; it is a raging torrent of shit, piss, blood, pus, and bile, carrying putrescent drifts of meat mixed with hair, toenails, marrow, and human fat. Smoke and flame billow up from the churn. Crocodilian monsters and giant ravenous fish swim in this foul soup, while monstrous flesh-eating birds fly above it, grating the air with horrisonant squawks and screeches.

The condemned souls may have to wait by the banks of the Vaitarna for many years, but eventually the Yamadutas will drag them through the river and into one of the twenty-eight different hells of Naraka. There the demons proceed to torture the souls in various innovative ways as per the nature of their sins in life.

In Hindu art, Yamadutas are usually pictured as looking similar to **Rakshasas**—humanoid, but with animal heads, horns, tusks, manes, and tails. They often have two long, curved protruding fangs pointing downwards from the corners of their upper jaw.

Yamadutas are the minions of Yama, the Hindu god of death, and obey his every command. Yamaraj rides a black buffalo and is surrounded by a halo of flames. In one hand he carries a mace and in the other he holds a noose of rope, which he uses to capture the souls of the dying.

Ref: 278

YANTRA-PURUSHA

Tala pattachitra is an art form from Odisha in which intricately detailed pictures—usually mythological scenes or animals—are carved into a canvas made from sewn-together palm leaves.

One of the more unusual subjects traditionally depicted by tala pattachitra artists are what appear to be alien robots. The designs vary from artist to artist, but they are usually roughly anthropomorphic. Some common elements include pincer-like hands, spheroid or domed bodies, and wheels beneath the feet.

According to local lore passed down by tala pattachitra artists in the city of Puri, these representations were originally inspired by a spaceship that landed in a sparsely populated region of Nayagarh district in 1947. The incident occurred during the chaos leading up to Indian independence (and just a few weeks before the famous UFO crash in Roswell, New Mexico).

The story goes that "Yantra-Purusha" (robot men) left the ship and surveyed a few square kilometres of the surrounding area. They later invited some locals inside their craft. After a few hours of an apparently friendly visit, the creatures bid the crowds of gathered villagers farewell, and their ship rose into the sky.

Ref: 175, 565

YATUDHANA

Yatudhanas are demonic beings mentioned in the *Rig Veda*, the oldest of the ancient Sanskrit texts. They are also mentioned in old Iranian scriptures. They are night-stalkers, thought to be powerful wizards who once were human, but who turned themselves undead through evil and abhorrent acts of necromancy.

Yatudhanas carry spears, eat human flesh, and have the ability to fly. One hymn describes them as having "three extremities" and a "triple root", though there is some dispute about what exactly this means. Neither the male Yatudhanas nor the female Yatudhanis wear clothing. They keep their hair long and loose.

Believed to inhabit the island of Lanka in large numbers, Yatudhanas seem to have originally been considered a separate class of entities from the Rakshasas, though later texts lump them together.

The apamarga plant (*Achyranthes aspera*; the devil's horsewhip) is said to ward off these spirits.

There is a legend that Jayasimha Siddharaja, who ruled the Western Chalukya Empire in the 12th century CE, once defeated the king of the Yatudhanas, named Barbaraka, in a battle in a cremation ground. His trophy from this battle was the *siddha* or magic power referred to in his royal title.

In Tibetan Buddhism, Yatudhana is the spirit of witchcraft and the guardian of the southwestern corner of the cremation ground. He appears with blue-black skin, standing on a corpse, holding a sword and a skull-cup full of blood.

Ref: 119, 566, 567, 568

YETI

Of all legendary South Asian monsters, the Yeti has probably achieved the highest level of international fame, making appearances everywhere from Ramsay Brothers films to Tintin comics to American Christmas specials to a ride at Walt Disney World.

The word derives from Tibetan, but similar creatures are known by other names from the folklore of ethnic groups across the Himalayan Plateau, from Kyrgyzstan to Mongolia to Bhutan. When Himalayan mountain-climbing became more popualr in the early 1900s, sightings of Yetis or their tracks became more frequent, and were eagerly picked up by international newsreels. In India, Yeti sightings have been reported in Ladakh, Sikkim, Himachal Pradesh, and Arunachal Pradesh.

The legend is very much alive. On 29 April 2019, an Indian Army expedition found what they said were Yeti footprints near Makalu Base in Nepal. Pictures of the tracks were posted on the army's official Twitter account.

There are three main varieties of Yeti in Tibetan lore. The largest and fiercest is the **Nyalmo**. It resides at the highest altitudes, on the snowy peaks of the very tallest mountains. These creatures stand about fifteen feet tall and have black fur. The second-largest is the **Chuti**, which lives from about 8,000 to 10,000 feet above sea level and stands about eight feet tall. Finally there is the Rang Shim Bombo, which is only three to five feet tall, with reddish-brown fur. These often descend low enough to raid human settlements for grain and milk.

All Yetis are nocturnal and see perfectly well in the dark. Most have flattened, ape-like faces. The males have matted locks falling over their eyes which may block their vision. Some Yetis have a small horn in the middle of their forehead.

Their legs are short in comparison to their torsos. Their feet are turned inwards towards the centre line of their bodies, and the toes point backwards.

In all varieties of Yeti, the female is considered more dangerous than the male, and is usually larger. Nyalmos in particular are described as living in matriarchal societies.

Most Yetis are thought to be brutish and stupid. They fear fire and gunpowder, and they eat their food raw. But there is also a legend of a wise teacher-shaman Yeti, **Ban Jhakri**, considered by some to be a spiritually advanced Rang Shim Bombo. His wife, Ban Jhakrini, on the other hand, may be a Chuti or Nyalmo.

Other creatures which may be considered as types of Yeti are the **Mande Burung** of Meghalaya and the Jyamphi **Mung** of Lepcha folklore.

Ref: 269, 298, 365

⊱── ZASAM ──⊰

In the folklore of the Hmar and other Kuki tribes of Mizoram and Manipur, Zasam is a female demon who wears tattered clothing and has dirty, messy hair. She lives in a secret hut deep in the jungle.

Zasam has huge, full breasts and is constantly lactating. She abducts people and tries to suckle them and care for them as if they are her children, but she inevitably ends up murdering them by mistake.

Ref: 16

⊱── ZOTING ──⊰

In the folklore of Maharashtra and along the Konkan coast, a Zoting is the ghost of an unmarried man who dies an accidental death with no living heirs.

Zotings are notoriously untrustworthy spirits. They make promises in return for various offerings (young goats, chickens, clothes) but then don't hold up their end of the bargain. They are more bothersome than they are fearsome, harassing people for food or money for no real reason other than having a cantankerous nature.

A Zoting's favourite target is a pious person who is very meticulous about observing religious rites. The ghost will find ways to snip the person's *janeu*

thread, steal his pooja items, blow out all his diyas as soon as they are lit, put worms in his kumkum powder, and replace his sandalwood paste with fæces.

Zotings usually haunt old empty houses. On the rare occasions that they are found outside, they stand with their legs spread apart, with one foot on each of two trees.

Ref: 92, 115 , 575, 576

 ## ZOUMI

In Kuki folklore from Northeast India, a Zoumi is a kind of evil spirit that lives in the hilly forest. There are reports of both male and female Zoumis. They are sometimes classed among the **Thilha**.

The Zoumi has an elastic body that can stretch into all sorts of different shapes. Usually, it appears standing as tall as a tree, but it can also shrink itself down to a tiny size. Zoumis rarely show their faces, and this is a blessing, for they are so horrible to look upon that the sight can shock a person to death.

Zoumis get mad cravings for chicken blood, and they often come to human villages late at night to steal hens or roosters, twisting off the heads and sucking the blood out through the neck. They also love bean flowers. For some reason, however, they are mortally terrified of women's petticoats; it is said that the best way to keep a Zoumi from stealing one's chickens is to keep a few petticoats hanging outside one's house.

There are occasional news reports from the Manipur hills of trespassing Zoumis being shot by homeowners, accompanied by photographs of mysterious-looking corpses.

Ref: 569, 570

ZUNHINDAWT

In the folk stories of Mizoram, Zunhindawt is an incorporeal spirit that possesses individuals and causes them to develop a very specific and extremely disgusting habit: drinking from puddles of other people's urine.

In the days before plumbing and outhouses, people used to step out of their bamboo houses and relieve themselves in the jungle. Late at night, people possessed by Zunhindawt would go into a sort of sleepwalking trance and creep around outside, waiting for someone to feel the call of nature. As soon as the person was done and went back inside, the Zunhindawt would emerge from the undergrowth and eagerly lap up the piss.

If the Zunhindawt was ever caught in the act, they would snap out of the trance—to their extreme mortification.

Some say this affliction was due to sexual perversion. Others blame it on a rare dietary deficiency. Whatever the truth, Zunhindawt reportedly affected people of all genders and ages. In fact, in some stories, it is a **Phung** that goes to drink from the puddle; so it is possible that this bizarre spirit did not discriminate between man and monster, either.

It is said that the knees and elbows of a Zunhindawt glow faintly in the dark.

Ref: 6, 150, 324

BIBLIOGRAPHY

1. A Peep into the World of Ghosts! (2 March 2021). *Indus Ladies*. https://indusladies.com/community/threads/a-peep-into-the-world-of-ghosts.21713/

2. A.M.T. Jackson. (1914). *Folk Lore Notes. Vol. I: Gujarat*. British India Press, Bombay.

3. Abdulla, F. and O'Shea, M. (2005). *English-Dhivehi and Dhivehi-English Dictionary*. Maldives Culture.

4. Agarwal, Deepa. (2008). *Folk Tales of Uttarakhand*. Children's Book Trust.

5. Aijazuddin, Shahnaz (trans.). (2009). *Tilism-e-Hoshruba*. Penguin UK.

6. Almeida, Rhea. (13 March 2017). We Illustrated 10 of Mizoram's Mythical Creatures & Their Fascinating Stories. *Homegrown*. https://homegrown.co.in/article/53190/from-giants-to-goblins-mizo-folklores-mythical-creatures-illustrated

7. Ambardar, Upender. (23 November 2020). The Winter Rituals of Kashmiri Pandits: The Legacies of Past. *Kashmiri Pandit Network*. http://ikashmir.net/uambardar/rituals.html

8. Anafafictionworld (17 February 2018). Shai: The Giant. https://anafanovelsworld.wordpress.com/2018/02/17/shai-the-giant/

9. Anafafictionworld. (2 August 2016). U Ksuit Tynjang. https://anafanovelsworld.wordpress.com/2016/08/02/u-suid-tynjang-an-imp/

10. Andileser. (6 November 2017). Rhino, lion & Co. Today: The Odontotyrannos. https://alexikon.wordpress.com/2017/11/06/odontotyrannos/

11. Anonymous. (2008). Dangerous magic: Muth/Handi. https://www.indiaforums.com/forum/topic/963575

12. Antares. (1998). The A Bao A Qu Mystery. *Magick River*. http://www.magickriver.net/abaoaqu.htm

13. Arni, Samhita. (2016). Dancing With Spirits: Encountering Karnataka's Supernatural Bhoothas. *National Geographic Traveller India*. http://www.natgeotraveller.in/encountering-the-spirit-of-karnatakas-supernatural-bhoothas/

14. Atsma, Aaron J. (n.d.). Indian Dragon (Drakon Indikos). *Theoi Project*. https://www.theoi.com/Thaumasios/DrakonesIndikoi.html

15. B. (7 September 2013). The Unavoidable Facts About C.W. Leadbeater. *Blavatsky Theosophy*. https://blavatskytheosophy.com/the-unavoidable-facts-about-c-w-leadbeater/

16. Bachaspatimayum, Mary. (2008). *Religion and Society of the Kuki Tribes in Manipur*. [Doctorate dissertation, Maharaja Sayajirao University of Baroda]. Shodhganga. http://hdl.handle.net/10603/59178/

17. Bainbridge, R.B. (1905). The Saurias of the Rajmahal Hills. *Memoirs of the Asiatic Society of Bengal*. The Asiatic Society.

18. Baite, Chungkhosei. (2015). Christianity and Indigenous Practices: A Brief Sketch of the Baites of Manipur. *Global Journal of Human-Social Science: C. Sociology & Culture*.

19. Baloch, Nabi Bakhsh. (1967). وڑروم ۽ مانگر ڇﻣ: Sindhi Adabi Board.

20. Banerjee, P. (2017). Why Dracula Fails to Get a Bite of India but Atmas, Dayans Make Us Shiver. *Hindustan Times*. https://www.hindustantimes.com/art-and-culture/dracula-didn-t-come-to-india-why-atmas-and-dayans-have-us-spooked/story-TNYKHxXVtsjDEOO6TcrwsK.html

21. Banjare, Ajit Kumar. (4 May 2014). बैगा और गोंड जनजाति में जादू एवं जादू करियाएं. *Research Journal of Humanities and Social Sciences*. https://rjhssonline.com/HTML_Papers/Research%20Journal%20of%20Humanities%20and%20Social%20Sciences__PID__2014-5-4-17.html

22. Bareh, Hamlet. (2001). *Encyclopaedia of North-East India, Vol 1*. Mittal Publications.

23. Barpujari, Indrani. (2010). *Customary Laws Among the Tiwas of Assam* [Doctoral dissertation, Gauhati University]. Shodhganga. http://hdl.handle.net/10603/116427/

24. Baruya, A. (2005). *Belief in Witch: Witch-killing in Dooars*. Northern Book Centre.

25. Basu, Helene. (2008). *Journeys and Dwellings: Indian Ocean Themes in South Asia*. Orient Black Swan.

26. Beggiora, Stefano. (2013). Tigers, Tiger Spirits and Were-tigers in Tribal Orissa. *Religions of South Asia*, vol. 7.

28. Bentley, Jenny. (2008). Láso Múng Sung: Lepcha Oral Tradition as a Reflection of Culture. *Bulletin of Tibetology*, vol. 44. http://himalaya.socanth.cam.ac.uk/collections/journals/bot/pdf/bot_2008_01-02_05.pdf

29. Bernadette, Maria. (1993). *Ethnomedicine and Healing Practices in Goa* [Doctoral dissertation, Goa University]. Shodhganga. http://hdl.handle.net/10603/31594/

30. Bhargava, Gopal (ed.). (2003). *Encyclopaedia of Art and Culture in India (Assam)*. Isha Books.

31. Bhasin, Veena. (2007). Medical Anthropology: Healing Practices in Contemporary Sikkim. *Anthropology Today: Trends, Scope and Applications*.

32. Bhat, Suneel. (2004). Bangane, Karnataka: School Building Construction and Well-Being Study. *Princeton1991*. http://www.princeton1991.com/imupload/documents/91FundProjectSummary-Bhat.pdf

33. Bhatia, Lakshmi. (2012). *Education and Society in a Changing Mizoram: The Practice of Pedagogy*. Routledge.

34. Bhattacharya, Rohit. (9 August 2018). 11 Scary Ghosts from Indian Folklore That are the Stuff Nightmares are Made of. *ScoopWhoop*. https://www.scoopwhoop.com/supernatural-beings-from-indian-folklore/

35. Bhattacharya, Rohit. (17 November 2014). 15 Bizarre "True Stories" From India That Will Keep You Up All Night. *Scoopwhoop*. https://www.scoopwhoop.com/inothernews/bring-on-the-shivers/#.kmvpe8uay

36. Bhavishya Purana. (15 December 2015). Pratisarg Parv: Chapter 45 [Notes]. *Facebook*. https://www.facebook.com/notes/bhavishya-purana/pratisarg-parv-chapter-45-krishnaamsa-udal-age-ninereads-sastras-parimala-pays-t/152590685102033/

37. Bhuyan, Avantika. (30 March 2018). The Little Fish in Big Rivers. *LiveMint*. https://www.livemint.com/Leisure/TB9AouNDcXASwUdc7ObL3H/The-little-fish-in-big-rivers.html

38. Binusivan. (2016, October 2). Odiyan. *Write Words*. https://binusivan.wordpress.com/2016/10/02/odiyan/

39. Biswas, P., and Thomas, C.J. (2012). *Construction of Evil in North East India: Myth, Narrative and Discourse*. SAGE Publications India.

40. Black, Andrew. (3 March 2011). Know Your Ghosts: The Ghosts of the Bengali. https://maskofreason.wordpress.com/2011/03/03/know-your-ghosts-the-ghosts-of-the-bengali/

41. Blackburn, Stuart. (2008). *Himalayan Tribal Tales: Oral Tradition and Culture in the Apatani Valley*. Brill.

42. Bobo. (7 March 2017). The Demoness (Lai-khutsangbi). http://folktalesofmanipur.blogspot.com/2017/03/the-demoness-lai-khutsangbi.html

43. Bond, R. (20 August 2019). Ruskin Bond Presents a Real-life Crime Story in "In a Crystal Ball: A Mussoorie Mystery." *Scroll*. https://scroll.in/article/934381/ruskin-bond-presents-a-real-life-crime-story-in-in-a-crystal-ball-a-mussoorie-mystery

44. Bond, Ruskin. (1986). Hotel Savoy: India's Largest Mountain Holiday Resort Hotel. *Internet Archive*. http://web.archive.org/web/20021101210311/http://www.freeweb.hu/gergoe/savoytxt.htm./

45. Borah, Jadabendra. (2015). *Representation of Tribal Life of Assam in the Assamese Novels: A Study with Special Reference to Four Novels* [Doctoral dissertation, Tezpur University]. Shodhganga. http://hdl.handle.net/10603/134922/

46. Borang, Asham. (1999). *Studies on certain Ethnozoological Aspects of Adi Tribe of Arunachal Pradesh India* [Doctoral dissertation, Gauhati University]. Shodhganga. http://hdl.handle.net/10603/69523/

47. Borges, Jorge Luis and Guerrero, Margarita. (1957). *Manual De Zoología Fantástica*. Fondo De Cultura Económica, Mexico-Buenos Aires.

48. Bose, N.K. (1964). *Cultural Contours Of Tribal Bihar*. Punthi Pustak Printing Press.

49. Boyce, Mary. (2012). Fravasi. *Encyclopaedia Iranica, Vol X*. https://iranicaonline.org/articles/fravasi-

50. Brar, Gurnam Singh Sidhu. (2007). *East of Indus: My Memories of Old Punjab*. Hemkunt Press.

51. van Breugel, Seino. (2014). *A Grammar of Atong*. Brill.

52. Brighenti, Francesco. (2017). Traditional Beliefs About Weretigers Among the Garos of Meghalaya (India). *eTropic* (16.1). https://journals.jcu.edu.au/etropic/article/viewFile/3568/3457

53. Brighenti, Francesco. (2011). Kradi Mliva: The Phenomenon of Tiger-Transformation in the Traditional Lore of the Kondh Tribals of Orissa. *Lokaratna, Vol IV*. Folklore Foundation. https://www. repository.cam.ac.uk/bitstream/handle/1810/244857/Lokaratna_04.pdf

54. Radcliffe-Brown, Alfred. (1922). *The Andaman Islanders: A Study in Social Anthropology*. Cambridge University Press.

55. Campbell, A. (1891). *Santal Folk Tales*. Santal Mission Press.

56. Campbell, James MacNabb. (1885). *Notes on the Spirit Basis of Belief and Custom (Rough draft)*. Government Central Press.

57. Chandra Roy, Sarat. (1928). *Oraon Religion And Customs*. Ranchi.

58. Changkija, Narola (2007). *From Oral Tale to Graphic Novel: Re-animating the Tiger-Soul* [Doctoral dissertation, Griffith University]. http://hdl.handle.net/10072/366646/

59. Changsan, D.M. (1992). Basic Beliefs of the Traditional Kuki Religion. *Journal of Dharma*, vol. 17. http://www.dharmaramjournals.in/ArticleFiles/Basic%20Beliefs%20of%20the%20Traditional%20 Kuki%20Religion-D.M.%20Changsan-April-June-1992.pdf

60. Charkraborty, Sumitabha. (2011). Traditional Health Practices: A Study among the Lepchas of Sikkim. *Jr. Anth. Survey of India*, vol. 60, pp. 83–101.

61. Charkraborty, Sumitabha. (2016). The Nature of Lepcha Traditional Festival: An Overview. *Jr. Anth. Survey of India*, vol. 65, no. 1, pp. 39–54.

62. Charles, Yuhlung Cheithou. (2010). *Indigenous Religion of the Chothe of Manipur: A Sciological Study* [Doctoral dissertation, North-Eastern Hill University]. Shodhganga. http://hdl.handle. net/10603/5515.

63. Chatterjee, A. (3 August 2016). The Ghosts of the Savoy: The Mussoorie Murder Mystery that Inspired Agatha Christie's First Novel. *Scroll*. http://scroll.in/article/812971/the-ghosts-of-the-savoy-the-mussoorie-murder-mystery-that-inspired-agatha-christies-first-novel

64. Chatterjee, A. (2 March 2017). Strychnine at the Savoy: Was Agatha Christie's Mysterious Affair at Styles Inspired by an Indian Murder? *The Conversation*. http://theconversation.com/strychnine-at-the-savoy-was-agatha-christies-mysterious-affair-at-styles-inspired-by-an-indian-murder-73326

65. Chelseylobo. (15 April 2014). Rakandhar. *Your Ghost Stories*. https://www.yourghoststories.com/real-ghost-story.php?story=19558

66. Chengappa, Raj. (18 July 2013). Mysterious Killer Stalks Pavagada Taluk in Karnataka, Five Young Girls Brutally Killed. *India Today*. https://www.indiatoday.in/magazine/indiascope/story/19830831-mysterious-killer-stalks-pavagada-taluk-in-karnataka-five-young-girls-brutally-killed-770954-2013-07-18

67. Chhatre, A., Lakhanpal, S., Prasanna, S. (2016). Heritage as Weapon: Contested Geographies of Conservation and Culture in the Great Himalayan National Park Conservation Area, India. *Annals of the American Association of Geographers*. doi:10.1080/24694452.2016.1243040.

68. Chingtamlen, Wangkhemcha. (June 2011). How the name "Sanamahi" Came into Existence: Discovery Of Kangleipak – 24. *E-Pao*. http://www.e-pao.net/epSubPageExtractor.asp?src=manipur. Manipur_and_Religion.How_the_name_Sanamahi_came_into_existence

69. Chophy, G.K. (2019). *Constructing the Divine: Religion and World View of a Naga Tribe in North-East India*. Routledge.

70. Chowdhury, Ruma Roy. (1995). *The Donyi-Polo Cult of Arunachal Pradesh: A Study in Textualising Tribal Oral Religion* [Doctoral dissertation, North-Eastern Hill University]. Shodhganga. http://hdl. handle.net/10603/65764

71. Claus, P. J., Diamond, S., Mills, M. A. (2003). *South Asian Folklore: An Encyclopedia: Afghanistan, Bangladesh, India, Nepal, Pakistan, Sri Lanka*. Routledge.

72. Collins, Steven. (16 September 2008). Pretas/Petas. *H-Net Humanities and Social Sciences Online*. https://lists.h-net.org/cgi-bin/logbrowse.pl?trx=vx&list=h-buddhism&month=0809&week=c&msg=A PHh7pIKyVM0mPTTUoIxnA&user=&pw=

73. Comes Lamta, Time to Drive Evils. (17 February 2018). *Pothashang*. http://www.pothashang. in/2018/02/17/comes-lamta-time-drive-evils/

74. Crooke, William. (1896). *The Popular Religion and Folk-Lore of Northern India*. A. Constable & Co.

75. Curators of the University of Missouri. (2015). Questionnaire: Lepcha, Sino-Tibetan. In *Database for Indigenous Cultural Evolution (DICE)*. University of Missouri.

76. Curse of Zayn Khan: The Djinn. (5 December 2014). *Amroha Books.* http://www.amrohabook.com/2014/12/curse-of-zayn-khan-djinn.html

77. Daimary R. (2017). *Witch Hunting in Bodo Society of Kokrajhar District Assam: A Socio Political Study* [Doctoral dissertation, Bodoland University]. Shodhganga. http://hdl.handle.net/10603/207239

78. Dalal, Roshen. (2014). *The Vedas: An Introduction to Hinduism's Sacred Texts.* Penguin UK.

79. Damon: The Malabar Slave (Historic Alleys). (2016, November 30). *South African History Online.*

80. Daniel, J. (2015). *Sex and Culture.* Lulu Press.

81. Das, Jayanta. (2015). *Folk Literature of the Karbis of Assam: A Study* [Doctoral dissertation, Gauhati University]. Shodhganga. http://hdl.handle.net/10603/152822/

82. Das, Sur. (2017). An Unpublished Account of Kinnauri Folklore (Moran, Arik, Intro.). *European Bulletin of Himalayan Research.*

83. Datta, Birendranath. (1973). *A Study of the Folk Culture of the Goalpara District of Assam* [Doctoral dissertation, Gauhati University]. Shodhganga. http://hdl.handle.net/10603/67892/

84. Debnath, D. (2003). *Ecology and Rituals in Tribal Areas.* Sarup & Sons.

85. Desai, Mahalaxmi S. (2002). *A Study of Maternity and Child Care in a Rural Setting of North Karnataka* [Doctoral dissertation, Karnatak University]. Shodhganga. http://hdl.handle.net/10603/96541/

86. Devchar in a bottle. (2020, June 17). http://talkingmyths.com/the-spirit-in-the-bottle/

87. Devi, K. Bidyarani. (2013). *The Religion of the Meiteis: A Historical Perspective* [Doctoral dissertation, Manipur University]. Shodhganga. http://hdl.handle.net/10603/26523/

88. Dharma Ashoka. (13 July 2019). NIRAYA !!! [Image Attached]. *Facebook.* https://www.facebook.com/Dharmaashokakingdom/photos/a.1820988844788158/2354625694757801/?type=1&theater

89. Do You Think Ghost Has a Sex Ratio Problem too? What is Some Light on this Serious Issue? (n.d.). *Quora.* https://www.quora.com/Do-you-think-Ghost-has-a-sex-ratio-problem-too-What-is-some-light-on-this-serious-issue

90. Rajagopalan, C.R. (2013). Performances, Art, Folk Narratives and Sustainable Environment Management. *Centre for Environment and Development.* http://cedindia.org/wp-content/uploads/2013/08/KEC-2013.pdf/

91. Maharana, Bhabani. (2017). Beliefs of Kondhs Concerning Diseases. *Odisha Review.* http://magazines.odisha.gov.in/Orissareview/2017/Sep-Oct/engpdf/116-120.pdf

92. *Gazetteers of the Bombay Presidency (Facsimile Reproduction), Kolhapur District Vol.* XXIV. Gazetteer Department Govt. of Maharashtra. https://gazetteers.maharashtra.gov.in/cultural.maharashtra.gov.in/english/gazetteer/Kolhapur%20District/appendix_d.html

93. Timung, Longkiri. (9 May 2020). The Most Frightening (Creepiest) Evil Figures of the Karbis. https://voleng.com/the-most-frightening-creepiest-evil-figure-of-the-karbis/

94. Drabu, Onaiza. (2019). *The Legend of Himal and Nagrai: Greatest Kashmiri Folk Tales.* Speaking Tiger Publishing Pvt Ltd.

95. Dungur. *Tripura Kshatriya Samaj.* http://www.tripura.org.in/dungur.htm

96. Edezhath, Edward A. (n.d.). Kappiri Myth: A Living Remnant of Luso–Dutch Encounter in Cochin. https://www.academia.edu/9544403/Kappiri_Myth_a_living_remnant_of_Luso_Dutch_encounter_in_Cochin.

97. Edingo, D.B. (2007). A Pragmatic Glimpse at Limbu Mundhum. *Contribution to Nepalese Studies,* vol. 32, no. 2. Research Centre for Nepal and Asian Studies. http://himalaya.socanth.cam.ac.uk/collections/journals/contributions/pdf/CNAS_34_02_08.pdf

98. Ekta. (8 June 2018). इस मंदिर में नारियल-फल नहीं, चढ़ाए जाते हैं गाड़ियों के पुर्जे. *Punjab Kesari.* https://himachal.punjabkesari.in/himachal-pradesh/news/in-this-temple-coconut-fruit-no-are-offered-carriage-part-815722

99. Elwin, Verrier. (1947). *The Muria and Their Ghotul.* Oxford University Press.

100. Elwin, Verrier. (1949). *Myths of Middle India.* Oxford University Press.

101. Elwin, Verrier. (1958). *Myths of the North East Frontier of India.* Presses Universitaires De France.

102. Evening Star · Page 24. (1912). *Newspapers.Com.* https://www.newspapers.com/image/331501159/

103. Ezung, Mhabeni. (2014). *Traditional Religion of the Lotha Nagas and the Impact of Christianity* [Doctoral dissertation, Nagaland University]. DSpace Repository. http://www.nagalanduniv.ndl.iitkgp.ac.in/bitstream/handle/1/93/T00076.pdf?sequence=1&isAllowed=y

104. Steingass, F. (2018). *Persian-English Dictionary: Including Arabic Words and Phrases in Persian Literature*. Routledge.

105. Faesal, Shah. (14 March 2015). It Symbolizes a Ghost Prodigy of Kashmiri Origin. *Greater Kashmir*. https://www.greaterkashmir.com/news/opinion/it-symbolizes-a-ghost-prodigy-of-kashmiri-origin/

106. Farooqi, Musharraf Ali. (26 June 2012). Mischief Makers: The Devils and Demons of the Islamic World. *Lapham's Quarterly*. https://www.laphamsquarterly.org/roundtable/mischief-makers

107. Ferro-Luzzi, G. (1998). Demonology in Tamil Folktales. *Anthropos*, vol. 93, no. 4/6, pp. 405–15. http://www.jstor.org/stable/40464840

108. Furtado, Joseph. (1942). *Selected Poems*. Printed by Paul Pereira.

109. Gadyachi Jatra: A Tribute to the Ghosts and Holy Spirits. (2016). *The Goan*. https://www.thegoan.net//gadyachi-jatra-%E2%80%93-a-tribute-to-the-ghosts-and-holy-spirits/13751.html

110. Gazetteers of the Bombay Presidency: Kolhapur District. Vol. XXIV. (1886). https://gazetteers.maharashtra.gov.in/cultural.maharashtra.gov.in/english/gazetteer/Kolhapur%20District/appendix_d.html

111. George, Goldy M. (2015). *The Duma Among the Gandas of Western Odisha* [Doctoral dissertation, Tata Institute of Social Sciences]. Shodhganga. http://hdl.handle.net/10603/103849/

112. Gerlitz, Peter. (1984). *Religion Und Matriarchat: Zur Religionsgeschichtlichen Bedeutung Der Matrilinearen Strukturen Bei Den Khasi Von Meghalaya Unter Besonderer Berücksichtigung Der National-religiösen Reformbewegungen*. Otto Harrassowitz Verlag.

113. Girish, M.B. (31 July 2017). Superstition Kills, Nokanalli Villagers Target Chameleons. *Deccan Chronicle*. https://www.deccanchronicle.com/lifestyle/pets-and-environment/310717/superstition-kills-nokanalli-villagers-target-chameleons.html

114. Gogoi, Shrutashwinee. (2011). *Tai Ahom Religion: A Philosophical Study* [Doctoral dissertation, Gauhati University]. Shodhganga. http://hdl.handle.net/10603/116167

115. Gole, Sushant. (7 October 2016). Spirits and Ghosts of Konkan Culture & the Chakwa Experience. https://sushantgole.wordpress.com/2016/10/07/spirits-and-ghosts-of-konkan-culture-the-chakwa-experience/

116. Gorer, Geoffrey. (1938). *The Lepchas Of Sikkim*. Cultural Publishing House.

117. Goswami, Hirendra Kumar. (1984). *Rabhas: A Sociological Study* [Doctoral dissertation, Gauhati University]. Shodhganga. http://hdl.handle.net/10603/66746/

118. Granoff, P., and Shinohara, K. (2010). *Images in Asian Religions*. UBC Press.

119. Griffith, Ralph T.H. (1895). *The Hymns of the Atharvaveda*. E.J. Lazarus & Co.

120. Roychoudhury, Priyanka G. (5 November 2012). Some Folk Beliefs of the Moran Community of Assam. *India Study Channel*. https://www.indiastudychannel.com/resources/156599-Some-folk-beliefs-Moran-community-Assam.aspx

121. Joshi, H.G. (2005). *Arunachal Pradesh: Past and Present*. Mittal Publications.

122. Hall, James. (2015). The Cryptid Zoo: The Buru, Giant Lizards and Giant Crocodiles. *New Animal*. http://www.newanimal.org/buru.htm

123. Haokip Sonkhojang, D. (2006). *A Study on the Traditional Religion of the Kukis before the Advent of Christianity* [Doctoral dissertation, Manipur University]. Shodhganga. http://hdl.handle.net/10603/103667.

124. Harding, Luke. (18 May 2001). "Monkey Man" Causes Panic across Delhi. *Guardian*. https://www.theguardian.com/world/2001/may/18/lukeharding

125. Harlan, Lindsey. (2003). *The Goddesses' Henchmen: Gender in Indian Hero Worship*. Oxford University Press.

126. Hasan, Rameeza. (2008). *Ethnomedicine among the Garos of North East India Aspects of Traditional and Modern Health Care Practices in Two Village Settings* [Doctoral dissertation, Gauhati University]. Shodhganga. http://hdl.handle.net/10603/42099/

127. Haughton, Henry Lawrence. (1913). *Sport and Folklore in the Himalaya*. Edward Arnold.

128. Hembrom, T. (1996). Maran Buru Bonga – Satan Equation a Theological Crime. *Indian Journal of Theology*, vol. 38, no. 2.

129. Heneise, Michael. (2017). The Naga Tiger-man and the Modern Assemblage of a Myth. In *Anthropology and Cryptozoology: Exploring Encounters with Mysterious Creatures (Multispecies Encounters)* (ed. Hurn, Samantha). Routledge

130. Higley, S.L. (1997). Alien Intellect and the Roboticization of the Scientist. *Camera Obscura: Feminism, Culture, and Media Studies*, vol. 14, no. 1–2, pp. 40–1). https://doi.org/10.1215/02705346-14-1-2_40-41-129

131. Hiltebeitel Alf. (2009). *Rethinking India's Oral and Classical Epics: Draupadi among Rajputs, Muslims, and Dalits*. University of Chicago Press.

132. Hindustani, Thangjam. (8 December 2011). The Demoness with the Long Hands: Lai Khutsangbi. http://magickalmusings-thangjam.blogspot.com/2011/12/lai-khutsangbi.html

133. Hindustani, Thangjam. (9 September 2017). Chaobi, the Pheiding-ga Lallonbi's Daugter: A Meitei Folktale Retold. https://magickalmusings-thangjam.blogspot.com/2017/09/chaobi-pheiding-ga-lallonbis-daughter.html

135. Hopkins, E. Washburn. (1915). *Epic Mythology*. Strassburg Verlag Von Karl.

136. Christensen, Michael. (28 December 2017). Gandharvas. *Mahavidya*. http://www.mahavidya.ca/2017/12/27/gandharvas/

137. Delhi Man Kills Family Friend for Doing "Black Magic" on His Sister. (23 February 2018). *Hindustan Times*. https://www.hindustantimes.com/delhi-news/delhi-man-kills-family-friend-for-doing-black-magic-on-his-sister/story-LfbYgKnbJVzSpSHycHTlsI.html

138. Hunt on for Alusive "Ape" in Meghalaya Hills. (25 July 2008). *Mumbai Mirror*. https://mumbaimirror.indiatimes.com/news/india/hunt-on-for-elusive-ape-in-meghalaya-hills/articleshow/15834662.cms

139. Huttmann, G.H. (1828). *Asiatick Researches: Or, Transactions of the Society Instituted in Bengal, for Inquiring Into the History and Antiquities, the Arts, Sciences, and Literature of Asia*. Bengal Military Orphans Press.

140. Hutton, J.H. (1921). *The Sema Nagas*. Macmillan and Co., Limited.

141. Hutton, John Henry. (1921). *The Angami Nagas, with Some Notes on Neighbouring Tribes*. Macmillan and Co., Limited.

142. ఈశాన్య ప్రాంతపు దెయ్యాలు. (2012). Red Squid Press, Guntur.

143. భరత దేశ చరిత. (1995). Red Squid Press, Guntur.

144. Indpaedia contributors. (17 March 2019). Witch-Hunting in India. In *Indaepedia*. http://indpaedia.com/ind/index.php/Witch-hunting:_India

145. Izzard, Ralph. (2001). *The Hunt for the Buru*. Craven Street Books.

146. Jacobs, Joseph (ed.). (1910). *The Demon with the Matted Hair. Indian Fairy Tales*. G. P. Putnam's Sons.

147. Jah, Syed Muhammad Husain. and Qamar, Ahmed Husain. (2009). *Hoshruba: The Land and The Tilism* (trans. Musharraf Ali Farooqi). Penguin Random House.

148. Jamkhothang Haokip, T. (2002). *The Concept of God in Traditional Thadou Kuki Religion* [Doctoral dissertation, Manipal University]. Shodhganga. http://hdl.handle.net/10603/105308/

149. Jarrett, H.S. (1949). *Ain-i-akbari Of Abul Fazl I Allami, Vol. 2*. Royal Asiatic Society of Bengal.

150. Jerusha. (10 February 2011). Say Hello to the Demons in my Head. http://dignifiedcow.blogspot.com/2011/02/say-hello-to-demons-in-my-head_10.html

151. JK. *We Know What We Did Last Summer, And We Want To Forget*. (n.d.). https://www.101india.com/horror/we-know-what-we-did-last-summer-and-we-want-forget

152. John, Haritha. (15 June 2016). The Sacred Spirits of African Slaves: Kochi's Unique History. *The Quint*. https://www.thequint.com/voices/blogs/the-sacred-spirits-of-african-slaves-fort-kochis-unique-history-portuguese-kappiri-muthappan-kerala

153. Jose, Thommen. (1 November 2013). *Halloween Travels: Ghosts Tales from the Road*. Wanterink.

154. Joseph. (2005). *History and Culture of Vaiphei Tribe of Indo Myanmar* [Doctoral dissertation, Manipur University]. Shodhganga. http://hdl.handle.net/10603/103879

155. Joshi, H.G. (2005). *Arunachal Pradesh: Past and Present*. Mittal Publications, Delhi.

156. Joshi, S. (13 August 2014). *Story of Kuldhara: The Abandoned "Chudail" Village of Rajasthan!* https://www.sid-thewanderer.com/2014/08/chudail-witch-trail-legend-of-kuldhara.html

157. Kaisuvker, Suraj P. (9 November 2014). A Cultural Treasure in the Woods. *Goa News – Times of India*. https://timesofindia.indiatimes.com/city/goa/A-cultural-treasure-in-the-woods/articleshow/45084108.cms

158. Kala Bhairava. (16 March 2016). *Kateri Amen* [Image Attached]. *Facebook*. https://www.facebook.com/748636691839047/photos/kateri-amenkateri-ma-the-good-the-bad-and-the-fairorigins-of-indias-kateri-ameni/974345882601459/

159. Kalita, Dilip Kumar. (1992). *A Study of the Magical Beliefs and Practices in Assam With Special Reference to the Magical Lore of Mayong* [Doctoral dissertation, Gauhati University]. Shodhganga. Retrieved from http://hdl.handle.net/10603/115253

160. Kalla, K.L. (1985). *The Literary Heritage of Kashmir*. Mittal Publications.

161. Kambale, Sadashiv S. (2003). *A Study of Ethnomedicine in a Karnataka Tribe* [Doctoral dissertation, Karnatak University]. Shodhganga. http://hdl.handle.net/10603/95808/

162. Kamkhenthang, H. (1988). *The Paite: A Transborder Tribe of India and Burma*. Mittal Publications.

163. Kanwal, Pushkar Singh. (2014). *Vanraji of Kumaun: A Historical Study* [Doctoral dissertation, Kumaun University]. Shodhganga. http://hdl.handle.net/10603/63811.

164. Kappakkattu, Asokan. (26 June 2012). Gulikan. http://asokanastro.blogspot.com/2012/06/gulikan.html

165. Kapur, Tribhuwan. (1988). *Religion and Ritual in Rural India: A Case Study in Kumaon*. Abhinav Publications.

166. Karabi, Goswami. (2016). *Folklore Materials in the Novels of Lummer Dai and Yeshe Dorjee Thongchi* [Doctoral dissertation, Gauhati University]. Shodhganga. http://hdl.handle.net/10603/195595/

167. Kashyap, Samudra Gupta. (18 March 2008). All That Haunts Assam Now in a Thesaurus. *Indian Express*.

168. Kato, Naoki. (Director). (2007). *A bao a qu*. [Film]. Tokyo National University of Fine Arts.

169. Katteri Scare Keeps Villagers Indoors. (25 March 2012). *News18*. https://www.news18.com/news/india/katteri-scare-keeps-villagers-indoors-458826.html

170. Kennedy, W. (2012). Motherland Ghost Stories. *Issuu*. https://issuu.com/wkdelhi/docs/motherland_ghost_stories

171. Little Badger, Darcie. (29 July 2019). Killer Echinoderms in Indian History by Virender Murkblob (Review). *Strange Horizons*. http://strangehorizons.com/non-fiction/reviews/killer-echinoderms-in-indian-history-by-virender-murkblob/

172. Khaidem, Rajit. (24 July 2015). Poubi Lal: The Story of a Giant Python, Exhibition Begins at National Museum in New Delhi. *Khbuzz*. https://www.khbuzz.com/2015/07/24/poubi-lai-the-story-of-a-giant-python/

173. Khaleque, K. (1982). *Social Change Among the Garo: A Study of a Plains Village in Bangladesh* [Master's thesis, Australian National University]. Open Research Repository. https://openresearch-repository.anu.edu.au/bitstream/1885/11265/1/Khaleque_K_1982.pdf

174. Khanna, Rakesh (ed.). (2010). *The Blaft Anthology of Tamil Pulp Fiction: Vol II*. (trans. Pritham K. Chakravarthy). Blaft Publications.

175. Khanna, Rakesh. and Devadasan, Rashmi Ruth (eds.). (2012). The Nayagarh Incident. In *The Obliterary Journal Vol. 1*. Blaft Publications.

176. Kharbangar, Sarabha. (2006). *A Study of Khasi Indigenous Religion: A Period of Transition (1897–1997)* [Doctoral dissertation, North-Eastern Hill University]. Shodhganga. http://hdl.handle.net/10603/61322/

177. Kharlukhi, W R. (1994). *An historical analysis of the political development in Jaintia Hills* (1835-1972) [Doctoral dissertation, North-Eastern Hill University]. Shodhganga. http://hdl.handle.net/10603/60607/

178. Khongsai, L. Jonah. (2012). *Rediscovering Folk Music in Worship in Kuki Christian Church* [Master's thesis, The Senate of Serampore College (University)]. http://lunkimjonahkhongsai.blogspot.com/2018/07/rediscovering-folk-music-in-worship-in.html

179. Kikon, Myanbemo. (2002). *Culture Change Among the Lotha Nagas: A Case Study of Wokha and Akuk Village in Nagaland* [Doctoral dissertation, North-Eastern Hill University]. Shodhganga. http://hdl.handle.net/10603/65767/

180. Kipgen, Paominlien. (2010). The Thadous: Part 1. *E-Pao*. http://e-pao.net/epSubPageExtractor.asp?src=manipur.Ethnic_Races_Manipur.The_Thadous_1/

181. Kishore, Usha. (2015). Pangolin & Other Poems. *East Lit Journal*. https://www.eastlit.com/eastlit-may-2015/eastlit-content-may-2015/southlit-supplement-may-2015/pangolin-other-poems/

182. Kloss, C. Boden. (1903). *In the Andamans and Nicobars*. John Murray.

183. Kressing, Frank. (2003). The Increase of Shamans in Contemporary Ladakh: Some Preliminary Observations. *Asian Folklore Studies*, vol. 62, no. 1. http://www.jstor.org/stable/1179079

184. Krishna, Nanditha. (2008). *Book of Demons*. Penguin Global.
185. Kukreti, Bhishma. (11 May 2013). Jagar: Calling of God. *Mera Pahad Forum*. http://www.merapahadforum.com/culture-of-uttarakhand/jagar-calling-of-god/130/
186. Kumar, A. (12 July 2015). What Brought the Original James Bond to Upper Assam after World War II. *Scroll*. http://scroll.in/article/717269/what-brought-the-original-james-bond-to-upper-assam-after-world-war-ii
187. Kumar, Chandra. (1961). *A Village Survey of Naachar*. Linguistic Survey of India, Vol XX-Part VI-No.16. http://lsi.gov.in:8081/jspui/bitstream/123456789/4832/1/44191_1961_NAC.pdf.
188. Kumar, N. Dilip. (2014). *On Top of the Old Tak*. Dorrance Publishing.
189. Kumar, Surendra. (2008). *Issues of Identity and Assimilation of African Diaspora in India: A Study of Siddi Community of Karnataka* [Doctoral dissertation, Jawaharlal Nehru University]. Shodhganga. http://hdl.handle.net/10603/32295
190. Kuttichathan. The Dance of the Divine. (n.d.). *Kerala Tourism E-Books*. https://www.keralatourism.org/ebooks/dance-of-the-divine/kuttichathan/7
191. Lakhnavi, Ghalib. and Bilgrami, Abdullah. (2012). *The Adventures of Amir Hamza* (trans. Musharraf Ali Farooqi). Penguin Random House.
192. Lalthangliana and B. (2005). *Culture and Folklore of Mizoram*. Publications Division, Ministry of Information & Broadcasting, Government of India
193. LangtukTRC (8 June 2017). The Myth of Kenglongpo. https://langtuktrc.wordpress.com/2017/06/08/the-myth-of-kenglongpo/
194. Latham, Robert Gordon. (1859). *Descriptive Ethnology, Vol. 2: Europe, Africa, India*. John Van Voorst.
195. Lavers, Chris. (2010). *The Natural History of Unicorns*. Harper Perennial.
196. Laycock, Joseph P. (2015). *Spirit Possession around the World: Possession, Communion, and Demon Expulsion across Cultures*. ABC-CLIO.
197. Legend Vishnumaya. (n.d.). *Kanadiaku*. https://www.kanadikavu.com/legend.html/
198. Lenin, Janaki. (6 July 2010). The Smokey Cat: My husband and Other Animals. *The Hindu*. https://www.thehindu.com/sci-tech/energy-and-environment/The-Smokey-Cat-ndash-My-husband-and-other-animals/article16188057.ece
199. Lepcha, Charisma Karthak. (2013). *Religion Culture and Identity: A Comparative Study On The Lepchas of Dzongu Kalimpong and Ilam* [Doctoral dissertation, North-Eastern Hill University]. Shodhganga. http://hdl.handle.net/10603/67279/
200. Lloyd, Keith (ed.). (2020). *The Routledge Handbook of Comparative World Rhetorics: Studies in the History, Application, and Teaching of Rhetoric Beyond Traditional Greco-Roman Contexts*. Routledge.
201. Longchar, Talilula. (2018). *She Who Walks With Feet Facing Backwards and Laughs in the Wilderness: Ao Naga Narratives of Aonglemla*. Zuban Projects. https://zubaanprojects.org/wp-content/uploads/2020/02/SPF-2018-Grant-Papers-Ao-Naga-Narratives-Of-Aonglemla.pdf.
202. Lorrain, J. Herbert. (2012). *A Dictionary of the Abor-Miri Language*. Mittal Publications.
203. Lungchuang, Ruata. (1 September 2018). 5 Nasty Mythical Creatures From Northeast India. https://zolistblog.wordpress.com/2018/09/01/5-nasty-mythical-creatures-from-northeast-india/
204. Lyngdoh, Fabian. (23 November 2017). Psychology of "Ka Rngiew" in Khasi Thought. *The Shillong Times*. https://theshillongtimes.com/2017/11/23/182286/
205. Lyngdoh, Margaret. (2012). The Vanishing Hitchhiker in Shillong Khasi Belief Narratives and Violence Against Women. *Asian Ethnology*, vol. 71, pp. 207–24. https://asianethnology.org/downloads/ae/pdf/a1754.pdf
206. Lyngdoh, Margaret. (2013). Alternative Perceptions of Belief Among the Khasis: The Weresnake and the Weretiger. *International Society for Ethnology and Folklore*. https://nomadit.co.uk/conference/sief2013/paper/16635/
207. Maaker, Erik de. (2009). *Traditions on the Move*. Rozenberg Publishers.
208. Maaya Pasuvai Vathaitha Padalam. *Dinamalar*. https://temple.dinamalar.com/en/news_detail.php?id=2250
209. Mackintosh-Smith, Tim. (2010). *Landfalls: On the Edge of Islam from Zanzibar to the Alhambra*. Hachette.
210. Maddy. (February 2010). The Bewitching Yakshi. *Maddy's Ramblings*. https://maddy06.blogspot.com/2010/02/bewitching-yakshi.html

211. Maddy. (1 November 2020). The European Demon. *Historic Alleys Blogspot*. https://historicalleys. blogspot.com/2010/10/european-demon.html

212. Madhav, Athira. (9 August 2016). Madan: A Collection of Kerala Ghost Stories. https:// keralaghoststory.blogspot.com/2016/08/madan-shutyour-stupid-mouth-mocked.html?m=1

213. Mainwaring, and George Byres. (1898). *Dictionary of the Lepcha-language*. Unger Bros.

214. Malsawmdawngliana. (2012). *Aspects in the Cultural History of the Mizos During the Pre-British Period* [Doctoral dissertation, University of Hyderabad]. Shodhganga. http://hdl.handle.net/10603/106134/

215. Malsawmluangi, Nancy C. (2018). *Understanding the Socio Cultural Heritage of the Kuki in Assam in the Light of Christianity: An Anthropological Approach* [Doctoral dissertation, Gauhati University]. Shodhganga. http://hdl.handle.net/10603/206990

216. Mang, Hlon Khua. (2007). *The Belief and Practice of Ahmaw (Witchcraft) and its Effects in the Mara Community* [Bachelor's thesis, Eastern Theological College]. https://hlonkhuamang.blogspot.com/

217. Mann, Rann Singh (ed.). (1981). *Nature-man-spirit Complex in Tribal India*. Concept Publishing Company.

218. Marak, Fameline K. (2006). *Major Folk Festivals of Garos With Special Reference to Cultivation: A Critical Study* [Doctoral dissertation, North-Eastern Hill University]. Shodhganga. https://shodhganga. inflibnet.ac.in/handle/10603/61420/

219. Marathi, Rajshri. (10 March 2016). कोकणातली १४ भुतं | *Popular 14 Styles Of Ghosts In Konkan, Maharashtra | True Or False* [Video]. *YouTube*. https://www.youtube.com/watch?v=72HcWWohaW0

220. Maung Saw, U. Khin. (2005). On the Evolution of Rohingya Problems in Rakhine State of Burma. *Network Myanmar*. https://www.burmalibrary.org/

221. Mawrie, H. Onderson. (1981). *The Khasi Milieu*. Concept Publishing Company.

222. Mibang, T., Chaudhuri, S. (2004). *Understanding Tribal Religion*. Mittal Publications.

223. Miller, Robert. (24 May 2018). Alexander the Great vs. the Odontotyrannos, aka Dentityrannus, aka the Tooth Tyrant. Add MS 15268 f. 208r @BLMedieval. [Image Attached]. Twitter. https://twitter. com/robmmiller/status/999446997621932032/

224. Mills, J.P. (1922). *Lhota Nagas*. Macmillan and Co., Limited.

225. Miñja, Divākara. (2010). *Muṇḍā Evaṃ Urāṃva kā Dhārmika Itihāsa*. Gyan Publishing House.

226. Mishra, Mahendra Kumar (ed.). (2018). *Lokaratna, Vol XI-1*. Folklore Foundation.

227. Misra, Kamal K. (1987). *Khamti Elites and Social Transformation in Arunachal Pradesh* [Doctoral dissertation, Utkal University]. Shodhganga. http://hdl.handle.net/10603/189333/

228. Misra, Ram Nath. (1981). *Yaksha Cult And Iconography*. Manishram Manoharlal Publishers.

229. Mizogurl. (5 March 2008). Sichangneii: A Mizo "Swan Lady" tale. http://tochhawngmizogurl. blogspot.com/2008/03/sichangneii-mizo-swan-lady-tale.html

230. Moazami, Mahnaz. (2016). NASU. *Encyclopædia Iranica*. http://www.iranicaonline.org/articles/nasu-demon

231. Modi, Jivanji. (1922). *The Religious Ceremonies and Customs of the Parsees Part 5*. Avesta.

232. Mohrmen, H.H. (26 June 2013). Traditions and Modernity: Beyond Superstition. http://hhmohrmen. blogspot.com/2013/06/traditions-and-modernity-beyond.html

234. Moran, Arik. (2011). An Unpublished Account of Kinnauri Folklore by Sur Das. *European Bulletin of Himalayan Research*. http://himalaya.socanth.cam.ac.uk/collections/journals/ebhr/pdf/EBHR_39_01. pdf.

235. Morris, John. (1938). *Living With Lepchas*. William Heinemann Ltd.

236. Mukhia, Terence. (2017). *Impact of Christianity on the Lepcha and Tamang Tribal Communities in the Darjeeling District (1841 to 2012): A Philosophical Perspective* [Doctoral dissertation, Assam Don Bosco University]. Shodhganga. http://hdl.handle.net/10603/176401

237. Mumford, Stan. (1989). *Himalayan Dialogue: Tibetan Lamas and Gurung Shamans in Nepal*. University of Wisconsin Press.

238. Muralidharan, Sharath. (16 April 2012). Odiyan – someone who can change to anyone and anything – based on 1930's belief! *When Vinu Writes*. http://storiespoemsandvinu.blogspot.com/2012/04/odiyan-someone-who-can-change-to-anyone.html

239. Murder at the Savoy. *Telegraph India*. (n.d.). *Newspapers.Com*. https://www.telegraphindia.com/culture/style/murder-at-the-savoy/cid/1550005

240. Murkblob, Virender. (2019). *Killer Echinoderms in Indian History*. Blaft Publications.

241. Nadkarni, Vithal C. (28 May 2003). British Scientists Say Boo to Spooks. *Times of India*. https://timesofindia.indiatimes.com/city/mumbai/British-scientists-say-boo-to-spooks/articleshow/47706283.cms

242. Namboodiri, Narayan. (6 February 2019). Mumbai: Key Conspirator in Black Magic Murder Case Held. *Mumbai News – Times of India*. https://timesofindia.indiatimes.com/city/mumbai/key-conspirator-in-black-magic-murder-case-held/articleshow/67858511.cms

243. Nandakumar, R. (24 June 2014). Thumbi and Thendan. http://nandakumarr.blogspot.com/2014/06/thumbi-and-thendan.html?m=1

244. Nath, Govind. (20 February 2016). Bhoot Mantra Siddhi Sadhana. https://ssd-sadhnaye.blogspot.com/2016/02/bhoot-mantra-siddhi-sadhana.html

245. Nath, R. (2018). *Jaina Kirtti-Stambha of Chittorgadh (c.1300 A.D.): The Form and the Idea*. Mughal Architecture Publications.

246. Nathan, D., Kelkar, G. and Xiaogang, Yu. (1998). Women as Witches and Keepers of Demons: Cross-Cultural Analysis of Struggles to Change Gender Relations. *Economic and Political Weekly*, vol. 33, no. 44. http://www.jstor.org/stable/4407326

247. Nattupurapattu. (20 February 2017). *Arakkan Kathai Villu Paadal* [Video]. *YouTube*. https://www.youtube.com/watch?v=9Z77WGHzH90

248. Navrang India: Colonial British ghosts!! – Spooky, Haunted Places in India. (2015). http://navrangindia.blogspot.com/2015/08/colonial-british-ghosts-spooky-haunted.html

249. Neetika. (2015). Old Spirits in the New Context: The Supernatural Narratives From The Folklore of Kinnaura Tribes of India. *International Journal of English Language, Literature and Humanities*, vol. III. http://ijellh.com/papers/2015/April/40-386-392-April-2015.pdf

250. Nehkholun Haokip, S. (2013). *Folk Dances of the Thadou Kukis: A Case Study in the Cultural Significance* [Doctoral dissertation, Manipur University]. Shodhganga. http://hdl.handle.net/10603/39991

251. Nichols, Andrew. (2008). *The Complete Fragments of Ctesias of Cnidus: Translation and Commentary with an Introduction* [Doctoral dissertation, University of Florida]. The University of Florida Digital Collections.

252. Niraj. (27 June 2011). Yaksha and Jainism. Perspectives on Pan-Asianism. https://ariseasia.blogspot.com/2011/06/yaksha-and-jainism.html

253. Nissim, P.S. (2017). *Brown Boy*. Blaft Publications.

254. Nongkynrih, Kynpham Sing (ed.). (2007). *Around the Hearth: Khasi Legends (Folktales of India)*. Penguin.

255. Notermans C., Nugteren A. and Sunny S. (2016). The Changing Landscape of Sacred Groves in Kerala (India): A Critical View on the Role of Religion in Nature Conservation. *Religions*. https://doi.org/10.3390/rel7040038

256. Oinam, James. (2016). *New Folktales of Manipur*. Notion Press.

257. Oldenberg, Hermann. (1988). *The Religion of the Veda*. Motilal Banarsidass Publ.

258. Ondaa: Folk Tale of Tea-tribes of Assam. (11 June 2016). *Nezine*. https://www.nezine.com/info/Ondaa%20-%20Folk%20tale%20of%20Tea-tribes%20of%20Assam

259. Parry, N.E. (1932). *The Lakhers*. Macmillan & Co., Limited.

260. Patel, Mailal H. (2020). ભૂસાતાં ગ્રામ્યમંત્રો. R.R. Sheth & Co. Pvt. Ltd.

261. Pathak, R.K. and Sinha, A.K. (2008). *Bio-social Issues in Health*. Northern Book Centre.

262. Patnaik, S. (2006). "Nyibu Agom": The Sacred Lore of the Adi of Arunachal Pradesh. *Indian Anthropologist*, vol. 36, no. 1/2, pp. 45–62.

263. Pattnaik, Devdutt. (18 November 2017). Tulu-Nadu's Bhootas. https://devdutt.com/articles/tulu-nadus-bhootas/

264. Pegu, Binita. (2015). Changing Beliefs and Practices of the Missing Tribe of Assam: A Case Study of the Majuli Island [Doctoral dissertation, Dibrugarh University]. Shodhganga. http://hdl.handle.net/10603/199429

265. Penzu, Tsuknug. (2009). *Ancient Naga Headhunters: Lives and Tales in Prose and Poetry*. Mittal Publications.

266. Pereira, Biula V. (2007). *Cultural Location of Alcoholic Beverage in the Goan Society* [Doctoral dissertation, Goa University]. Shodhganga. http://hdl.handle.net/10603/11854/

267. Pertin, Odol. (2015). Folk History on Origin and Early Migration of the Adi-Paadam Tribe of Arunachal Pradesh. *IJIRSSC*, vol. 1, no. 2. http://ijirssc.in/pdf/1451387434.pdf

268. Perwad, Abdul., Theruvath, AQM. and Dr. Amanullah, Adoor. (2017). *Kaasrote Baase*. Self-published.

269. Peters, Larry G. (2017). The "Calling," the Yeti, and the Ban Jhakri ("Forest Shaman") in Nepalese Shamanism. *Association for Transpersonal Psychology*. http://www.atpweb.org/jtparchive/trps-29-97-01-047.pdf

270. Philostratus. (1870). *Opera*. Lipsia Teubner.

271. Philostratus. (1912). *The Life of Apollonius of Tyana*. (trans. F.C. Conybeare). Sacred Texts.

272. Picerni, Federico. (2020). Urban Poetics and Politics in Asia. *International Quarterly for Asian Studies*, vol. 51. https://crossasia-journals.ub.uni-heidelberg.de/index.php/iqas/issue/view/761.

274. Plaisier, Heleen. (2007). In Awe of So Many Múng: Halfden Siiger in the Sikkim Himalayas. *Bulletin of Tibetology*, vol. 43. http://himalaya.socanth.cam.ac.uk/collections/journals/bot/pdf/bot_2007_01-02_02.pdf

275. Playfair, A. (1909). *The Garos*. David Nutt.

276. Pokhrel, Raju. (2014). *A Study of the Folklore of the Karbis: An Aesthetic Appraisal* [Doctoral dissertation, Gauhati University]. Shodhganga. http://hdl.handle.net/10603/116527/

277. Powell, Ken. (5 December 2012). A Christmas Carol? Ghostly Tales for the Season – Part II. https://kenthinksaloud.wordpress.com/2012/12/05/a-christmas-carol-ghostly-tales-for-the-season-part-ii/

278. Prabhupada, A.C. Bhaktivedanta Swami. "Bhagavata Purana 5.26". The Bhaktivedanta Book Trust International, Inc. Archived from the original on 13 November 2012.

279. Prasad, Saikia Shyamal. (2016). *Witch Craft, Witch Trials and Witch Hunting Perspectives: A Review With Special Reference to the Rabha Community of Assam* [Doctoral dissertation, Gauhati University]. Shodhganga. http://hdl.handle.net/10603/152219/

280. PraveenMohan (30 December 2014). Aliens Attack India, Kill 7 People: "Muhnochwa" UFO caught on film. [Video]. *YouTube*. https://www.youtube.com/watch?v=AcpDqJm1oGw

281. Purkayastha, Nabarun. (2012). *Oraons in Barak Valley* [Doctoral dissertation, Assam University]. Shodhganga. http://hdl.handle.net/10603/30214/

282. Putul, Alok Prakash. (23 September 2015). क्या आपने कभी 'भूत' खरीदा है?. *BBC News Hindi*. https://www.bbc.com/hindi/india/2015/09/150921_ghostsellers_of_chhattisgarh_pm

283. Qurratulain Shirazi. (n.d.). *Themes and Motifs in the Adventures of Amir Hamza*. Minds@UW, University of Wisconsin.

284. Lal, R.B. (2003). *Gujarat, Part 1*. Popular Prakashan.

285. R., Daimary. (2017). *Witch Hunting in Bodo Society of Kokrajhar District Assam: A Socio Political Study* [Doctoral Dissertation, Bodoland University]. Shodhganga. http://hdl.handle.net/10603/207239

286. Friar Jordanus. (c.1330). *The Wonders of the East* (trans. Colonel Henry Yule, 1837). The Hakluyt Society.

287. Rafy, K.U. (1920). *Folk-Tales of the Khasis*. Macmillan and Co., Limited.

288. Rahmann, R. (1959). Shamanistic and Related Phenomena in Northern and Middle India. *Anthropos*, vol. 54, no. 5/6, pp. 681–760. http://www.jstor.org/stable/40453635

291. Rajanarayanan, Ki. (2008). *Where Are You Going, You Monkeys? Folktales from Tamil Nadu* (trans. Pritham K. Chakravarthy). Blaft Publications.

292. Rajanarayanan, Ki. (2016). நாட்டுப்புறக் கதைக் களஞ்சியம். Annam-Agaram Pathippagam Books.

293. Rajendran, Abhilash. (7 June 2012). Odiyan Concept in Kerala. *Hindu Blog*. https://www.hindu-blog.com/2012/06/odiyan-concept-in-kerala.html

294. Rajkhowa, Benudhar. (1905). *Assamese Demonology*. Patrika Press.

295. Ramirez, Philippe. (2005). Enemy Spirits, Allied Spirits: The Political Cosmology of Arunachal Pradesh Societies. *North-Eastern Hill University Journal*, vol. 3, no. 1.

296. Ramnath, Madhu. (2015). *Woodsmoke and Leafcups: Autobiographical Footnotes to the Anthropology of the Durwa People*. Harper Litmus, Delhi.

297. Rath, Bibasini. (2004). *Social Structure of the Kutia and the Dongria: A Comparative Study of the Kondh* [Doctoral dissertation, Utkal University]. Shodhganga. http://hdl.handle.net/10603/119597

298. Redfern, Nick. (10 January 2017). The Biggest Yeti Of All? *Mysterious Universe*. https://mysteriousuniverse.org/2017/01/the-biggest-yeti-of-all/

299. Redij, T., and Joglekar, P. (2010). Origin and Development of Alakṣmī and Alakṣmī Concept. *Bulletin of the Deccan College Research Institute*, vol. 70/71, pp. 107–24. http://www.jstor.org/stable/42931240
300. Reisch, Gregor. (2017). Technical Devices in Ancient Alexandria and their Equivalents in the Indian Cultural Area. https://www.academia.edu/33891339/Technical_Devices_in_Ancient_Alexandria_and_their_Equivalents_in_the_Indian_Cultural_Area
301. Rev. Kittel, Ferdinand. (June 1873). Coorg Superstitions. *Indian antiquary, Vol 2*. Popular Prakashan.
302. Richet, C. (1923). Materialisation of "Bien Boa". https://www.survivalafterdeath.info/photographs/richet/bienboa.htm
303. Romero-Frias, Xavier. (2012). *Folk Tales of the Maldives*. NIAS Press.
304. Ronghang, Ronjit. and Ahmed, Rezina. (2010). Edible Insects and Their Conservation Stratergy in Karbi Anglong District of Assam, North East India. *The Bioscan*, vol. 2.
306. Rongmuthu, Dewan Sing. (1960). *Folk Tales of the Garos*. Department Of Publication, University of Gauhati.
307. Rout, J., Sajem, A. and Nath, M. (2009). Some Superstitious Botanical Folklore of Different Tribes of North Cachar Hills, Assam (Northeast India). *Ethnobotanical Leaflets Vol 13*. http://www.ethnoleaflets.com/leaflets/folklore.htm/
308. Roy, Babul. (1998). *Sociocultural and Environmental Dimensions of Tribal Health: A Study Among the Dimasa Kacharis and the Zemi Nagas of North Cachar Hills District in Assam* [Doctoral dissertation, Gauhati University]. Shodhganga. http://hdl.handle.net/10603/67935/
309. Roy, Sarat Chandra. (1928). *Oraon Religion and Customs*. Cambridge. Office.
310. Ruhela, Satya Paul. (1960). *Gaduliya Lohars of Rajasthan: A Study in the Sociology of Nomadism*. Impex India.
311. Russell, R.V. (1916). *The Tribes and Castes of the Central Provinces of India*. Macmillan and Co., Limited.
312. Saletore, Rajaram Narayan. (1981). *Indian Witchcraft*. Abhinav Publications.
313. Sandal, Veenu. (2 September 2018). Need to Control Hostile Water Spirits. *Sunday Guardian*. https://www.pressreader.com/india/the-sunday-guardian/20180902/282359745585177
314. Sangma, Milton S. (1975). *Development of Political and Social Institutions in the Garo Hills* [Doctoral dissertation, Gauhati University]. Shodhganga. http://hdl.handle.net/10603/67610/
315. Saravanan, V. Hari. (2014). *Gods, Heroes and their Story Tellers: Intangible cultural heritage of South India*. Notion Press.
316. Sarma, Bobby. (Director). (2018). *Mishing (The Apparation)* [Film]. BB Entertainment Trade Private.
317. Sasmal, Kartik Chandra. (2016). *A Study of Eight Bauri Villages in West Bengal: An Exposition of Their Socio Economic Life* [Doctoral dissertation, University of Calcutta]. Shodhganga. http://hdl.handle.net/10603/162698
318. Scheid, Claire S. (2015). Desires of the Recently Dead: Preliminary Observations on Post-mortem Possession Among the Adi of the Eastern Himalayas. *Irish Journal of Anthropology*, vol. 18. http://anthropologyireland.org/wp-content/uploads/2018/06/IJA_18_2_2015.pdf
319. Selby, M., Peterson, I. (2008). *Tamil Geographies: Cultural Constructions of Space and Place in South India*. SUNY Press.
320. Sen, Orijit. (27 June 2012). The Night of the Muhnochwa. *The Pao Collective*. https://paocollective.wordpress.com/2012/06/27/the-night-of-the-muhnochwa/
321. Sengar, Resham. (25 October 2018). Would You Dare to Stay in This Palace in Kota Known for its Harmless Ghost? *Times of India*. https://timesofindia.indiatimes.com/travel/destinations/would-you-dare-to-stay-in-this-palace-in-kota-known-for-its-harmless-ghost/as66363364.cms
322. Sengupta, A. (2020). Ghosts: Good, Bad and Gluttonous. *The Hindu*. https://www.thehindubusinessline.com/blink/cover/glossary-of-indian-ghosts/article32980324.ece
323. Sevea, Terenjit Singh. (2013). Pawangs on the Malay Frontier: Miraculous Intermediaries of Rice, Ore, Beasts and Guns [Doctoral dissertation, University of California]. eScholarship. https://escholarship.org/uc/item/3m42v60c
324. Shakespear, John. (1912). *The Lushei Kuki Clans*. Macmillan & Co., Limited.
325. Shama, S. R. (1915). *Kautilya's Arthaśastra* (trans. R. Shamasastry). Government Press.
326. Sharath, L. (15 September 2012). Omkareshwar Temple: One of the Places to See in Coorg. https://lakshmisharath.com/omkareshwar-temple-places-to-see-in-coorg/

327. Sharma, Chhavi. (23 February 2017). 5 Haunted college campuses of India. *Shiksha*. https://www. shiksha.com/b-tech/articles/haunted-college-campuses-of-india-blogId-8868.

328. Sharma, Jatin. (2016). *Values in Karbi Folk Literature: An Evaluation* [Doctoral dissertation, Gauhati University]. Shodhganga. http://hdl.handle.net/10603/160624/

329. Sinha, Shashank. (2007). Witch-Hunts, Adivasis, and the Uprising in Chhotanagpur. *Economic and Political Weekly*, vol. 42, no. 19. http://www.jstor.org/stable/4419566

330. Shrivastava, R.K. (n.d.). चटयिामटयिा-भाग-२. *Pratilipi*. https://hindi.pratilipi.com/read/%E0%A4%9 A%E0%A4%9F%E0%A4%BF%E0%A4%AF%E0%A4%BE%E0%A4%AE%E0%A4%9F%E0%A 4%BF%E0%A4%AF%E0%A4%BE-%E0%A4%AD%E0%A4%BE%E0%A4%97-%E0%A5%A8-5z4ibim9swhc-4521953423d9h14

331. Sikhiwiki contributors. (26 December 2009). Kauda Bheel. In *SikhiWiki, Encyclomedia of the Sikhs*. https://www.sikhiwiki.org/index.php/Kauda_Bheel

332. Singh, Anurag. (29 January 2016). Indian Ghosts & Legends – Part 1. *Fitnessexpertz*. https:// fitnessexpertz.wordpress.com/category/uncategorized/

333. Singh, Huirem Behari. (1985). *A Study of Manipuri Meitei Folklore* [Doctoral dissertation, Gauhati University]. Shodhganga. http://hdl.handle.net/10603/68226/

334. Singh, U. Nissor. (1906). *Khasi-English Dictionary*. Shillong, Eastern Bengal and Assam Secretariat Press.

335. Sinha, Shashank. (2007). Witch-Hunts, Adivasis, and the Uprising in Chhotanagpur. *Economic and Political Weekly*, vol. 42, no. 19. http://www.jstor.org/stable/4419566

336. Sinha, Upasana. and Manna, Nirban. (2018). Being and Believing: Santhal World of Gods and Spirits. *Journal of Ethnography and Folklore*.

337. Skeat, Walter William. (1965). *Malay Magic: An Introduction to the Folklore and Popular Religion of the Malay Peninsular*. Psychology Press.

338. Sky Stories: Indigenous Astronom. (2008). http://www.virtualmuseum.ca/edu/ViewLoitDa. do;jsessionid=C235472ED86FCF1A69A1BD75E2E379C1?method=preview&lang=EN&id=5169

339. Social, Culture and Economical Dimension Of Kurukhs. (n.d.). *Kurukh World*. https://kurukhworld. com/portray/social,%20culture%20&%20economical%20dimension/index.html

341. Soraparachil. (2 May 2015). Thendan Thenttikkum! *Tumblr*. https://soraparachil.tumblr.com/ post/120677817746/thenttan-thettikkum

342. Sreesobhanam. (17 September 2013). The Legend of Melancottamma. https://sreesobhanam. wordpress.com/2013/09/17/the-legend-of-melancottamma/

343. Srivastava, Priya. (18 January 2018). The Scary Saga of Haunted Dumas Beach in Gujarat. *Times of India*. https://timesofindia.indiatimes.com/travel/destinations/the-scary-saga-of-haunted-dumas-beach-in-gujarat/as62550736.cms

344. Srivastava, Priya. (24 June 2018). The Haunted Tale of Chain Tree in Kerala's Wayanad Will Keep You Awake All Night Long! *Times of India*. https://timesofindia.indiatimes.com/travel/destinations/the-haunted-tale-of-chain-tree-in-keralas-wayanad-will-keep-you-awake-all-night-long/as65119903.cms

345. Srividhya Samakya, V. (2017). *Mother and Child Health Care Practices of the Parengi Porja: A Particularly Vulnerable Tribe In Andhra Pradesh India* [Doctoral dissertation, Pondicherry University]. Shodhganga. http://hdl.handle.net/10603/240067/

346. Stack, E., Lyall, C. J. (1908). *The Mikirs: From the Papers of the Late Edward Stack*. D. Nutt.

347. Indian Police Say Hysteria Created "Monkey-Man". (21 May 2001). *CNN*. http://edition.cnn. com/2001/WORLD/asiapcf/south/05/21/india.monkey.man/index.html

348. Standing, Hillary. (2017). *Munda Religion and Social Structure* [Doctorate dissertation, SOAS].

349. Stegmiller, P. (1921). Aus dem religiösen Leben der Khasi. *Anthropos*, vol. 16/17, no. 1/3. http://www. jstor.org/stable/40446050

350. Stocks, C. De Beauvoir. (1925). Folk-lore and Customs of the Lap-chas of Sikhim. *Journals and Proceedings of the Asiatic Society of Bengal*.

351. Stonor, Charles Robert. (1955). *The Sherpa and the Snowman*. Hollis and Carter.

352. Strong, John S. (2004). *Relics of the Buddha*. Princeton University Press.

353. Subba, J.R. (2009). *Mythology of the People of Sikkim*. Gyan Publishing House.

354. Sumi, Hitoka H. (2011). *Beliefs and Practices of Naga Life: A Religio Philosophical Study With Special Reference to Sumi Tribe* [Doctoral dissertation, Gauhati University]. Shodhganga. http://hdl.handle.net/10603/110913

355. Surendranath, Nidhi. (17 June 2013). Once a Slave, Now a Deity. *The Hindu.* https://www.thehindu.com/news/cities/Kochi/once-a-slave-now-a-deity/article4820623.ece

356. Swaminathan, London. (16 August 2016). அரக்கர்கள் யார்? கம்பன் தரும் உண்மைத் தகவல்! (Post No.3066). *Tamil and Vedas.* https://rb.gy/wxqmyc

357. Swarup, Shubhangi. (30 December 2010). India's Most Haunted. *Open The Magazine.* https://openthemagazine.com/art-culture/indias-most-haunted/

358. Tadu, Rimi. (2017). *Writing Local History of Apatanis* [Doctoral dissertation, Tata Institute of Social Sciences]. Shodhganga. http://hdl.handle.net/10603/174513/

359. Talengale, Shobha. (2016). *Bobbare Bhuta: The Spirit That Straddles a Sea.* Conference: *Re-Centring Afro-Asian Musical and Human Migrations in the Pre-Colonial Period 700–1500 AD.*

360. Tani, Rubu. (2019). *Resistance Movements in Eastern Arunachal Pradesh* [Doctoral dissertation, Rajiv Gandhi University]. Shodhganga. http://hdl.handle.net/10603/247907/

361. Mahoraga. *Wisdom Library.* https://www.wisdomlib.org/definition/mahoraga

362. Tanti, Bulu. (2009). *Social Folk Custom of the Tea Garden People of Oriya Origin of Assam with Special Reference to the District of Tinsukia* [Doctoral dissertation, Gauhati University]. Shodhganga. http://hdl.handle.net/10603/69746

364. Tayeng, Obang. (2003). *Folk Tales of the Adis.* Mittal Publications.

365. Taylor, D.C. (2018). *Yeti: The Ecology of a Mystery.* Oxford University Press.

366. Faith That Still Resides in Goa's Villages. (28 March 2017). *Neutral View.* http://theneutralview.com/faith-that-still-resides-in-goas-villages/

367. Teron, Dharamsing. (2007). The "Môsêra" Tradition and the "Egg Origin" of the Karbis. *Karbis Of Assam.* https://karbi.wordpress.com/2007/11/05/the-%E2%80%98mosera%E2%80%99-tradition-and/

368. Teron, Dharamsing. (2008). Understanding Karbi Folk Religion. *Karbis of Assam.* https://karbi.wordpress.com/2008/02/26/understanding-the-karbi-folk-religion/

369. Teron, Dharamsing. Invisible Man and the Myth of Tiso-Jonding. *Scribd.* https://www.scribd.com/document/462583853/Invisible-Man-and-the-myth-of-Tiso-Jonding

370. Teron, Robindra. (2009). Influence of the Evil Figure: Tisso Jonding on the Socio-religio-cultural Life of the Karbis. *India Folklore Research Journal*, vol. 9.

371. Tetrapodzoology. (18 January 2009). The Pogeyan: A New Mystery Cat. *Science Blogs.* https://scienceblogs.com/tetrapodzoology/2009/01/19/pogeyan-the-cat-in-the-ghat

372. The Deities of Tipra of Independent Hill Tipperah. (2020). *The History of 185 Kings of the Tripura Kingdom.* https://www.185tripurakings.in/the-deities-of-tipra-of-independent-hill-tipperah/

373. The Kansas City Star · Page 3. (1912). *Newspapers.Com.* https://www.newspapers.com/image/653657183/?terms=garnett-orme&match=1

374. The Observer · Page 11. (1912). *Newspapers.Com.* https://www.newspapers.com/image/258831860/?terms=garnett-orme

375. Parrat, Saroj Nalini. *The Religion of Manipur: Beliefs, Rituals and Historical Development.* (1980). Firma Klm.

376. The Vina's Main Structures. (n.d.). *The South Indian Veena.* http://southindianveena.net/making.html

377. The Witch Hunt. (2017). https://www.tribuneindia.com/news/archive/features/the-witch-hunt-447786

378. The Wolves of Pavagada: A Mystery That Was Never Solved. (11 May 2005). *Wolf Song of Alaska.* https://www.wolfsongalaska.org/chorus/node/259

379. Thurston, Edgar. (1912). *Omens and Superstitions of Southern India.* T. Fisher Unwin.

380. Timung, L. (9 May 2020). The Most Frightening (Creepiest) Evil Figure of the Karbis. https://voleng.com/the-most-frightening-creepiest-evil-figure-of-the-karbis/

381. Tiwari, S.K. (2002). *Tribal Roots of Hinduism.* Sarup & Sons.

382. Tochhong, Rini. (2008). Chawngchilhi. *Mizo Writings in English.* http://mizowritinginenglish.com/2008/04/chawngchilhi.html

383. Tom Cat. (20 August 2012). *Ghosts in Assam, India.* http://biobid737.blogspot.com/2012/08/ghosts-in-assamindia.html

384. Tripathy, B. and Dutta, S. (2008). *Religious History of Arunachal Pradesh.* Gyan Publishing House.

385. Tuli, Priya. (14 July 2015). Ghost of Gata Loops & Other Mysteries of Leh & Ladakh. *GoMissing.* http://gomissing.in/blog/travel/ladakh/ghost-of-gata-loops-other-mysteries-of-leh-ladakh/

386. Tyagi, K. Shriti. (20 March 2017). Ghosts, Ghouls and Graveyards: Stories from 6 Feet Under in India. *Ecophiles.* https://ecophiles.com/2017/03/20/ghosts-ghouls-graveyards-stories-india/

388. Van Helvert, L. (1950). Burial Rites of the Gonds. *Anthropos,* vol. 45, no. 1/3, pp. 209–22. http://www.jstor.org/stable/40450839

389. Vancouver Daily World · Page 34. (1912). *Newspapers.Com.* http://www.newspapers.com/image/64834270/?terms=garnett-orme&match=1

390. Varma, Aditya. (22 July 2016). The Wolves Of Pavagada: The 3-Decade-Old Mystery Of Karnataka's Unsolved Murders. *Scoopwhoop.* https://www.scoopwhoop.com/The-Wolves-Of-Pavagada/#.z2m8l24ky

391. Vetschera, T. (1978). The Potaraja and Their Goddess. *Asian Folklore Studies,* vol. 37, no. 2, pp. 105–53. doi:10.2307/1177634

392. Vidyarthi, L.P. (1938). The Sacred Complex in a Maler Hilly Village of Santhal Pargana. In *Aspects of Religion in Indian Society.* Kedar Nath Ram Nath.

393. Vidyarthi, L.P. (1961). *Ghaghra: A Village in Chotanagpur.* Census of India.

394. Viehbeck, Markus. (2018). *Transcultural Encounters in the Himalayan Borderlands: Kalimpong as a "Contact Zone".* Heidelberg University Publishing.

395. Vitebsky, Piers (1980). Birth, Entity, and Responsibility: The Spirit of the Sun in Sora Cosmology. *L'Homme.* https://www.persee.fr/doc/hom_0439-4216_1980_num_20_1_3680266

396. Vitebsky, Piers. (1993). *Dialogues with the Dead: The Discussion of Mortality among the Sora of Eastern India.* Cambridge University Press.

397. Vohra, R. (1982). Ethnographic Notes on the Buddhist Dards of Ladakh: The Brog-Pā. *Zeitschrift Für Ethnologie,* vol. 107, no. 1, pp. 69–94. http://www.jstor.org/stable/25841799

398. Singhal, Arundhuti Dasgupta. (2013). Alha Udal and the devi of Maihar. *The Mythology Project.* https://themythologyproject.com/alha-udal-and-the-devi-of-maihar/

399. Wagner, Bryan. (2017). *The Tar Baby: A Global History.* Princeton University Press.

400. Waterfield, William (1923). *The Lay Of Alha: A Saga of Rajput Chivalry as Sung by Minstrels of Northern India.* Oxford University Press.

401. What is "Chathan Seva" in Kerala? (n.d.). *Quora.* https://www.quora.com/What-is-Chathan-Seva-in-Kerala

402. What is Muthkarni. (n.d.). *Vashikaranspecialist.* https://vashikaranspecialist.info/what-is-muthkarni/

403. Whitehead, G. (1924). *In the Nicobar Islands.* Seeley, Service & Co., Limited.

404. Wikipedia contributors. (10 July 2017). Kimpurusha Kingdom. In *Wikipedia, The Free Encyclopedia.* https://en.wikipedia.org/w/index.php?title=Kimpurusha_Kingdom&oldid=789977306

405. Wikipedia contributors. (28 August 2018). Hemaraj. In *Wikipedia, The Free Encyclopedia.* https://en.wikipedia.org/w/index.php?title=Hemaraj&oldid=856987307

406. Wikipedia contributors. (16 August 2020). Maring Naga. In *Wikipedia, The Free Encyclopedia.* https://en.wikipedia.org/w/index.php?title=Maring_Naga&oldid=973285616

407. Wikipedia contributors. (28 February 2020). Nale Ba. In *Wikipedia, The Free Encyclopedia.* https://en.wikipedia.org/w/index.php?title=Nale_Ba&oldid=943005132

408. Wikipedia contributors. (29 June 2020). Tsat Tsz Mui. In *Wikipedia, The Free Encyclopedia.* https://en.wikipedia.org/w/index.php?title=Tsat_Tsz_Mui&oldid=965094443

409. Wikipedia contributors. (4 June 2020). Gold-digging ant. In *Wikipedia, The Free Encyclopedia.* https://en.wikipedia.org/w/index.php?title=Gold-digging_ant&oldid=960689681

410. Wikipedia contributors. (9 March 2020). Odontotyrannos. In *Wikipedia, The Free Encyclopedia.* https://en.wikipedia.org/w/index.php?title=Odontotyrannos&oldid=944727092

411. Wikipedia contributors. (18 May 2020). Gajasurasamhara. In *Wikipedia, The Free Encyclopedia.* https://en.wikipedia.org/w/index.php?title=Gajasurasamhara&oldid=957309445

412. Wikipedia contributors. (5 May 2020). Chir Batti. In *Wikipedia, The Free Encyclopedia.* https://en.wikipedia.org/w/index.php?title=Chir_Batti&oldid=955055605

413. Wikipedia contributors. (7 November 2020). Kalakeyas. In *Wikipedia, The Free Encyclopedia*. https://en.wikipedia.org/w/index.php?title=Kalakeyas&oldid=987449550
414. Wikipedia contributors. (1 November 2020). Yali (mythology). In *Wikipedia, The Free Encyclopedia*. https://en.wikipedia.org/w/index.php?title=Yali_(mythology)&oldid=986456060
415. Wikipedia contributors. (15 November 2020). Maricha. In *Wikipedia, The Free Encyclopedia*. https://en.wikipedia.org/w/index.php?title=Maricha&oldid=988800812
416. Wikipedia contributors. (16 November 2020). Makara. In *Wikipedia, The Free Encyclopedia*. https://en.wikipedia.org/w/index.php?title=Makara&oldid=988938320
417. Wikipedia contributors. (2 November 2020). Manticore. In *Wikipedia, The Free Encyclopedia*. https://en.wikipedia.org/w/index.php?title=Manticore&oldid=986776943
418. Wikipedia contributors. (20 November 2020). Ghosts in Bengali culture. In *Wikipedia, The Free Encyclopedia*. https://en.wikipedia.org/w/index.php?title=Ghosts_in_Bengali_culture&oldid=989659431
419. Wikipedia contributors. (22 November 2020). Sumbha and Nisumbha. In *Wikipedia, The Free Encyclopedia*. https://en.wikipedia.org/w/index.php?title=Sumbha_and_Nisumbha&oldid=990006957
420. Wikipedia contributors. (7 November 2020). Susna. In *Wikipedia, The Free Encyclopedia*. https://en.wikipedia.org/w/index.php?title=Susna&oldid=987499305
421. Wikipedia contributors. (14 October 2020). Khonds. In *Wikipedia, The Free Encyclopedia*. https://en.wikipedia.org/w/index.php?title=Khonds&oldid=983406092
422. Wikipedia contributors. (15 October 2020). Preta. In *Wikipedia, The Free Encyclopedia*. https://en.wikipedia.org/w/index.php?title=Preta&oldid=983626679
423. Wikipedia contributors. (21 October 2020). Mehandipur Balaji Temple. In *Wikipedia, The Free Encyclopedia*. https://en.wikipedia.org/w/index.php?title=Mehandipur_Balaji_Temple&oldid=984671809
424. Wikipedia contributors. (23 October 2020). Gandaberunda. In *Wikipedia, The Free Encyclopedia*. https://en.wikipedia.org/w/index.php?title=Gandaberunda&oldid=985074620
425. Wikipedia contributors. (26 October 2020). Kanjirottu Yakshi. In *Wikipedia, The Free Encyclopedia*. https://en.wikipedia.org/w/index.php?title=Kanjirottu_Yakshi&oldid=985538778
426. Wikipedia contributors. (3 October 2020). Naraka (Jainism). In *Wikipedia, The Free Encyclopedia*. https://en.wikipedia.org/w/index.php?title=Naraka_(Jainism)&oldid=981704209
427. Wikipedia contributors. (30 October 2020). Ichchadhari Naags. In *Wikipedia, The Free Encyclopedia*. https://en.wikipedia.org/w/index.php?title=Ichchadhari_Naags&oldid=986171259
428. Wikipedia contributors. (12 September 2020). Pari (2018 Indian film). In *Wikipedia, The Free Encyclopedia*. https://en.wikipedia.org/w/index.php?title=Pari_(2018_Indian_film)&oldid=977956352
429. Wikipedia contributors. (29 September 2020). Phaya Naga. In *Wikipedia, The Free Encyclopedia*. https://en.wikipedia.org/w/index.php?title=Phaya_Naga&oldid=980916225
430. Wojkowitz, R. von Nebesky. (1951). Ancient Funeral Ceremonies of the Lepchas. *The Eastern Anthropologist, Vol.*(5), No. 1. Lucknow.
431. Wolflanq, Barrylia Mesha. (2003). *Khasi Myths: An Interpretative Study* [Doctoral dissertation, North-Eastern Hill University]. Shodhganga. http://hdl.handle.net/10603/60928
432. Wylie, T. (1964). Ro-Langs: The Tibetan Zombie. *History of Religions*, vol. 4, no. 1. http://www.jstor.org/stable/1061872
433. Xaxlo, Prem. (2007). *Complementarity of Human Life and Other Life Forms in Nature: A Study of Human Obligations Toward the Environment with Particular Reference to the Oraon Indigenous Community of Chotanagpur, India*. Gregorian Biblical BookShop.
434. Yandell, Keith E. and Paul, John J. (2013). *Religion and Public Culture: Encounters and Identities in Modern South India*. Routledge.
435. Yungdrung, Kalden. (30 December 2017). Spirits in the Sky and on Earth. *Dharma Wheel*. https://www.dharmawheel.net/viewtopic.php?t=27472
436. Ziggy the Blue. (29 January 2019). The Quest for A Bao A Qu. *Quests: Looking for the Improbable*. https://quests.home.blog/2019/01/29/the-journey-begins/
437. المسالك: Ibn Battuta Relates of the Magicians Called Jugis. (n.d.). http://www.almasalik.com/locationPassage.do?locationId=33384&languageId=en&passageId=15361

438. Swaminathan, London. அசுரர்கள், அரக்கர்கள் அகராதி. (23 October 2014). *Tamil and Vedas*. https://rb.gy/wxqmyc

439. Swaminathan, London. இந்தக்களின் 18 பிரிவுகள் : பதினெண் கணங்கள். (9 November 2014). *Tamil and Vedas*. https://rb.gy/wxqmyc

440. ആറാമിന്ദ്രിയം. (8 February 2009). Ghosts: True or Fake? http://prethanubavangal.blogspot.com/2009/02/ghost-true-or-fake.html

441. What are Ancient Alternative Tamil Words (Sanga Thamizh Sorkal) for Ghosts or Horrors? *Quora*. https://www.quora.com/What-are-ancient-alternative-Tamil-words-Sanga-Thamizh-Sorkal-for-ghosts-or-horrors

442. தேமொழி. (26 May 2018). அணங்க. http://siragu.com/%E0%AE%85%E0%AE%A3%E0%AE%99%E0%AF%8D%E0%AE%95%E0%AF%81/

443. Duchesne-Guillemin, J. "Ahriman". *Encyclopædia Iranica*. http://www.iranicaonline.org/articles/ahriman

444. Apasmara. *Yogapedia*. (27 July 2017). https://www.yogapedia.com/definition/9098/apasmara

445. Choudhary, Sagarika. (15 May 2020). Mahabharat: Is Ashwatthama Still Alive? *Mumbai Mirror*. https://mumbaimirror.indiatimes.com/entertainment/tv/mahabharat-is-ashwatthama-still-alive/articleshow/75754593.cms

446. Who Is Ashwathama? Why Was He Cursed by Krishna? Is He Still Alive? *Mythgyaan*. https://mythgyaan.com/ashwathama-curse-still-alive/

447. Krishnan, Nandhita. (2007). *The Book of Demons*. Penguin, UK.

448. Sharma, Jayanta Kumar. (1985). Oxomor Bhootor Kotha (On Types of Ghosts in Assam). *Pathshala Xophura*, 22nd edition.

449. Prabhupada, A.C. Bhaktivedanta Swami. (1970). *Krsna, The Supreme Personality of Godhead*. https://krsnabook.com/author/

450. Save, K.J. (1945). *The Warlis*. Padma Publications, Bombay.

451. संपादक. (9 September 2018). बायंगी - मराठी भयकथा. Marathi Mati. https://www.marathimati.com/2018/09/bayangi-marathi-katha.html

452. Ghosh, Amitav. (1994). *In an Antique Land*. Vintage Books.

454. Atsma, Aaron J. Blemmyes. *Theoi Project*. Retrieved 15 November 2020 from https://www.theoi.com/Phylos/Sternophthalmoi.html

455. Miñja, Divākara. (2010). *Muṇḍā Evaṃ Urāṃva kā Dhārmika Itihāsa*. Gyan Publishing House.

456. Dey, Lal Bihari. (1912). *Folk-Tales of Bengal*. Macmillan and Co., London.

457. Native Fibs: A Revisiting (Tales in Kashmiri Folklore). (2015). *The Troubled Waters*. https://syedaqeel.wordpress.com/2015/10/18/native-fibs-a-revisiting-tales-in-kashmiri-folklore/

458. Dollfus, Pascale. (2006). The Seven Rongtsan Brothers in Ladakh. *Études mongoles et sibériennes, centrasiatiques et tibétaines*, vol. 36–37, pp. 373–406.

459. Marak, Preetty Ch. (21 August 2020). Folk Tale from Garo Hills: Dombe Wari – The Story Behind the Iconic Calm & Foreboding Lake. *The Northeast Today*. https://www.thenortheasttoday.com/dont-miss/folk-tale-from-garo-hills-dombe-wari-the-story-behind-the-iconic-calm-foreboding-lake

460. Bullet Baba. *Rajasthan Direct*. https://www.rajasthandirect.com/tourism/temples/bullet-baba

461. Bullet Baba: Story of A Strange Temple. (28 March 2019). *Biking Mystery*. https://bikingmystery.com/blog/bullet-baba/

462. Atsma, Aaron J. Ketea Indikoi. *Theoi Project*. https://www.theoi.com/Thaumasios/KeteaIndikoi.html

463. Enthoven, R.E. (1915). *Folk Lore Notes Vol. II: Konkan*. British India Press, Bombay.

464. Census of India, Volume X. (1961). Scheduled Tribes in Maharashtra Ethnographic Notes. Maharashtra Census Office, Bombay.

465. श्रीकांत आनंदी सधिदार्थ ओहोळ. (15 September 2017). चेटकीण. Pratilipi. https://marathi.pratilipi.com/story/%E0%A4%9A%E0%A5%87%E0%A4%9F%E0%A4%95%E0%A5%80%E0%A4%A3-q1520zg8g00i?uitype=old

466. नारायण धारप. (2017). चेटकीण. Saket Prakashan.

467. Man, Edward Horace. (1885). *On the Aboriginal Inhabitants of the Andaman Islands*. Royal Anthropological Institute, London.

468. Strabo (1924). H.L. Jones (ed.). "Strabo, Geography". The Perseus Digital Library. Tufts University. http://www.perseus.tufts.edu/hopper/text?doc=Strab.+toc

469. Dakini. *New World Encyclopedia*. https://www.newworldencyclopedia.org/entry/Dakini
470. Dakini. *Khandro.net*. http://www.khandro.net/dakini_khandro.htm
471. The Bundahishn: Knowledge from the Zand. (1897). Wisdom Library. https://www.wisdomlib.org/zoroastrianism/book/the-bundahishn/d/doc4479.html
472. Williams, A.V. Dew. (1994). *Encyclopedia Iranica*. https://www.iranicaonline.org/articles/dew
473. What is the Best Ghost Story You Have Ever Read? *Quora*. https://www.quora.com/What-is-the-best-ghost-story-you-have-ever-read
474. Surana, Pingali. (2003). *The Sound of the Kiss: Or, The Story that Must Never be Told*. (ed. Velcheru Narayanan Rao and David Dead Shulman). Translations from the Asian Classics. Oxford University Press.
475. Ganguly, Pranab Kumar. (1961). Religious Beliefs of the Negritos of Little Andaman. *The Eastern Anthropologist*.
476. Sharma, Richa. (10 August 2015). 25 Lesser Known Mythical Creatures from Hindu Mythology. *Speaking Tree*. https://www.speakingtree.in/allslides/25-lesser-known-mythical-creatures-from-hindu-mythology
477. Muscato, Christopher. Indian Mythological Creatures. *Study.com*. https://study.com/academy/lesson/indian-mythological-creatures.html
478. Wang, Phub Dorji. (22 October 2019). The Mystical Lion Fortress Singye Dzong. http://www.phubdorjiwang.com/2019/10/the-mystical-lion-fortress-singye-dzong.html
479. Mundhra, Navneet. (6 September 2019). Real Story Behind the Horrifying Legend of Gata Loops. *Yahoo News*. https://in.news.yahoo.com/real-story-behind-the-horrifying-legend-of-gata-loops-091922265.html
480. Westrem, Scott D. (1998). Tomasch, Sylvia and Sealy, Gilles (eds). *Against Gog and Magog*. Text and Territory: Geographical Imagination in the European Middle Ages. University of Pennsylvania Press
481. Mindry In. (2013). Goggayya Interview (Kannada Comedy). [Video.] *YouTube*. https://www.youtube.com/watch?v=ionLQyjeX3U
482. राजन गायकवाड. (2018). हडळ. Pratilipi. https://marathi.pratilipi.com/story/%E0%A4%B9%E0%A4%A1%E0%A4%B3-2nirl3wxjpq0
483. Indian Ghosts and Evil Spirits: How Superstitions Have Gripped the Country. (7 September 2013). *Daily Bhaskar*. https://daily.bhaskar.com/news/DEL-indian-ghosts-and-evil-spirits-how-superstitions-have-gripped-the-country-4368512-PHO.html
484. Bagulboowa. (30 June 2020). वहिरीवरची हडळ. [Video.] *YouTube*. https://www.youtube.com/watch?v=KuzwS_P_2As
485. Chapekar, L.N. (1960). *Thakurs of the Sahyadri*. University of Bombay.
486. Ramesh, B.M. (15 January 2017). The Killing of Hidimba. *VyasaOnline*. http://www.vyasaonline.com/2017/01/15/the-killing-of-hidimba/mahabharata/
487. Pachuau, Margaret L. (9 June 2008). Nucchimi. *Mizo Writing in English*. http://mizowritinginenglish.com/2008/06/nuchhimi.html
488. Chawnghilh. (16 December 2009). Nuchhimi. *Chawnghilh's Blog*. https://chawnghilh.wordpress.com/2009/12/16/nuchhimi/
489. Lawmsanga. (2010). A Critical Study on Christian Mission with Special Reference to Presbyterian Church of Mizoram. Univerity of Birmingham. https://etheses.bham.ac.uk/id/eprint/767/1/Lawmsanga10PhD.pdf
490. Mr. Light. (7 January 2013). Jinns. *Angels and Jinns*. http://angels-jinns.blogspot.com/2013/01/jinns.html
491. The Strange Life of Mary Warwick. (2016). *Chowkidar*, vol. 14, no. 4. British Association for Cemeteries in South Asia.
492. Vohra, Rohit. (1989). *The Religion of the Dards in Ladakh*. Skydie Brown International, Ettelbruck (Luxembourg).
493. Agastya-2. (November 2008). Maharishis Of Ancient India. https://maharishis.blogspot.com/2008/11/agastya-2.html
494. Smith, John D. (2005). *The Epic of Pabuji*. Katha, New Delhi.
495. Lebling, Robert. (2011). *Legends of the Fire Spirits: Jinn and Genies from Arabia to Zanzibar*. Counterpoint.

496. Taneja, Anand Vivek. (2017). *Jinnealogy: Time, Islam, and Ecological Thought in the Medieval Ruins of Delhi*. Standford Univerity Press.

497. McGregor, Richard. (2012). *The Case of the Animals versus Man Before the King of the Jinn*. Oxford University Press.

498. El-Zein, Amira. (2017). *Islam, Arabs, and Intelligent World of the Jinn*. Syracuse University Press.

499. Sharif, Ja'far. (1921). *Islam In India, Or The Qanun-i-Islam*. Oxford University Press.

500. Olomi, Ali A. @aalomi (Entire Twitter feed). https://twitter.com/aaolomi

501. What Are the Type of Ghosts and Evil Spirits Known in Tamil Nadu? *Quora*. https://www.quora.com/What-are-the-types-of-ghosts-and-evil-spirits-known-in-Tamil-Nadu

502. Kabandha. *Wisdom Library*. https://www.wisdomlib.org/definition/kabandha

503. Wikipedia contributors. Kabandha. In *Wikipedia, The Free Encyclopedia*. https://en.wikipedia.org/wiki/Kabandha

504. Shaw, Willam. (1929). *Notes on the Thadou Kukis*. Government of Assam.

505. What is Karna Pishachini Vidya? Does Anyone Know Who Has Mastered This? *Quora*. https://www.quora.com/What-is-Karna-Pishachini-Vidya-Does-anyone-know-who-has-mastered-this

506. Karna Pishachini to Get Answers for Everything (26 December 2014). *Speaking Tree*. https://www.speakingtree.in/allslides/karna-pishachini-to-get-answers-for-everything

507. Kirtimukha, the Face of Glory. http://kirtimukha.com/devilsMask.htm

508. Chhangte, Cherrie Lalnunziri. (2018). *The Blaft Book of Mizo Myths*. Blaft Publications.

509. Kum Chirui. (2017). Kenglongpo. [Video.] *YouTube*. https://www.youtube.com/watch?v=2IcpGn45oKU

510. Wikipedia contributors. Ketu (mythology). In *Wikipedia, The Free Encyclopedia*. https://en.wikipedia.org/wiki/Ketu_(mythology)

511. Oakley, E. Sherman. (1905). *Holy Himalaya: The Religion, Traditions, and Scenery of a Himalayan Province (Kumaon and Garhwal)*. Oliphant Anderson & Ferrier.

512. Rohit. (14 January 2012). Khavis (खवीस) – The Messenger of Death: An Age Old Myth. *Indian Horror Tales*. http://indianhorrortales.blogspot.com/2012/01/khavis-messenger-of-death-age-old-myth.html

513. Wikipedia contributors. Kinnara. In *Wikipedia, The Free Encyclopedia*. https://en.wikipedia.org/wiki/Kinnara

514. Studio Kokaachi. (2019). 30 Days of Kokaachi. *Facebook*. https://www.facebook.com/pg/studiokokaachi/photos/?tab=album&album_id=2386000844797525&__tn__=-UC-R

515. கல்கி கிருஷ்ணமூர்த்தி. (1955). பொன்னியின் செல்வன் #1. கல்கி.

516. Ayya Narayanan. Ucchippadippu. (16 February 2011). Ayya Narayanan – Vaikundar. https://ayyanarayanan.blogspot.com/2011/02/ucchippadippu.html

517. N. Vivekanandan (2003), *Akilathirattu Ammanai Moolamum Uraiyum (Part 1)*, Vivekananda Publications.

518. Gurdon, P.R.T. (1914). *The Khasis*. Government of Eastern Bengal and Assam.

519. Mundkur, Ravindra and Vishwanatha, Hosabettu. (8 October 2015). Kāle and Kāle kola. *Tulu Research*. https://tulu-research.blogspot.com/2015/10/350-kale-and-kale-kola.html

520. Mundkur, Ravindra and Vishwanatha, Hosabettu. (21 October 2015). Kule Madime. *Tulu Research*. https://tulu-research.blogspot.com/2015/10/351-kule-madime.html

521. Amrita. (3 August 2012). Traditional Demon Worship. *Coorg Chronicles*. http://thetaleofkodagu.blogspot.com/2012/08/traditional-demon-worship.html

522. Paniyan in India. (2020). *Joshua Project*. https://joshuaproject.net/people_groups/17834/IN

523. Mills, J.P. (1951). The Story of Shambili: A Chang Naga Folk Tale, *Folklore*. https://doi.org/10.1080/0015587X.1951.9718048

524. Wiktionary Contributors. Reconstruction. Reconstruction: Proto-Sino-Tibetan/m-hla. https://en.wiktionary.org/wiki/Reconstruction:Proto-Sino-Tibetan/m-hla

525. Haokip, L. Paul and Haokip, N. Esthar. Brief History of Khulmi Kuku. https://www.academia.edu/7806299/BRIEF_HISTORY_OF_KHULMI_KUKI

526. Moriro Graves Destruction Remains a Mystery. (22 July 2006). *The News*. https://www.thenews.com.pk/archive/print/16611-moriro-graves-destruction-remains-a-mystery

527. City Secret: Moriro Mirbahar and His Brothers' Graves, Gulbai Chowk. (13 July 2019). *The Karachi Walla*. https://thekarachiwalla.com/2019/07/13/city-secret-moriro-mirbahar-and-his-brothers-graves-gulbai-chowk/

528. Fernandes, Domnic. (5 August 2010). DISTH! Goanet. https://www.mail-archive.com/goanet@lists.goanet.org/msg65241.html

529. Doma, Yishey. (2010). *Legends of the Lepchas*. Tranquebar Press.

530. Elwin, Verrier. (1945). Funerary Customs in Bastar State. *Man in India*, vol. 25.

531. Elwin, Verrier. (1955). *The Religion of an Indian Tribe*. Oxford University Press.

532. Naskar, Sanjukta. (July 2020). The Dynamic Nature of Folklore in Issues of Nationalism. *Design for All*, vol. 15, no. 7. Design for All Institute of India.

533. Das, Sarat C. (20 May 2008). Dead Prisoners Make Merry at Salimgarh Fort. https://www.hindustantimes.com/delhi/dead-prisoners-make-merry-at-salimgarh/story-MZdDdeCAIOgfLblCMT6O1M.html

534. Das, Sarat C. (29 May 2008). A Ghost Funeral in Chandni Chowk. *Hindustan Times*. https://www.hindustantimes.com/delhi/a-ghost-funeral-in-chandni-chowk/story-QPLv2cnA9fs1Ou0KoWS23H.html

535. Khan, Vargis. (25 June 2014). The Hauntings of Khooni Darwaza. https://vargiskhan.com/log/hauntings-khooni-darwaza/

536. Wikipedia contributors. Nazar. In *Wikipedia, The Free Encyclopedia*. https://en.wikipedia.org/wiki/Evil_eye

537. Lhanghal, Ngulminthang. (19 February 2012). The Kuki Mythologies. https://archive.vn/20130217041923/http://ngulminthang.blogspot.de/2012/02/kuki-mythologies.html

538. Shaki, Mansour. (15 December 1996). Duzak. *Encyclopaedia Iranica*. https://iranicaonline.org/articles/duzak

539. Dhema, K.S., Shalini, S. and Nair, Aishwarya J. (January 2020). A Study of Magical Realism in Odiyan through the Collective Conscious of Paruthipulli. *International Journal of English, Literature and Social Sciences*, vol. 5, no. 1. https://dx.doi.org/10.22161/ijels.51.54

540. Delhi Exhibition Showcases Manipur's Mythical Giant Snake Poubi Lai. (22 July 2015). *Business Standard*. https://www.business-standard.com/article/news-ians/delhi-exhibition-showcases-manipur-s-mythical-giant-snake-poubi-lai-115072200463_1.html

541. Elwin, Verrier. (1944). *Folk-Tales of Mahakoshal*. Oxford University Press.

542. Berger, Peter. (2015). Feeding, Sharing, and Devouring: Ritual and Society in Highland Odisha, India. *Religion and Society*, vol. 59. De Gruyter.

543. Contractor, Huned. (2015). Pune and its Ghosts: Are You Brave Enough to Visit These 5 Haunted Places? *Folomojo*. http://www.folomojo.com/pune-and-its-ghosts-are-you-brave-enough-to-visit-these-5-haunted-places/

544. Wikipedia contributors. Pitrs. In *Wikipedia, The Free Encyclopedia*. *https://en.wikipedia.org/wiki/Pitrs*

545. Tripathi, Shailaja. (7 December 2014). Give the Devil His Due. *The Hindu*. https://www.thehindu.com/features/metroplus/give-the-devil-his-due/article6668169.ece#!

546. Wikipedia contributors. Talk:Printer's Devil. In *Wikipedia, The Free Encyclopedia*. https://en.wikipedia.org/wiki/Talk:Printer%27s_devil

547. Viramma, Josiane Racine. (1997). *Viramma, Life of an Untouchable*. Verso.

548. Blogger Manado. (November 2013). Dead Girl living, Saffron BPO. *Airinband*. https://mysterynewstory.blogspot.com/2013/11/dead-girl-living-saffron-bpo.html

549. Wikipedia contributors. Saamri. In *Wikipedia, The Free Encyclopedia*. https://en.wikipedia.org/wiki/Saamri

550. 12 Types of Funny and Scary Ghosts That Are Found Only in India. (27 November 2017). *The Daily Moss*. https://www.dailymoss.com/types-of-funny-and-scary-ghosts-found-only-in-india/

551. Niali Again: Mystery Creature Strikes Again, 14 Sheep Killed. (22 November 2017). *Orissa Post*. https://www.orissapost.com/niali-again-mystery-creature-strikes-again-14-sheep-killed/

552. Blavatsky, Helena P. (1892). *From the Caves and Jungles of Hindostan*. Theosophical Publishing Society.

553. Gutschow, Kim. (1997). Unfocused Merit-Making in Zangskar: A Socio-Economic Account of Karsha Nunnery. *The Tibet Journal*, vol. 22, no. 2. Library of Tibetan Works and Archives.

554. Roy, Abhishikta Ghosh, Mukherjee, Shreya and Behera, Banita. (December 2018). The Socio-Cultural Belief of the Lepchas of Pedong, West Bengal, India. *International Journal of Social Science and Humanities Research*, vol. 6, no. 4.

555. Dym, Jeffery A. (12 September 2012). Commonly Seen. *Retold.* https://storiesfrombackhome.tumblr.com/post/31392184014/commonly-seen

556. Wikipedia contributors. Svarbhanu. In *Wikipedia, The Free Encyclopedia.* https://en.wikipedia.org/wiki/Svarbh%C4%81nu

557. Tatelman, Joel. (2000). *The Glorious Deeds of Purna: A Translation and Study of the Purnavadana.* Motilal Banarasidass.

558. Walter, Michael. (2004). Of Corpses and Gold: Materials for the Study of the Vetāla and the Ro langs. *The Tibet Journal*, vol. 29, no. 2. Library of Tibetan Works and Archives. https://www.jstor.org/stable/43302556

559. Moonlight, Alexia. (13 March 2009). Danny Phantom: Your Guide to All Things Ghostly. *FanFiction.net.* https://www.fanfiction.net/s/4917322/1/Danny-Phantom-Your-Guide-to-All-Things-Ghostly

560. Hamilton, Francis. (1807). *A Journey from Madras Through the Countries of Mysore, Canara and Malabar.* East India Company.

561. Wikipedia contributors. Vritra. In *Wikipedia, The Free Encyclopedia.* https://en.wikipedia.org/wiki/Vritra

562. Kincaid, C.A. (1993). The Werewolf. In *The Penguin Book of Indian Ghost Stories* (ed. Bond, Ruskin). Penguin Books India.

563. Smith, R.V. (6 December 2018). When the "Werewolves" Rode Again. *The Statesman.* https://www.thestatesman.com/supplements/section/when-the-werewolves-rode-again-1502714254.html

564. Musharraf Ali Farooqi. (5 September 2015). The One-Eyed Yeti. *Mint.* https://www.livemint.com/Leisure/JFfxyKiHDgYavYbMUYhOVP/The-oneeyed-Yeti.html

565. Routroy, Saswat. (2 November 2018). An Interesting Blog on Alien Sighting in Nayagarh and Pattachitra. *Bhubaneswar Buzz.* https://www.bhubaneswarbuzz.com/updates/odisha-news/interesting-blog-alien-sighting-nayagarh-pattachitra-saswat-routroy

566. Griffith, Ralph T.H. (1896). *The Hymns of the Rigveda.* E.J. Lazarus & Co.

567. Jacobsen, Knut A. (2011). Yoga Powers: Extraordinary Capacities Attained Through Meditation and Concentration. Brill.

568. Yatudhana, Yātudhāna, Yatu-dhana: 12 definitions. *Wisdom Library.* https://www.wisdomlib.org/definition/yatudhana

569. Haokip, Telsing Letkhosei. (2015). Ethnic Separatism: The Kuki-Chin Insurgency of Indo-Myanmar/Burma. *South Asia Research*, vol. 35, no. 1. Sage Publications.

570. Kipgen, Paominlien. (19 September 2004). Religious Beliefs and Practices Among the Kukis in Olden Days. *Kuki Forum.* http://kukiforum.com/2004/09/religious-beliefs-and-practices-among-the-kukis-in-olden-days/

571. Wikipedia contributors. Hinn (mythology). In *Wikipedia, The Free Encyclopedia.* https://en.wikipedia.org/wiki/Hinn_(mythology)

572. Kharmawphlang, Desmond L. (2004). From Tigermen to Tourism: Changing Narratives. *NEHU Journal*, vol. 2, no. 2.

573. Kharmawphlang, Desmond L. (2006). *Khasi Folk Songs and Tales.* Sahitya Akademi, Delhi.

574. Noble, William A. and Jebadhas, A. William. Irula. *Encyclopedia.com.* https://www.encyclopedia.com/humanities/encyclopedias-almanacs-transcripts-and-maps/irula

575. *Maharashtra State Gazetteers (Facsimile Reproduction), Kolaba.* https://cultural.maharashtra.gov.in/english/gazetteer/KOLABA/home.html

576. *Gazetteers of the Bombay Presidency (Facsimile Reproduction), Pune District Vol. XVIII.* Gazetteer Department Govt. of Maharashtra. https://gazetteers.maharashtra.gov.in/cultural.maharashtra.gov.in/english/gazetteer/Poona%20District/Poona-I/appendix_a.html

577. Soundar Rajan, Indra. (2019). *The Aayakudi Murders* (trans. N. Rajagopalan). Blaft Publications.

578. Sen, Amrita and Mukherjee, Jenia. (2020). Bonbibi: A Religion of the Forest in the Sundarbans. *Environment and Society.* https://www.environmentandsociety.org/arcadia/bonbibi-religion-forest-sundarbans

579. Patel, Utkarsh. (1 September 2015). Cigarette Baba of Junagadh. *The Mythology Project.* https://themythologyproject.com/cigarette-baba-of-junagadh/

580. Ray, Joydeep and Khanna, Summit. (14 June 2013). Cigarettes Get a Holly Touch at this Surat Temple. *Business Standard.* https://www.business-standard.com/article/economy-policy/cigarettes-get-a-holly-touch-at-this-surat-temple-104121501090_1.html

581. Srinibash Samal. (31 July 2019). Rituals And Beliefs On Chitalagi Amavasya. *Bhubaneswar Buzz.* https://www.bhubaneswarbuzz.com/citizen-bloggers/rituals-beliefs-chitalagi-amavasya

582. Hajongs. *Banglapedia.* https://en.banglapedia.org/index.php/Hajongs

⤳⊶ LIST OF ILLUSTRATIONS ⊷⤷

p. 7: **Airi** by Appupen

p. 12: **Aleya** by Rashmi Ruth Devadasan

p. 17: **Anchheri** by Appupen

p. 24: **Arakkan** by Shyam

p. 29: **Baak** by Shyam

p. 35: **Balishtamaru (Rav)** by Samita Chatterjee

p. 39: **Ban Jankhri** by Pankaj Thapa

p. 58: **Bhoota (Panjurli)** by Misha Michael

p. 62: **Bhurey** by Samita Chatterjee

p. 75: **Bram Bram Chok** by Vidyun Sabhaney

p. 79: **Bugarik** by Samita Chatterjee

p. 81: **Bullet Baba** by Shyam

p. 84: **Cetea** by Samita Chatterjee

p. 87: **Chedipe** by Shyam

p. 89: **Chetnik** by Samita Chatterjee

p. 93: **Chordeva** by Shyam

p. 103: **Crocotta (Leucrocotta)** by Samita Chatterjee

p. 138: **Ginggrek Mikdalong** by Samita Chatterjee

p. 140: **Goggayya** by Misha Michael

p. 158: **Iliphru** by Shyam

p. 161: **Indus Worm** by Samita Chatterjee

p. 163: **Iwi-Pot (Hanta)** by Samita Chatterjee

p. 165: **Jadaamuni** by Samita Chatterjee

p. 166: **Jhunjharji** by Shyam

p. 173: **Jurua** by Samita Chatterjee

p. 175: **Kabandha** by Samita Chatterjee

p. 178: **Kalystrioi** by Samita Chatterjee

p. 180: **Kanni Pey** by Samita Chatterjee

p. 186: **Keerthimukha** by Misha Michael

p. 193: **Khond** by Samita Chatterjee

p. 198: **Kokaachi** by Priya Kuriyan

p. 200: **Kollivay Pey** by Shyam

p. 202: **Kuntomasali** by Samita Chatterjee

p. 204: **Ksuid (Ka Ñiangriang)** by Samita Chatterjee

p. 211: **Kundra** by Samita Chatterjee

p. 216: **Kuttichathan** by Shyam

p. 220: **Lai Khutsangbi** by Pankaj Thapa

p. 223: **Lasi** by Samita Chatterjee

p. 230: **Man-Eating Boulder** by Samita Chaterjee

p. 238: **Mayel** by Samita Chatterjee

p. 250: **Muhnochwa** by Rashmi Ruth Devadasan

p. 271: **Naale Ba Bhoota** by Samita Chatterjee

p. 280: **Newand Dokka** by Appupen

p. 288: **Nyalmo** by Samita Chatterjee

p. 291: **Odontotyrannos** by Rashmi Ruth Devadasan

p. 299: **Penchapechi** by Samita Chatterjee

p. 313: **Pisacha** by Shyam

p. 338: **Rulpui** by Samita Chatterjee

p. 358: **Simekar (Girha)** by Osheen Siva

p. 361: **Songduni Angkorong Sagalni Damohong** by Misha Michael

p. 369: **Takte Ragre** by Samita Chatterjee

p. 382: **Timitimingala** by Samita Chatterjee

p. 384: **Tsine Nat** by Shyam

p. 394: **Unicorn** by Misha Michael

p. 398: **Vetal** by Shyam

p. 415: **Yakshi** by Shyam

p. 429: **Yatudhani** by Appupen

p. 431: **Zoumi** by Appupen